# THE
# HIGHLANDER'S
# FALLEN ANGEL

# ALSO BY HEATHER MCCOLLUM

## SONS OF SINCLAIR SERIES

*Highland Conquest*
*Highland Warrior*
*Highland Justice*
*Highland Beast*
*Highland Surrender*

## THE BROTHERS OF WOLF ISLE SERIES

*The Highlander's Unexpected Proposal*
*The Highlander's Pirate Lass*
*The Highlander's Tudor Lass*
*The Highlander's Secret Avenger*

## HIGHLAND ISLES SERIES

*The Beast of Aros Castle*
*The Rogue of Islay Isle*
*The Wolf of Kisimul Castle*
*The Devil of Dunakin Castle*

## HIGHLAND HEARTS SERIES

*Captured Heart*
*Tangled Hearts*
*Crimson Heart*

# THE
# HIGHLANDER'S
# FALLEN ANGEL

# HEATHER
*USA TODAY* BESTSELLING AUTHOR
# McCOLLUM

Entangled Publishing, LLC
644 Shrewsbury Commons Ave., STE 181
Shrewsbury, PA 17361
Visit our website at www.entangledpublishing.com.

Amara is an imprint of Entangled Publishing, LLC.

Edited by Alethea Spiridon
Cover design by LJ Anderson and Bree Archer
Photography by Shirley Green
Stock art by Fodor90/GettyImages
and Mlenny/GettyImages
Interior design by Britt Marczak

Print ISBN 978-1-64937-747-0
ebook ISBN 978-1-64937-687-9

Manufactured in the United States of America

First Edition May 2025

AMARA

*To Barb/Aunt Bop*

*I have no doubt that you'd steal a set of wings
(and a Highlander) to save your family.*

*We are a stronger clan with you in it. Love always.*

*The Highlander's Fallen Angel* is book two in the Brothers of Solway Moss series from *USA Today* bestselling author Heather McCollum. The story includes elements that might not be suitable for all readers. The book contains references to kidnapping, drugging, being held against one's will, and hints of past domestic abuse not on the page. Readers who may be sensitive to these elements, please take note.

# OLD ENGLISH AND SCOTS GAELIC WORDS USED IN *THE HIGHLANDER'S FALLEN ANGEL*

daingead - dammit

mo chreach – my rage

mo Dhia – my God

rachamaid dhachaidh – let's go home

sgian dubh – black-handled dagger with one sharp edge, used more as a utility knife than a weapon

Sneachda (pronounced Snek-da) – Snow (name of Tierney's Great Pyrenees dog)

Siuthad – Go on

tapadh le Dia – thank God

# PROLOGUE

The Battle of Solway Moss occurred on 24 November 1542. "Losses as a direct consequence of the battle were relatively few, however several hundred Scots were believed drowned and around 1,200 taken prisoner."

*Historic-UK.com*

25 May 1544
Carlisle Castle Dungeon, Northwest England

Kenan Macdonald stretched his arms overhead as he turned from a barred window where he'd been watching the wind blow the budding branches of a hawthorn tree outside. "'Tis almost dark." He looked at the figure sitting on one of the two cots the four of them had rotated through using over the past year and a half of this hellish existence. For the last two weeks, Asher MacNicol had taken up one continuously while they nursed his flayed skin and fever to the point he could escape Carlisle prison with them.

Kenan nodded to him. "Will ye be able to walk with us?" He studied the quiet man that had been caught trying to escape on his own and had suffered a flaying that had left his back torn apart. He still fought infection.

"Aye," Asher said. "I would foking fly out of here

if given the chance."

Cyrus Mackinnon chuckled. "If we had the wings that Kenan says da Vinci has planned, perhaps ye could. But we do not, and so 'tis important for ye to remember—"

"We work together," Rory MacLeod interrupted, his words like a growl. "None of this running off alone shite. Got it, Ash?"

The man had found a short blade sewn into a blanket that had been given to him at Beltane from an anonymous source. Each of them had received a similar blanket, but they all held different hidden treasures: the blade, eight crowns, skeleton keys, and the name of a ship at a port relatively close by. Together, they had a chance to escape England. Separately, they'd end up like Ash or dead, dumped into the moat surrounding Carlisle Castle.

Fury itched inside Kenan, and his hands clenched. Fury at King Henry for imprisoning Scotsmen because they refused to bow before England, fury at his father for trading him to stand in his place after the Battle of Solway Moss, and fury at Ash for trying to escape on his own. But Kenan had learned during eighteen months of imprisonment that old grudges and hatreds against each other's clans on the Isle of Skye meant nothing when facing a larger enemy.

If Scotland kept fighting amongst themselves, England would surely rule them. They must work together to survive, as four individual men and as a country.

Ash nodded, and Kenan looked at the other two. "Then we go tonight." Kenan withdrew his skeleton key that they had already confirmed could open the cell.

Rory held up one of the gold coins sewn into his blanket, and Cyrus held up the scrap of paper scrawled with the name and location of a ship that would take them home. In silence, Kenan's hand wrapped around the key into a fist, which he pressed against his chest over his heart. Rory and Cyrus followed his pledge, and the three looked at Ash. He no longer had his dagger, but he formed a fist and, meeting their gazes, pressed it against his own heart.

*Together.* Who would have guessed that men from four feuding clans on the Isle of Skye would work together? They had each been taught since the cradle to view the others as deadly enemies who must be conquered. But these brutal months together had changed everything.

Kenan sat next to Ash, Cyrus and Rory on the other cot, and they all four leaned back against the damp walls to rest. There was no fear they'd sleep until morning; none of them did with the cold and dampness and the scurrying vermin. But Kenan managed a couple hours of dreamless sleep before someone nudged him, and his eyes flew open.

Ash stood and gingerly stretched his arms overhead. 'Twas a good sign he could keep up with them. They wouldn't leave him behind, and the man was too heavy for them to carry with any speed.

With barely a whisper of sound, all four men gathered their meager things, tying their blankets like capes around their necks. Kenan's heart thumped hard like it did right before a raid. But instead of winning a half dozen sheep or a shaggy cow, he'd be winning his freedom. Or at least an end to this cold, grimy, hungry existence.

Rory slid the key into the heavy iron lock on the cell door. They had used grease from the chicken legs they'd each received for dinner to make the hinges silent so the door didn't squeak as it swung slowly outward. One by one, Rory, Cyrus, Ash, and Kenan crept in their agreed order out the door into the dark corridor. Kenan closed the door behind him, although it would be obvious the cell was empty. There was no way to make it look like they remained since they would need their blankets. They'd rely on speed and silence for this to work.

With practiced light tread, they moved through the darkness like silent shadows. If other prisoners saw them, they could raise an alarm. Step by step, the four moved in the darkness, thankful for the torches having sputtered out by that time of night. After so much time in the dark, their eyes scanned the dungeon's landscape easily, and they maneuvered without issue to the door into the guard room.

Before Kenan even entered the alcove, Rory had already grabbed the sleeping English guard by the throat. The man's eyes bugged out, but no sound issued from his mouth with his breath cut off. Within a minute, his eyes shut, and Rory released him to his cot where Kenan gagged him with the man's own handkerchief and then helped Cyrus tie him to the metal frame.

Taking his ring of keys, Kenan waved the others to follow him out through the gate. He yanked out the greasy chicken bone from his sock, sliding it along the hinges before unlocking and pushing the door open. No squeak. His heart pounded with the scent of freedom.

*So close.*

A guard dozed in a chair at the far end of the corridor. With three footfalls, Ash was on him.

"What the —" the man said questioningly, but then Ash twisted his neck, the sound of its *crack* stark in the silence. He let the man slump back to the chair and spit on him. From the brutal retaliation, Kenan was certain the English soldier had participated in Ash's flaying.

Creeping through another set of locked doors, the four Highlanders found themselves outside in the cool spring night. Kenan inhaled the sweetness of it even with the stench of the moat water so close. They had already decided to brave the River Eden that flowed into the moat instead of going across the stone bridge that was guarded by six English soldiers with weapons.

They crept near the ground along the rough stone wall. Their filth-darkened clothes and skin helped them blend in with the shadows, as if they would become dirt-covered corpses in that hellhole, digging their way out to freedom. Under the bridge, they walked hunched over until they dropped to their knees to crawl unseen through the tall grass that flanked the Eden away from the castle. Kenan looked behind them, but only darkness filled the space, the night breeze rustling the grasses.

The water was cold, but after a year of cold, it hardly registered to Kenan's body. They lifted their blankets over their shoulders to keep them dry and waded across the swift flow, holding hands to make certain Ash made it. At least this water was clean and not the putrid liquid on the other side of the castle where shite and dead bodies soured the water.

They crawled out the far side, all four of them lying flat, three on their backs and Ash on his stomach, to rest, warm up under their dry blankets, and listen to the night. Kenan counted in his head up to five hundred and then knocked Ash's shoulder next to him. Ash would knock Cyrus, who would knock Rory.

Rory rose first, staying crouched, and they each followed in order. Hiking up the steep bank, Kenan kept low like the rest, his gaze continuously scanning behind and to the sides. His blood rushed, making him want to run off into the night, but he held himself in line, his discipline winning out. Because it was discipline and sticking to their plan that would see them survive the night.

The wind bent the grasses over as they crawled, stopping in line behind Rory when he felt they might be seen. They each crept with a swaying motion to mimic the movement of the tall weeds and catkins at the ends of their stalks. Suddenly, Ash stilled before Kenan, and he almost crawled into the heels of his boots. Ash shot quickly forward, coming up on his feet in a hunched sprint. Kenan watched as the man veered away from their line toward the two soldiers standing guard at the very front of the bridge in the dark.

Rory, Cyrus, and Kenan watched as Asher stalked them while the men chuckled softly, their profiles relaxed. *Foking Ash.* He'd alert the battalion inside the guard house if he didn't take out his revenge in total silence.

Rory looked back at Kenan, and Cyrus followed suit. Rory pointed his finger toward the forest. He wanted to leave the arse to his fate. *Daingead*. If they left him, if the man survived and they all still got away, the distrust and fury between the MacNicol Clan might continue on the Isle of Skye. If they remained and they were all caught, they would all die. Or if they lived, Rory and Cyrus would despise Kenan and Ash for their torture.

But Kenan and Cyrus had talked well into the night about uniting Scotland so the humiliating defeat at Solway Moss wouldn't happen again. Kenan gave a slight shake of his head. He would stay. They would stay to help Ash. With a silent exhale, Kenan followed Ash through the grasses.

Ash glanced back to see the three of them following, and he halted as if surprised they weren't abandoning him. Recovering quickly, he slunk forward until he was close. He still swayed with the wind in the grass, a perfect camouflage, waiting for his opportunity. When Kenan came even with him, Ash nodded to him and then pointed at one of the men. Kenan gave a quick nod to the other man and held his fist before his chest. Ash waited while he unfurled each finger: one, two, three.

They stood together at the same time, each of them grabbing their guard's mouth, holding in their surprised yells. Kenan heard Ash's whisper beside his guard's ear. "Ye shouldn't order another five lashes because a prisoner doesn't plead for mercy." *Crack*. The man wouldn't have a chance to reform himself, because Ash had broken his neck, too. He released him to fall and turned away, leaving Kenan to decide the other man's fate.

The guard struggled in his hold. Kenan could break his neck, but instead he wrapped his arm around the man's neck, cutting off his breath until his head nodded. He lowered him to the ground next to his dead comrade. Kenan grabbed the two swords along the men's sides while Cyrus tied the breathing man's wrists together and gagged him with strips he'd torn from the man's tunic.

Keeping low, the four Highlanders jogged through the grass until they reached the forest edge. Standing, they ran toward the west for half a mile until they reached a river.

"Far enough," Cyrus called, his voice seeming strange in the silence.

Using one of the swords, Kenan cut off four long pine boughs from different trees, handing them around. "Cover the tracks," Rory said, and they dragged their pine boughs gently over their footprints as they headed east back into the forest.

*Home.*

For the first time in eighteen months, Kenan thought he might just see his isle again.

# CHAPTER ONE

"Fair is foul, and foul is fair: Hover through the fog
and filthy air."

*William Shakespeare – English playwright, 1564–1616,
spoken by the three witches in Macbeth*

THREE MONTHS LATER - 22 AUGUST 1544
WATERS OFF CLAIGAN BEACH, ISLE OF SKYE

Kenan Macdonald stared in disbelief at the woman
dangling from his flying machine over the choppy
sea. How had she gotten the huge wings airborne?
More importantly, why?

Kenan had weighted his set of canvas wings,
based on Leonardo da Vinci's sketches, down on the
top of the hill overlooking the beach where his sister's wedding had just concluded. He was to fly for
the first time in Sara and Rory MacLeod's honor
later that day.

"She is going to crash into the sea!" Sara yelled,
grabbing her brother's arm and trying to shake it.
She clearly remembered the terror of flying herself.

"There is little chance she won't," their aunt
Morag said, her voice curious but cheerful.

The sound of the woman's splash was muted by
the constant crash of waves.

"I wonder who she is," Eleri MacLeod said,
clasping her twin sister's hand as they watched with

wide eyes.

"She won't be anyone if she drowns," Rory said and began to yank his boots off.

"Stay here with yer bride," Kenan yelled, yanking off his own boots. "'Tis my folly." Clearly, he should have left guards up on the hill. He charged through the breaking waves with his knees high, keeping the floundering woman and her splashing arms in his sight. He yanked off his tunic, unbuckled his belt, and let his plaid drop just before rushing into the froth of the churning sea.

With a shove against the sharp bottom, he propelled himself in a dive over the next wave, the cold enveloping his heated body. *Bloody, foking thief!* She might not be successful in stealing his flying machine, but she was tearing it apart. Even though she'd managed to get her feet in the stirrup to keep her body from dangling, she'd let the nose of the glider tip downward, sending his creation into the sea.

He sucked in air when he surfaced and stroked through the icy north Atlantic, blowing bubbles out of his nose and ignoring the ache of cold in his bones. He would save her even though he'd rather throttle her. Once again, his sister's wedding had been disrupted, the first time by fire, and now by his glider plummeting through the air, ruining her happy day.

*Pull. Kick. Breathe. Dive.* He continued his strokes, the taste of salt on his tongue, the burn of seawater in his nose.

"The useless thing won't hold me up," the lass yelled, not toward him but toward the sky as if she cursed God for not saving her. Her curled fingers clawed at the canvas wings.

"'Tis not a bloody boat," he yelled back, and her face snapped around toward him. "'Tis a glider made for air, not water."

Wide eyes stared at him over the spread of canvas just under the surface. Light-colored hair was plastered around a pale oval face. Droplets of seawater made her eyelashes dark under gently arching brows. With a white tunic, soaked through and clinging to her slender shoulders, she almost looked naked like a mermaiden.

Her full lips looked pale with the cold and parted. "Are you Kenan Macdonald of Sleat?" She coughed against the water that had lapped into her mouth.

"Aye." He stroked past his dying creation until his hands bumped into the warmth of her soft body. Kenan pulled her to him, her legs kicking his as she tried to keep herself afloat.

Green eyes stared into his, her long lashes spiked with seawater. Her hands encircled his arms as she abandoned the canvas wings. Perhaps she couldn't swim.

*She's definitely not a mermaiden.*

"Are you Kenan Macdonald?" she asked, her brows pinching together.

"Aye, the creator of the wings ye've ruined."

"I need you," she said, her grasp on him tightening as if she feared he'd swim away without her.

"Aye, ye do." His tone added "foolish lass" without him having to say it. "Else ye'd sink like my violated wings."

At first, he attempted to hold her with one arm and drag his glider, but the saturated wings and the heaviness of the control bar and leather straps meant he'd inch his way back to shore. The woman was already shivering in the sea's unwelcome embrace.

"Daingead!" he roared and released his glider to float along the undulating surface. He slid both his hands up the woman's form, unwilling to release her in fear she'd sink. Her waist was slim but not thin. No petticoats hit his legs, but she wasn't naked like him. "Hold onto my shoulders," he said, turning and placing her hands there. Her fingers pinched into his skin, holding tight, and he began to swim back to shore.

A glance above the waterline showed the whole wedding party and the curious villagers of Dunvegan pointing and staring at them from the white beach made of sharp crystalized, bleached seaweed. Kenan's muscles bunched and pulled, keeping him warm enough as he kicked and stroked to shore. When he'd yanked off his tunic before wading into the water, they had all gotten a look at the lashing scars across his back, including Cyrus's sister, Grace Mackinnon. Well hell, if she was going to marry him, she'd see his back anyway.

The thief clung to him, and he felt her kicking at the surface as she let her legs float out behind her. When her legs collided with his, it made him even more ornery.

*Foking hell.*

She'd destroyed the glider he'd built, based on Leonardo da Vinci's plans for wings. It had taken him months to measure, cut, and stitch together, assembling it in secret while his father still lived. The glider had saved his sister's life, surviving the flames that had engulfed his castle at Dunscaith only to be destroyed by this slip of a lass who'd flown it into the sea.

"Are you naked?" she asked and then sneezed, the saltwater no doubt stinging her nose.

Kenan breathed past the rise and fall of the lapping waves, not bothering to answer. She was just lucky he'd braved the waters for her. For her or for his glider? He wasn't sure. He'd like to think he'd dove into the icy Atlantic to save the life of the lass who was a thief at worst and a curious fool at best.

When he got to the underwater shelf where the waves broke, he lowered his feet, finding the sharp sand and shells. He pulled the lass around before him as the water gave way, exposing his shoulders and chest. No need to shock the ladies who may not know how a man's cock and ballocks crawl up inside him when exposed to the brutal cold. He sure as hell didn't need rumors about him having a small pisser.

The woman was shorter than him by almost a foot and half his width. The heavy water slicked her hair back and only fell to the middle of her back, much shorter than most lasses he knew who coiled their arse-length hair up into intricate buns and crowns on their heads.

Kenan's sister, Sara, the newly wedded Lady MacLeod of Dunvegan, lifted her voluminous petticoats to meet them at the shore's edge with her husband, Rory MacLeod.

"Holy Mother Mary," Sara said. "Let's get you up

to the castle and into a warm bath."

Dunvegan's housekeeper, Margaret, also helped to guide the bedraggled, sodden woman from the sea. "Ye poor thing."

Poor thing, his arse!

"Lass, your element is definitely not water," Aunt Morag said.

Without a word, Kenan turned and trekked back into the water, giving everyone on shore another view of his naked arse and twisted scars.

"Where are ye going?" Rory yelled.

Kenan's friend, Tomas Duffie, called, "Damn fool is going back for the glider."

"Ye bloody dolt," Cyrus Mackinnon said. For a split second, Kenan wondered what Cy's sister thought of the man her brother wanted her to wed. Grace was standing there on the shoreline with all the rest, watching him charge naked back into the sea after his creation.

Of course, he was going back for the glider. At least he needed to try to save it. He hadn't yet had a chance to fly with it and yet already his sister and this unknown lass had flown. Who was she? No mythical mermaiden. She was too water-logged for that. And too warm. Her body heat had covered his back like a mantle of soft curves.

Kenan dove through the breakers and surfaced, the cold Atlantic numbing him. Having grown up on the Isle of Skye, he'd become used to swimming numb, and he stroked back out toward the glider.

How had she gotten pulled into the air? Had she been trying to steal his creation, or was it an accident born of curiosity? She was light. His wings were meant to be caught by the air, and he'd left them unattended under rocks at the top of Cnoc Mor a Ghrobain, a hillside above the shoreline.

*Stroke. Kick. Breathe.*

He'd never seen her before. She was not a Macdonald of Sleat. Perhaps she lived here at Dunvegan with the MacLeods. The lass's almond-shaped eyes were the green of a spring glen and framed by long lashes that any lass would envy. Her nose was straight and slightly tipped at the end, her nostrils flaring as she sucked in air over the rising and falling water surface. Would they flare like that when she ran or gasped on a passionate moan?

Kenan's hands hit the canvas floating just below the surface, and he raised his head, treading water. Her ire-filled curses had revealed the fire within her even with the threat of drowning. She would be just as passionate in a warm nest of blankets.

Despite the frosty depths, Kenan felt his cock twitch. Lord, it had been too long since he'd tupped. "Shite," he said, and gripped the canvas wing, turned toward the shore, and began to kick. A small group of women surrounded the sopping lass as they climbed the shoreline to the path leading to Dunvegan Castle. Sara waited with her new husband, Rory's two uncles, and some Macdonald and MacLeod warriors to see him pull in the glider.

"We need to get you into a warm bath, too," Sara called as he found his footing.

Kenan had planned to ride back to Dunscaith an hour into the wedding feast. He'd left his castle in ruins and his clan weak after his father was killed and his brother ran away with a known murderess.

He couldn't be away from Dunscaith for long.

But for the first time since the battle for the Fairy Flag several months ago, Kenan wasn't thinking about renovations and reaffirming clan alliances. His gaze relocated the group taking the woman away. Grace Mackinnon was amongst them, her yellow petticoat flapping in the wind. But Kenan could only think of the mystery woman's green eyes: inquisitive, annoyed, and then…determined.

*I need you.*

That's what she'd said.

And Kenan didn't think she was referring to his rescuing her from the North Atlantic.

• • •

Tierney MacNicol shivered and dripped as she walked with several ladies toward the foreboding two-towered form of Dunvegan Castle. The ten-foot-thick curtain wall made it impenetrable with the only entrance from the water side.

"What is your name, lass?" the middle-aged woman named Margaret asked.

"Tierney," she said, her gaze scanning the crowd that seemed to be dressed in their best, waiting for the bride and groom. Tables were set up everywhere, and garlands of summer wildflowers swooped along houses lining the path through the village.

"Now what's happened?" an elderly woman with a tight-lipped frown asked. "Another attack?" She looked Tierney up and down with a disapproving glare.

"A mishap in the water, Mistress Bounce,"

Margaret said. "The bride and groom will be along shortly."

"'Tis about time we had something to celebrate," the frowning woman called after them.

Tierney crossed her arms over her chest, which was only covered with a tunic over a simple binding. The chill was making Tierney's nipples sharp enough to show. The men's trousers she wore also stuck to her. She hadn't wanted to wear petticoats while trying to fly.

"'Twas a beautiful ceremony," one of a pair of remarkably identical twin girls said and smiled as if dragging a woman from the sea who'd crashed a flying machine were an everyday affair.

The other twin smiled, too. "I sketched the scene and will create an oil painting of it." She held a rolled scroll up as they marched toward one of three waiting ferries tied to the dock next to the castle wall.

"A blanket, mistress." The familiar voice made Tierney's face snap to the far left as a young woman pulled a woven blanket from her wagon and ran it over to her.

*God bless Cora.*

Tierney's gaze connected with her wide eyes. Cora Wilson had been her friend since they were no taller than a Highland calf. Despite her reticent questioning, she always ended up helping Tierney with her wild plans. So of course she hadn't abandoned Tierney to the MacLeods.

"Thank you," Tierney said, and raised two fingers, rubbing them along her lips as if the drying saltwater made them itch. But this was no random scratch; it was a signal to Cora.

Cora's eyes opened wider, but then she fished around in her pocket for a vial. "A tincture against fever, milady," she said, pressing it into Tierney's hand.

Tierney smiled, even though she trembled both from the cold and what was to come. "Thank you." Plan number one had failed with the glider crashing into the water, so it was on to plan number two.

# CHAPTER TWO

"A great wind is blowing, and that gives you either
imagination or a headache."

*Catherine the Great – Empress of Russia 1729–1796*

"Where is she?" Kenan asked when his twin sisters
ran up to him at the wedding feast. Not wanting to
take the time for a real bath, he'd bathed in a fresh-
water stream and redressed. His gaze rose over Eliza
and Eleri as he took in the gathered crowd.

Eliza propped hands on her hips, which were beginning to curve outward with her thirteenth
birthday drawing near. The girls were nearly identical, except Eleri had suffered from a bending spine,
which their aunt Morag was trying to strengthen.
Eliza frowned. "You mean Tierney? And most civilized people start with a greeting before throwing
questions about."

"Apologies," he said, raking his hand through his
wet hair. "Greetings, Lady Eliza, Lady Eleri." He
bowed to each of them, winning himself smiles and
curtseys. "Her name is Tierney, then?" he asked.
"Tierney what?"

"She has not told us," Eleri said, with a wave toward the castle. "Mistress Margaret took her inside
to bathe in warm water and drink some hot broth."

"Have either of ye seen her before?"

They shook their heads in unison, one with coiled

braids and one with cascading curls.

Kenan rubbed his short beard. "Did she say why she tried to steal my glider?" He still couldn't believe the audacity of the woman.

"I think it was an accident," Eliza said.

"Surely, she didn't mean to fly over the ocean, crash, and nearly drown," Eleri said.

"Surely," he murmured, looking toward the castle.

"Greetings and good tidings to ye all," Rory called after leaping up on one of the tables. "I offer a toast to my lovely bride." He raised his cup with one hand and pulled Sara up with the other so that she stood beside him. "To Sara, the Flame of Dunscaith, the Lady of Dunvegan, and my wife!"

The hundreds of villagers and warriors in attendance roared their approval, raising their cups or finding one to join in. The twins hurried toward the couple, and Simon and John Sutherland, the two elderly advisors, cheered loudly. Simon thumped John on the back as if they had some part of bringing Sara and Rory together.

Kenan turned toward the ferries that took people into Dunvegan Castle and stopped short as Cyrus pressed a tankard into his hand. Cyrus raised it with the mass behind Kenan and took a drink. "Grace is on the hunt for ye," Cyrus said, holding onto Kenan's arm. "After seeing yer naked arse, I think she's convinced my idea for ye two to wed has merit despite her inheriting Father's dislike of Macdonalds."

So, the lovely, flirtatious Grace Mackinnon didn't mind the scars on his back.

Cyrus patted his jacket. "I already have the documents drawn up to unite Clan Macdonald and Clan Mackinnon through marriage."

"I am not planning to stay here the night, Cy," Kenan said. "Leaving Dunscaith in ashes and unprotected doesn't show me to be an excellent chief to my clan."

"Ye need to look at the betrothal contract before ye leave, then, and sign it if it all looks right to ye."

Kenan's friend had proposed the alliance-forming union behind his father's back. Old Hamish Mackinnon hated the other clans on the Isle of Skye, especially the Macdonalds. Cyrus's older brother died from a tainted wound after a skirmish with Kenan's father's forces. Hamish held all Macdonalds responsible. A union between his daughter, Grace, and the new chief of the Macdonalds of Sleat would be a considerable step to mending that festering hatred. When they escaped Carlisle Dungeon three months ago, Cyrus, Kenan, Rory, and Asher had sworn to unite their isle.

"Yer father will rage, Cy. I'm surprised Grace and ye were able to sneak away from Dun Haakon Castle without raising suspicions."

Cyrus's usual grin turned into a tight line of determination. He set his tankard on a table and drew out a folded missive. "Our oaths to bring Skye together, to make our isle strong against the foking English, are stronger than any of Da's rages. 'Tis been over a year since Patrick died. Grace agrees with me and the Brotherhood that 'tis time to bring the isle together."

The humiliating loss at Solway Moss, fifteen

thousand Scots to three thousand English, showed
the deadly problem of Scottish disloyalty to one another. And then the four men had been abandoned
by their clans as they rotted in a dungeon in
England, so they'd formed a brotherhood. The loyalty between the Highlanders was stronger than clan
blood. They would work around old prejudices and
blood feuds to strengthen their isle.

"When ye marry Grace, she will come with thirty-
thousand crowns, which will go a long way in helping
ye resurrect Dunscaith," Cyrus said. "She will also
bring twenty head of—"

"Good eve." Grace Mackinnon's voice broke
through her brother's description as she walked up
to them with a practiced smile. With dark hair swept
partly up, allowing a drape of curls down her back,
she was pale perfection with stained red lips. "'Twas
gallant of you to rescue that bedraggled child from
the sea, Kenan."

"She's actually a woman," Kenan said. "I need to
find out why she tried to steal my glider."

"Madness," Cyrus said. He returned the folded
parchment to his jacket.

Madness was one possibility, but there'd been a
look of sane determination in the lass's eyes that
made Kenan think there was more to her story.

"I'll be able to tell after an interview with her,"
Kenan said.

Grace slid her arm through Kenan's. "Later,
Chief Macdonald. Right now, I'd like to interview
*you*."

Her smile was firm and her dark eyes confident.
Grace was used to getting her way. As much as

Kenan would like to learn more about the woman who could cement an alliance between their two large, feuding clans, his mind was being tugged like his canvas glider in the wind.

"I hear Dunscaith will be beautiful once 'tis cleaned and repaired," Grace said.

"Uh, aye," he replied.

The lass's name was Tierney, but Tierney what? And if the woman wasn't mad, why would she risk her life trying to steal his glider? Could she possibly know how important the machine was to him? Had someone sent her to take the wings after seeing how they could be used in battle? Did she have a clan that was waiting to attack?

Kenan had to find answers sooner rather than later.

"Will there be a festival to celebrate its completion?" Grace asked.

And what had Tierney meant when she said she needed him? Was that said through fear of drowning? It hadn't sounded that way.

Kenan patted Grace's hand and then lowered his arm so that she had to pull it back or look like she was trying to drag him somewhere. "I will seek ye out after I question the woman," Kenan said.

Grace's bottom lip protruded like a pout. "Very well, but I might not be available later. Several men have asked me to dance."

He bowed over her hand, making up his mind to stay at Dunvegan a few hours, maybe until morning if the whisky was flowing. He kissed her soft knuckles and smiled at her. "I will battle the men away, Lady Grace, to win an interview with ye."

"How nice of you to stay for Grace," Cyrus said, raising his eyebrows.

Kenan held her gaze. "I was going to leave soon for Dunscaith, but ye've made it too difficult to leave immediately. I will be sure to see ye before I must away."

Her frown softened with the words he knew she wanted. He could charm the petticoats off a woman as easily as Cyrus. The difference was that Kenan rarely did.

Grace turned away before he could, and Kenan strode toward the dock where ferries waited to be poled over to the castle's entrance.

Cyrus followed him. "Kenan." His voice was heavy with warning. "Ye don't know my sister well yet, so let me enlighten ye. She's the jealous type."

"I picked up on that." Kenan's boots crunched on the pebbles. Would Tierney be sleeping? The ordeal may have worn her completely out.

"Grace has Father's tenacity and can be…vindictive if she feels slighted. That golden-haired lass that looked like an angel falling from the sky will, I fear, bring out the worst in her."

The woman had looked like an angel, although wearing trousers, before plunging from sky to sea. Kenan jumped onto one of three ferries. He set his tankard down to unhitch the barge from the dock. "Be careful, Cy, else ye make me reconsider marrying her."

Cyrus rubbed a hand down his face. "Grace is a good woman with high moral standing and a need to create the perfect world for herself, perfect betrothal, perfect wedding, perfect marriage. I love her, but…she's a challenge, Kenan."

"I like challenges," Kenan said, although Grace Mackinnon was starting to sound like more than he had time for. "But she needs to know I have a castle to rebuild and a clan to strengthen." He looked over at his friend as he grabbed up a pole. "They are my priority right now."

Cyrus crossed his arms and gave him a dubious look as Kenan pushed off. "It looks to me like a fallen angel is suddenly yer priority."

"Curiosity, not priority."

"Curiosity for beautiful lasses will see ye without a wife," Cyrus called.

"Says the man known as the biggest rogue on the isle."

Cyrus smiled but shook his head. He couldn't refute it. Cyrus Mackinnon had women practically sneaking into his bed with his chiseled body and handsome face. For the most part, the man was full of wit and affable. Few saw the darker side of him, the side Kenan had seen at Carlisle. If he let that fury out, even a little, he wouldn't be so sought after by the lasses.

Kenan pushed down on the pole. "I promise to seek out Grace as soon as I come back across. But this mystery woman owes me an explanation."

Cyrus huffed and called after him. "Thirty thousand crowns and twenty head of prime Highland beef, Kenan. Yer clan would be strong again by Christmastide."

Cyrus was right. Kenan's clan was his priority, and Grace Mackinnon would help strengthen his clan and bring further peace to Skye. Mackinnon territory stretched from the Sleat Peninsula up through the center of Skye to MacLeod territory. It was vast, and the clan's warriors were powerful. Cyrus's father didn't plan on dying anytime soon. A marriage to Grace would align all three great clans on Skye. Kenan should go find her now and tease a kiss out of her.

But Kenan continued to propel the barge across the distance to the spit of land that served as a shoreline and entrance to the castle. "I'll return to her quickly."

No guards stood at the peer to Dunvegan today, and he hopped off, securing the ferry before climbing the many stone steps to pass through the iron gate. Kenan's father, Walter Macdonald, who'd wanted to besiege Dunvegan his entire life, was probably throwing a fit down in Hell that Kenan could walk into the castle with such ease. Friendships and alliances opened doors where violence and threats closed them. Kenan had learned that and more from his time imprisoned in England with men from each of the warring clans on the Isle of Skye.

Gus, Rory's old wolfhound, barked as Kenan entered, but nobody else was in the Great Hall. Not even a hearth fire had been kept going. The dog snuffled around Kenan's legs, realizing who he was, and walked back to find his bed beside the cold hearth where a blanket had been laid for him. Footfalls came from a corridor, and Margaret entered. "Oh, Chief Macdonald, everyone's out at the wedding feast."

"Not ye, though."

She smiled. "I'm on my way now."

"Is Tierney tucked away somewhere?" Kenan glanced upward.

"She finished her bath and a meal in the kitchen. I left her up in the east tower room to rest from her ordeal."

"I need to ask her some questions."

"She does not seem inclined to give answers," Margaret said, hesitating. "And you shouldn't rebuke her for the accident."

"Does she say it was an accident? Her moving the heavy rocks away from the wings and grabbing hold of the control bar to fly my glider?"

Margaret shook her head. "She hasn't given answers to any questions, but I don't think she was trying to take her own life. She is too…high-spirited for melancholia to be her ailment." She looked back at the stairs. "I can chaperone if you'd like to—"

"Ye can go to the feast," he said, waving her toward the door. "If she's sleeping, I'll leave her be. If she's awake, I will ask some calm, non-threatening questions. Since I saved her, maybe she'll be more forthcoming."

Margaret looked pointedly at him. "If you weren't Sara's beloved brother, and known to be honorable, levelheaded, and kind, I wouldn't allow you to visit her, but both she and Rory swear to your integrity, Chief Macdonald."

The word "kind" irked him. It shouldn't, but his father had said it was his weakness. He didn't throw rocks at barn kittens or punch lads if they laughed at him. Kenan's mother once called him a kind lad, and his father had jumped on the word, using it to point out how weak he was. But right now, it worked in his favor.

Kenan tried to look as honorable as he could by standing straight and keeping a serious but contented look on his face. "I'll do the lass no harm."

"Very well, then. Join the festivities when you can. I know Sara will be looking for you." She smiled. "And Grace Mackinnon."

Sara would know that he wanted answers from the lass, and Cyrus would make certain his sister was entertained. As soon as Kenan heard Margaret go through the iron gate down the stairs to the ferry, he turned toward the alcove where the steps rose to all three levels and the tower rooms. His sister had stayed in the same tower where the mysterious Tierney now rested. After his lengthy swim against the current, towing a woman and then the water-logged glider to shore, his legs burned with his fast climb. But pain meant little to him, and the exertion would merely make more muscle, so he surged up the stairs almost as if running.

He slowed as he climbed the last turn leading to the tower door, stopping outside. Listening, he heard a quiet voice through the thick wood. Singing? He couldn't make out the words, but it meant Tierney wasn't asleep. He brought his knuckles to the door.

*Rap. Rap.*

The song stopped. "Who is it?"

"Kenan Macdonald."

Silence. He crossed his arms, waiting. After long seconds, the latch clicked, and the door swung outward, making him dodge to the side so it wouldn't hit him. Rory MacLeod sometimes used the room as a prison, so the door had been reversed. When Kenan came back around the door, his breath caught.

The woman stood before him in a thin robe over a smock. *Look away.* But he couldn't. She'd rendered him still as a marble statue, leaving only his gaze moving across her form. Tierney's hair was damp but starting to curl around her lovely face. Clear green eyes blinked slowly. Cheeks rosy, nipples hard through the linen and begging to be kissed, she was a siren luring him to a quick but thoroughly enjoyable death.

"I… Pardon," Kenan said and finally forced his gaze upward. "I did not know ye were undressed. I can come back."

She moved closer, her hands outstretched as if she'd cling to him again like when she was in the sea. But she stopped before reaching him and crossed her arms over her chest, which only pushed her breasts higher until he could see the swell above the lace edging of her smock. "No. Stay."

Her full bottom lip slid slightly out, not in a playful way but more authentically. "Is your flying machine at the bottom of the sea?"

"Nay," he said, dropping his hands to his sides. "I dragged it to shore, but 'tis likely destroyed."

She grimaced. "I am sorry for that. 'Twas a magnificent machine."

Kenan's jaw hardened as his teeth clamped tightly for a moment. "Were ye trying to steal it? Is that why ye took the stones away?"

"No," she said. "Will you stay at Dunvegan to fix it? Surely it can't be dragged back to Dunscaith torn up."

"Nay," he said. His priority was rebuilding Dunscaith, not fixing his wings no matter how badly he wanted to feel the wind pick him off the earth. "Why did ye remove the stones?" he asked.

"I can help you fix them. Here at Dunvegan."

He huffed a wry exhale. "Ye owe me an explanation, Tierney."

Her head tipped slightly. "You know my name."

He felt like a dog chasing its tail in a never-ending game he couldn't win. "So ye went to the top of Cnoc Mor a Ghrobain, used force to remove the stones from my glider, and then took hold of the control bar so the wind could pick ye up. And ye did all this to *not* steal my glider."

"No, but I feel responsible, so I will help you fix it. Here at Dunvegan," Tierney said, sitting on the edge of her cot. Her fingers curled inward, propping herself forward on her knuckles, her shoulders higher to her ears.

Kenan narrowed his eyes, trying to ignore how beautiful she looked sitting there as the breeze from the open window ruffled her curls. As the air dried her hair, the color lightened to a pale gold color. "If ye didn't mean to steal it, ye meant to destroy it."

The space between her brows furrowed slightly, and he had the outlandish desire to smooth it with his thumb.

"I noticed the rock cutting into a wing and moved it," she said. "I was worried it would injure the material. And then the wind blew up and yanked the glider from the other rocks, and I managed to grab the bar to stop it from escaping when it snatched me off the ground."

He inhaled deeply. "The rocks were not sharp-edged." He'd checked them all.

"One was." She kept his stare, challenging him like no other person besides his sister, Sara, had ever done. Men respected his leadership, and the lasses, although boldened by his easy smile and reputation for honor, never ignored his questions or argued against what he knew to be true.

"What is yer surname?" He knew very well he wouldn't get any further with questioning her about the accident or sabotage, whichever it truly was.

"Bruce."

His brows rose. "From what clan do ye hail?"

"I was visiting a distant cousin here at Dunvegan and saw the glider placed on the hill."

Kenan studied her, but the lass didn't look away. She met his eyes without blinking. If she was lying, she was a good liar. "I will take ye back to yer cousin, then."

She took a full breath as if she were shoring up her courage and smiled, bringing mischief to her eyes. He wondered if his aunt Morag had some tonic that would make Tierney Bruce tell all her secrets, because she no doubt had a head full of them. "I would like that, thank you. I was so bedraggled from my crash in the sea that I didn't resist the ladies when they brought me here. Truth be told, I wanted a warm bath and some food. My cousin's family doesn't have much to spare."

Kenan frowned. "They should report their need to Rory MacLeod. 'Tis his responsibility to make sure all the people in the MacLeod Clan are fed and hearty."

She waved a hand. "Oh, I'm sure he does, but they hadn't planned on me being another mouth to feed this eve."

"Yer cousin will be worried. I'll visit to let—"

"I already sent word. A message as soon as I arrived here. One of the kitchen maids who helped me with my bath swore she'd let my cousin, Eleanor MacLeod, know I was safe and up at Dunvegan. Maybe for another whole day."

They stared at one another, Tierney grinning and tilting her head. Would her hair look flaxen or golden in the sun? "Thank you again for saving me," she said and pulled her knees up, tucking her feet under her. "I apologize about your glider, Kenan Macdonald, and I want to atone for my mistake. I will help you rebuild it here. You are staying for a few days at Dunvegan, aren't you?"

Kenan stared at the woman who fluctuated between remorse and requests. "Nay," he said, following the trail of her hair over one shoulder to lie on her breasts. Och, but they were perfect and full enough to fill his palms. Lord! He was staring at her breasts! He turned, walking to the door. "I will take ye to yer cousin's, but then I must ride south to Dunscaith immediately."

She stood abruptly. "You will leave tonight?"

"Or at dawn tomorrow. Even though the wolves are well fed this time of year, I prefer to avoid them."

Tierney blinked rapidly. "You won't stay at Dunvegan?"

"I have a castle to rebuild on Sleat Peninsula and a clan to guide. I can't tarry."

"But you'll come with my meal this eve?" Tierney asked quickly. "You won't take your leave without seeing me again?"

The woman's hair spread around her shoulders like a golden cape, her face smooth, and her lips the color of summer roses. Whether from the mystery of the lass or her beauty or strange ways, Kenan was certain he'd be the one to return. He nodded. "I'll return this eve."

She smiled with what looked like relief, and somehow Kenan's plans to return to Dunscaith that afternoon blew away.

# CHAPTER THREE

"It is not in the stars to hold our destiny but in ourselves."

*William Shakespeare – English playwright, 1564–1616*

Tierney stood at the tower room window, letting the breeze ruffle the curls that refused to be captured by the braid she'd tied down her back. Margaret had brought her a dry smock, stays, socks, petticoat, bodice, and jacket, all in a light blue that reminded Tierney of a summer sky.

'Twas a whole new ensemble. She looked down at it, shaking her head. It would be yet another sin since she'd be stealing it. "I'm not a good lass, never will be." Her father had said as much. But stealing an ensemble wasn't too terrible compared to her second plan.

She cringed, shutting her eyes as she exhaled. "But I need him. I can't let him leave for Dunscaith." People depended on her. Cora, Gabriel, Jacob, even ornery old Henry needed her plan to work. And Maggie.

Tierney fished the chain out from her new smock and pried her fingernail between the two halves of the locket. The tight-fitting seal had kept the picture inside safe from saltwater. Maggie's small face smiled out from the tiny portrait, surrounded by haphazard blond curls.

Tierney slid her thumb over the picture, thankful it wasn't washed away and whispered, "We need him, Maggie." Just saying her name soothed the guilt about what she must do.

The celebratory noise of the wedding festival had calmed as the sun descended, although an occasional shout of merriment carried to her on the breeze coming through the open windows. She turned away, and her gaze fell on the two tarts sitting on a square of cloth on the table. Two tarts, both with sweet blackberries in them but one with the addition of Doris MacNicol's potent tincture.

The frowning cook named Fiona gave Tierney the tarts after her bath in the kitchen. *No lass deserves to fall from the clouds into a briny, icy, tumbling sea*. And she'd handed her the two tarts with a third for good measure, which Tierney had eaten right away.

After Tierney implemented her brash plan, Fiona would change her mind. It happened every time she was forced to employ one of her plans. *'Tis a wonder Wallace even wants ye*, her father had said. And now that her father was dead, there'd be no changing his mind about her. She would always be a devilish woman who took brash risks, but she had a plan to prove to her clan that she was clever and brave. And it would save them from annihilation. Something she wouldn't let happen without a fight. If she was going to succeed in this fight, she needed a weapon. That weapon was Kenan Macdonald.

Tierney had soaked one tart in the tincture Cora had handed to her. The powerful sleeping concoction was made with henbane, hashish from a trader from the Far East, valerian root, and vinegar. She even removed some of the berry filling, mixing it with the potion and scooping it back inside, careful not to lick her fingers.

Now, she had to get Kenan Macdonald to eat the tainted tart. She glanced at the door. "And carry him down five flights of stairs and row him over to shore," she murmured. "Without anyone seeing us." She rubbed her face. "Bloody impossible."

Footsteps stopped outside her door. *Rap. Rap.*

Tierney hurried to the table, wrapping the tarts but making sure there was cloth between them to prevent them from touching. She'd cut a corner off her own to know which one was safe. Her hands trembled as she worked.

"I have yer supper, lass." Kenan Macdonald's voice rumbled, making her heart jump.

Could she really do this? 'Twas the most audacious plan she'd ever had. "Maggie. For Maggie," she whispered.

Tierney opened the door and smiled despite her charging pulse. "Good eve," she said, and her gaze dropped to the wooden basket held with his two hands. Another plan coalesced inside her. "Why, yes," she said, with a jubilant smile, "a picnic would be a lovely way to eat my supper."

He frowned. "Picnic?"

"The basket," she said and then lifted the cloth in her other hand. "I even have tarts to contribute." She set them inside.

"I didn't come to take ye on—"

"And then you can take me back to my cousin's cottage."

His lips clamped shut, and his gaze bored into her, so she turned, grabbing the square of blanket she'd folded. Hugging it to her chest, she walked toward the door. "What a gallant surprise."

"No one knows of ye in the village, Tierney Bruce," Kenan said, but she kept walking down the turning steps. Kenan followed. "Nor yer cousin."

"My cousin is private, and her cottage is up in the forest behind the village." She kept amusement in her voice. "No wonder they don't know of us yet. I arrived two days ago and Eleanor a month ago." She glanced over her shoulder to give him another smile. *Keep the details brief. Too many and he'll pick up on the lies.* "I'll show you where her cottage is, but I'll return here in the morn to help you fix your glider."

"I'm heading back to Dunscaith at dawn," Kenan said.

She stopped and offered what she hoped was a playfully seductive smile. "Are you sure you must go so soon? I'd like to get to know you better." *Holy Joan!* What did she know about being seductive? Nothing.

His brows knitted as he studied her, and then the corner of his mouth turned upward. "I wish I could, because ye're the most interesting person I've met in a long time, Tierney Bruce."

But not interesting enough to keep him there so she could persuade him to help her cause. If she couldn't get him to stay an extra day, there was no way merely asking him would make Kenan agree to coming back to Scorrybreac with her. Plan number two must be executed.

"Is your castle terrible? The burning?" she said and reached the corridor at the bottom. Her head turning left, then right, Tierney exhaled in relief at the emptiness. For her plan to work, she must get Kenan alone and preferably without anyone seeing her with him.

"Ye heard about Dunscaith burning?"

She stood before him on the third-floor level. In the shadows, Kenan seemed even larger. It didn't bother Tierney, who had stopped growing early when she'd started her women's courses. Every adult she met was taller than her. The flame of a sconce flickered, showing golden brown strands in the darker brown fullness of his hair. It looked thick and soft. Would it tickle if she rubbed her cheek against it?

Tierney blinked. Why would she want that? She stayed far away from virile men. "Uh…yes," she said, recalling his question. "I heard about it from a bard who came…to my clan's castle on the Isle of Lewis a fortnight ago. He said there was a fire, but I didn't know it was extensive." She needed to give just the right number of details, and these were true.

Kenan's lips hovered open for a second before he spoke. "Was the bard's name Reid Hodges?"

"Yes, Reid Hodges. He wasn't a good singer, but he brought all the news from the southern part of Skye. This was why I visited my cousin, hoping to see your flying machine." She gave a dramatic shiver and then hoped it wasn't too false. "I had no idea how dangerous the whole encounter would prove."

She spun to keep descending the stairs before he could ask her anything else. The lower they climbed, the quicker she walked.

*Good Lord, please don't let anyone stop us.* Would God help her in her deceit? Doubtful. *Please, Holy Joan, help my plan work.* She prayed instead to the fifteenth-century French peasant woman who'd become a military leader under God's guidance. She'd been martyred and deserved to be made a saint in Tierney's opinion. And Tierney had decided that Joan D'Arc wouldn't mind if she occasionally swore upon her name.

Her hand moved to the hard locket under her bodice. *Holy Joan, bless me with your courage to fight for my people.*

• • •

After the boisterous, whisky-flowing wedding celebration, which had started before noon, the town seemed to have retired early. Kenan had spent time dancing with Grace and avoiding Cyrus, who kept waving the betrothal contract at him. Kenan's mind was too full of the mystery of Tierney Bruce to concentrate on crowns and heads of cattle and how he could possibly keep Grace Mackinnon happy.

He'd asked Rory MacLeod about Tierney and her MacLeod cousin. Rory was the chief and had grown up at Dunvegan, but he'd never heard of her, although he did have clan members living in cottages beyond the forest line.

Now Tierney assumed they would picnic before he took her to her cousin's cottage somewhere in the MacLeod woods. "What's yer cousin's name?" Kenan asked as he led his large Percheron horse,

Freya, through the dark village. He'd asked before but wanted to see if her answer would change.

"She is so large," Tierney said, sliding her hand down Freya's neck. "I can't even reach her head unless she lowers it."

"Freya is a Percheron. 'Tis a large breed and very effective in battle and able to haul heavy weights."

"I can imagine," she said, seemingly unafraid of the black giant walking next to her. Freya's wide eye kept track of the woman as if trying to avoid stepping on her.

"What is yer cousin's name?"

"I told you already, Eleanor MacLeod. She married a MacLeod from another isle, and they journeyed here a couple months ago." The words rolled out of Tierney's mouth easily, and yet something in Kenan warned him the name was false.

"And she lives at the edge of the forest?"

"Just inside, but let's have our picnic out under the stars first. Eleanor won't be happy I have caused such a spectacle today, and probably won't let me go back out after I walk over her threshold."

Kenan had delayed his departure for Dunscaith until the morning because of Tierney, the mystery about her and that mischievous smile that made him want to keep questioning her until he managed to dig out all her secrets. He doubted Cyrus would be happy with him riding out with the lass after Kenan had basically agreed to wed his sister. Nothing had been signed yet, and he was merely taking Tierney back to her cousin's house. Time was short with her, and his curiosity huge.

The stars were out, with stray clouds cutting

across the black sky. A sliver of curved moon sat low above the tree line. Perhaps if the lass relaxed, he'd get more answers from her. For someone who seemed to talk easily, she gave no information.

"I'll help ye mount." *Mo creach.* Just the word "mount" sent a sizzle through Kenan as his mind turned to another picture of him mounting this warm, curvy woman. Lord, 'twas like he was a randy lad again. *Daingead!*

Tierney yanked up her skirt, shoving her toe into Freya's stirrup, and bounced. Kenan's hands wrapped around her waist, lifting her higher. Her other leg swung around, and he ducked at the last second to avoid it, but the petticoat caught his head. "Bloody hell," he said.

She laughed lightly. "You're under my skirts."

"'Twas yer doing," he called from under the light wool layers, ducking down, his hands swatting the material off his head. The lass straddled his large horse, her skirts nearly up to her knees to accommodate the mare's girth.

Tierney looked down at him. "Are you climbing on top?"

His mouth went dry. Why did everything having to do with horses and riding suddenly sound scandalous?

Without answering, Kenan slid her foot from the stirrup and replaced it with his own to swing easily up behind her in the saddle. Unfortunately, that brought his cock right up against her arse. She wiggled in her seat, making him grit his teeth. He swallowed hard and leaned in to her ear, inhaling the warm scent of her. "Hold on," he said, his deep voice sounding too aroused to his ears. But if she noticed, she didn't show it as she grabbed hold of the pommel of the saddle with both hands as if she were holding onto his—

"Blast it," he murmured and tapped Freya with his heels. The horse took off into the night. He'd ridden the meadow above Dunvegan before and knew it to be flat from the daily training Rory's warriors practiced. So he let Freya have her head, the cold wind hitting his face and clearing his mind of the carnal images Tierney's nearness had conjured.

He heard her laugh, and she released the pommel to open her arms wide to the sides. She held onto Freya with only her thighs as she tipped her face upward, the wind tugging even more curls out from the braid she wore. Kenan wound one arm around her middle, keeping her seated, but she seemed to have no fear of falling from his giant mare.

Freya cantered, and Tierney's body seemed to absorb the rolling gait easily. She was an experienced horsewoman. Perhaps that's why she'd been wearing men's breeches when she fell into the sea.

She pointed to the right, toward the tree line. Could her cousin live along the coast? He turned Freya, and after a few more minutes of climbing, Kenan slowed her to a walk.

"That was wonderful," Tierney said, her words warm with authentic happiness. "Like flying."

Kenan's jaw was still tight from holding himself against the onslaught of sensation the ride had riddled him with like arrows of lust. He didn't answer, just stopped his mare and quickly jumped to the ground. He looked out at the shadowed landscape.

"You should never dismount and turn away when someone else is on your horse," she said. "Your beautiful mare might get stolen."

He reached up for her, his hands clasping around her waist to pull her toward him. "Are ye a horse thief, Tierney Bruce?"

In the thin light from the slivered moon, he saw the edge of her white teeth as she smiled. "Not usually, but I do know a thing or two about these amazing beasts." She ran a hand down Freya's neck. "And Freya is a beauty, strong and no doubt courageous."

*Not usually?*

An owl hooted from inside the woods, and Tierney dropped her hand from Freya. "Let's set out our picnic. I'm famished."

Kenan studied the shadows but saw nothing. Owls hoot, he told himself, but not when hunting at night. Perhaps it was calling to its young. He stopped to listen but only heard the wind rattling the leaves in the trees.

Tierney dragged the blanket off the horse's back and snapped it out to fall into a square on the trodden grasses. Walking to the middle of it, she sat so abruptly that her petticoat billowed out as it caught the night air beneath it. She pulled the fabric in toward herself to make room for him. "Bring the basket." He did, and with the efficiency of a battle general, Tierney set out the contents between them.

Dunvegan's cook, Fiona, had placed within the basket warm chicken pie, now cool, boiled vegetables with butter, and cheese with bread. "I have dessert," Tierney said, unwrapping the tarts she'd set inside. "One for you and one for me." She pinched her lips as if considering them. "They are small. I bet you can gobble yours in one whole bite."

She held hers up to her wide-open mouth, and all Kenan could do was stare. He could remain at Dunvegan another day, let the wings dry out, and see what else Tierney said or did that made him mad with lust. Could she be doing it on purpose?

"Are ye married?" he asked.

Her mouth closed, and she set the tart down next to her plate of food. "Not anymore."

"Ye're a widow?"

She nodded. "Wallace died three years ago."

"I am sorry for yer loss."

"I'm not," she said, and her brisk tone gave truth to that. "He was…not someone I loved."

Anger built inside Kenan. "Was he cruel?"

She took a bite of her supper and chewed for long seconds. "Let's talk of happy things." The brief discussion had brought a heavy veil over their picnic.

Kenan felt his jaw ache and relaxed it, rubbing it through his beard. His father had been a cruel husband, possibly killing his mother. Those with power who abused people and animals in their care should be made to suffer. As chief of the Macdonalds of Sleat, he would never allow such criminal actions within his clan to go unpunished.

"If he was," Kenan said, "I am heartily sorry, Tierney."

She stared across at him, her head tilting, studying him in the dark. "You may call me Tier if you like," she said. "My friends sometimes call me that, and Wallace never did."

His chest opened. "We are friends, then?"

She nodded, giving a winsome smile.

Kenan felt a powerful need to protect Tierney from the cruelties of the world, and there were many.

*Daingead.* This wasn't a leisurely picnic to look at the stars with a lover or to mentally swear to protect a mysterious woman. Cyrus was certain Kenan was going to wed his sister now after watching them dance and talk at the wedding feast. Spending any time with Tierney, especially alone under the stars, could start a war if Cyrus thought Kenan was being dishonorable to his sister. As part of the brotherhood they'd formed, they had all pledged to respect and honor each other. Tupping another lass or even thinking about it or looking like he might after he'd wooed Cyrus's sister could break that pledge, something Kenan wouldn't risk.

Best to get this strange meal over with quickly and get Tierney to her cousin's. He ate some of the pie and vegetables. Even though Dunvegan's cook had given Tierney large portions, they were still portions for one, so he didn't eat much. He let Tierney eat all she wanted, which was a hearty amount.

"I'm happy ye haven't lost yer appetite." A well-fed woman's beauty was enhanced by health and soft curves. And the lass had luscious curves. He'd felt her strength as she battled against the sea, but she was also soft and would mold perfectly to his hard body. *Mo chreach*. He purposely looked up at the stars.

"Meals can be intermittent sometimes," she said, "and Fiona cooks delicious offerings." She held up a tart. "Like these. Have one with me."

Kenan looked toward the dark forest, but he saw no light within. There were wolves out, but during the summer months they weren't as hungry with a healthy population of deer and hares. Even so, he was on guard. "How far is it to yer cousin's cottage?" The sooner he delivered Tierney, the sooner he could start forgetting about those damnably soft curves of hers.

"Not far," she said, holding out one of the tarts to him. "Let's see if you can fit this whole thing in your mouth at once." She held her own before her lips. "Together, but I'm sure you'll be faster."

He looked at her fingers holding the small confection. They were delicate but strong if they'd held onto his glider's control bar for as long as she did. "The whole thing at once?"

She stuffed her whole tart between her lips, smiling around it as it sat stuffed in one cheek like a squirrel. Her childlike, wicked glance challenged him to do the same. He looked back at her fingers gripping the soft pastry. If he took it all, he might suck on those fingers for a moment. Any thoughts of Grace, Cyrus, and honor faded.

He opened his mouth and let her shove the whole tart inside. An herbal mix of sweet blackberries and bitterness flooded his tongue just before he swallowed it. He had been so struck by the strange taste that he hadn't paid attention to her fingertips, and the moment was gone. Disappointment tightened his stomach.

Tierney smiled, watching him closely for a moment. "Your mouth is bigger than mine. Let's lie on our backs and look at the stars for a few minutes before going."

Kenan took a swig of ale from the bladder they had shared to wash away the bitter tart. Whatever the Dunvegan cook had put inside to complement the blackberries had only made the dessert foul. He listened to Tierney chatter.

"I think apple with cinnamon spice is my favorite," she said. "Blaeberry, too. I add lemon to it. My father used to trade with a man from the East. He brought us all sorts of spices and foreign fruits."

Kenan drank more of his ale, his tongue sliding around his mouth, which suddenly felt smaller than normal. "That was a foul…tast…ting thart," he said, hearing the slur in his words. He cleared his throat and repeated it properly, but it was difficult with his mouth shrinking.

A sudden weight hit his shoulders. It felt a bit like when he'd been struck with influenza years ago, as if he had to lie down immediately because his body had declared war. He tilted to the side, and Tierney was suddenly before him, helping him lie down, pushing him onto his back. His open eyes stared at the tail of the Ursa Minor constellation. He blinked. Bloody hell, what was happening? He closed his eyes, listening to the dark moor around him.

Something brushed his thigh, and Tierney bent

over top of him. "You rest now," she said, her face close to his. And then he felt her lips brush against his. They were warm, and the kiss was too brief as cold replaced them when she sat up. "Soft, like I thought," she whispered.

Her words seemed to echo in his head, growing farther away until everything faded to black.

# CHAPTER FOUR

"Though the sex to which I belong is considered
weak you will nevertheless find me a rock that
bends to no wind."

*Queen Elizabeth I – Queen of England and Ireland
1533–1603*

"Good Lord, he's heavy," Cora Wilson said as she
lifted under Kenan's arms. "Dead weight."

The light from the lantern cast gold and shadows
across Kenan. He was breathing fine through gently
parted lips. "A heavy sleep does that," Tierney said,
stomping down the guilt that rose up her throat like
bile. "Henbane, hashish, valerian root, vinegar, and
sweet wine. It won't kill him." Holy Joan, she hoped
not. She wouldn't be able to live with herself if she
killed an innocent man.

"Bleh," Tierney's twelve-year-old brother,
Gabriel, said. "That sounds terrible."

"He won't even have a headache when he
wakes."

Sneachda, their white Great Pyrenees dog, ran in
circles around them but kept quiet. He knew when
they whispered that he should stay silent unless a
warning was required. He was five years old, having
come on a ship from the Basque region of France,
and fierce enough to protect them from wolves. He'd
been small and helpless when he'd arrived and had

grown so large. Even though she loved him greatly, he was Gabriel's dog. Her brother had a way with all animals. If given the choice, they chose Gabriel to love most.

"Let me take the top half of him," Gabriel said, lifting one of Kenan's arms. Tierney's brother was agile, strong, and despite the grime looked like the golden-haired angel he was named after.

"I'm still stronger than you both," Tierney said, although the last day had taken a lot out of her. "You each lift a leg, and I'll pull his top part into the wagon." With Gabriel grumbling the whole time about soon growing stronger than her, he and Cora followed Tierney's direction. The back of the wagon was low, and she put all her oddly tingling strength into lifting Kenan's head and shoulders while digging her heels into the cold grass to pull him backward with her to the wagon lip.

His shoulders were massive, and the heat from his skin came through his tunic. Even in sleep, he was handsome with perfectly symmetrical features and groomed brows. His beard was cropped short, showing a strong jawline. She longed to touch his lips again. If only she'd been able to convince him to stay and listen to her. But there was no time.

Working together, the three lifted and shoved the Highlander all the way in, but the effort made Tierney's head spin. Sneachda jumped into the back of the wagon, sniffing Kenan, his nose sliding up the woolen wrap around his hips, until the Highlander was nearly exposed.

"No, Sneachda." Tierney pushed his big head away. She wouldn't add baring Kenan's jack or letting her dog sniff him indecently to her sins against the man. He'd been kind, just like her cousin, Asher, had said. Hopefully he'd be kind when he woke, although she doubted it. She'd be anything but kind if someone drugged and stole her away. *For Maggie.* She touched the hard cover of her locket through her bodice.

"Look, look, look," Gabriel whispered.

Tierney's gaze snapped to Kenan, her heart leaping into a panicked run. She expected his eyes to be open and damning. She exhaled in a huff of relief when she saw them still closed.

"What?" she asked, turning back to her brother, who had picked a lizard-looking creature, with a jagged dorsal ridge, off the side of the wagon and placed it on his shoulder.

"No time for adopting lizards," Cora said. "We need to get Chief Macdonald farther into the wagon."

"He's a newt, not a lizard. Newts have four toes and no claws." Gabriel stretched carefully, looking back at Kenan. "He's as heavy as a boulder."

"He must weigh two hundred pounds," Cora said. "He's about six foot four inches and all muscle." Her tone was appreciative even though she panted with exertion.

Tierney pulled him as she scooted backward into the flat wagon half filled with hay. Her arms felt heavy, and she leaned against the wall encircling the wagon bed with Kenan's head on her lap. The darkness of the night moved strangely before her, and she let her head loll, her fingers resting on Sneachda's furry back. "I must have licked my finger," she said, shaking her head. "Got a bit of the tincture in me." But she knew it was because of the foolish kiss.

What had made her risk ingesting any of the henbane concoction? The hardness of the warrior's body, the kindness in him giving her most of the food, the guilt she harbored for destroying his glider and then rendering him unconscious. Whatever the reason, her impulse was foolish beyond measure. Her rash actions had certainly gotten her into trouble before.

Cora leaned over the wagon wall. "Oh no," she said and shook Tierney's shoulder. "You licked some of Doris's henbane mixture?"

"Just a bit," she said, blinking wide, but the darkness around them made closing her eyes so easy. "I'll rest back here while you two drive us through the forest. Keep Sneachda with you. She'll growl to scare away any stray wolves."

"What about his horse?" Cora asked.

"I will ride him," Gabriel called, and Tierney was too tired to deny her little brother anything. She sank into the comfortable darkness, cradling Kenan's head on her lap.

Her body was so heavy, and she felt adrift in the night. The familiar coldness of dread wrapped around her as she fell into sleep.

*The ship went down. They are dead and you're alone.*

Tierney's dreams brightened behind her closed eyes and then receded, snatches of real life and worries that plagued her. Her father's advisor, Henry Macqueen, featured in many of her nightmares.

*He will send Maggie and Gabriel away. You know that, don't you? He will steal Scorrybreac Tower and scatter the clan.*

*She tried to shake her head, the heaviness of grief and fear pressing on her chest, making it hard to draw breath. And then she was in the icy sea again, floundering, forgetting how to swim. Everything pulled at her. Her father's frowning face swam before her. "Ye need to listen to yer husband."*

*His face turned into Wallace's handsome features, which turned cruel. "Ye're mine, Tierney, and I can do whatever I want to ye." She gasped, trying to swim away.*

Arms went around her, and she struggled against the hold. *"Ye drugged and stole a man." Her father's voice pursued her through the waves. "'Twas sinful."*

*"But I had to take him. For Maggie."*

*"For ye, too, daughter. Selfish!"*

*With a sob, Tierney let herself go underwater. Surrendering to the punishment of the sea.*

*Her father's voice changed to a deep resonance, reaching her ears under the surface. "We're here." The words made no sense. They were in the middle of the choppy sea. Her body shook with the rapid to and fro motion of the waves as her mind justified her rash plan.*

"Tier. Wake up. We're here."

The dream faded to darkness, and then she blinked against a gray light. More shaking.

"All right," she murmured and blinked wider, her fingers rubbing at her dry eyes. The heaviness of dread weighed her down before she could even remember what was going on. What was truth, and what was nightmare? She could feel the cold of the sea on her skin, the heavy drowning in her chest.

Cora's face was set with concern warring with exhaustion. "We need to get him secure before he wakes." Her gaze shifted to Kenan, his head still on Tierney's lap.

"Bloody hell," Tierney whispered, realizing it was dawn. Understanding swelled through her, nearly swamping her. "I slept the whole night?" She rubbed her palms over her face, aware of the ache in her back and neck. Despite the rest, her nightmares had left her exhausted.

Cora nodded. "Sneachda ran all night, and the warrior's horse followed us, even when Gabriel fell asleep. And that lizard rode on his back."

Gabriel frowned at her as he straightened, stretching his arms. "He's a Great Crested newt, and I named him Betrim."

"And you had to stay awake by yourself all night. I'm sorry, Cora." Tierney slowly moved Kenan's head from her lap. In repose, he was beautiful to look at, his warrior hardness smoothed away, but there was no time to study him. She shook her head. How could she have been so foolish as to kiss him after he ate the tart? Tierney groaned softly. "Again, Cora, I'm so—"

"I can't believe you abducted the chief of the Macdonalds of Sleat," Cora said, shaking her head as she stared at Kenan. "And I can't believe I went along with doing it." Her wide eyes softened the severe frown she wore.

Tierney couldn't believe it, either, but she forced confidence into her voice. As if she had everything under control. "You always go along with my plans." Tierney scooted out the back of the wagon. "Because they're good plans."

Cora snorted. "Your plans are risky and only work half the time."

"But they are so unpredictable that I can do something like abduct a warrior chief without him suspecting it." *Holy Joan!* What had she done? Seriously, what had she actually done…

Cora's hands rested on her forehead as she stared. "We were going to steal his glider and then send a note to ransom it back so he'd come to Scorrybreac. Although I don't know how you would have kept him there or planned to get him to fight off Ranulf for you after you stole his glider."

"The wind throwing me into the sea made me have to enact my second plan." She exhaled. "Perhaps this one is better anyway. I'll have more time to convince him to help us," Tierney said, running her fingers through her tangled mess of hair.

Cora dropped her hands. "Or it will be another catastrophe, Tier." She motioned to her head. "Like when you cut your knee-length hair completely off to scare Wallace from tupping you."

Tierney frowned, ruffling her hair. "'Tis grown back."

"And the time you baked that plant that trader brought from the Far East into Bannocks for the guards so you could sneak out of the tower house without anyone raising the alarm."

Tierney looked at Kenan in the wagon as Cora continued. "Instead of them falling asleep, they all became very hungry and foolish, eating everything they could find in the kitchens, but they still wouldn't let you leave, and then your father woke—"

"I remember," Tierney cut her off, not wanting to think about her father. "Some of my plans are unconventional, so they carry a certain amount of risk. But with great risk comes great reward."

"Or great disaster," Cora said, both hands planted on her hips.

*Ye're a selfish disaster.* Tierney's father's words followed Cora's into her mind, but she stomped them down. No time for questioning her actions. Not now. Not when she was already in the thick of plan two.

Tierney threw her arms around Cora like she used to when they were children and one of them was angry at the other. She held on tightly, and finally Cora's stiff body relaxed. "You're my best friend, Cora Wilson, and I love you even if you say you'll never help me again."

Cora exhaled through her nose, making a little whistle, and sniffed, squeezing Tierney back. "Friends 'til the end. It helps that I know why you're doing this."

Tierney let her go, and Cora pressed the back of her hand over her mouth as she yawned. "I'll be kinder after a nap. Sneachda can sleep with me after we get Chief Macdonald inside."

Gabriel untied the rope he'd used to keep himself in the saddle and slid off the tall horse. He checked Betrim, who'd toed his way back up to his shoulder. "I think Tier's plans are good, risky, too, but at least she's doing something instead of old, grouchy Henry."

"Thank you, Gabriel." She gave her brother a big smile, his easy acceptance of her plan lifting her confidence that this was the right choice. "Let's get our savior inside before he wakes." She pointed toward two massive oaks that flanked an arched doorway covered with vines. The cottage was visible when one was upon it, but from a distance, the moss-covered roof and vines draping the stone walls of the squat structure made it blend into the surrounding forest. She'd visited often with her father when she was a child, before Gabriel was born, before her father had decided a girl didn't matter.

"I'll feel safer once he's restrained," Tierney said. She'd given Kenan a large dose because of his size and the need to knock him out quickly. Thank goodness she hadn't given him any more. "I had no other choice," she whispered but knew he couldn't hear her. She rubbed her face, wishing for water to wash away the sourness of her mouth.

"Go find a worm or bug, Betrim," Gabriel said, setting the newt on a log.

Tierney turned to the old cottage, the bittersweet memories floating like ghosts around her. Before he had a son, Douglas MacNicol taught her to shoot her bow and throw a dagger so it would stick. She touched the weathered gash in the oak door where she'd hit it with a sgian dubh before her father reminded her only to throw blades away from people. The wood held a scar just like Tierney's heart.

Early on, Tierney had received a son's education and knew how to read and write and cipher. But once Gabriel was born, her father's lessons stopped. She was to be a polite, agreeable lass and do girl things since he had his son. Tierney continued to practice archery on her own and learned more outdoor survival skills from her friend, Jacob Tanner. But with each skill she mastered, her father frowned more.

On the way down to Dunvegan, where they'd learned Kenan would be attending the wedding of his sister to Rory MacLeod, Tierney and her accomplices had stopped at the vine-covered cottage. Preparing for all possible scenarios, Tierney had hammered the link of a heavy chain to attach it to a rafter inside. Another chain and shackle were waiting as well, making the cozy cabin look a bit like a dungeon. She never actually thought she'd be using the chains, but here she was.

They lowered Kenan to the ground without dropping him. Gabriel helped her drag him by the arms while Cora lifted his legs, and the three of them got him inside the cool, dark room.

"He's too heavy to lift onto the cot," Cora said with a grunt.

"Stretch him out here," Tierney said. "And we can move the mattress to the floor."

Once the hay-filled tick was on the floor next to the cot, the three rolled Kenan. Tierney caught her foot in her petticoat and fell over, landing directly over him, her pelvis pressed to his where she felt the bulge of his jack. She hadn't gotten a look or feel of it while in the sea, but riding before him across the moor had introduced her to the hard ridge rubbing against her arse. She scooted back, ignoring the flush rising into her cheeks.

"Get him chained," Cora said, rubbing her arms

as if she felt a chill. It was her nature to worry and her poor luck to have a friend like Tierney who made her worry most of the time. It was another nugget of guilt that Tierney shoved down into the pit of her conscience.

Tierney picked up the iron cuff chained to the floor. "I hate to shackle him, I really do," she said. "Especially after Asher told us what they endured in Carlisle Dungeon. That might be too far."

Her cousin, Asher MacNicol, had returned from England scarred and bitter before leaving Scorrybreac with a vow never to return.

"He'll walk out when he wakes if we don't," Gabriel said, sounding much older than he did less than a year ago when life was still calm and their lives were relatively happy. "There is no other choice."

"Or skewer us." Cora pointed to the sword sheathed at his side.

Tierney threw her palms to her forehead. "Holy Joan." She hadn't even taken his weapon away from him. "Help me get it off him. I'm not made for such crimes!"

• • •

Kenan's mouth was dry, his tongue sticking to the roof like one of the worst crapulous mornings he'd ever endured. What the bloody hell had he drunk last eve? Where had he even been?

Images of a blond angel swam in the darkness before his closed eyes. Tierney Bruce, under the stars. She had kissed him. Or was that a dream?

He kept his eyes closed, taking in his surroundings without giving away that he'd woken. The bed was lumpy, but he was definitely inside, not sleeping on a mossy bed because he wasn't damp with dew. Carlisle Dungeon?

*Nay. It doesn't smell like shite and death.*

He inhaled and smelled a musty vegetation scent, no fire, but the heaviness of a blanket weighed on him. His fingers slid against his side. Damn, his sheath and sword were gone.

A door creaked open. "He's still asleep." It was a woman's voice, and one he didn't recognize.

"You and Gabriel must go," another woman answered. That voice he did recognize. Tierney Bruce, the lass he was taking back to her cousin's cottage just inside the woods from Dunvegan. *Fok.* The taste in his mouth was bitter with the rancid blackberry flavor of the horrid tart she'd nearly shoved into his mouth.

*I'm a foking idiot.* The lass had drugged him.

Rage bloomed inside Kenan, rage at her and rage at himself for falling for a teasing grin and soft curves. He wanted to leap up and grab her, growl in her face, and demand she tell him the truth. Had anything she said been true? Had she been married before, or had she created the whole story to garner his pity and lower his defenses? Had she heard he was kind and played on the weakness?

*Ye're weak, boy.* His father's words ground through his head.

"You and Gabriel took a nap, so head back now to make it home before nightfall," Tierney said. "Please go and make sure Maggie is safe. The bastard might have already arrived."

"Doris and Edith will hide her," the other lass said. "When will you bring him?" He could feel their eyes on him and concentrated on even breathing.

Bring him? Not bloody likely. Not now that his guard was up and his cock wasn't doing his thinking, or lack of thinking. He forced himself to remain still.

They walked closer. Was she close enough to grab?

"As soon as I convince him to help me," Tierney said.

The muscles in his body tightened, and his eyes snapped open. "How the fok are ye going to do that, ye lying, thieving, bloody witch?"

Both women jumped, hands flying to cover their hearts. He was surprised his voice held force considering the desert in his mouth. He rolled to his side, pushing up to sit, and realized he was on the floor in a cottage. The sound of a chain dragging made prickles rise along his arms and red-hot fury ignite inside his chest. He threw off the blanket to see his leg was in a shackle attached to a chain that ran all the way up to the bloody ceiling.

His face swiveled toward the two women. The one he didn't know had brown hair sticking haphazardly from a braid and wide eyes in a thin face full of fear. She'd retreated to the far wall and attempted to hold his heavy sword before her. Tierney remained on the other side of a partial circle chalked out on the gray floorboards.

Kenan rolled easily onto his heels to stand in a fluid motion, ignoring the slight dizziness still plaguing his head. He strode toward her, his fingers bent like talons on a bird of prey to grab her shoulders, to demand she remove the shackle. But the attached chain caught him. Even lifting his leg behind him and stretching his arms out, he couldn't go past the chalk drawn in a semicircle around his side of the barely furnished room. She must have measured it based on his height.

He dropped his arms, feeling ridiculous, but his lips curled back in a snarl like an avenging wolf. "Release me now."

"I cannot do that." The woman's hair fell in wild, golden waves around her oval face. She folded her hands before her, hands he remembered thinking were delicate but strong. They weren't what made her dangerous. 'Twas her mind and her poison.

Eyes narrowed, he spoke as if to a child. "Ye can take the little key from yer little pocket and hand it to me."

She exhaled through her nose, her small nostrils flaring. "So you can ride off without hearing—"

"I don't need to hear anything! Just release me." The words thundered through his head, bringing back the dungeon's dank smell of human waste and disease.

"I can't do that," she said, her words infuriatingly calm. His roars and flashing anger, once triggered, were known to make men quake, and yet she just stood there, hands folded with quiet patience. "I'm sorry. I am."

"Aye, ye *can* do that. And ye are *not* sorry."

"I should say I *won't* do that. I can't do that."

He wanted to roar, stomp his feet, and scare the piss out of her. But she could just leave, and he needed answers.

"Who the bloody hell are ye? Where are we? And where do ye think ye're going to make me go without me snapping ye in two like a brittle stick?" His words flew out of him like javelins meant to kill. The woman against the wall flinched, but Tierney just stood with her hands fisted by her sides as if waiting to see how many hits she could take before falling.

When he stopped, she inhaled and crossed her arms. "So you *do* need to hear something."

Kenan breathed through his nose like a trapped boar ready to yank his own leg off to charge. "I would know who my enemies are."

"We are allies, not enemies."

"The hell we are," he said, trying to keep control. "And ye," he pointed at the lass against the wall, "are going to cut yer own foot off with my sword if ye don't put it down carefully."

Tierney, if that was even her name, looked at her. "Be careful, Cora." Cora lowered his sword, sliding it into the scabbard across the table they'd scooted over to their side of the chalk circle, and Tierney looked back at him.

"My name is Tierney MacNicol from Scorrybreac. We are in a hidden cottage in the forest. You are going to come back with me to Scorrybreac because…you are going to save our clan."

# CHAPTER FIVE

"People reveal themselves completely only when they are thrown out of the customary conditions of their life."

*Leonardo da Vinci — Italian artist and scientist*
*1452–1519*

Tierney's heart thumped as she stood just outside the man's reach, thankful that she'd measured correctly while he slept off the draught. Apparently, Cora hadn't trusted her measurements, because her friend flattened herself against the far wall. Tierney couldn't really blame her. Kenan Macdonald was as close to a furious mythological Zeus that she'd ever seen.

Glinting blue eyes threw daggers at her as he stared her down from his great height. His dark hair brushed the low ceiling of the cottage and fell around his head in waves that looked styled by the wind. But it was his broad shoulders and well-muscled arms that she could see bunching under his tunic that really made him look like a sculpted king of the gods. The man was every bit a warrior, ready to throw lightning bolts—at her.

"Tierney MacNicol, not Tierney Bruce," he said. "Whatever yer name, ye will release me now." His words ground out from a clenched jaw in such a way that goose bumps rose along her arms.

"I'll go check on…" Cora flapped her hand at the door and hurried out, dragging his sword behind her.

Tierney studied him. At present, he didn't look kind, but who could blame him? "First, hear me out."

He raised his hands to catch the chain attached to the low beam above his head. Yanking, it didn't even move, so he rested his hands on the beam and leaned toward her while holding on. It made his muscles bulge. "Ye poisoned me. Why would I help ye?"

She stared at him without blinking even though the knot in her stomach ached. "Because you are kind."

"I'm bloody hell not kind, and I'm not helping ye." He narrowed those long-lashed eyes. "MacNicol? Are ye related to Asher MacNicol of Scorrybreac?"

"Yes, but he's no longer of Scorrybreac." If her cousin was still there, she wouldn't have had to resort to any of this.

Kenan's biceps bunched as if he would rip the beam down from the ceiling. She needed to distract him from destroying everything around him, which included her, though she completely understood why he'd want to.

Tierney held out both hands. "I will explain."

"There is no explanation good enough for drugging a man and—"

"There are good reasons. To me, anyway. Hear me out."

"—dragging him out to… Where the bloody hell am I?" Their voices continued to rise until they were yelling back and forth, him in anger and her in frustration.

"I need you to save—"

He released the beam. "First ye try to steal my glider—"

"I wasn't stealing it, just trying to lure you—"

He paced to the window. "—and then ye destroy it in the sea and feed me a tart laced with poison—"

"A sleeping brew. Not poison. Sleeping brew. Very different."

"Poison!"

"You wouldn't have just come with me."

"Nay, I wouldn't go anywhere with a mad thief and poisoner to be shackled in a dingy cottage."

"Again, I'm sorry." The words flew from her mouth only to dissolve in the face of his fury.

He looked like a chained bear being baited, nostrils flaring, muscles ready to explode in violence. His jaw was granite, and his face flushed red. He wacked the half-open shutter with his hand.

With a *thunk*, the shutter fell off the window to the floor. They both looked at it, giving them a chance to breathe.

Tierney inhaled. "Chief Macdonald of Sleat, I need your help, please. For the sake of many. For the sake of my clan, I beg of you. I had to resort to capturing you before you returned to Dunscaith. There was no other way, and I am out of options and ideas." She waited for another thrust of yelled curses. He took long breaths, turning to pace away from her. He grabbed up a bladder of spring water she'd left within his reach along with oatcakes. He uncorked the bladder and sniffed it.

"'Tis fresh spring water. Untainted, I promise," she said.

"Like I would trust yer promise."

"I don't want to have to carry you again, so I have no reason nor desire to render you unconscious."

"Ye carried me?" His brows rose, and she felt a flush rise along the skin of her neck as he perused her more diminutive form.

"I had help," she snapped out.

He threw an arm out. "The mousy lass who can barely lift my sword?"

"And my brother, Gabriel."

He rubbed the side of his fist against the grimy glass of the window, causing a squeak. "The child out there?" Straightening, he turned back to her. "Ye three carried me from the moor? 'Tis a wonder I don't have a cracked head from being dropped."

She huffed. "We had a wagon, lifted you in there and then out of it once we reached here. As you can see, we had to leave you on the floor instead of the bed."

"To chain me like a prisoner." He sniffed the drink once more.

"I promise I don't want you unconscious again," she said and crossed her arms. "You're too cumbersome, and your plaid kept riding up."

He stared at her, his tongue pushing into his cheek for a moment before he tipped the bladder up to his lips. She watched him swallow down the entire thing. He wiped his mouth with the back of his hand, tossing the empty bladder on the floor. Looking around, Kenan strode to a privacy screen, ducking behind it.

The rushing sound of pissing made Tierney rub a hand down the side of her face. He wasn't going to scare her off with natural bodily functions. She'd braved her father, her late husband, her horrid suitor, and most recently the sky and freezing sea. Piss, wind, and vomit couldn't hurt anyone. Only a brutal temper and unchecked fists. Would Kenan Macdonald be as terrible as Wallace?

*Asher said he was kind.* Tierney closed her eyes and imagined breathing in courage and pulled the locket up from her smock, clasping it. *Courage.*

*Splash.* He'd found the water pitcher and washstand. Kenan walked back around, his arms across his now-naked chest. Well-developed, honed muscles were emphasized by nicked scars here and there. A circle of dark pigment lines sat on one thick bicep with a Celtic design that just made the muscle look larger. Small rivulets ran down his chest from where he'd washed, and his hair looked slightly damp as if he'd run wet fingers through it. His short beard held droplets.

Kenan braced his boots apart, and his wrap slung low across his narrow hips. Lines of muscle slid diagonally across his abdomen as if pointing below the edge of his plaid, daring her eyes to drop. But Tierney kept her gaze on his face.

"Speak."

His tone sounded like he was the captor and she was the one shackled. What would it be like to be this sculpted man's captive? *Never again.* She'd never let anyone trap her again, not after what she'd endured. She would never trust anyone with a jack between their legs.

She wet her lips. "I need your help to save Scorrybreac Tower from Ranulf Matheson, brother to the new Chief Murdoc Matheson on the mainland. He's come to Skye to take over the MacNicol Clan now that my father, Chief Douglas MacNicol, and mother, Fannie, have been lost at sea."

"The MacNicol Clan is strong and won't give up their land to an interloper without legal—"

"Some of our warriors were lost at Solway Moss, and the sweating sickness took half of those who remained last winter." She swallowed. "And my father, in a mistaken attempt to keep Clan MacNicol strong, requested a betrothal before he died."

Kenan's hard gaze focused on hers. "Ye're to marry Matheson. Which one?"

"I never agreed, but the contract was sent to Ranulf, who now thinks we are betrothed when we are most definitely not."

"Which has nothing to do with me." Kenan's voice was still hard as granite, but it was devoid of curses and not an ear-splitting bellow. Progress.

"My father included a clause in the contract that says if I wed another clan chief, the betrothal contract is void." Douglas MacNicol was determined to align with another clan to save his own, and he would use Tierney to do it with another marriage alliance. But she'd yelled so much about the hideousness of Ranulf that he'd added the clause to try to get Tierney actively interested in marrying with the leader of a powerful clan.

"He's coming to take over my home and clan," she said, trying to keep panic out of her voice. "I cannot allow it. I have a younger brother, Gabriel, who is still too young to lead the MacNicol Clan." She glanced toward the door where he waited outside.

"Asher MacNicol can lead yer clan and chase off this Matheson if ye don't consent to marry him." Kenan looked wholly dispassionate, as if her problem was easily solved.

Frustration pinched Tierney's mouth. "Asher disappeared soon after he came home from England. Off Skye, from what I've been able to discern. When he accused my father of abandonment after the battle at Solway Moss, we were almost at civil war, but then Asher withdrew and left without a word, taking four of our best warriors with him. I've spent the last month trying to find him to no avail. Ranulf is due within the fortnight."

She crossed her arms to mimic Kenan. She must make him understand. The silence in the room was thick with waiting while thoughts churned inside Tierney. Why wouldn't anyone help her? She was clearly expendable to everyone, a pawn to be surrendered.

No one had ever saved Tierney before, not her father who'd turned his back on her because she wasn't a son and then refused to help her once she was wed. Not her mother when she wept after shaving her head in efforts to keep Wallace away from her. Even Cora abandoned her when her plans fell apart, shaking her head, afraid to do anything to help. Jacob had helped only when it was almost too late. But this time it wasn't just for her. She had to save Maggie, too.

She took a breath. "Asher said you were

honorable and clever, that you wanted to see the Isle of Skye united. If Clan Matheson gets a foothold on Skye, they will be yet another clan to convince to unite. The Matheson Clan values conquest over peace."

Crossing his arms, Kenan's gaze bored into her. A light sprinkling of hair curled over his chiseled chest. Was it soft? Nothing about Kenan Macdonald was soft except the hair on his head that she'd run her fingers through. She shifted, trying to banish the flutter of anticipation that muddled her thoughts when he looked at her so intensely. He was assessing her, judging her cause…judging her. So far, she hadn't made a great impression.

"Asher said you were kind."

Kenan's lips pulled back like she'd just said he ripped the heads off kittens and drowned newborn bairns. "I am not kind." His voice came low and threatening. "And I have no time to venture to Scorrybreac and deter Ranulf Matheson. My clan needs its leader, especially right now as we rebuild Dunscaith Castle." He stalked to the window, kicking aside the shutter on the floor. Looking out, he said, "Ye can claim sanctuary at Dunscaith on Sleat."

"Ranulf will take Scorrybreac if I abandon it!" Her words flared out of her like a blaze of fire, her guilt at abducting him taking a back place to the need she had to save her clan. He turned back to her. "It belongs to Clan MacNicol," she said.

"Those who wish to flee may accompany ye down to Sleat. My sister can take in some at Dunvegan, too."

She was already shaking her head. "You will be

allowing Ranulf Matheson a foothold on Skye, a thorn that will never go away. You won't be able to unite all the clans on Skye with him here." Her nose scrunched at the thought of the cocky man. "He's not a reasonable person."

"Not reasonable," Kenan murmured, although his ferocity had dulled. "Ye two should pair together nicely."

"All you need to do is act like we wed, telling Ranulf you're leading Clan MacNicol and that Scorrybreac Tower is my dowry. It will negate the betrothal contract, and I'm certain the chief of the mighty Macdonald Clan of Sleat can chase him off Skye. The MacNicol Clan will continue under my control until Asher can be found or until my brother reaches his majority."

"What if I don't care about the MacNicol Clan?"

He was baiting her. Wasn't he? Asher had said Kenan Macdonald was a good person who wanted to unite all of Skye and even all of Scotland. 'Twas why she'd targeted him for this audacious, morally gray plan.

"You care about uniting the Isle of Skye to strengthen us," she said, her toe tapping with pent-up worry. What was wrong with her that no one wanted to help her?

"And assisting ye will do this?"

"Yes," she shouted but then took a deep breath to take the sting out of her voice. She'd always been headstrong, a risk taker as Cora said, but the stress of Ranulf's suit and threats against her family had resurrected her sudden outbursts. 'Twas as if she were still married to Wallace or trying to prove she was capable to her father. "Yes," she repeated, lowering her voice. "But I can offer you more."

"More?" His brow rose, and he let his gaze slide down her form as if he were mentally stripping her naked. "More of ye?"

A blush flew up her neck and into her face. Unfortunately, those damn embers of heat within her flared as if fanned by the fluttering of her heart. Wallace had called her cold to a man's attention, but Tierney was feeling anything but cold under this wickedly handsome Highlander's gaze. It was like a stroke along her skin, purposely inciting her unprecedented lust.

He was trying to embarrass her, and despite Tierney's hot cheeks, a simple look would not fluster her. This was a battle of gazes, words, and wills. And her will was iron. It had to be.

"I don't bargain with my body, so let's plan to make you Lord of the Isles, the leader of all the clans on Skye and throughout the Hebrides."

Kenan's jaw fell open, and he dropped his arms so that they once again mimicked each other's stance. "Lord of the Isles is a title that died out a century ago, stamped out by Scottish royalty."

"Scotland is a ridiculous dictatorship," she said, dismissing it. "We should govern ourselves out here, far away from Edinburgh. They know nothing of the Highlands nor the isles."

"And *ye*," he paused to point at her, "are going to make me Lord of the Isles?"

Her smile turned tight, and she kept her spine straight with confidence. Men respected confidence and stomped all over meekness. "I will endeavor to do so." He opened his mouth to retort, but she held up a hand. "And when I endeavor to do something, like abducting a fierce warrior, I am successful." At least she hoped so. Her success was still in limbo.

"Like stealing a man's glider?" he asked, frowning fiercely. "Flying it successfully and landing on dry land?"

"Your glider was an unknown entity," she said. "Besides, da Vinci's drawings showed the nose to be severed into two wings. I had no way to research—"

"Ye looked at da Vinci's plans?"

"Of course," she said, hands propping on her hips even though that made her look like a scolding fishmonger's wife. "I wouldn't risk my life without any forethought." She wasn't daft or a fool even though some thought she was. "I had planned to sail the wings out past Dunvegan to the moor beyond, landing near the tree line where Gabriel and Cora would be waiting for me. We would take the glider and send word that we would trade it for your help. That was plan number one, but when it went askew, I had to go with plan number two."

"Poisoning and abducting me was plan number two," Kenan said.

She nodded, swallowing past the tightness in her throat. "Which is working." Perhaps if she said it enough, it would. And he'd not be so cross with her.

He scoffed. "'Tis not."

She pointed to the shackle at his bare ankle. "That says it is."

His clear blue eyes hardened until his gaze looked like it could slice her from throat down her belly so that all her bloody innards rolled out onto the floor. An involuntary shiver coursed through her, followed immediately by regret. Her foolish mouth got her into so much trouble.

"I spent over a year shackled by the English," he said, his words soft and hard. "I escaped with red-hot vengeance in my heart. An inconsequential slip of a lass won't hold me for long, and when I find my freedom again…" He let the threat hang in the air between them.

The heat of her shame clashed with the ice in his words, releasing chill bumps all over Tierney. She spun around in an effort to break his spell that threatened to eviscerate her courage. If this didn't work, then she would die anyway.

Cora's face appeared in the cracked door. She pushed it farther open and cleared her throat, peeking in, her eyes wide. "I heard yelling."

"He's not cooperating." Tierney marched out of the cottage, making Cora back up.

Gabriel stood behind Cora, the lizard-creature back on his shoulder.

"Plan number three, then?" Cora asked, her voice a squeak.

"What's plan number three?" Gabriel asked, glancing at Betrim as if the newt had the answer. It tipped its head as it stared back at him.

"Never you mind," Cora said to him.

"I should know all the plans," Gabriel said, frowning.

Cora shook her head. "'Tis not for a young lad's ears."

"I'm almost three and ten. I know all sorts of things."

Tierney's cheeks burned as she remembered telling a wild story of seduction to Cora that would be plan number three. She would tie the Highlander to the bed, stripping in front of him until he was wild with lust, thrusting his hard jack into the air, begging her to sit upon it. Then she would wring his oath to help her in exchange for her sliding down upon him as he roared his promises to save their clan as long as she stayed with him.

The image of Kenan, naked, tied to the bed, and aroused while straining to pounce on her made the shiver from before turn into a full-blown ache.

"I'm not resorting to plan number three," Tierney said, to stop the mild bickering between them. She glanced at the open door, wishing she'd closed it. Kenan stood listening, naked except for the wrap around his hips. His hands fisted at his sides matched the hardness of his muscles. He was the perfect specimen of a warrior, and she had no doubt he could conquer on the battlefield and in bed. Tierney found it challenging to swallow and turned away from him.

"No plan three, then," Cora whispered, flattening her hand over her heart as if relieved. She needn't be so worried over something Tierney could never actually imagine doing. Not after the horrors of Wallace looming over her, tearing into her as he growled that she better learn what it meant to be married. The nightmares still worked their way into her dreams.

"You two will have to take his glider and his horse back to Scorrybreac as hostage. And his sword." She met Kenan's hard stare. "You'll get everything back if you help us."

"Freya won't pull a wagon," Kenan said, his voice strong even though he was inside the cottage. It reached her as if stone walls were no real barrier against his force. "She's a Percheron horse, a charger made for war."

Tierney pierced her lips. "Percheron horses were originally bred for heavy hauling."

"But I've only trained her to charge into battle and stomp the life out of thieves and their helpers."

Cora gasped, so Tierney rolled her eyes as if her heart wasn't in her throat. "He's making that up," she whispered.

"Do *not* take Freya," Kenan said.

He apparently loved his mare more than his sword, perhaps even more than his glider. Something they had in common, then. Tierney would give her life for her horse, Fleet, so she understood this weakness.

"Take Freya and Sneachda with you to Scorrybreac," she said to Gabriel and Cora. "If Freya won't take the rigging, then just ride her and leave the wagon. Fleet will pull it." Her preference was for the wagon to go since it had Kenan's glider and sword, two more things to draw him to Scorrybreac.

"How will you get him to cooperate?" Gabriel asked her. Tierney knew he didn't doubt her abilities, but Kenan Macdonald was not pliable, and her own conscience wouldn't permit her to force him physically any more than she'd already had.

"I have a plan," she said with false cheer, because her plans were flimsy and depended on Kenan's cooperation, which he didn't seem inclined to give.

"But not plan number three, whatever that is," Gabriel said, a pout in his tone. He held a small worm before Betrim, whose tongue snagged it immediately.

"Leave my bow and arrow," Tierney said. "We'll be along once I convince him 'tis in his and our whole isle's best interest to help us."

Her brother and Cora turned to start soothing Freya to accept the wagon gear. Tierney had confidence that her animal-loving brother would be able to coax the giant horse to do anything.

With a full inhale and exhale, Tierney walked to the cottage and clipped across the floorboards back to the edge of Kenan's allowable range.

Kenan sat on the small bed where he'd returned the tick. He leaned against the wall with his arms folded over his chest. "Stealing a man's horse is a hangable offence."

"I'd rather hang than see Ranulf Matheson take over Clan MacNicol by forcing me to wed him or through military strength."

"And drugging a clan chief and abducting him and his horse might see ye drawn and quartered," he said, his voice as stubborn as his hard face. "'Tis completely dishonorable."

His brittle condemnation reminded her of her father. No matter what she did to try to prove herself to Douglas MacNicol, he always made her feel small and inconsequential. In frustration, born out of desperation and a need so deep it made her stomach feel hollow, Tierney's hands flew out to either side of her to emphasize her words.

"Since the beginning of time, women have been

abducted, assaulted, knocked unconscious, and forced to marry men they abhor. You're enduring a small portion of that horror." She'd endured years of it with Wallace. Because she'd been his wife, no one, not even her father, interfered. No one risked saving her, except her friend Jacob.

Tierney stalked outside, letting the door bang closed. It made Freya's head shoot up out of Gabriel's hands, and Tierney silently chided herself for letting Kenan fluster her.

*I am in charge of this situation. My plan will work.* Holy Joan, maybe she was truly losing her mind. Cora had asked that of her when she'd first explained her plans about abducting a powerful clan chief who was said to also be kind and reasonable. She ran hands down her face and slowed her breathing. The movement of air in and out helped her regain her focus.

Gabriel held out an apple to Freya as Tierney approached, slowing her stride. "There now, Freya," Gabriel said, his voice soothing. Betrim's head bobbed for a slight second as if he were agreeing. "My sister makes a lot of noise sometimes, but she's doing what's right."

Did he really think that? Her brother was only twelve, but he understood that she was doing this for him, too.

Cora was quietly hooking up the wagon along her side. She smiled at Tierney, nodding to Gabriel.

Her father hadn't thought anything she did was right, but this time she was. "I'm going to save us all."

"You will," Cora said. "If heart and cleverness

can win over evil, you'll do it."

*Think of how you want things to be.* Her mother's advice repeated in Tierney's mind. *Think hard on it and then create plans to make it happen.* She sniffed slightly at the memory. She hadn't allowed herself time to mourn the loss of the woman who'd loved her so much and soothed her when her father finally had his son.

Fannie MacNicol had been strong but sweet, cajoling people into doing things she wished. Even her father had relented under her gentle persuasion, except when it came to Tierney. Then he'd become as stubborn as a mule, insisting she wasn't acting like a proper lass. In his mind, a proper lass wouldn't complain about being knocked about by her horrid husband, and she'd accept her father's betrothal plans to another brute when the first one died.

Tierney straightened and blinked against the ache of tears. "I guess I'll never be a proper lass, but we will win this." Because the only option if this didn't work was death.

# CHAPTER SIX

"Anger is a wind which blows out the
lamp of the mind."

*Robert Green Ingersoll (American Lawyer 1833–1899)*

"Ye may look like an angel, but ye're a bloody devil," Kenan said, imagining himself snarling. Although, if he turned berserker and frightened her away, he'd have a hell of a time getting loose from the shackle around his ankle before he died of thirst.

He watched the golden-haired woman brush out her tresses before the fire. She had changed from her petticoats and bodice into trousers that revealed her well-shaped arse and long legs. The white tunic was that of a lad's and untied to show her lovely, kissable throat. Was she trying to tempt him, knowing he was properly shackled and unable to reach her? He had to keep imagining his middle-aged aunt, Morag, naked to keep his cock from rising up.

"If I'm an angel, I'm a fallen one," she said, turning her back to him. "In fact, I'm cold and a nuisance and not a proper lady." She used her brush to point toward the trout she'd caught. "But I can keep us fed." She'd cleaned and roasted it over the fire she'd started. She'd seasoned it well with herbs from a packet she'd brought, and he'd waited until she ate it first before partaking. The fish was delicious. Bread and berries had been included in the meal, as well as fresh spring water.

"A resourceful devil," Kenan said. He sat on the small bed, his back against the wall and arms crossed over his chest. The woman had left the door wide open earlier so he could see his beloved horse being ridden away, hauling his glider and sword in the back of a wagon. The other lass, Cora, had sat in the wagon while the young lad rode on Freya's back, their white dog trotting alongside as if on sentry duty.

Tierney looked over her shoulder at him. "I'm just a dead chief's daughter who needs your help to save her people."

He'd heard desperation in her voice before, but he'd been too incensed to listen. Which wasn't his fault. She'd foking abducted him. "Ye don't know much about men if ye think ye can force me to do anything to help ye after ye've drugged and shackled me and then stolen my horse and sword."

She exhaled through her pert little nose and lowered her gaze to the floor as if the weight of thousands of lives sat upon her shoulders. "Freya will be treated with care. My brother has a calm way with animals and will likely sleep in her stall to keep her company when they arrive at Scorrybreac. I even sent Sneachda with them to keep the wolves away. But I need a reason to get you to accompany me to Scorrybreac since you've refused."

Tierney raised her gaze and held her arms out, lifted from her sides with palms exposed. "I haven't the physical strength to force you to do anything, Kenan Macdonald, so I must use whatever weapons I have. Cleverness, resourcefulness, and a vast knowledge of living in the forest."

"And how to drug a man."

"Which falls under all three categories," she said. She pointed to his plate. "Shove your plate over the line so I can wash it."

He could refuse, but it would come across as childish pouting. Kenan stood, the sound of the chain sending a ripple of memory and anger up his spine. He'd been shackled whenever he was moved from his cell at Carlisle Dungeon. A year and a half of cold, hunger, diseased surroundings, and torture. Despite greatly outnumbering the English that day, the disastrous loss to the Scots at Solway Moss had reinforced the need for Scotland to stop fighting each other and unite. Something Kenan had sworn to do at least on Skye.

Helping this woman would bring the MacNicol Clan in as an ally, but from how she described her ailing clan, it wouldn't be much to celebrate. Clan Mackinnon, on the other hand, was vast and powerful. Daingead. Did Cyrus think he left Dunvegan without wishing his sister farewell?

Tierney picked up his plate and moved about the cabin with agile grace, skirting the perimeter of his invisible cell as if she'd been doing it all her life. The woman was clearly athletic and fairly strong, but her body was also full of soft hills and valleys. Bloody hell! He needed to keep his mind away from how soft and warm she'd felt clinging to him in the sea.

*She's a thief and a liar.*

What else was she? "How is it ye know how to fish and start fires if ye're the daughter of a chieftain?" Perhaps her story was all a lie.

Tierney left the door open as she scraped the fish bones off the side of the stoop and squatted to wash the plates in a bucket set outside the door. For a long moment, he thought she wouldn't answer. Without looking up, her voice came out crisp. "I thought one day I'd run away, live wild perhaps. To be prepared, I set out to learn how to survive in the woods."

"Ye do seem quite feral," he said. She ignored his insult. "Why would ye have to run away from Scorrybreac?"

She turned her face to him, still in her crouched position. "I was living at Uig then, in Tuath Tower, with the Macqueens, and it was…inhospitable. My first plan to…" She shook her head. "Well, it didn't work. Plan number two was to run away, and I wasn't about to die in the woods of starvation and cold or be eaten by wolves."

His brow rose. "Ye can fight off a wolf?"

"We might both die in the process, but yes, yes, I can."

He tipped his head to the side, considering her. "His pack would just eat ye, then."

She straightened, drying her hands on her thighs, ignoring his taunt. "I can hunt, fish, start a fire, slice a beast trying to eat me or a man trying to attack me. I can shoot a bow with practiced accuracy and climb trees. I know which berries and mushrooms are safe to eat and how to collect herbs to heal or put a captive to sleep. I am self-sufficient." Her beauty glowed as pride infused her words. She walked back inside, barring the door.

"But ye still need me," he said. Even though

she'd learned much about survival, she knew when she needed help. Not only able, intriguing, and lush, but also clever. *Liar and thief. Don't forget that.*

She nodded slowly. "I need a warrior who will deter a war. I could slice Ranulf's throat, but it would bring his brother bent on revenge." He watched her swallow and wondered if she'd actually be able to kill someone. Or was she putting on a confident face?

"The simplest way to solve this issue is for you to pretend to be my husband. If I'm already wed to a strong chief on Skye, the betrothal contract my father wrote will be void. There will be nothing Ranulf can do about it."

"Except try to kill me," Kenan said. "Is there a clause in the contract about that?"

"Your reputation as a warrior says you'll survive anything Ranulf throws at you."

But if Kenan killed him, it would cause more strife between the clans of Scotland.

Tierney looked at him. "Please," she said evenly. There was no begging. Just determination.

"One of yer MacNicol warriors could act as yer husband."

She hesitated near the tiny cupboard where she stored the two plates away. "The clause says it must be someone in power, like a chief with a large enough army to keep Clan Matheson from taking over Scorrybreac and my clan." She looked at him. "And I need a warrior who is honorable, a man able to deter a formidable enemy but who also won't just take us over." She stepped right up to the line marking his prison. "And you, Kenan Macdonald, fit that role. I need you. Please."

The words wrapped around in his chest like a ribbon that could change into a noose. "Ye need me, lass? Only me?"

She inhaled, and he caught a slight tremble in her shoulders. "Your position and the force you command, your acceptance of this quest, can save us. Your refusal will see the MacNicol Clan wiped off Skye, replaced by a powerful foe."

And see either Tierney taken by Ranulf Matheson against her will or her living in the forest, taking shots from trees at the invaders until someone kills her. Neither of which was something Kenan wanted to see happen despite what she'd done to him. She had reasons for her plan number two, reasons he could understand. Somewhat.

Kenan rubbed the short beard over his jaw. "Capturing and shackling a man who has survived and escaped an English dungeon will not sway him to help ye."

She stared at him for a long moment. "Then what will?"

"What's yer third plan?"

"Pardon?" she asked, blinking. Blotches of color rose first in her cheeks and then slid up her neck as if heat bloomed under her skin.

"I heard yer friend ask if ye were going to implement plan three before she and the lad stole Freya—"

"Borrowed," she interrupted. "You'll get her back unharmed."

"She said something about ye resorting to plan three, and she'd looked aghast as if it involved force-feeding me kittens."

Tierney waved her hand. "Cora looks aghast at most of my plans."

"Maybe that means all your plans are mad."

The lass smiled meekly. "Maybe they are, but some of them work."

He opened his eyes wide. "Good God, ye *are* going to suffocate me with kittens."

A little hiccough of a laugh came out of her. It sounded almost musical, and Kenan wanted to hear it again.

"I might have unique ideas," she said, "but I would never torture kittens or any animal." She flapped her hand. "And all ideas have merit. Without the irrational idea of man flying, Leonardo da Vinci would never have made his plans that you used for inspiration."

He crossed his arms. "So yer third plan doesn't involve torturing me or my horse."

"Of course not. What do you think I am?"

"Seduction, perhaps? Is that more like you?" he asked, watching the color that darkened in her cheeks.

"I know nothing about seducing horses." She rolled her eyes, but the stain of embarrassment slid across the exposed skin at her collar.

"How about men?"

A small burst of air escaped her lips, and she shook her head, returning to the fire without an answer. Keeping her legs straight, she bent over to stir the embers, adding another dry peat square. The trousers cupped her perfect round arse like his palms itched to do. Would she like to be mounted from behind? His hands fisted, and he sat back on the cot, his back against the wall while he adjusted his rising cock. When she stood, her hair fell to her midback in waves of gold. It looked soft, and he suddenly imagined pressing his face in it.

*Bloody hell.* She might not have kittens to suffocate him with, but a man could lose himself in those glorious tresses.

"We will just have to stay here until you agree to act as my husband to void the contract and dissuade Ranulf from invading, until you see that it will benefit you to keep him off Skye."

"And how exactly does a husband act? Do I carry ye over a threshold or throw yer skirts up without ye skewering me with a sgian dubh, slicing me right where ye know a man would bleed to death?"

She stared unblinking at him.

When she didn't speak, Kenan continued, hoping to shock her. "Do I ask ye, wife, to take me in yer mouth before this obstinate suitor?"

"Is that what being wed to you would look like? You telling me to suck on your jack before people? Or you throwing my skirts up for a quick mating in corners of a barn?"

"Probably not in a barn. Hay makes me sneeze."

Her lips pursed, and her face reddened so she looked like she might pop.

"Bloody hell, Tierney," he said with a dramatic sigh, "I would never embarrass a woman like that, but I don't know how ye think me saying, 'Good day, Ranulf Matheson, many pardons but I wed her first,' will make him believe that we are wed. We have no paper that says we are married."

"You can tell him we are wed, and I'll say it as well, that the priest has the document. Then you can promise to rally the might of Clan Macdonald against him if he doesn't leave Scorrybreac and Skye completely, never to return."

"I could start a war with the Matheson Clan," he said, which was opposite of what he wanted. His castle was destroyed, and he was just gaining confidence from his clan as the new chief. He couldn't just jump into a clan war, especially when he'd sworn to help bring Scotland together.

"No." She shook her head. "Ranulf, with his brother, Chief Murdoc, would be starting a war. They are bent on war anyway, either with my clan or yours, and your clan is powerful while mine is nearly non-existent." A slight shine of unshed tears came to her eyes. "You will be victorious, Kenan Macdonald, and I will help you become the new Lord of the Isles, in charge of all of Skye and beyond."

"Again, saying the words into the air doesn't make them true."

"Putting the words out there helps them manifest into reality."

"Even if that really worked," he said, shaking his head, "I'm not greedy and prefer the clans rule themselves. They should be united, helping each other out of joint loyalty, not being ruled by one man." He tipped his head. "Perhaps ye should try plan three instead of luring me with a promise of power. That is if plan three involves something... pleasantly carnal."

She blinked at him, which made her look almost innocent and certainly not a woman who would trick and abduct him. She was soft and curved and looked like someone who could use saving, not that he was foolish enough to say that. Instead, he wondered what it be like to sink into the softness of Tierney MacNicol. She looked like a true fallen angel with golden hair framing smooth features, large eyes, and full lips.

"Plan three is…complicated and risky," she said. "'Tis hard to bargain with seduction when a man is physically stronger than a woman and likely to take what he wants and walk away."

Kenan frowned. "I don't take anything from a lass that isn't freely given."

One slender finger rose to her lips, the tip tapping them in thought. "So, if I remove my clothing and unshackle you…"

Kenan stood, moving to the line, his chain dragging behind. "And I kiss ye and stroke yer fine skin until yer heart races and ye tremble in my arms, pleading me to bring ye to thrashing climax."

Her hand dropped to her side. "Or you throw me down and push into me, bruising me as you take your pleasure before leaving me on the floor while you steal my horse and ride back to Dunvegan and Dunscaith." She shook her head. "Plan three has major flaws."

Had someone told her that was how tupping worked? "I don't hurt my lover, and if I…push into ye, 'tis because ye want me to. With me loving ye, ye'll be begging me to touch ye inside and out."

She swallowed, her gaze dropping to the floor. "I can't imagine that." She fluttered her hand in the air as if brushing away his description. "I'm sticking with plan two and will come up with plan four."

Kenan released a long exhale and shifted on the bed. "Tell me why ye chose me again."

Tierney clasped her hands before her. "Asher MacNicol said," she hesitated, "said you were honorable and the kindest of the four of you imprisoned in Carlisle Dungeon."

"Would an honorable man fok ye and steal yer horse?" He watched her closely as he cursed. She didn't flinch. The lass was tough and brave, and she didn't look convinced. "Nay, I wouldn't, and I must get Freya back. She's more to me than a mount. She's a friend." He shrugged. "And Goliath, her stallion mate, would mourn her."

Tierney's eyes fastened back on his, and he saw a gleam of hope there before she hid it with indifference. "You would go to Scorrybreac to save your horse even with your need to return to Dunscaith?"

There was also the betrothal Cyrus had brokered with his sister. He needed to make sure his sudden absence hadn't ruined a possible alliance with the Mackinnons.

"I will retrieve Freya."

"Then just come to Scorrybreac for her. My father's advisor, Master Henry Macqueen, will see we are married and hear your pledge to help our clan. He will swear to it before Ranulf and request the contract be destroyed. It won't be as good as you being there, but it will help. Perhaps you could send some warriors to help deter Ranulf when he arrives."

"'Tis not that simple, lass." Nothing about this plan of hers was simple. He needed to marry Grace

Mackinnon to bring peace to Skye. Joining with the Mackinnons could also stop a Matheson incursion. But that plan didn't sit well in his gut suddenly. Could Grace catch and skin a rabbit? Climb a tree? Risk her life to save her clan? Bloody hell. Those things weren't important.

"'Tis simple. We can be done with all this," she motioned to the chain, "if you just promise you'll help me."

He lifted the end of his chain, his fist firm around the iron. "Ye could have asked me nicely for help. That works."

She leaned, bringing them close across the border but still out of reach. "If I had asked you at the wedding, you would have said no and ridden away to Dunscaith. You said you were leaving at dawn. I didn't have time to follow you to Sleat Peninsula. Ranulf could land any day."

"Ye should have tried."

"And put you on guard against my strategy?" She snorted as if that were preposterous.

"I can assure ye I would never have imagined..." He swooped the chain through the air. "...this."

She didn't look convinced. This was getting nowhere. He turned, forgetting he'd taken off his tunic, and sat on his cot to drop his face in his palms.

"Your back," she said. "Does it still pain you?"

She'd obviously seen the flay marks. You couldn't miss them. "Nay, but the tightness is a reminder that Scotland will always be weak if we don't unite as a nation." This was why he needed to ally with the powerful Mackinnon Clan.

He watched her bite the cuticle of her finger and

wondered if she did it without being aware.

Lowering her hand, she said, "I will work hard to help you strengthen Scotland if you help me save my clan."

"And ye want me to marry ye to do that."

She shook her head. "Not really marry. I will never marry again. Merely act like we are married."

"So that part wasn't a lie. Ye've been married before?" She was fairly young to be a widow.

"I wish it were a lie." Her voice was soft and pinched but also swollen with anguish.

Darkness pressed in on Kenan. "Did he give ye bruises when ye were wed to him?" Did the lass think that all tupping involved pain and a man being violent?

She moved her hand in the air as if washing away the topic. "We are not discussing my past marriage."

"Tupping is not about pushing and ending up with bruises."

Her eyes squeezed shut, and she shook her head. "We aren't discussing tupping. We are discussing you helping me deter Ranulf Matheson from taking over Scorrybreac and my clan. And you keeping Skye strong and united."

He nodded slowly when she opened her eyes. Inside though he was gripping his temper with both hands, wishing he could meet this dead husband and thrash him. No wonder Tierney knew better than to wed Ranulf Matheson. From what he'd heard, the man was brutish, too. Any investigation would have revealed that to her father. Had Douglas MacNicol failed his daughter a second time?

"An honorable man doesn't hurt any woman, and

he protects his wife."

"I've learned to protect myself because honorable men are quite rare."

"Ye certainly don't have a good opinion of my sex."

She held up three fingers, and for a moment, he hoped she was telling him she'd try plan number three with him. "I know three people who are male and also honorable." She counted on her fingers. "My brother, Asher, and a friend, Jacob. That's it." She dropped her hand. "I'm hoping you will be a fourth." She looked hopeful and sad and desperate. It all pulled at his chest like something trying to yank his heart out. 'Twas his weakness. This blasted kindness.

He inhaled. "After ye poisoned me, chained me, and robbed me." The reminder stirred some anger in him, and he tried to hold onto it.

She placed her palms together before her. "I am sorry." She bit her bottom lip. "It was the only way to keep you here to listen to me."

He wanted to continue to be furious with her. She foking shackled him. But his fury had mellowed to annoyance. "I may have listened if you'd tried plan three," he said. "I appreciate a good seduction, and I'd never hurt ye."

The moisture cleared from her eyes, and she frowned at him. "Do women ply you with seduction often, or are you the seducer?"

"Usually 'tis I doing the seducing." He studied her as she considered his words. How far would she go down this path?

"Oh?" she said, crossing her arms. "And what do

you do during this seduction?"

He allowed a seductive grin to spread across his lips. "I'd kiss ye from those lush lips to yer long neck," he said and watched her lips part slightly. "My warm touch would cause a tingling to run just under yer skin." His words came slowly as if he truly was tasting her skin. "I'd stroke and trail the warmth of my breath over to capture one of yer peaked nipples before sliding down yer tingling body with feather-like, teasing touches and heated nibbles."

Her cheeks brightened again in the glow of the hearth light. He liked it, knowing he affected her.

"I'd reach yer inner thighs that would spread on their own as ye squirm under my mouth, my fingers—"

"I will give you some time for privacy before sleep." Her voice was high-pitched, and she turned away, striding toward the door. "We ride to Scorrybreac in the morn."

"To do that, ye'll have to get close to me, lass." His voice was still husky, and he realized his cock had been listening. It rose up, and he adjusted it. "Close enough to feel all the heat ye're feeling now."

She slammed the door on the way out, and he stroked his hard cock. Daingead, it would be an uncomfortable night, not because of the shackle but because of his own foolish words.

• • •

*By Holy Joan's sword!*

Tierney lay on her side facing the stone wall of the cottage as dawn turned the darkness to gray in the room. She'd spent much of the night unable to sleep. First, she'd had to fight off the strange achiness his carnal description had woken in her. That must be lust, something she barely remembered from those days before she knew that behind Wallace's good looks was a monster.

And once her body had calmed enough for her to go back into the cottage where Kenan seemed to be sleeping on his cot, she'd spent hours trying to work out a way to get Kenan to Scorrybreac. She'd have to be close to him to make certain he was bound tightly. If she was close to him, he could just grab her, taking her away from Scorrybreac and those who desperately needed her plans to work.

She couldn't drug him again. Just the thought brought such guilt that she nearly gagged. And despite this new-to-her heat that Kenan's words had ignited in her, plan three was just too risky. He could certainly overpower her before, during, and after…

*I'd stroke and trail the warmth of my breath over to capture one of yer peaked nipples before sliding down yer tingling body with feather-like, teasing touches and heated nibbles.*

And what was that about him doing something with his mouth? More kissing, but on her inner thighs?

She'd ask Vera about it when she got to Scorrybreac. Vera, who helped in the tower, giggled about frolicking with the lads in the village. But she couldn't trust Kenan to really do any of that. Asher had said Kenan Macdonald was honorable and kind, but she'd pushed the powerful Macdonald chief too far by drugging and chaining him. Honor and kindness could dissolve in the shackles of an enemy.

The iron links of Kenan's tether rattled as he rose from the cot, and she heard him pissing in the pot behind the screen. Each minute he wore it made the man angrier and more deadly. She hadn't figured that into her plans, how Kenan must feel being chained after his year and a half in an English dungeon. She grimaced as she heard him curse.

She rolled over to see him sitting on his cot, the foot raised as he inspected his binding. "Is it chafing?" she asked, pushing up out from the blanket.

"Of course," he said. "Have ye spent any time shackled?" His eyes rose to meet her gaze.

Tierney had been shackled, trapped in a horrible marriage, but he was talking about irons and chains, not vows and threats. "No." She stood slowly. "I have some ointment for it." She ached from lying on the hard wooden floor and stretched as she went to her leather satchel to retrieve another clay vial.

When she turned back, he leaned upright against the wall behind him. "Or ye could toss me the key to get the bloody thing off." Even though his tone was milder than the night before, there was still an edge to it she couldn't miss.

"And then you take my horse and return to Dunvegan."

He exhaled. "I've already told ye I would go to retrieve Freya and my sword, and if possible, my glider." Kenan wiped a cloth over his teeth with some of the gritty polish she'd left for him with the pitcher. He stood and went behind the screen again where she heard him swish water and spit into the privy pot. When he came back around, he was raking his fingers through his thick hair.

"And you will act like my husband?"

Kenan crossed his arms and stared at her as he took his battle stance. "I cannot stay at Scorrybreac until this suitor of yers comes calling." His arms went out. "I have a clan to guide, a castle to rebuild, a brother to find, and now my glider to repair."

Panic shot through her stomach. She must convince him. "What if I help you with all of that? All you have to do is act like we are wed before witnesses at Scorrybreac."

Tierney took a full breath, her breasts rising above the binding under her tunic. "Then when Ranulf Matheson comes, people will say 'tis true that I wed the powerful Macdonald chief, and he will leave me and my clan alone." It may not be enough to deter Ranulf, but the threat might stop him from moving into the tower house. She would just have to stay on guard until he left Skye.

"Will ye cut the hides and stretch them?"

Her eyes narrowed. "Pardon?"

"To rebuild my glider."

"Yes." She nodded. "I can do that."

"And wash soot from Dunscaith's stone walls?"

The speed of her words increased. "I can, but I'll have to spend time at Scorrybreac to make certain Ranulf is truly gone. But I can help you from there by commissioning new tapestries and writing songs about the great Macdonald chief."

"Songs?" he asked. "Ye think ye can help me with songs?" His eyes opened wider as if he worried about her being mad.

She pinched her lips together in impatience.

Even now, Ranulf may be arriving in Scorrybreac. "Yes. I write songs that touch the hearts of people, and I'm a very good singer."

"Sing then."

She stopped herself from grabbing her hair by fisting her hands at her sides. "Right now?"

"Aye. Sing."

Her mouth fell open, and then she waved her hand. "There's no time for that."

He crossed his arms. "If ye don't sing, I don't help."

Her lips opened with hope. "If I sing, you *will* help?"

"Ye will scrub Dunscaith's charred walls, assist in the re-creation of my glider, order tapestries and furniture for Dunscaith, and write ballads about my bravery, honor, and fairly handsome looks. Feel free to exaggerate—"

"I will write you a song—"

"And possibly plan three if ye're curious about the heat and aching ye've been feeling."

"Wha…I…" Her lips remained parted on an unfinished denial. Had she moaned in her sleep, or had he seen her try to rub away the ache between her thighs? She finally snapped her lips shut, pinching them hard for a moment before she spoke. "There will be no seduction. Plan number three is off the negotiation table, but I agree to the rest."

His lips curled in as if he were disappointed. Then he shrugged. Holy Joan! What had she gotten herself into? "Very well," he said, "so go ahead. Sing."

"And you will help—?"

"I will go to Scorrybreac to see yer copy of this betrothal contract. I'll spend a day assessing yer clan's strengths and devising a plan with ye and anyone there who cares."

"And a letter to Ranulf and his brother the chief," she continued.

"Ye can write yer letter and use my signet ring to seal it. Now sing."

He would do it. He would help her in exchange for servitude. The relief that washed through her was muted by the anxiety still tying her in knots.

"I'm waiting," he urged, and annoyance warred with her relief. She'd sworn never to make herself serve another man. Was breaking an oath to oneself a sin? She'd add it to the rest of them on her list.

Tierney had sung to entertain her clan when she was young. She'd even sung when Wallace Macqueen, young and handsome, had come to call, when he pretended to be honorable. She'd been excited that a man wanted her, someone she hadn't grown up with, someone she didn't think of as a brother. Wallace had said she was beautiful and clever and smiled at her, so she sang often before she found herself in a soul-killing marriage. Then there'd been silence for years as she plotted her escape.

She inhaled and closed her eyes, her lips opening with an exhalation of song. She worked the long notes expertly, ignoring any reasons why she wanted to impress him.

"How we grieve the sight, the grayness of his skin. May the angels paint his cheeks anew and carry him to rest with his kin."

After two more stanzas, she let the final perfect note fade and opened her eyes to find Kenan staring at her, no emotion on his handsome face. "A funeral dirge?" he asked, leaning forward. "Ye sing me a funeral dirge right after I agreed to help ye?"

"It matched my mood."

His lips twitched as if he fought a smile. "Toss me the key."

She frowned. "Your word, Chief Macdonald, on your mother's soul."

He tipped his head to the side. "What if I hated my mother?"

She imitated the tilt. "Your mother was kind and loved you. 'Twas your father you hated and are certain burns in Hell." Before he could ask her how she knew anything about his immediate family, she held up a hand. "The bard who came through."

Kenan Macdonald stared into her eyes and slowly nodded. "On my mother's soul, I will come for a day to Scorrybreac and help as much as I am able."

The tension that she'd been holding for so long lessened its hold on her, and she nearly sank to the floor. Her plan was working.

"And then," he continued, "ye will sing me a joyful song."

# CHAPTER SEVEN

"Look at the stars lighting up the sky: no one of
them stays in the same place."

*Seneca (Roman philosopher 4BC–65AD)*

Luckily, Tierney's charger was strong and seemed to
carry them both without trouble. The saddle was
large and allowed them to ride together, the lass before Kenan even though she held the reins. She sat
with her back rigid as if trying to keep herself from
smashing into his chest, but it was her nicely rounded arse, her curves on display in the trousers, that
drove him nearly mad. No matter how hard she tried
to scoot forward, the movement of the horse made
her slide backward, and that sweet arse wriggled
against his groin.

"Bloody hell, stop doing that," he said.

"I can't keep high enough on—"

"Just stop trying to scoot away. All that…move-
ment is making this ride damn uncomfortable. Let
yerself press into me. 'Tis far better than the friction."

She stilled, and they rode while he took several
breaths of the fresh mid-morning air. "Friction?"
Her voice held a restrained laugh. She'd been smiling ever since leaving the dungeon-cabin together.

"Rubbing, brushing, sliding, grinding—"

She held up a hand, glancing quickly over her

shoulder at him. He could see her cheeks had grown flushed. "Friction," she repeated. "Understood. I will try to stay still."

He grumbled. "Impossible."

"I'd ride faster, but I'm afraid the friction will increase," she said, keeping her face forward.

"Ride faster, then," he said, not caring that he sounded terse. "I would get Freya back as soon as possible. And my grandfather's sword."

"Great."

"Great?"

"Your *great*-grandfather's sword."

She looked over her shoulder again, her eyes looking greener under the canopy of late summer leaves. Long lashes framed them in perfect little spikes. He wondered if they ever stuck her in her eyes.

"Aye, my great-grandfather's sword."

She nodded as if relieved she had the correct information. Tierney gathered details like a general surveying the terrain to tweak the battle plan. "And you will say we married right after your sister's wedding."

"Why would we do that?" he asked, being sure not to agree. He wouldn't lie to Tierney no matter that she'd lied to get him out on the moor. Although misleading was just another way of lying.

His head tipped back as if he stared up at a laughing God. Kenan was supposed to be marrying Grace Mackinnon. If Cyrus learned about this... whatever this was, abduction, mission of mercy, way to keep the Isle of Skye from being invaded. Kenan doubted that Cyrus would be forgiving if word got back to him about Kenan marrying someone other than his sister. After Kenan had all but signed the betrothal contract.

Tierney spoke in succinct words as if instructing a warrior before battle. "You lusted after me but knew that I would not give myself to you unless you married me."

"So instead of finding a willing widow to relieve my uncontrollable lust, I married ye after ye tried to steal my glider and destroyed it in the sea?"

He heard her sigh heavily and grinned. The lass was finding out how difficult it was to get people to conform to a plan without input. And no matter what she said, he couldn't say they were wed, not without jeopardizing a treaty with Clan Mackinnon.

"You can add that you were drunk on whisky," she said without looking at him.

"How about ye? Were ye drunk on whisky and lustful and therefore agreed to wed a stranger, albeit a handsome, possibly honorable stranger?"

She tossed a glare over her shoulder. "My clan knows I don't drink to excess. And, anyway, they knew I planned to find someone who could save us."

He leaned in to her ear, feeling the tickle of her hair brush against him. "Do they know about plan number three?"

Her back straightened. "I don't tell them my plans. Word could get into enemy hands."

Which was exactly why he didn't want word out that he'd married someone else. He could be at war with Clan Mackinnon before he even made it home.

"Hmmm…" he said, understanding her secrecy. "Although, if someone had ridden down to

Dunvegan to tell me a lovely, angel-haired lass with curves as lush as the Highland slopes was coming to seduce me into helping her, I certainly wouldn't have ridden away to Dunscaith."

She didn't turn toward him so he couldn't see her expression. "You said you were leaving the next morning. I asked you twice to stay." Had she?

"If ye told me what was going on, I might have changed my mind."

They rode in silence for long minutes. "Ye know, lass," he said, "saying that we are wed before witnesses pretty much makes us wed in truth. With or without a cleric."

"Not if we haven't consummated it."

A lazy grin quirked up one side of his mouth. "'Tis a good thing ye didn't enact plan number three, then."

His smile broadened when he heard her snort.

She rubbed a hand dramatically down one side of her face. "The letter to Ranulf will order him to abandon his plans to take over Scorrybreac Tower and leave me alone. We will seal the letter with your signet ring." She turned enough to reach for his hand where he wore the Macdonald chief's ring etched with a fist holding a cross with three little crosslets.

He let her turn the ring on his finger. "Ye could have taken my ring and left me to wake on the moor," he said.

Her gaze rose from the ring to his eyes. "That wouldn't have been enough. I need you to say we are working on nulling the contract with Ranulf Matheson." He saw the little speckles of gold amongst the green in her irises. "I need you, Kenan

Macdonald." The words rippled through him. His sisters needed his protection, and the same was true for his clan. But, somehow, the words coming from this self-reliant woman felt powerful as if she'd grabbed some vital organ of his and tugged. It mixed with the hollowness of guilt for misleading her, but he really didn't have a choice.

He shook off the feeling and relaxed his mouth into an irksome grin. "And ye'll be overcome by happiness and sing me a joyful song."

"I will hold to my promise."

"And then ye'll come to Dunscaith by Hogmanay to help me clean my castle and rebuild my glider." In truth, he wanted to see her again. The most surprising things came from her mouth. He'd never met a lass brave enough to attempt flying nor abduct a warrior almost twice her weight. What other surprises were inside Tierney MacNicol?

"Yes, I promise, by Hogmanay."

He hoped to have Dunscaith put back together before then. The fire had burned through the three stories of floors and the furnishings, but his men had already rebuilt the roof and disposed of the burned beams and ruined interior. They were moving quickly before word spread that the Macdonalds of Sleat were weakened. And yet he was riding north instead of returning to help them.

"'Tis the least ye can do for breaking my glider, drugging me, shackling and threatening me, stealing my horse, and throwing my schedule completely off track." *Fok*. Why was he doing this? He should still be fuming with lethal ire even if Tierney was the most interesting person he'd come across, a trouser-wearing, emerald-eyed devil who had curves that were still driving him to lust. Even her damn hair smelled like some flower. He ran both hands down his face.

"What the bloody hell am I doing?" he murmured.

"Asher was right," Tierney said without turning to him. "You are remarkably kind to help me."

He snorted, the sound startling some wood pigeons that flapped in the bushes beside them. "Ye twist the blade."

"Hold on," she said. "Let's end this torture quicker."

Before he could ask if she meant his torture or hers, she leaned over her mare's neck, her nicely plump arse pressing into his already hard cock. And the horse shot forward into a gallop.

• • •

Tierney guided her courser, Fleet, rolling with his gait while she tried to ignore the powerful man and his hard jack behind her. No wonder her mother never allowed Tierney to ride with her friend, Jacob, like that.

The constant feel of Kenan's warmth against her back and the proof of his virility rubbing against her nearly bare bottom had caused the carnal heat to rise in her again. She'd thought Wallace Macqueen, with his cruel words and bruising hands, had pushed and pumped all desire out of her forever. But Kenan Macdonald was nothing like Tierney's dead husband.

The most obvious difference between them was that she'd angered Kenan without being struck. Asher was right. Kenan was honorable and kind under his lethal-looking bluster. And every time he stared into her eyes, he captured her breath. What did that mean?

The forest opened more, and the stream to her right was familiar. As much as she needed to reach home, Fleet needed a drink, and Tierney needed to change out of her manly clothes. Her clan would find it hard to believe she'd found a husband to wed her in trousers. She'd already sent word to Ranulf that she wouldn't honor her father's betrothal plans, that she'd never signed the contract, and they were void. Now she just needed Kenan to act his part for her father's advisor, Henry, to believe it.

She'd send another letter once she reached Scorrybreac telling Ranulf she'd wed the Macdonald chief, and Kenan was allowing her to govern Scorrybreac and its tower for her brother, Gabriel. If she convinced Henry it was true, he'd support Gabriel.

Mind spinning, Tierney guided Fleet to the free-flowing water. He bowed his head to slurp, and she looped the reins around the pommel of her saddle.

"We'll reach Scorrybreac within the hour," she said, pointing in the easterly direction. "I must change back into petticoats." Pulling a leg around over Fleet's bent neck, she pushed off, landing in a crouch in the soft moss flanking the stream.

When she turned, Kenan already had the reins off the pommel and clasped in his hands even as Fleet drank. He smiled down at her, his eyes hooded slightly as he shook his head. "Ye should never leave a person on yer horse or they might steal it," he said. The same warning she'd given him upon the dark moor.

Tierney's heart leaped in her chest. She grabbed the reins closer to Fleet's harness as if that might give her some control. Her horse raised his head, water dripping from his lips. "I still have your horse, Macdonald," she said. "And your great-grandfather's sword at Scorrybreac."

"Perhaps I'll take yer horse in exchange."

She shook her head, panic flashing through her like lightning. "Freya means too much to you." The words came out with desperate force.

"Since I have the upper hand now," he tipped his head, "I would say ye're *my* prisoner instead of me being yers, Tierney MacNicol. And since I am an honorable man, I release ye." He flicked his hand as if shooing her away.

She grabbed onto Fleet's neck with both her arms. The horse nickered as if questioning her sanity, something Tierney did herself. She felt the cold water from the horse's lips drip down her back.

"Bloody hell, Kenan. All I need you to do is say we're married before witnesses."

He lifted his gaze to the trees, staring there. She watched the masculine bulge in his throat move up and down on a swallow before he looked back at her. "I'm already betrothed. I cannot say I am wed to ye. If that gets back to Grace Mackinnon, it could ruin the union between Clans Macdonald and Mackinnon."

"Bbbb...betrothed? You never said—"

"It happened at the wedding celebration."

She moved around to his side and swatted his calf above his boot planted in the stirrup. "And you bloody hell went on a moonlit picnic with me." *Daingead!* "You're a dishonorable rogue, Kenan Macdonald."

His gaze narrowed. "I was taking ye back to yer cousin who doesn't exist."

"But you stopped to lie beneath the stars when I asked."

"When ye badgered me to eat. I didn't lie down until ye poisoned me."

She slapped at the air momentarily like she was shooing away stinging bees. Her plan was crumbling. "Holy bloody Joan!" The words came out loud and unladylike. "You could have said something about this betrothal problem at the cottage."

He shrugged. "I already knew I had to come to retrieve my horse and sword." He guided Fleet to turn away from the stream.

"Don't go. I have to change," she said.

"I'll give ye a few minutes," he said, taking on the tone of a stern jailor. "Ye may change behind that rock or right here if ye wish."

She narrowed her eyes at him and caught the satchel that he'd pulled from the back of Fleet and thrown to her. "Your betrothed would not be happy with me stripping down here before you."

"Grace is most certainly unhappy with my sudden disappearance. She and her brother, with whom I'm supposed to be making an alliance."

Tierney pulled her wrinkled petticoats out of the bag, shaking them. Sweet Holy Joan. She could be making more enemies. "Which clan?"

"Mackinnon," he said.

Another clan her father used to complain about, saying the old chief was bent on seeing every MacNicol in his grave. It was a powerful clan, with a vast territory on Skye, a monster that fed children's nightmares. "Mackinnons are vicious," she said and shimmied her petticoat up over her trousers.

"The chief is, especially after his oldest son died. But his second son, Cyrus Mackinnon, understands the need for alliances to strengthen Skye and Scotland." Kenan watched her as she reached under her petticoat to untie the trousers. Tierney shimmied until they dropped, and she stepped out of them. Without help, she wouldn't be able to tie her stays behind her back, but her bodice had lacing in the front. "Grace agrees with him," Kenan said.

"I grew up with a girl named Grace," Tierney said, looking askance at him. "She picked her nose."

"I'm sure she was a different lass."

She crossed her arms. "You trust Cyrus Mackinnon enough to make an alliance? I've heard he's a rogue only interested in bedding lasses."

Kenan rubbed his short beard. "There's more to him than that." He was still watching her. She could go behind the rock, but it was bad enough that she'd let him take control of Fleet so easily. She couldn't stand the thought of hearing him ride away.

Shrugging the bodice over her tunic, she slid a hand underneath to pull the band around her breasts loose. An ache of relief tingled in her breasts as she released them. An involuntary sigh escaped her lips, and the white cloth unspooled around her, sliding out from her tunic. Pulling the bodice closed, Tierney tugged the ties crisscrossing down the front. She pulled the locket out to settle on her breastbone.

Kenan watched her the entire time. She felt heat from his gaze. He didn't leer nor even smile at her, merely studied her. Did he know she was missing her stays and a proper smock underneath? He may not have dressed a woman before, but there was no doubt he'd undressed some. But he didn't say anything as she strode back over, shoving her men's clothes into the satchel and attaching it behind the saddle.

For a moment, Tierney considered trying to push him off Fleet's back, but having ridden up against the granite form through the morning, she was aware of how futile the attempt would be.

He never turned to look back at her, but when she returned to the stirrups, his hand was out. Without a word, she accepted his assistance to lift her onto her large horse. His hand, warm, calloused, and reliable, wrapped around her own. With him by her side, she knew she wouldn't fall. The luxury of security almost made her dizzy even if it was temporary. She couldn't remember a time when she felt secure and happy. *Before Gabriel was born.*

She still sat astride, even though in the petticoats it was more scandalous than in trousers, especially without a smock under the petticoat, leaving her bare. She bunched some of the petticoat before and under her for cushion.

"All settled?"

"No, not without the reins in my hands."

"Ye'll get them back when I release ye at Scorrybreac."

Tierney turned to glower at him, twisting in her seat. "Release me? You are *my* prisoner."

"I have the reins."

"And a shackle mark on your ankle," she retorted and felt shame heat her cheeks instantly.

The teasing glint in his eyes hardened. Before she could apologize, he tapped Fleet, sending him into a run. Only Tierney's strong thighs and quick grab of the pommel kept her from falling off the saddle. He probably wouldn't have even stopped, just left her in the pebbles and tall grass with a cracked head.

When they broke out of the forest, Kenan urged her horse on, giving him his head as if to see how fast he could race. The wind in her face normally wiped the worry from her mind, but this was a completely knotted situation, and she was once again without a plan.

*Damn Mackinnons.* And damn poor timing. Kenan was betrothed? Which woman at the celebration was Kenan supposed to wed? There'd been a comely lady in bright yellow with dark hair who'd smiled and talked with him. Was that Grace Mackinnon? *Bloody Hell!* Her stomach flipped with an uncomfortable clench that was different from anger. Disappointment? Jealousy?

Tierney pointed east, and Kenan followed her direction without question. A few minutes later, the top of Scorrybreac Tower jutted into the sky where it sat along the sea's edge as if growing from the rocks surrounding it. It wasn't as defensive as a castle since it didn't possess a moat or thick walls, at least not intact enough to keep invaders out. That project had come to a halt with the sickness. But it was still impressive, soaring four floors up with an accessible slate roof.

Kenan slowed to a walk, and his mouth came close to her ear. "I will send Macdonald warriors up here and do what I can to keep Clan Matheson out of Scorrybreac, Tierney, but do not say we are wed."

Disappointment and dread swirled in her gut. If she wasn't wed, then the contract was still valid, and Henry would say she still must surrender to Ranulf. Maggie's sweet face rose up in Tierney's mind, bringing desperation with it up her gullet like bile. She kept her face straight ahead. "I could say that you did wed me. Swear to it before a priest." She'd risk her soul to save her people. "Send word to Grace Mackinnon if you don't tell a small lie now."

With a finger on her chin, he turned her face to his. For a moment, she couldn't draw breath at the restrained fury she saw in his dark blue eyes.

"I will not be forced to do anything." His tone sent ice along her spine. "I wouldn't sign King Henry's pact to support him to gain my freedom in England even when they tortured me, and I won't be forced to say I'm wed to gain my freedom from ye. If I help the MacNicol Clan, it will be on my own terms and not yers. If ye lie, ye risk Clan Macdonald going to war against yer clan, too."

# CHAPTER EIGHT

"Adversity is like a strong wind. It tears away from us all but the things that cannot be torn, so that we see ourselves as we really are."

*Arthur Golden – American Writer, 1956–*

Kenan allowed the fury inside him to show on his face. The anger was more at himself for getting into this situation, letting the mystery of Tierney lower his guard enough to be abducted by two lasses and a lad. He was also angry at himself for allowing the guilt to rise within him, gnawing at his gut. He was a warrior and a clan chief, and he wouldn't jeopardize his friendship with Cyrus nor an alliance with the Mackinnons to help this woman who lied easily enough to be the serpent in Eden's Garden. She could definitely be a fallen angel.

Tierney's green eyes opened the smallest bit wider. It didn't matter that she possessed a vulnerability that made him want to protect her. He wouldn't be forced to lie to help her.

"Asher was wrong," she said. "You have no honor, Kenan Macdonald."

"Grace and Cyrus Mackinnon would say I have immense honor."

"The Mackinnon Clan is not about to be utterly destroyed."

Kenan kept his sigh silent. He'd talk with Rory

and Cyrus about the Matheson Clan, and he'd send Macdonald warriors, maybe ask for MacLeod warriors, too. Tierney was right in that they didn't need any land-hungry clans infiltrating the Isle of Skye. He would deposit Tierney home and speak with her people about Clan Macdonald supporting them against Ranulf Matheson, but he wouldn't say they were wed. If word got back to Cyrus, it could jeopardize everything.

More of Scorrybreac Tower was exposed as they rode closer, and soon the meadow of tall grass gave way to a village, a silent village. Kenan slowed Tierney's horse, and they walked down a winding pebble path toward the tower in the distance. Doors and shutters were closed. No voices. No children running between cottages. Only a few gardens were plotted out behind them. No sheep in the fields. The village looked deserted.

"Where is everyone?" he asked, his voice sounding too loud in the silent town.

"Half are buried behind the chapel." Tierney tipped her head toward a stone building on a rise with a modest bell tower over it. "Twenty-six are lost to the bogs of Solway Moss and twenty went down with the *Rosemary*."

Kenan remembered the swampy mud sucking him down during that disastrous battle. Cold slid up his spine, and he could smell the dankness of mold and muck mixed with blood.

"And the rest are too frightened to show their faces," she said. "They have no chief, no allies, and a powerful clan ready to defeat them." Her voice lowered. "I thought I was bringing them a savior, but once again, my plan has failed."

Guilt dissolved the armor inside his chest that he'd built out of fury. The remorse was corrosive, eating away at his resolve against playing a dangerous farce to scare away a suitor. It was one thing to know a clan had been decimated by war and disease. It was another thing to listen to the telling silence and feel the fear, sorrow, and defeat emanating from the cottages as he rode through. The heaviness of it weighed over his shoulders. There was no hope left here at Scorrybreac.

She rode straight-backed before him, hair blowing to tickle and lash his face with the increased wind off the sea, and her petticoat hitched up her shins. *Bloody hell.* Sometimes, he hated that he cared. His father, Walter Macdonald, had said it was Kenan's weakness that he took after his mother that way. But Kenan would never wish to be vicious like his father. Otherwise, there'd be no hope for peace on Skye.

Up ahead, near the front of Scorrybreac, a small group was gathered. He saw the wagon with his crippled glider resting in it, but Freya wasn't there. The young woman, Cora, and Tierney's brother, Gabriel, stood to the side, their faces pale with what looked like fear. A handful of warriors stood with swords sheathed and an older man dressed in finer clothes who frowned.

Kenan needed to understand the players here in what looked like a theatrical tragedy.

"Oh, Tierney," Cora called, a keening in her voice that sounded twisted with tears.

A man stepped out from a stable, holding a wee

lass's hand, and Tierney gasped, her whole body going rigid like a cat arching its back, its fur on end.
The man was tall and had an untrimmed beard down
his thick neck, his hair long. The lass looked about
five years old and had golden hair tied back with a
blue bow to match her simple dress. Her eyes were
wide in a cherubic face.

"By all the saints, no," Tierney whispered. She
turned in her seat, her fingers biting into his thighs.
"Please, Kenan. That's Ranulf Matheson."

Kenan had already figured that from the cocky
expression the man wore and the fear in her people's
eyes. "And the child?" he asked.

"Maggie," Tierney said. "My daughter."

Tierney's heart pounded with a need to jump
down and race to her daughter, pulling Maggie into
the safety of her arms. But here amongst Ranulf and
his men, her arms weren't safe enough. She needed
Kenan.

Throat strained, her plea came out higher pitched
but full of honest fear, not for herself but for the
child that had become everything to Tierney.
"Please." The adage was horribly true. When a
woman gives birth to a child, her mother's heart
forevermore lives on the outside. If anything bad
happened to Maggie, Tierney would die, too.

"He will hurt her to get me to cooperate. Maggie
was hidden." She shook her head. "He must have
found her." Doris and Edith were guarding Maggie
until Cora could return and get her away from
Scorrybreac Tower.

Kenan searched her pleading eyes, and his gaze
darkened into a look that made Tierney shiver. The

kind man that hadn't retaliated with physical strength now looked like the harbinger of death. "I will help."

She breathed in through her nose as if her body sought air to fuel her muscles. "She's frightened. I need to get to her. If you anger him with her in his arms, he might just kill her, snap her neck like a rag doll. The devil has no conscience." She waited until he gave the slightest nod and turned forward, her gaze fastening on her frightened little girl as prickles of fear poked under her skin.

Kenan nudged Fleet to walk forward amongst the silent group. Behind Ranulf, six warriors she didn't recognize stood staring at their approach. Mathesons.

"Ye don't happen to know where my sword is, do ye?" he said near her ear.

Her gaze shifted. "It should be in the wagon bed under the glider."

*Unless a Matheson took it.*

Neither of them said it, but the possibility hung in the air. Kenan steered Fleet over to the wagon behind the small group of MacNicols. Were other of her men hiding, waiting to ambush the Mathesons? There were only four young ones with swords, Jacob being the leader of the small army. He frowned hard at Kenan but didn't say anything.

"Welcome home, Tierney, love," Ranulf called. "Who's our visitor, and why is he holding my betrothed against his cock?"

Kenan dismounted and reached up to lift Tierney down. His hands were tight around her waist as if trying to dissuade her from leaving his side, but when she turned, she made to lunge toward Maggie. Kenan's grip around her wrist stopped her, her shoulders aching at the tug she made against it.

"Let go," she said. Everyone could hear her, but she didn't care. Her heart ached to wipe the tears from her child's face.

"Nay," Kenan said.

"Mama," Maggie called, her one hand lifting as if to grab for her.

The little voice clawed at her heart. "'Twill be all right," she said with as much confidence as she could produce.

"Lady Tierney," Ranulf said, his mouth turning downward into a fierce frown that promised retribution. "Come to greet yer betrothed properly, and ye can hold sweet Maggie. She's been asking for her absent mother." He *tsk*ed. "I thought ye a better woman than to leave her without proper guards."

Absent only because she was desperately trying to find help. Tierney walked stiffly next to Kenan, still tethered to him with his grip.

"I am Kenan Macdonald, chief of the Macdonald Clan of Sleat Peninsula on the Isle of Skye. Release the child so she can come to her mother."

"Release the mother to come to her child." The men behind him drew their swords, and Tierney heard the four MacNicols doing the same behind her. And her sweet little Maggie was right in the middle of it all. "Tierney MacNicol is soon to be my wife. Take yer hands off her," Ranulf said.

"I never signed the betrothal contract, Sir Ranulf," Tierney said, her voice strong despite feeling like she couldn't breathe. She blinked against the sparks of light in her periphery and forced herself to take even breaths.

"A minor issue," he answered, his gaze on Kenan.

"'Tis no issue at all," Kenan said, holding up their two clasped hands, "because…we are wed, and that negates the contract."

Cora gasped somewhere behind Tierney, and she could imagine her friend slapping two hands over her mouth as if that would pull the sound back inside. Two of the Matheson warriors cursed out loud. Kenan had done something he said he wouldn't, but Tierney was too focused on Maggie to care.

"Tierney married the Macdonald chief?" Henry Macqueen said somewhere to the right. Tierney glanced over at her father's old advisor and watched him draw his own sword. She'd told him her wild plan to bring Kenan Macdonald back to defend them. He'd just scoffed and rubbed his balding head like he always did when he was worried.

Ranulf's lips pulled back in something of a snarl, yanking Maggie to stand against his legs. Before Tierney could try to pull away again, Kenan squeezed her hand, speaking at the same time.

"Release my daughter," Kenan said, "or feel the full wrath of the Macdonald Clan of Sleat."

"Are they hiding in the trees, Macdonald?" Ranulf asked, and his men laughed. "Because it looks like ye're a clan of one, far away from Sleat Peninsula."

"Let my daughter go," Kenan repeated, "and return to the mainland, never to visit Skye again unless invited. I am Tierney's husband and protector of Scorrybreac now."

Ranulf's face reddened, his gaze going to Tierney. "Ye're a whoring bitch. Scorrybreac is mine." He held up the missive she recognized as her father's letter about the betrothal.

"That paper means nothing," Tierney said. "The chief who signed it is dead. I am his rightful heir. I did not nor will I ever sign that betrothal contract."

"The clause of her marrying someone else has made the contract void. Scorrybreac belongs to the MacNicols and who they choose to lead their clan," Kenan said. "And Tierney belongs to me."

"Then she'll simply become a widow again," Ranulf said, pulling out his sword, his other hand still clutching Maggie's shoulder, his fingers long enough to pinch her collarbone. Maggie tried to sink under his hold, but he must have pinched harder, because she grimaced and straightened.

"The threat against the chief of a clan is a declaration of war, Matheson. Does yer brother, Chief Murdoc, know ye and yer little band here are at war with the Macdonalds of Sleat, who are able to call upon the MacLeods and Mackinnons to assist?"

While Ranulf made some remarks about his brother backing whatever he did, Kenan lowered his lips to Tierney's ear. "Get the child out of the fray as soon as he releases her hand." Oh, she definitely would, or if she couldn't, she'd cover Maggie, shielding her. Tierney's body coiled with waiting energy.

Kenan nudged Tierney to move closer to Ranulf but without leaving him. She thought he'd want to go for his sword in the wagon, but he wasn't going in that direction. Tierney wished she had her bow, training a deadly arrowhead on Ranulf's broad forehead. Although killing the brother of the Matheson chief could bring a war swarming over Scorrybreac. Had Kenan considered that?

"Chief Douglas MacNicol," Ranulf said, "signed our betrothal contract for Tierney because he knew what was good for her and his clan. He—"

"I've heard that yer brother wants ye to fail, Ranulf Matheson." Kenan's voice broke into and over Ranulf's. The man stopped speaking mid-sentence, his mouth open. He snapped it closed, and Kenan continued. "That ye two have competed since ye were scrawny lads, but that Murdoc was always better than ye and tires of having to prove it to ye. He would be glad to see ye dead."

Ranulf's face bloomed red, and his hand came off of Maggie's shoulder to hold his sword with both hands. His knuckles were white as he clasped it hard. "Ye foking liar," he said, his lips curled. Whether Kenan had the information or was just guessing, he'd poked a wasp's nest with his words.

Kenan took several strides toward Ranulf, speaking as he stepped. "Murdoc left on campaign to aid King James before Solway Moss…" One, two, three. "The man spoke of…" Kenan's stride was long and powerful, reaching Ranulf before his sentence was finished. Kenan's fist shot through the air while he still spoke, catching the still fuming Ranulf by surprise.

*Crack!* The sound of the punch was like the crack of a pistol, and Tierney ran forward, grabbing her daughter as Ranulf flew backward and hit the ground, his sword clattering beside him.

Maggie's little arms and legs wrapped around

Tierney as she ran off to the side, Henry and Gabriel meeting her, their own weapons drawn, and they ran toward the cottages along the road. Behind her cursing and shouting flew up like birds being flushed from a bramble, but she didn't hear the clash of swords. Several more MacNicol men came running as if they had just heard of the invaders, young and old. They held knives and pitchforks and even a scythe.

At the door of the second cottage up the lane, Doris waved them inside. "Hide in here," she said.

"Take Maggie," Tierney said.

"No, Mama." Maggie's grip was as if she'd grown a dozen more appendages and would never let go.

"Go back to the mainland," Kenan called, making Tierney spin toward the confrontation, Maggie wrapped around her. "When he wakes, tell Ranulf not to step foot on Skye shores or the Macdonalds, MacNicols, and the MacLeods will rise against him and his clan. Let Murdoc know too."

With a row of MacNicols standing behind Kenan, two of the Matheson warriors lifted Ranulf under his arms, carrying him between them as his head lolled. Another grabbed up the fallen betrothal contract.

"That is worthless," Kenan said. "Void."

"Ballocks," the man said and spat in the dirt.

The group of MacNicols followed the six Mathesons with Ranulf back toward the shore. In the distance, a carrack ship was anchored in deeper water.

"When did they arrive?" Tierney asked Doris, who had stepped outside with her to watch the spectacle. Maggie raised her little face from Tierney's neck and twisted to look behind her. Tierney inhaled her daughter's scent, her heart squeezing with gratitude that she was safe in her arms.

"The ship was seen yesterday before the sun sank, and they rowed up to shore this morn. Ranulf and his men ordered the doors to the tower opened, and Henry opened them." Doris shook her head. "Thought he could reason with them, the fool. He's lucky to be breathing."

"How did they find Maggie?" Tierney watched Kenan turn, his gaze moving about until they found her. He was a hero, just what she needed. Thank God she'd brought him back with her. She kissed Maggie's golden head, tucking her snugly against her, although her usually brave little girl didn't seem like she'd be letting go of her anytime soon.

"Went door to door," Doris said. "Frightened Edith to within an inch of her life when they saw the doll left on her table. Tore her cottage apart and found Maggie under a bed in the back."

"Is Edith well?" Tierney asked about the eighty-year-old woman.

"Aye," Doris said, "although she's ordered Gerald to make her a sword light enough she can wield it." Perhaps Tierney should have the blacksmith make one for each woman in the village.

Kenan jogged over. "Was the lass harmed?"

Tierney looked down at her daughter. "Maggie? Are you hurt?"

Her clear, blue eyes blinked, and she glanced down at her front to see if there was anything amiss. "No, Mama."

Doris slid a finger into the child's neckline,

exposing her pale skin where bruises from Ranulf's hold were blooming. The woman's lips pinched tight, and fury filled her gaze. "I'll skewer the bastard myself as soon as Gerald makes me a sword."

Tierney hugged Maggie against her, her gaze going to Kenan. "Bruises will heal easier than nightmares." She certainly knew that herself.

Doris's gaze trailed up and down Kenan, inspecting him as if he might be some useful weapon that she'd learn to work. "So you wed our Tierney?"

*Holy Joan.* In all the panic with freeing Maggie, the fact that Kenan had done the exact thing he said he wouldn't hadn't registered in Tierney's mind. She turned, breath stuck in her chest, to look at Kenan. The man's face was unreadable.

"'Tis not official," Tierney said, glancing at Doris when he kept silent.

"A handfasting, then?"

"Pardon us, Mistress Doris," she said. "I must speak with Master Henry." She turned, striding away, hoping Kenan would know enough to follow without her tugging him because Maggie was heavy enough now to need two arms to hold.

Doris's voice followed her. "Ye should talk to Master Henry about us older ladies helping. Our bairns are grown and out in the world. All the energy we had keeping our children safe, we can turn to protecting the clan. A slice to the jugular could be quite unexpected coming from one of us."

Kenan strode next to her. Gabriel and a few of the MacNicol men followed them toward the tower where Henry waited, watching the Mathesons row away from shore. Jacob Tanner was one of them, and he frowned fiercely. "Ye've married?" he asked and looked at Kenan. "Him?" He asked it like Kenan was some weak, old man with a hump, a putrid eye, and a strange growth on the side of his neck.

Tierney knew Jacob was sweet on her. With his dark hair and long, angular nose, she'd thought she could like him back when they were young. But each time she considered it, she'd get a sick feeling as if he were her brother. Unfortunately, Jacob did not view her as a sister.

"Let's sit down so Master Henry can fill us in on what's occurred," Tierney said, shifting Maggie to her other hip.

"Tier," Jacob said, not accepting her non-answer. He grabbed her upper arm to stop her.

"She would like to sit down, lad," Kenan said, stopping next to them to stare into Jacob's tight face.

"I'm no *lad*," Jacob said, sounding very much like a boy trying to act the part of a man.

Without a word, Kenan slid his arm around the back of Tierney's shoulders, guiding her and Maggie into the shade of the keep. Jacob made a sound of disgust as they walked away.

They stopped inside the Great Hall with its vaulted ceiling and dusted iron chandeliers, unlit with the daylight shining through the narrow window slits cut high up. A fire hadn't been started despite the cold that the stone walls held inside. Tapestries depicting Norse mythology and biblical scenes covered the smooth, white plaster walls. The wooden floor was swept, but the tower held a stagnant odor like the inside of a tomb.

A single half-eaten meal sat on the long wooden

table where Henry must have been interrupted that morning.

"Thank the good lord ye came when ye did," Henry said to Kenan, offering him a tankard from the sideboard. Her father's advisor didn't offer her one. "A clan chief, a powerful chief with armies." Henry looked gleeful. "Voiding Ranulf's betrothal contract." His face turned to Tierney. "See, yer father was right to put that clause in. He knew ye would help find us a powerful chief."

Kenan stared at Tierney. She couldn't read what was behind those angry eyes. He'd refused to lie for her, and then lied directly. To save Maggie? Tierney felt torn, dragged in two different directions by horses. If word got out on Skye that he'd wed her, Kenan could truly incite war with his friend. She'd be responsible for war between two large clans on Skye.

Maggie finally released her squeezing hold on Tierney enough for her to lower her daughter to sit on the tabletop, her small, booted feet on the bench. "Gabriel has a crested newt," Maggie said. "His name is Betrim."

Tierney brushed blond curls back from her face, the ribbon having come loose. She would keep her daughter safe even if they had to run.

"And now," Henry said, raising his tankard high, "we have the mighty Macdonald Clan of Sleat to—"

"We are not wed," Tierney said over his words.

# CHAPTER NINE

"Oaths are but words, and words are but wind."

*Samuel Butler – British poet, 1835–1902*

Kenan watched the faces of the MacNicol people who'd followed them into Scorrybreac Tower. Henry Macqueen looked an age to be Tierney's father, with a bald head framed by gray, thinning hair that he kept trimmed and a white beard that came to a point. He was soft around the middle, but a few scars on his cheek and hairline spoke of battle in his youth.

The relief on Henry's face slid off as his brows pinched. "Not wed? But—"

"Kenan said as much to distract Ranulf and re-trieve Maggie," she said. "And it worked."

"But…word will get back to the Matheson Clan that ye lied," Henry said, pinching the bridge of his large nose. His words came faster as if they were boulders rolling down a hill. "Without a union to someone else, yer father's betrothal contract still stands. The clause will not take effect to void it."

"I never signed it," Tierney said with obvious frustration as if she'd already said it a million times to no avail. "I will not honor it."

Kenan noted the small gathering. Were these all that was left of the MacNicol army? Old men and lads with four young men with swords? Were there more on farms far enough away that they hadn't heard of the invading Mathesons? This clan was going to die out in another generation without help. Tierney's father must have deduced this, which prompted him to contact the Matheson Clan.

Douglas MacNicol hated the other clans on Skye as much as Kenan's father had, so of course he would look to mainland Scotland for a clan with whom to ally. And he'd been trying to use his non-cooperating daughter to do so when he died at sea.

Tierney stood tall, arms lowered to her sides and her hands in fists. Even though she once again wore a petticoat, Kenan imagined her legs were braced and ready. The horrific sweating sickness and the battle at Solway Moss had crippled their once-fearsome clan, and she was doing everything her wild imagination could create to save it. Perhaps she would have left and escaped the inevitable end, but she had a brother to support and a wee daughter who looked like a little angel with bright blue eyes and golden hair.

Tierney's little lass hopped nimbly from the table and took her mother's hand. Tierney immediately uncurled her fingers, winding them with Maggie's. Kenan watched the young mother's chin firm with determination. Aye, Tierney MacNicol would do anything to save her daughter and clan, even stealing a flying machine, even abducting a clan chief with her decoctions and shackling him. And Kenan could not stand to see her brought to heel by men such as Ranulf Matheson.

Henry's voice rose. "We must have an ally to strengthen—"

Tierney waved her free hand at Kenan. "The

Macdonald Clan is going to be our ally."

"We need more than an understanding—"

"We are betrothed," Kenan said, cutting into the man's ranting. "Tierney and I are handfasted for a year and a day. 'Tis the same as marriage in these remote parts, and it activates the clause to break the betrothal to Ranulf."

No one moved. Silence sat between everyone, and Tierney stared at him with her rosy lips parted. After he'd lied and said he was betrothed to Grace already, her shock was genuine.

"In a year and a day," Kenan continued, "I will have demonstrated the support of Clan Macdonald of Sleat and deterred the Matheson Clan, and Tierney may decide whether to wed me officially or end the…ordeal."

Tierney's little girl, Maggie, let go of her hand and stepped up to him. She tipped her chin up so she could look into his face, her blond ringlets falling down her back. "You made that horrid man go away, so I think Mama should wed you," she said. "If you treat her well and I get to stay with her." The lass had as much courage as her mother. "And I like the swirly decoration on your arm." She pointed to the ancient design of pigment etched into his skin, a reminder to him of the need for strength and his commitment to his people. "'Tis pretty."

His war design was pretty?

"'Tis a pigment etched into his skin to show how brave he is," Tierney said.

Maggie's head tilted. "'Tis still pretty."

Kenan kept his face serious. "And I think yer golden curls are pretty."

Maggie smiled broadly. "They're just like Mama's."

Kenan met Tierney's still questioning gaze. "Aye, two golden-haired angels."

The young warrior with the dark hair, who seemed to feel he had some claim on Tierney, cleared his throat. "Tier? Is this true? Ye've handfasted?"

Tier? Kenan's gut tightened. Had she given this upstart permission to shorten her name? "Her name is Lady Tierney MacNicol."

"Not to me," the man said without looking away from her. Accusation twisted in his tone.

Angry heat spread within his chest, and Kenan resisted the urge to grab him by the throat. This judging lad had no idea what Kenan had just done to help their floundering clan. *Foking hell.* Kenan had offered a year of help, and with it, he might be igniting war with Clan Mackinnon if he couldn't calm Cyrus and Grace.

"Yes, Jacob," she said. "We are handfasted for a year and a day."

"From what day?" Jacob countered.

"The day of the glider crash, so two days ago."

Jacob's gaze moved between them; his lips pulled back so that a flash of teeth could be seen. "So ye crashed his mad flying machine into the sea, and he said, 'Let's get handfasted'?"

The gazes kept volleying between Tierney and Jacob and then to Kenan.

"I…" Tierney began, hesitating at first, but then her words came smoothly. "I spoke with Kenan at length about our plight. He wishes to keep Skye free of other clans and unite us. Then he kissed me, and I demanded a handfasting before I'd submit to anything else."

Everyone looked at Kenan. Condemnation shot from Jacob's narrowed eyes. He'd decided Kenan was a conniving lech. Good bloody Lord. She'd been the one to drug and drag him off, shackling him.

He opened his mouth to say as much but stopped. It would show Tierney to be mad and criminal. And he certainly didn't want this group of strangers to think he was so foolish as to let a curvy fallen angel trick him.

Confusion was on Gabriel's cherubic face, and the other warriors had taken on Jacob's menacing stare, forgetting how he'd just sent their enemies flying from their land.

He met Henry's gaze. "A united Skye is the first step toward a united Scotland to stand strong against England or any other foreign invaders. So 'tis in the best interest of the MacNicol Clan that they unite with Clan Macdonald of Sleat to keep the Matheson Clan from invading yer shores."

Jacob shook his head. "I don't believe it. Tierney, even ye couldn't convince him to handfast so quickly. Cora said he'd been talking to another woman at the wedding festival, Grace Mackinnon."

"I have no agreement with Grace Mackinnon," Kenan said and saw Tierney stare at him. She either thought he was lying now or back on their journey.

Kenan walked over to Tierney. "My sister, Lady Sara MacLeod, and her husband, Chief Rory MacLeod of Dunvegan, were there as witnesses." All lies, but with the suspicious looks from Jacob and the other MacNicol warriors, they were necessary.

Kenan's arm slipped around Tierney's stiff form, pulling her closer. He bent his face to hers. Her eyes were wide open as he pressed his mouth against her warm lips. The kiss was short, but he felt desire jolt through him. She was warm and sweet-smelling, and he wanted to kiss her until she softened. And he needed to explain his declaration, but now wasn't the time.

Kenan straightened but kept his arm locked around her as he looked at Henry. "Binding enough to break the contract and keep Ranulf away from Tierney and yer clan. I will write a letter to Chief Murdoc Matheson to that effect."

Henry nodded, relief relaxing his bushy eyebrows. "That will be quite helpful."

Cora hurried inside the front double doors, her gaze finding Maggie quickly as if she'd lost her. The older woman from the village who'd appraised him walked in on the arm of another woman. Both carried short swords. "There's wee Maggie," one said, glancing at Cora. "Safe with her mama."

"I am so sorry, Edith," Tierney said, "that Ranulf's men went through your cottage."

The elderly woman swiped her sword through the air, nearly hitting the other woman. "If I'd had this, they wouldn't have dragged Maggie from under the bed. I would have sliced right through their Achilles tendons, and they wouldn't be able to walk."

"Good Lord," Henry said, looking aghast at the ladies. "Edith, ye almost sliced Doris's nose off."

Edith lowered her blade, patting her friend's arm. "Sorry, Doris."

"No bother," Doris said and looked at Tierney.

"We are setting up a celebration in the bailey to honor yer union."

"'Twas a handfasting," Jacob said, "not a wedding."

"In my day, that was the same thing."

Jacob crossed his arms. "I don't believe it. Their two witnesses aren't here. No witnesses mean it didn't happen."

*Blast the fool.*

Cora looked with wide eyes between Tierney and Kenan, her cheeks reddening in her pale face. "I...I witnessed it. A handfasting?" She said the last word like a question, but then she nodded. "The binding with a sash and the promises. I saw it between Tier and Chief Macdonald."

Doris smiled at Tierney. "Well, perhaps they will do it again before the village. We need something to celebrate."

Tierney felt stiff, wound tight enough to explode if poked. She pulled away from him, and he felt her absence like a cold breeze. "No need for that, but we can celebrate."

"A festival," Maggie yelled with glee, jumping up and down. "Mama, Cora, let's find wildflowers to make into crowns."

Tierney took up Maggie's hand; Cora took the other. Tierney gave Kenan a small smile. It was clearly a thank-you, and he nodded back. She walked with her daughter and beckoned the two ladies back outside.

Henry dropped a weathered hand on Kenan's shoulder. "Ye have yer work cut out for ye, Chief Macdonald."

Kenan looked at him. "She did not get along with her first husband, Maggie's father?"

Henry shook his head, his bushy eyebrows like two clumps of cattail fluff stuck over his squinty eyes. "Nay. She agreed to wed at first, but then she begged her father to get her out of it. Even sheared all her glorious hair off to get him to release her, but he wouldn't be deterred. It's grown back as lovely, but it had been down past her hips. Her mother cried when she'd done it." Henry shook his head. "To her pale scalp in some parts."

"'Tis a wonder she didn't run away," Kenan said, walking with the man toward the door.

Gabriel stood beside him, his newt still on his shoulder. "She was locked up most of the time, and then Maggie came along." The lad's eyes held quiet anger. "She poured all her love into Maggie, and Wallace died shortly after she was born."

"He was a Macqueen?" Kenan met the elderly man's gaze. "Like ye?"

Henry nodded. "I came with Wallace here as escort." He moved his head left and right. "An envoy per se, but I became friends with Douglas MacNicol and remained even when Tierney returned to Uig in Macqueen territory with Wallace. He was the young chief and moved them to Tuath Tower."

"He was young? How did he die?" Kenan kept his voice even.

Jacob's words came clipped and hard from behind Kenan, like stones being thrown at him. "An accident along the cliffs."

Henry walked with Kenan out into the courtyard. "After her husband died, her parents took Tierney and Maggie back in here at Scorrybreac, and Clan Macqueen has not lived up to their promise to support Clan MacNicol. Apparently, Wallace Macqueen was not a respected chief. Since Maggie is a girl, they're not offering any support against Clan Matheson."

The Macqueens lived in the northernmost part of Skye and were renowned fishermen. Perhaps Kenan could use the link with Tierney and Maggie to approach them about uniting as allies.

"Since the sweating sickness hit our clan, they've had nothing more to do with us," Henry finished. "I rather think they're waiting for us to die out so the new chief can take over this land."

Their boots crunched along the pebbles in the bailey as they caught up to Tierney, Cora, and Maggie. Tables were being carried into the space, and at least thirty more people had come out of their homes with colorful cloths to lay over them.

"Riders were sent out?" Tierney asked Doris.

Doris nodded. "We sent some lads out on horses to tell the farmers in the area of the celebration."

Edith gave a little sniff. "I wager they will come quicker for tarts than for fighting."

Maggie twirled, skirts whirling out and stopped before her mother. "They're coming because you've saved us, Mama."

"I... Uh..." Tierney's words trailed off, and she looked at Kenan.

"Aye," he said, meeting her gaze, "yer brave mother's plan has worked."

At least for the time being.

# CHAPTER TEN

"Marriage brings one into fatal connection with
custom and tradition, and traditions and customs
are like the wind and weather, altogether
incalculable."

*Soren Kierkegaard, Danish Philosopher, 1813–1855*

The entire clan came to Scorrybreac to congratulate
Tierney and Kenan. With each farming family trek-
king in from the countryside, Tierney cringed
inwardly at the lie. Even if she hadn't lied about a
wedding, a handfasting was still a union, and she'd
done neither.

She'd sworn never to bind herself to a man again,
not after the horrors with Wallace. She had her
sweet Maggie to love, and that would be enough.
She'd also sworn never to give a man any power
over her again. She'd sworn it to Jacob, which was
why he was so suspicious of their story.

Tierney's heart squeezed with each handmade
gift and food offering the people brought. Jars of
blackberry preserves and buttery cheeses, woven
handkerchiefs, and even a bolt of silk. And each gift
was given with their heartfelt thanks for creating
such a strong alliance through Kenan. She couldn't
turn them away, so she just smiled.

'Twas amazing how fast news traveled within her
dispersed clan. People had come to gather within

two hours when hardly any had come to fight off Ranulf.

There'd been too much loss, and her people needed time to heal. Hopefully this lie would give them time to regain their strength to fight for their clan. Parents had lost sons at Solway Moss, men and women of all ages had died with the sweating sickness, and everyone had watched Asher MacNicol ride away from their clan with some of their mightiest warriors. It had all become too much for her people when they realized that the Macqueens had abandoned them, too, and then learned Tierney's parents had perished at sea. 'Twas as if God had forsaken them.

Tierney felt cursed. All her plans had twisted into failures, and with this last threat by Ranulf, she'd nearly succumbed to defeat. But having a daughter, a little life that needed her to be strong, had bolstered her determination to try some highly risky plans—like abducting a Highland chief.

"Things are finally turning to favor us," Doris said, walking with Edith, who been given a wool-lined sheath in which to store her blade.

"We still need to arm ourselves," Edith answered, tapping the sheathed blade as they joined their friends.

The day was waning as people continued to arrive on foot and in wagons. A large bonfire had been lit, and children laughed, running around it. Each home brought out a dish to share, even though Tierney knew they didn't have much. Without the muscle to help with the farming, only a quarter of their fields had been planted. But each household contributed what they could to celebrate the hope that Kenan had brought.

"I'll stay with Maggie," Cora said, coming up to Tierney and handing her a small cup of wine that Henry had opened.

Tierney pulled her gaze from Kenan who spoke with each warrior who arrived. "Tonight?"

Cora's brows rose above her doe-like eyes. "While you take over your parents' room." She lowered her voice even more. "To look like you're truly handfasted, you need to share it with Kenan."

*Holy Joan.* What did Kenan expect of her? Her gaze slid back to him where he listened to the farmers, nodding every once in a while.

Kenan was taller than all of them, as if God had given him extra height to lead his massive clan. He'd washed and been given a clean tunic to wear. His dark, trimmed beard gave him the look of a handsome rogue, and his rock-hard body was built for war or lust. When he wasn't staring daggers at an enemy, or a woman who'd drugged and shackled him, there was such kindness in his dark blue eyes.

It squeezed Tierney's middle. How much had he just ruined with Cyrus Mackinnon by proclaiming that he'd handfasted with Tierney for a year? Of course, he could still marry Grace Mackinnon soon if he revealed the truth or after the year if he kept up their farce. Would the delay cause strife between the two great clans when Kenan tried to bring the Isle of Skye together? Guilt washed around in her stomach.

Perhaps he expected her to thank him in bed? The man was virile with youth, just like Wallace had been. Kenan was even larger than her dead husband with defined muscles. Wallace had acted kind at first, but as soon as they married, his cruel side took over.

Wallace had teased her and called her a coward when he'd taken her virginity. He hadn't cared that she wasn't ready, and pain had made her stiff. After that he'd called her icy, not someone anyone would want in their bed. It hadn't stopped him, though. He'd been resilient to her frost and didn't care if she lay there unmoving while he pumped into her. She'd hated him through it all, and any feelings of desire she'd felt before had died away.

Tierney shivered, rubbing her arms. But Kenan had shown her kindness even after all she'd done to trap him. He'd said things that warmed Tierney instead of threatening her with the mating act. He'd said he'd kiss her and taste her, bring her to pleasure. An unfamiliar pulse of heat between her legs made her shift.

Tierney walked across the square before Scorrybreac Tower that had been hung with bowers of spindly, bright-colored wildflowers. She'd bathed and donned her favorite blue gown with birds embroidered along the neckline. It felt like Beltane again with the laughter and food, except with every well wish, the lie within twisted.

Tierney strode to Kenan, stopping behind to listen as he spoke to Henry and the few warriors gathered.

"I've written three letters to send in the morn. Tomas, my general at Dunscaith, will receive my letter within the week, asking for a hundred volunteers to march to Scorrybreac." Kenan held up a hand to stop Jacob. "They will bring their own supplies and are used to sleeping outdoors." Kenan glanced at Gerald, the blacksmith. "I request ye make certain every person above the age of ten at Scorrybreac be given a sword, the size based upon their weight and height."

Gerald nodded. "Ye'll have to teach them how to not stab themselves." He jutted a thumb toward Edith. "I gave her a sheath, but more should be fashioned."

"I can work leather sheaths," one newly trained warrior named Peter said. He was a tall lad, gangly but eager.

"Good," Kenan said, the word firm as if he was checking it off a mental list. "I will give the women and young some lessons on what to do with their weapons and how to protect themselves."

"I can help with that," Tierney said, making Kenan turn toward her. At his gaze, her heart thumped harder, but she kept a serious, focused expression. "I've wanted everyone to learn how to protect themselves for a long time." She was better at archery than thrusting a sword, but she knew the basics of where to slice a man to disable him.

Jacob spoke up. "Chief MacNicol didn't agree with ye, Tier."

After she'd turned fourteen, her father had disagreed with all her ideas, as if her turning from child into a woman had muddled her mind. Either that or the birth of a son made her obsolete, and he no longer wished to hear her voice.

She looked directly at Jacob. "My father believed we could survive with three quarters of our warriors dead from battle and disease." She tipped her head in question as she skewered her childhood friend with her questions. "Do you, Jacob? Can you handle five armed Mathesons all on your own? Maybe six? Or would you like Edith to at least come behind and slice above their heel to sever a tendon?"

The picture she painted was morbid and not something her mother would like her discussing. But this was reality, and her mother was gone. She didn't have time to acknowledge the lump in her throat. Her people would be slaughtered without help from somewhere, and she'd rather die than marry Ranulf for an alliance.

When Jacob didn't answer, she came to stand next to Kenan. "Will Macdonald warriors arrive here before Mathesons retaliate?"

Kenan's gaze remained on her, weighing her, and she felt a flush rise in her cheeks. Hopefully the waning light hid it. "I know his brother somewhat," Kenan said. "He won't react without thought, and he doesn't much like Ranulf."

Kenan hadn't lied when he'd goaded Ranulf earlier.

"I expect Chief Matheson will pause before returning to our shores." Kenan looked back out at the gathered men. "He became chief when his father died in 1539 helping the MacKenzies defend Eilean Donan Castle, and he's still proving himself to his council five years later. Even if Murdoc wants his brother gone and a foothold on Skye, he isn't foolish enough to immediately charge against Clan Macdonald, knowing all the clan resources we have even beyond Skye." He looked across at the small group of young warriors who seemed to hang on his words. "I believe Ranulf will convince him to send troops, even if 'tis to stop the torment of his brother's tongue."

Jacob crossed his arms. "Chief Murdoc won't mind if we kill his brother."

"I have a brother like Ranulf," Kenan said. "As much as I dislike Gilbert, if someone kills him without a good reason, Macdonalds will retaliate."

Jacob cursed. Within the last year, he'd become the most skilled MacNicol warrior, stepping up when Asher left to lead the remaining men. Jacob had helped Tierney and Maggie more than she could expose. She'd told Jacob that any hint of ardor in her had died with Wallace's abuse. She couldn't return the feelings he had for her, no matter how he felt about her. He must think she was a liar having handfasted a near stranger. She sighed, knowing she was, in fact, just that.

Kenan crossed his arms, too, his hands resting on his mountainous biceps. She noticed how they strained against the sleeves of his tunic. Such obvious strength used to worry her, but Kenan had held her gently before him as they rode, even when he was furious and lusty. "Our goal should be to unite Scotland, not continue to tear it apart from the inside. 'Tis why England is stronger."

The circle of men grumbled. "He's right," Tierney called out. "Think of how badly Scotland lost at Solway Moss when England had three thousand troops to Scotland's fifteen thousand. 'Twas the conflict within our own ranks that crippled our country.

"I agree with Kenan. We need a stronger Scotland. Asher tried to tell my father that." It wasn't the first time Tierney wished her cousin was still on Skye. "Our country will never be strong if we attack ourselves from the inside like a sickness."

Several of the men nodded grimly, and Kenan spoke. "I'll send a letter to Murdoc Matheson, too, explaining the need for us to stay strong and allied, and that Clan Macdonald of Sleat is assisting Clan MacNicol." He stared out at Jacob. "'Tis not my intent to take over at Scorrybreac." Everyone remained silent, and Kenan let his gaze wander over them. "'Tis yers to manage and build. I pledge to help with that in an effort to make every clan on Skye strong and aligned."

"Under a new Lord of the Isles," Tierney said.

Kenan rubbed a hand down his cropped beard. "I prefer it to be a council of chiefs who agree to work together for the good of Scotland."

She shrugged. "There's always a need for a leader of leaders, as long as he doesn't have absolute power. A leader does not have to be a king."

Henry stared at her, aghast. He didn't think she should be discussing politics and had told her father that. She'd continued reading strategy and governmental procedures even after her father had stopped discussing matters with her, preferring to school Gabriel in such matters.

Kenan didn't agree nor disagree, but he studied her as if she'd just revealed a new side of herself. So far, he'd seen her as a half-drowned thief, a trickster, a jailor, a cold liar, and a desperate mother. She was also a strategist, and he would eventually see her as a warrior.

Kenan looked at the men. "Let's meet on the field where ye train tomorrow, with all the able-bodied warriors, and we can plan defense."

"And the women," Tierney said. "Can we start lessons?"

Kenan nodded. "Ye can instruct them after I see yer skills."

She opened her mouth to remind him that her proven skills had seen him abducted and shackled but then remembered that these men didn't know that, nor should they. "Certainly," she said, sounding more like one of his soldiers than a handfasted betrothed.

They began to talk about crop productivity, and Kenan suggested the unused fields be burned to push back the old growth and put nourishment back into the soil. Bored with the mundane discussion that crept along for long minutes, Tierney wandered off to chat with some of the older ladies discussing a fulling party later in the week. They would work sheep urine into the wool to make it waterproof and soft. It was hard work that Tierney joined in often, as long as they sang while accomplishing the arduous task.

"Tierney."

She turned to see Jacob standing behind her and glanced past him. "Have you all stopped talking about crops?" She saw Kenan still listening to Henry, who flipped his hand about with his words.

"Aye. Can I speak with ye?"

"I will help at the fulling party," Tierney told the ladies.

"Unless we are needed to fight," one younger woman said with a vigorous nod. Everyone agreed, and Tierney walked off next to Jacob.

Jacob led her into the shadows behind Doris's cottage framed by a low, white-washed fence. "What is it?"

His hands scratched through his hair. "I don't like that ye were forced into handfasting with him. To help us, ye've given him a year of yer life. A year of…having to…having to let him bed ye when I know ye don't want that."

Lord help her. She didn't know what she wanted. She'd told Jacob she wouldn't suffer a man's touch ever again, but the thought of Kenan touching her didn't turn her stomach. Instead, the thought, which she'd been having more and more, made heat spiral through her, heat like she'd never known but recognized as lust.

"Jacob," she said, "I'm not some maiden to be protected, and Kenan is honorable. He won't hurt me like Wallace."

Jacob didn't seem pacified. "He could break yer heart, Tierney, use ye for a year and then throw ye away. A man like that has other women waiting for him. He won't be faithful to ye."

A twisting sensation ground in her stomach. Grace Mackinnon was waiting for him.

Jacob stepped closer. "I know men like him, powerful men who attract women. They use them and move on to the next. I won't do that."

"How do you know Kenan so well? Have you met him before, seen him do this attraction and using? Know his verified history?" Irritation had replaced her calm tone.

Jacob reached out, holding her arm. "I worry about ye, Tierney. I've always protected ye. I could still protect—"

"I thank you for…what you've done for me and Maggie," she said, laying her hand on his forearm, "but you don't have a clan with warriors ready to charge in and protect all of us."

He clasped her hand. "We can still run away together, the three of us. Even Gabriel and Cora could—"

"I won't abandon Scorrybreac, Jacob." She shook her head, trying to pull her hand back, but he wouldn't let go. "I will keep it safe until Gabriel can be chief."

He pulled her closer. "Ye have other options, Tier," he whispered. "Better options. Let the Macdonalds keep the Mathesons off Skye while ye and Maggie leave with me. Kenan Macdonald is a powerful clan chief, surrounded by lasses who want to wed him, lasses with large dowries and connections. 'Tis obvious he wants to unite Skye and Scotland more than he wants ye. I do not doubt that he will abandon ye in a year. Let me be the one to love ye. I will never leave ye, Tier."

His words shot like a punch to her chest, simultaneously stopping her breath and mixing her confusion with anger and pain. Jacob must have interpreted her silence for acceptance because his mouth descended onto hers. He tasted of whisky just like Wallace. Panic stalled her response, and she stood there remembering the feeling of being trapped with brute strength that far surpassed her own.

• • •

Kenan's hand gripped the rough-hewn picket of the fence where he stood in the dark, watching like a bloody peeper. He'd seen Jacob lead Tierney behind the cottage into the shadows from the other side of the square. Following was obvious to anyone paying attention, but he followed anyway. His pride was already down the privy having been trapped and abducted by a lass. He'd declared them handfasted to help her, never guessing that she might love another. Tierney had never even mentioned Jacob.

*She did. He's one of the three men she trusted.*

She'd said she didn't want a man, hadn't she? That she'd been released from a terrible marriage. Rising anger muddled his memories of their discussions in the hidden cabin. He breathed slowly to gain control of his swirling temper. How much humiliation could one man stand? Abducted, shackled, made to go against his own plans to unite Clan Macdonald and Clan Mackinnon, and now Tierney was with a man in the shadows at their handfasting celebration.

*Ye're too soft.* His father's words, even from the grave, prickled under Kenan's skin.

His hand clenched, and he knew if he released the picket on the fence, he'd charge forward and break Jacob Tanner in half. Kenan might be slow to anger, but once he was furious, his well-built frame and finely tuned abilities quickly became lethal.

And he was enraged. At Jacob Tanner, at Tierney, and at himself. It was a trinity of fury.

*Crack!* The sound of knuckles hitting flesh shot through the night.

"Fok, Tier!" Jacob's pained voice kept Kenan's boots planted on the grassy path. "My bloody eye!"

Tierney's voice was hushed but full of indignant fury. "You're lucky I don't have one of Gerard's short swords yet."

Jacob's voice returned as angry as hers, almost enough to make Kenan advance. "'Twas just a kiss. And ye need to know what ye've given up by tying yerself to that stranger."

"Given up?"

Kenan couldn't see more than her shadow, but it was stiff, and her fists were raised.

"I've given up sour, drooling kisses," she shot back.

"Fok," Jacob whispered. "Ye don't know what ye want. I taught ye to live in the forest. I said I'd help ye and Maggie run away. I even helped free ye from Wallace when yer father did nothing. And what do ye do? Leap into the bed of the enemy."

Jacob helped free her from her marriage to Wallace?

"I haven't leaped into anyone's bed, you arse, and Kenan's not our enemy."

"Yer father sure thought he was. Called the Macdonald chief the devil who was spit down from heaven to plague our isle."

"Kenan is a new chief, and my father only thought MacNicols were worthy of ruling Skye. But God disagreed when he took two thirds of our people through war and sickness."

Kenan held tight to the fence picket so he

wouldn't charge into what Tierney was handling quite well on her own. Fury impassioned her voice, and yet her arguments were sound. A warrior who could think while rage heated their blood was lethal.

Jacob swore, his words flying. "Spreading yer legs for the enemy to save yerself is exactly what yer father had planned for ye to do with Ranulf, and yet ye refused."

Kenan released the picket. Rather, he yanked it from the ground, letting it drop as he strode into the shadows. Jacob leaped backward as Kenan stalked around the corner like an avenging demon coming up from the blackness of Hell. Kenan grabbed the front of his tunic at the neck, fisting it tight as he lifted until Jacob was on his toes, his tunic biting into his armpits.

"Coward," Kenan said before Jacob's face, grinding the word out like a growl. "To corner a woman in the shadows, force a kiss on her, and then condemn her for saving her clan with slander because of yer own selfish jealousy."

"Foking let go," Jacob said.

"Ye've had all evening to challenge me, but ye wait to drag Tierney into the shadows and accost her."

"Let him go, Kenan," Tierney said behind him. "He's a fool who's had too much whisky and is muddled with regrets."

He held tight to Jacob, shaking him to remind him that he could break him easily if he wanted. Kenan remembered how Asher had broken the guard's neck at Carlisle. That wasn't Kenan, but it could be.

Jacob glared back in the minimal light, his teeth clenched between parted lips.

"Foolish coward." Kenan shoved Jacob back as he released him. He'd been Tierney's childhood friend and a MacNicol warrior. Killing him was the wrong thing to do or even consider.

Jacob found his footing and lunged at Kenan. So the pup had enough courage to make him stupid.

*Crack!*

Kenan's fist contacted Jacob's face, the charging man adding to the force of the impact. It swept Jacob right off his feet, and he landed on his back with a thump and a groan, his head lulling to the side.

"Mo chreach!" Tierney yelled and shoved at Kenan's arm so she could crouch down to check on the unconscious man.

"What?" Kenan asked, anger still making his voice hard. "Ye can punch him, but I can't?"

"Thank God he's breathing," she said and rose.

Instead of God, she should be thanking Kenan, because he could have broken the arse's neck.

She turned, and Kenan was startled when she yanked his hand, still fisted up in the air. She held her own fist next to it. "I hit him with this," she said, her small fist half the size of his. "And you hit him with this." She clutched his, her nails curling inward like the talons of a hawk wrapping around a squirrel.

Why had he reacted so quickly with such hardness? "I could have killed him, but I chose leniency," he said.

Tierney flapped her hand at Jacob, lying unconscious on the ground. "This is leniency?"

Irritation brushed away the guilt she hurled toward him. "He took ye into the shadows, kissed ye against yer will, accused ye of spreading yer legs for me, and then lunged at me. He deserved more than a punch in the face." Kenan's usual mellow temper had turned to ash under the fire raging through him, and his voice had risen to shouting. The day had been full of prickly trials, and his temper could stand no more.

Several men, including Henry, jogged around the corner with torches, lighting the scene. They looked from Kenan to Tierney to Jacob. Instead of questions, understanding seemed to relax their faces. Did everyone know of Jacob's fondness for Tierney?

Kenan grabbed her hand, noticing her flinch. She'd probably bruised her knuckles from hitting Jacob. His hand was so callused and toughened from abuse that the impact and bruising hadn't even been noticed.

"Come," he ordered, marching away. She dug in her heels, but he was not ready to placate. Kenan swept Tierney up in a move he'd used with his younger sister when she'd run from him while playing tag, lowering her over one of his shoulders. Unfortunately, he did it before half the village who had come around the cottage to see what was going on.

"Put me down, you addle-brained Goliath," Tierney called, and he felt her hair tickle the backs of his knees. One of her fists struck his back, and her booted feet began to kick. He grabbed her calves with one arm and her nicely rounded arse with the other to keep her firmly in place while she thrashed.

"My fence," Doris said with a condemning tone. "Did that Jacob Tanner yank out my fence post, too? I'm going to beat that boy."

Kenan didn't bother to explain but continued to stalk off toward the meadow beyond where the light from the celebration fire didn't reach.

It was time they had a private discussion.

# CHAPTER ELEVEN

"Come Fairies, take me out of this dull world, for I
would ride with you upon the wind and dance upon
the mountains like a flame!"

*William Butler Yeats – Irish Poet, 1865–1939*

Tierney wiggled one foot free and kicked it toward
her backside in an effort to hit Kenan's face, but her
petticoat got in the way. "Daingead!" she cursed.
"What are you doing?"

"Let's call it retribution."

"For me meeting in the dark with Jacob?" Was
Kenan jealous? Of Jacob? There was hardly a com-
parison between the boy she'd grown up with and
the man who was currently humiliating her.

"Nay. For drugging me, tying me up, and carrying
me off against my will."

"Are you going to hold that over my head forever?"

"For a year and a day."

She exhaled. *Daingead.* She'd done all that to
him, and he'd still said they were handfasted to help
her save face before her clan and break her father's
damn betrothal contract.

"Put me down, Kenan Macdonald." The press of
his shoulder against her middle made it hard to draw
deep breaths to feed her temper, and she rested, deciding to keep her energy for when she got her feet

under her again. Then Kenan would suffer even if he'd saved her, saved Maggie. Her anger ebbed with that reminder.

Kenan climbed onto the meadow where the warriors trained during the day. When he got to the edge of trees, the bonfire's illumination only a distant dot, he shifted her off his shoulder.

Tierney waited for her feet to touch the ground and shoved him with all her pent-up frustration, confusion, and anger at the whole situation. But the damn man didn't move. 'Twas like shoving a two-foot-thick oak.

Her hands pulled back, and she thumped her palms against his hard chest again. At the same time, she kicked his shin.

He grunted. "Bloody hell, Tierney."

She smiled with triumph at the pain in his tone.

"That's for carrying me off like a helpless child." She thumped his chest again. "In front of my whole clan, like a child. You...you barbarian."

"So ye've moved past being angry that I knocked Jacob down?"

"That, too."

In the dim light from a moon that tried to peek past the moving clouds, she saw Kenan cross his arms, his legs braced for battle.

"I was handling him," she said. "I don't need you to rescue me."

"So far, evidence refutes that statement." He flipped up fingers as he spoke. "First, I had to rescue ye from the ocean and drowning. Second, I saved ye from Ranulf and his men, and third I defended yer wild plan before Henry and yer clan, even though ye drugged and tricked me."

He really was going to hold that over her forever, although she did deserve that.

Kenan dropped her arm. "And that fool lad needed more than yer paltry punch to teach him not to force unwanted kisses, especially on a woman who belongs to someone else."

"Belongs to someone else?" she repeated; his territorial language reminded her of Wallace. Her heart beat wildly, but it was with anger, not fear. It felt refreshing, so she let her temper flare. "Would that be you? I *belong* to you?"

"Aye, for a year," he said, leaning closer, "and a day. That's what bloody handfasting means, Tierney. And if anyone is going to kiss ye, 'tis me, not some heartsick swain who's lost his head to whisky and regret. Me."

She could point out that they'd never really handfasted, but he would just throw back that everyone thought they had. Instead, she glared, taking a different route that plagued her more. "Will you force your kisses on me, then?" Her face tipped up to him with a scowl. She'd only been kissed by Wallace before and now Jacob, and neither of them had been pleasant at all. "Slobbery, sour kisses."

"My kisses are not slobbery and sour," he said. "Bloody hell." His hands went to his head, and his elbows jutted out as he tipped his face up to the sky. "This was a foking mistake."

Tierney's anger flipped to worry so suddenly that it caused a nauseous wave in her stomach. Was Kenan going to leave? Walk away like Asher had after he argued with her father? Would Kenan take his offer of support away and let Ranulf come in to do what he wanted with her and her people, with Maggie? Would he tell her people about the lie? A different kind of fear washed over her. Could she withstand another abandonment?

She breathed deeply, lowering her voice to a calmer tone. "I've only ever had slobbery, sour kisses before, so I know nothing else. Perhaps your kisses are dry and sweet."

He leveled his face back to hers. "Ye will never know unless ye want one." He leaned closer so that his lips were only inches away from hers. "Because I don't force them on anyone, and those who do force kisses deserve to end up on their arses in the dirt." The ending "T" was hard and final like he thought it was the last word of their disagreement.

Kenan didn't know yet that Tierney always had the last word, even if it wasn't spoken aloud. She grabbed his shoulders, her fingers curling into the muscles there. He met her gaze with curiosity, surrounded by a frown in all the angles of his face. Her hands slid up to cup his cheeks, her heart pounding, and she pressed her lips against his mouth. It was deliberately hard and closed. With a smacking sound, she pulled back still holding onto him. "Will you knock me on my arse now?"

For a moment, Kenan said nothing, and the smugness at leaving him speechless warmed her.

Tierney opened her mouth to tell him his kiss was lacking when he pulled her to him. A breathy gasp left her as his lips met hers. But his mouth wasn't hard and punishing. It was soft and warm. His fingers threaded through her hair to the back of her head while his other hand slid gently under her jawline to tilt her face.

The stiffness in her body dissolved in response, and she found herself pressing back into the kiss. *Not wet. Not dry. Just right.* The thought flickered through her as she sank closer into the comfort of his arm against his chest where her hands rested. The leaning helped to steady her, because her legs felt weak as if she'd had too much whisky.

Despite the breeze that had grown chilled as the sun surrendered to darkness, warmth slid down from her cheeks to her neck and farther. The fire of worry and embarrassment inside Tierney quickly changed into an inferno of sensation, a heat that melted her past.

Their mouths slid against each other, and when his tongue touched her lip, she opened with a soft moan. He dipped inside, and she momentarily worried that she tasted sour from the wine and Jacob's breath. But Kenan didn't seem to mind as his hands stroked through her hair and his mouth devoured her.

She inhaled through damp lips as he kissed her jawline. Tierney had always been ticklish, but the way he touched and left a trail along her neck just made her tip her head back farther, giving him greater access. Sensations sizzled under her skin that made her shift against him. Her hands slid over the muscles of his chest. They were firm and built into rock from training for war. Pressed so intimately against him with only one petticoat and his wool wrap separating them, she could feel the growing hardness of his jack, and he reached down to adjust it upward through the plaid.

Tierney stiffened slightly at the memory of Wallace brandishing his jack like a weapon, telling her to just lie there and spread herself for him. But the feel of Kenan's gentle strength holding her, not entrapping her, made her press more into him as if to escape her past.

Kenan's lips lifted from its path along her neck, leaving a chill with the dampness there. She inhaled the night breeze mixed with his now familiar scent. It pulled her instead of making her wish to escape.

*He's safe.*

His breathing was ragged as if the kiss had affected him, too. She liked that idea. He rested his chin on the top of her head as he held her in his arms.

"Slobbery and sour?"

She smiled against his chest. "No, which is unexpected."

A chuckle rumbled in his chest. "Dry and sweet?"

She sniffed the smallest laugh. "No."

"Then what?" he asked, his voice devoid of the anger from before. "Dry and sour? Slobbery and sweet?"

She arched back enough to look up into his face. With eyes adjusted to the scant light, she could see his handsome, angular features, the only imperfection being a bump over the bridge of his nose. He waited for her to answer with what looked like great patience. The hardness of his jack gave evidence that she might not be the only one feeling anything but patient. The thrumming in her body was becoming more insistent as her heart beat rapidly with what a romantic might call a flutter. The feelings were foreign to Tierney.

"No words to describe my kiss, then?" he asked, and she detected a light smugness. She certainly couldn't let him have the last word.

"Hmmm…" She tapped a finger against her lips as if she were judging a baking contest. "Not too wet or too dry. Soft but firm with a hint of whisky and ale, but not bad."

He reached between them to clasp her hand, bringing it up to where he could kiss her bruised knuckles gently. His dark eyes held a wicked glint. "There are many types of kisses, Tierney, given on many parts of the body. Do ye know about those?" The way he spoke sent shivers through her, a friction that ran across the embers that the kiss had lit.

Words abandoned her under the seduction of his tone. She shook her head slightly.

His face was serious again. "If we belong to each other for a year," he said, his voice rough and full of heavy promise, "we should spend it well."

"Well," she repeated, pushing away the thought that they weren't actually handfasted. She watched his lips, how they came together as he spoke. Where would those lips kiss her? Her breasts? The thought sent another thrill through her middle, making her nipples pearl.

He nodded, moving his face before hers. "And just to clear up any misperceptions, I belong to ye as much as ye belong to me during this year."

She remembered the fury that had burned

through her as he carried her, saying she belonged to him. "A mutual commitment, then."

"Aye."

"But we didn't handfast," she said, her voice just above a whisper.

"We can act as if we did, but then ye can decide if we end our year early. I would leave it up to ye."

"And there would be…education between us," she said, and the tip of her tongue slid briefly to her upper lip as if licking a sweet off it. His gaze dropped instantly to her mouth. The energy that seemed to radiate between them there on the dark moorland rippled through Tierney, changing any unease into molten honey.

"As much as ye want," he said. "Ye have freedom in the fact ye aren't a virgin, Tierney."

She swallowed, her heart thumping. "I should tell you I've been called cold in bed before." Tierney's cheeks flamed, and she was glad for the darkness. Her stomach curled inward. "Icy, in fact."

Kenan's brows lowered, bringing back a hint of the tight anger from before. She tried to take a step back, but he kept her close. "He was wrong." In the dim light from the moon, she could see his brows pinch and his whole face contract in contained anger. "And I hate that ye believed him."

She shrugged, as if Wallace's words hadn't hurt her. But they had, as much as his strikes against her flesh.

Kenan's hands came up to cup her cheeks. "Tierney, there was absolutely no ice in yer kiss just now."

He was right. She'd gone from fiery fury to

inferno passion without any dip in temperature. Perhaps it had been Wallace that made her icy.

He leaned in, kissed her cheek and then her temple and over to her ear. "I'm guessing the heat of that kiss traveled down through ye, down to where ye might have started to ache, where I want to kiss ye."

If the heat in her had faded somewhat, Kenan's words shot flaming arrows back into her. Her lips parted, and she brought in a trembling breath. Suddenly, she wished they were in her chamber at the tower or even back at the cabin where she'd originally shackled him. Anywhere alone with a soft floor or bed and the glow of firelight so she could see Kenan's rock-hard, beautiful body again.

Her fingers reached up to tug his face back to hers, and she kissed him. Not hard like before, not soft and timid, but with an unspoken need that turned the kiss wild from the start. Mouths opening, neither of them seemed to care what form the kiss took as long as they were linked.

As if waking from a long, frozen sleep, Tierney's body pressed against Kenan, her hips rocking into him in a natural, needful rhythm. With a growl, Kenan's hands lifted under her backside, fitting her against his hard jack. Arms around his neck, she held herself to him so intimately that, for a moment, it was as if their clothes had burned right off them.

Tierney's hands began to slide down his thick arms as he helped her grind into him. The friction against the sensitive crux of her legs made her want to strip the clothes away. Never before had she felt so strong and weak at the same time. Her hands landed at the base of his back, and she squeezed his arse.

A cool breeze slid against her bared legs, and she realized Kenan had rucked up the back of her petticoat, his fingers bunching the fabric at her hips. Warm hands covered her naked backside, stroking down. Her back arched without thought as if the hot ache in her cleft sought his touch. She breathed heavily as he expertly slid down over her cheeks to part her from behind. She moaned when his fingers found her.

He groaned, too, as he slid inside her tight sheath while kissing a path to her ear. "Wet, hot, and I'm guessing sweet."

Tierney shuddered at the erotic promise in his tone. When he moved his fingers in a mating cadence, she strained backward. He was building a fire inside her that was rampaging out of control. She valued her control, but with this feeling growing inside her, she eagerly surrendered it if this delicious heat continued to grow toward something she wanted so badly.

Kenan was wrapped around her as he taught her how to feel passion and embrace the surrender to it. Could she drag him inside the forest line where there must be a soft spread of moss? "Yes," she hissed into the night as he stroked her inside, his other hand freeing her breast.

His mouth dropped to her nipple, sucking, picking up the rhythm he'd started below until she felt like a cord connected both aching parts of her. "Oh, my sweet Joan, yes," she whispered.

*Crack!*

Kenan stiffened, his hand and mouth disappearing from her, leaving need so fierce she cursed with a ragged groan. But Kenan was cursing louder.

"What the bloody foking hell?" he yelled, as he pulled her behind him, shielding her. He lowered his hand from his head, and Tierney saw the darkness of blood on his fingers.

# CHAPTER TWELVE

"When once you have tasted flight, you will forever walk the earth with your eyes turned skyward. For there you have been, and there you will always long to return."

*Leonardo da Vinci – Italian artist and scientist, 1452–1519*

"Are you shot?" Tierney asked, panic taking her already coursing blood and channeling it into her muscles, preparing her to fight, even as her body begged for completion. But there'd been no *blast*.

"I've been hit with a rock." Kenan stared out at the shadows.

"By who?" she asked, tugging up her bodice and turning in a circle.

"And if ye don't step away from her, ye'll feel the sting of another." The threat came from just inside the forest, where she spied a thin man and a white wolf. No. A dog.

"Gabriel?" Tierney said and heard Sneachda growl. How did they get around them without her noticing? That's right. She'd been rather distracted. Holy Joan, what had her brother seen? The fire in her cooled quickly.

Gabriel released the dog. Kenan stepped before Tierney again despite being the beast's target.

"Sneachda," she called, slapping her leg to get

the dog to leave him alone and come to her. "All is well."

"Except that a rock hit me," Kenan said.

Tierney saw him reach down his wrap to adjust what must have been a very hard and aching jack. She ached so badly herself that she wanted to scream at Gabriel.

"He was attacking ye," Gabriel said, holding his arm up with another projectile. She could just make out a shape on his tunic that looked like his newt. "I heard you groan in pain."

Thank the Lord it was dark, because Tierney's face flamed. Her brother was young and did not know passion. What Kenan had been doing to her had been a type of pain, one of longing and need.

Kenan held a rag from his belt to his head. "I would never attack yer sister, lad, not in a bad way."

"We were kissing." Tierney tried to keep the frustration out of her voice. But if that was just kissing, then the biblical apocalypse was simply a bad day. No. She and Kenan were tupping upright, kissing with their whole bodies. But she wasn't about to explain that to her brother.

"His mouth wasn't even on yers," Gabriel said, but his arm lowered. "'Twas like he was chomping on yer neck."

"Let's go back to the village," Tierney said, even though she'd much rather continue her plan of finding some soft moss in the forest. But she'd been given the large bedchamber in the tower with soft ticks and luxurious blankets. Much better than moss.

"If he wasn't biting ye, what was he doing?" Gabriel gave Kenan a wide berth, and Sneachda trotted beside the boy.

"What are you doing up here?" She trudged toward the dot of fire marking the edge of the village.

"I believe yer brother saw me carry ye off in an ungentlemanly manner and came to make certain ye weren't being harmed," Kenan said.

Gabriel walked right next to Tierney. "Over yer shoulder." He looked at Kenan. "Ye don't know my sister well, Chief Macdonald, but she won't put up with being tossed around like that. Ye'll end up with poison in yer stew."

"Or a tart," Kenan said, his voice cool.

"That wasn't poison," she said, feeling the guilt flood her again. "Just something for a nice, long sleep."

"Which ye won't ever do to me again," Kenan said and leaned into her ear. "Else I tie *ye* up." The way he said the words made a shiver of carnal anticipation run through her, pulsing down to the crux of her legs that had just minutes ago been rubbing rhythmically against his raging jack.

Gabriel's head swiveled around to them, his eyes wide in the dark. "If ye're planning to tickle her, ye'll be in for some bruises, Macdonald. She's terribly ticklish and kicks and punches and might even bite ye like a poked wildcat."

Kenan said nothing for a moment, and then a rumble of laughter came from him. "Ticklish?"

"Gabriel," Tierney said, his name heavy with a sigh, "you've now given Kenan a weapon to use against me."

"Oh, bloody hell," her brother said. "Sneachda," he called and trotted faster to catch up with the white dog who'd broken ahead of them like a scout.

The wildflowers and tall grass hit against her petticoat as they strode along in the darkness, her on his arm as if they were truly handfasted. Handfasted and allowed to do whatever they wanted to do to one another. The thought blew across the coals inside her.

"Are you ticklish?" she asked.

"Nay."

"Maybe you're lying. Maybe I need to tie you to the bed and tickle you to see."

"Do ye keep ropes and chains in yer bedchamber?" he asked, a huskiness to his voice that hinted at a dark passion.

"No, but I know where I can find some."

"I think 'tis yer turn to get tied up." He leaned closer to her ear. "But I'll make sure ye like it."

If it was a threat, her body didn't care, because it continued to sizzle.

In the village, people stared as they walked by. Cora ran up, her eyes wide, and took her other arm as if to pull her away, but Tierney held fast to Kenan. Cora leaned to her ear. "Did he hit you?"

"No."

Cora released a breath. "But you look," she studied Tierney, "flushed." In the middle of the path, she yanked Tierney before her even though Kenan still held her arm. For a moment, Tierney felt tugged in two. Cora caught her head with both her hands and pulled Tierney's face to her and pressed her lips to Tierney's forehead like their mothers would do to test for fever.

Her gaze rolled upward to her friend as Cora

pressed her lips against her skin. "I'm not feverish, Cora." Well, she was, but not with sickness.

Cora released her and nodded. "Thank the heavens."

"I'm a bit tired is all."

"Tired?" Cora asked. "The celebration has barely started."

Tierney feigned a yawn. "You'll stay with Maggie tonight?"

Cora blinked, and in the light of the torches, her cheeks grew flushed. She glanced at Kenan where he stood silently next to them, his gaze roaming the shadows. "Yes, of course."

"Many thanks," Tierney said. "Tell her I'll pop in later to kiss her while she's asleep."

Cora hurried off, and Tierney tugged the slightest amount to get them striding toward the tower. No one stopped them, and Kenan followed without hesitation. Tongues would wag, but the only tongue she was thinking about was that of her mock-handfasted partner who'd detected her haste.

They pushed inside the double front doors into the silent entry that was lit with only one torch. Silence. Only Tierney's wildly beating heart sounded in her ears. Was everyone still out at the celebration? The sun had gone down, so it was late enough for Cora to bring Maggie in, but it seemed everyone was taking the opportunity to celebrate something good.

All she could do was think about what Gabriel had interrupted, how her blood had felt like it was racing through her, making her skin feel extra sensitive to Kenan's touch. Was he thinking the same thing? He was right. Being a widow gave her certain freedoms. She had no maidenhead to protect.

They'd paused in the entryway, and Tierney turned to him. Before she could even worry about his ardor cooling, he backed her against the stone wall, kissing her as if they hadn't been interrupted out on the moor.

"Is your forehead still bleeding?" she asked against his lips as she kissed back and wrapped her hands over his shoulders to steady herself.

"I don't care."

"You will if you grow faint."

A low growl in the back of his throat preceded him lifting her. She was jostled up against his hard chest, his arm under her knees. "Do I feel weakened by blood loss?"

Absolutely not, but she had no air to tell him that because he was kissing her again, striding into the keep, and crossing it to the stairs. He set her down two steps higher than him, so they were face to face.

"Do ye want me to stop?" he asked, and she noticed that his breath was as ragged as hers.

"No." She gave a quick shake of her head, amazed that heat coursed through her when she'd been told once she was made of ice. "Don't stop."

His warm palms caught her face, and he tipped it slightly to the side as he descended for a wild kiss. Despite his strength, he allowed her to press him backward against the side of the plastered stone wall that made up the spiral staircase.

She gasped in the air as he left her lips, kissing a path to her neck and then to her ear where his deep voice vibrated. "I think 'tis time to move on to plan number three." His words sent a sizzle shooting down her body.

Before she could answer, he lifted her up a step and turned her so that she stood pressed against the wall, his large, hard body before her as he rose.

In answer, her hand slid down between them until it cupped his erection so evident through his plaid wrap. He was no doubt as hot and achy as she.

With a groan, he grabbed her hand from his jack and led her up the steps behind him. "Where do I take ye?"

*Right here on the steps* perched on her tongue. But the thought of Cora and Maggie coming up changed her reply. "My parents' bedchamber is being refurbished for me, for us, to use. Third landing and to the left."

Her heart thumped from the climb, the sensations still spinning through her body. On the third landing, Kenan turned to her. "Left?"

*Or here on the floor.* "Yes," she said, and they hurried together down the dim corridor to the room that Henry had led her to earlier that day, saying it was to be hers and Kenan's as Lord and Lady of Scorrybreac Tower.

Kenan threw the door open, and a musty smell hung in the air from disuse. But it was private and had a large bed. Then he kissed her, and she didn't care where they were because he was warm, and sensations thrummed through her pulling her mind from the mundane to the need that took her over. They moved together, knocking into something that clattered on the floor. He broke the kiss. "Are there traps set about?"

"Just a snare to keep you here," she said.

"It sounds like ye're asking me to tie ye up."

Lord, help her. His words, said in his deep, teasing tone, made the fire in her burn brighter.

He led her toward the large, four-poster bed that she knew was swathed in heavy fabric drapes. They would be the first to go. Their heaviness felt like a cage. But the only light in the room came from the two glass-paned windows allowing in scant moonlight, enough to see the hulking forms of the bed, armoire, and privacy screen, but nothing else.

Yanking aside one drape, Kenan pressed her back on the lofty mattress that was dressed in quilts. The maids would have cleaned the bedding and room as soon as her parents left on their ill-fated voyage to mainland Scotland. It just needed to be dusted.

The sound of his boots being kicked off preceded his quick pull of each of her own boots. "I can't see you," she said, her heart flickering with panic as she saw the whiteness of his tunic pull off and fade into the darkness. For a split second she imagined Wallace, his whisky-soaked body coming at her.

Another thump on the floor may have been his heavy wool wrap and belt. "But can ye feel me?" The rumble of Kenan's deep voice soothed her. This wasn't the harsh man who'd wooed her with a handsome smile only to demand complete obedience once she was trapped in a marriage. There was nothing to trap her into being with Kenan, not even a pledge of handfasting. He wasn't conquering her body; he was freeing it to soar with every touch.

Kenan slid his hands up each of her stockings that encased her calves, slowly, stopping to massage the muscle there.

Holy Joan, his fingers pressed in all her tight spots. She groaned as he worked the soreness out of her legs. No one had ever rubbed her legs before. "Oh yesssss," she said and realized the pleasure in the words sounded like he was touching more intimate places.

He chuckled in the darkness. "Ye like to be rubbed."

Rubbed and kissed and touched and whatever else he wished to do that caused this pleasurable tightening within her. The darkness seemed to heighten her other senses. He tugged the ribbons at the top of each stocking, and his fingertips tickled her as he rolled the thin wool down her legs, leaving her long limbs bare. His fingers stroked up her legs, rucking up the petticoat, and she began to shift on the bed, anticipating his touch higher. Her legs moved apart on their own as her crux throbbed, waiting.

Kenan's hulking form was caught in shadow, poised over her. For a moment, he looked like Wallace, who would grab at her and shove himself between her legs, hissing in her ear that it was his right. The thought sent a wash of cold wind through her as if it had funneled up from Wallace's grave.

Kenan had reached above her knees but stopped. "Tierney? We can stop this right now if ye wish."

Had she tensed with the memory of torture?

She shook her head but knew he couldn't see her, and reached down to his hand, squeezing it where it lay on her bare thigh. "I need this," she whispered. She wanted Kenan to wash her skin free of the nightmarish memories. "Touch me and see if I feel like I want you to stop." The ache between her legs pulsed with her wicked words.

Kenan slid up the bed, pulling her with him against his body. His tunic was gone, and so was his wrap below. He was completely naked. Warm skin with a sprinkling of hair over solid muscle.

He wrapped his arms around her, rolling the two of them across the bed as his mouth found hers again. She held onto his neck, kissing him back until the wildness of passion took her captive in a way she welcomed. Tierney was lost in sensation, Kenan's hot, hard body against her. His scent was made of fresh air, leather, and a spice all his own.

She tugged at the front ties of her bodice until they loosened, her breasts craving the feel of his touch. Moving against one another in total darkness, Tierney listened to the brush of her skirt as he lifted it. She sighed against his mouth when her bodice loosened enough to allow her breasts to perch out the top. Her stays were next to loosen and open. Shifting down from the top and up from the bottom, she laughed softly. "I'm tangled in clothes."

"When ye should be out of them," he murmured, his head bowing to her breast.

She sucked in a gasp as his mouth pulled one hard, sensitive nipple in between his lips. The warmth of his mouth burrowed into her, rushing down to her pelvis. Her fingers raked softly through his thick hair, holding him to her, and she felt the tickle up her leg as his fingers continued their journey.

The soft bristle of Kenan's clipped beard brushed

her chin as he kissed her, their tongues touching, bringing a guttural groan from him. Her legs slid farther apart, and when he touched, she pressed her mound into his hand, begging him for more.

"Ye are ready, more than ready," he said, as his fingers rubbed and teased. She began a grinding rhythm into his hand as he played her expertly. His hard, long jack moved against her thigh.

Tierney whispered, "Ask me to take you inside. Beg me."

She'd never been asked. He had all the power, the strength, the jack to plunge into her. Control was something she'd never had in bed, and it was something she craved. She sought freedom from her past, and Kenan loving her was a path to liberation.

He kissed her neck, nibbling the skin there as he continued to stroke her, making her breath ragged. "Aye, lass. Can I plunge inside ye?" he asked. "Please." He held the head of his jack right at her entrance.

"Yessss," she said and gasped as his huge length thrust into her wet, open body.

Kenan groaned, his body taking over, bracing his forearms on either side of her face as he pumped into her. When she tipped her pelvis forward, he groaned again. He withdrew and thrust, starting a frantic rhythm that her body matched. Her legs rose to wrap around his back, her heels resting on his muscled arse.

"Oh God, lass," he said on a lusty exhale as they rode the pleasure together. "I want to see ye."

Without breaking his stride, he yanked on the curtains around the bed. Once. Twice. She imagined his biceps bunching with the power. He yanked a third time. *Crack!* The sound of wood cracking preceded the heavy drapes falling on two sides. She barely noticed the destruction as moonlight filtered in through the window. He looked nothing like Wallace.

Kenan's features were strained as they moved together, a rhythm of madness and lust. His eyes centered on her face, his lips parted like hers, and his nostrils flared like a galloping stallion. She felt like they were beasts mating with wild abandon, and the thought made her press hard, meeting his thrusts.

Shifting up higher on her body, his pelvis brushed her most sensitive nub, and she gasped. Each rub of friction shot more heat through her like the teasing tickle of lightning until she teetered on the edge of… What? She wasn't sure, but it felt urgent.

"Yes," she breathed. "More."

They moved faster, her whole body open to him, until all the sensation exploded within her. Tierney moaned a high pitch like keening. As if to answer her, Kenan released a deep, long growl. Heat flooded Tierney, and she held on tight around Kenan as they continued to ride the waves of pleasure together. In a sea of erotic oblivion, Tierney knew only one thing.

She didn't want to let go.

# CHAPTER THIRTEEN

"Never regret thy fall, O Icarus of the fearless flight
For the greatest tragedy of them all
Is never to feel the burning light."

*Oscar Wilde – Irish Poet & Playwright, 1854–1900*

*Rap! Rap!*

"Kenan Macdonald, are ye in there?" It was a man's voice, forceful and deep.

Kenan's eyes snapped open, plucking him from the hazy dream of riding across the moor on Freya's broad back with Tierney laughing before him. Talons of sleep, trying to hold onto his foggy mind, made it difficult to take in the destruction around him. Where was he, and what the hell had happened to this room?

Dark drapes lay in haphazard piles around the large bed he was sprawled across. He turned his face to see Tierney, her golden hair tangled around her as she pushed up with her hands, her full breasts hanging down looking warm and perfectly in need of more suckling. *Aye.* He knew exactly where he was.

"Who is that?" Tierney whispered as more voices could be heard in the corridor. She glanced around, blinking. "Holy Joan. Did we do all this?"

Suddenly, the door opened. Tierney squeaked and rolled her naked body away as if to grab the blanket edge, but she got too close to the bed's side.

Yelping, she rolled off, her bare legs flying through the air. She thudded onto the floor on the far side of the bed with a curse.

"Kenan?" the man asked, anger and surprise squeezed into his name.

"Aye," he said but looked over the edge to see Tierney lying flat, her wild hair tossed out like a sun goddess.

She rubbed an elbow but then motioned to the door, her eyes wide. "Who is it?"

Kenan rolled away, sitting up in a fluid motion, and someone near the door gasped. Four people stood just inside, Cyrus Mackinnon and his sister, Grace, being the least welcome. *Bloody hell.*

Kenan grabbed one of the throw blankets from the floor at his feet and began wrapping it around his naked hips. It was a white quilt and made him look like a sheep in need of a shearing.

"Sara," he said to his sister who stood next to Henry MacNicol. "What are ye all doing here?"

"I thought I was saving you from brigands or mercenaries," she said, her gaze shifting to the sheet slowly being pulled off the far side of the bed. They all watched the sheet disappear over the side like a shallow wave sliding along the shore.

"Ye found him?" Rory MacLeod jogged up, stopping abruptly at the scene. "Lord. Did a cannonball fly through the bed?"

Indeed, it looked like something had crashed through the room with the heavy drapes all yanked down, the wooden slats above splintered where the fabric wouldn't let go. Their clothes were also left in strewn heaps, displaying the haste of their removal.

A chair was knocked over, too.

Sara's hand covered her mouth. Her gaze scanned the mess, landing on Kenan. She dropped her hand. "Did you do all this destruction?"

"It wasn't like this yesterday," Henry said in a fluster. "We would never put Chief Macdonald and Lady Tierney in a broken bed."

Sara's hand flapped up and down at Kenan's naked state. "You broke it while you were —"

"Grace, go downstairs." Cyrus's face had turned hard and red.

"Lady Tierney?" Grace Mackinnon snapped with barely checked rage, her beauty slipping away as if she'd thrown off a mask.

And Tierney, being herself, could not stay hidden any longer. With golden, tousled hair, she rose, the sheet wrapped around her curvy frame. She walked out from around the destroyed bed with grace and dignity, reminding him of an angel draped in white who had apparently fallen from heaven into pleasurable sin. *Someone should sculpt her*.

"I am Tierney MacNicol."

"MacNicol?" Rory said. "Not Bruce, a cousin to Eleanor MacLeod who doesn't exist?"

Grace's face was pinched in a sneer as she looked down her nose at Tierney. "You're the flying thief from Rory's wedding."

"Go downstairs, Sister," Cyrus said again, his granite gaze on Kenan. His friend was furious. Kenan couldn't blame him. Not with a betrothal contract between Kenan and Grace probably folded inside his sash.

"Why didn't ye say ye were a MacNicol?" Rory

asked, frowning. "Trickery, then?"

"Nothing untoward is going on here," Henry called out, his words coming in a spluttering cadence. "Our lady went to Dunvegan for help and found Lord Kenan. They handfasted. As good as married."

"Handfasted!" Cyrus yelled.

"Married!" Grace said at the same time.

Suspicion still pinched Rory's brows. "We thought ye were taken by force."

He was, but he wasn't about to explain how he'd let Tierney abduct him. "There were unexpected circumstances," Kenan said. Hopefully, Rory trusted him enough not to press for more answers.

"But you left without a word," Sara said, frowning.

"Ye were busy, Sister, with yer wedding feast."

Sara narrowed her eyes. "You left your clothes behind." The woman could ferret out a secret like a pig after truffles. "Rory tracked your large-footed horse to an abandoned cabin in the woods where there was a chain attached to a loop in the wall and one wrapped around the rafters." Her voice had risen in volume as she spoke. "Chains, Kenan! And then there were wagon tracks, Freya's tracks, and boot prints, big and," she looked at Tierney, "small."

Cyrus's anger spiked off him. Grace stared daggers at Tierney. And Tierney looked like she was building up to answer, so Kenan did first.

"There are a lot of parts to this story," he said. "All of it better heard below."

"With yer damn arse covered," Cyrus said and turned. He looped his arm through his sister's and practically dragged her out of the room.

Henry frowned, looking between them. "Lady Sara and Chief Rory MacLeod? Ye two witnessed the handfasting after yer wedding."

Sara's face swung back to Kenan, and he let her see the request in the slight widening of his eyes.

*Lie for me, Sister. There's a good reason.*

Sara's lips parted, and she gave a rapid nod. "Yes, but then you disappeared."

Henry released an audible sigh of relief.

Kenan would owe her. Hopefully, Rory would go along with the lie, too. "If ye could give us a moment," Kenan said, "we'll come below and explain things." Or at least some things. His sister would not take kindly to hearing how Tierney had drugged and shackled him.

It was amazing how a night of incredible tupping could make those details, which were once important to him, seem diminished. When he glanced back at Tierney, still wrapped in the sheet with a bemused look of ravishment, they completely disappeared. In fact, if she was naked and wanting to do what they did last night, he'd let her shackle him again.

Rory moved his arm in a wide arc. "Let's all wait for them below, then."

"I will call for sustenance to break our fast," Henry said, leading the way out into the hall.

Sara followed after casting one more ominous frown at the broken bed and then Kenan. "I wonder if the story will include a cannonball breaking through the bed," she said.

Rory snorted and shut the door behind them.

Kenan ran a hand through his mussed hair. He

probably looked ravished, too. Glancing down to his naked chest, he saw a small bruise from Tierney sucking on his skin. He looked at her. "Are ye well?"

She nodded and glanced around the room. "Did we do this?" She lifted her hand to the bed.

"I'll help ye rebuild it," he said. He would have smiled, but his mind was focused on the fury etching Cyrus's face.

She shrugged as if light of heart. "I wanted to re-decorate anyway, starting with getting rid of the hideously heavy drapes."

He walked to her, and she lifted a finger, resting it lightly on the bruise on his chest. "I want to see what I'm doing." She glanced up into his eyes. "In bed."

"That was the plan when I pulled them down." His hand snaked around her back, hugging her into him for a gentle kiss. Then they rested their foreheads together. This morning should have been lazy and sweet. She might have been shy in the light of day at first, but Kenan would have stirred her to a frenzy again. But morning light had brought stark reality thundering through their door.

She stepped slightly back. "I think 'tis safe to say, your family and friends don't like me. Was the lady beside your sister…?"

"Grace Mackinnon." He sighed. "Cyrus's sister who I'm supposed to wed."

She inhaled hard through her nose. "Shite."

Shite was right. He rubbed his head, shutting his eyes as all the repercussions prickled through his now wide-awake mind.

"Your betrothed," Tierney said, dropping her

arms. "Catching you with a naked woman in a room that they obviously destroyed in passion."

"I hadn't yet signed the contract." He opened his eyes.

Tierney stared at him. He could almost see inside her head as she thought over what he'd told her before. "So you...aren't betrothed?"

He tipped his head. "Nay, not officially. But in Cyrus's mind, and maybe Grace's, I was."

Tierney slid a hand down her cheek, her eyes staring at the door. "Your sister lied for us."

"That she did," Kenan said with a long inhale. "I'm sure she'll make me pay for it somehow."

Tierney's slack face turned to him. "The foking Mackinnons will attack us, too," she murmured.

It was a possibility. "I'll try to smooth things with Cyrus, although his father would love any excuse to attack us." His night with Tierney could truly lead to civil war on Skye. Bloody hell, how had he let this get so out of hand?

She grabbed his arm, her other hand squeezing the gathered front of the sheet so it wouldn't fall. "I need the might of Clan Macdonald even more."

"We need diplomacy more than might."

"Powerful foes don't listen to diplomacy," she said, her words heavy with worry and turned away, striding to a trunk. The lid caught on hinges as she threw it open. She grabbed up and shook out a smock, dropping the sheet. It slid off her smooth pale skin, along her shapely hips like an artist revealing his masterpiece.

Kenan's gaze stroked along her naked legs and up her spine where her hair hung midway. As she tossed a smock over her head to settle down her form, she truly looked like an angel, an avenging one at present, with her frown and snapping eyes.

He dressed quickly, watching her choose a gown out of the armoire. The length was too long, so she tied the petticoat high up under her breasts. "'Tis my mother's," she said. "I can't walk down the hall in a sheet, and my gown from yesterday is," she indicated the rumpled mess on the floor, "in need of brushing."

Minutes later, he held the door open for her to precede him out of the disaster of a room into the dim corridor. Tierney wrestled with her wild hair, weaving it quickly into a braid that she tied with a leather strap.

They walked silently down the stairs that he barely remembered climbing last night, his mind completely on the sweet ball of fire pushing him against the curved wall and kissing him every few steps until he just lifted her up to charge ahead. Mo chreach, he'd lost all control, his whole bloody mind. And now he must convince Cyrus that he hadn't meant to disrespect his sister. If he failed, their freshly formed brotherhood might dissolve into hatred again.

"Do you regret last night?" she asked without looking back at him.

The question had played through his mind, and he answered quickly without thinking. "That depends on if all of Skye goes to war over it."

She said nothing and continued to descend, but he could feel the chill in the straightness of her back. He clasped her hand, pulling her to a stop.

"Tierney," he said, bending his knees to catch her

gaze. It was sad, and it pulled at his conscience. He didn't want her to think he regretted loving her. "Last night was…explosive, like fire hitting gunpowder."

She glanced away. "The bedchamber would agree."

"Do ye agree?"

She sniffed a little laugh, but it held darkness. She looked at him. "Yes, explosive."

He reached for her face, glad that she didn't pull away, and slid his thumb across the smoothness there. "I don't regret being with ye," he whispered. "I regret that I hurt my friend and his sister."

She gave the smallest nod, her features thoughtful.

His smile hardened into granite. "And if yer husband told ye that ye're cold, he was an idiot to think it was because of ye." His hand cupped her cheek as he leaned in. "Ye're all softness, sweet honey, and fire, Tierney MacNicol." He pressed a kiss to her lips and pulled back quickly before his cock rose, embarrassing them even further.

She smiled. "And I'm happy to learn you're neither slobbery nor sour, Kenan Macdonald." She took his hand, pulling him with her down the steps.

"Mama!" Maggie ran from Cora's side toward Tierney, her little arms out, her slippers slapping against the floorboards.

Tierney picked her up in a hug. "I'm right here, sweet. You weren't giving Cora any trouble, were you?"

"I thought you'd gone away again to find us more help."

"Not without a kiss goodbye." Tierney stroked the little girl's hair, holding her as if she wished she could pull her into her body to protect her.

Kenan knew the feeling, and it had increased as he held Tierney last night. Wanting to keep her safe. 'Twas dangerous to his plans to unite Skye. Could he trade protecting the Isle of Skye for protecting one woman, even if she was the most interesting person, the most delicious woman, he'd ever met?

Cora looked right at Tierney and rubbed three fingers against her nose as if scratching it. But it looked like a signal, and the lift of her brows asked a question. Three?

Kenan leaned toward Tierney's ear that was not pressed against Maggie. "If Cora's asking if ye implemented plan three, the answer is a resounding aye." He nodded at Cora himself, holding up three fingers, and the woman's eyes opened.

"What does three fingers mean?" Sara asked, her words snapping. His sister took in every detail.

"That we need three cups of small ale," Kenan said, indicating Maggie, Tierney, and himself.

His glance moved to the rest of the quiet hall. Cyrus and Grace stood reading an unfolded letter, as did Rory. They were the letters he'd written to be sent this morning.

Henry motioned to them. "They were addressed to them, so I gave them out."

"Has the one for Tomas gone?" he asked.

Henry shook his head. "We thought Chief MacLeod could take it back with him and send a runner. We have few men to spare if Matheson returns quickly."

Grace Mackinnon looked up from Cyrus's letter, her eyes flashing with anger. The letter had been to Cyrus, not her, and didn't discuss how she might feel over this change of plans.

"Lady Grace," he said, "I apologize for the last-minute reversal of what yer brother had set in motion."

She gave a tight smile. "I have many prospects, Chief Macdonald, and care little. Unfortunately for you, my father may not accept your apology."

"Yer father knows about the proposed betrothal?" Kenan asked, turning his pinched brows toward Cyrus.

Cyrus huffed, lowering the letter, his face grim. "I didn't know that ye'd run off with some…" He stopped himself, but his dark gaze went to Tierney who still held Maggie against her.

"Some brave, clever woman who's determined to save her clan," Tierney finished for him.

"From the Matheson Clan," Cyrus said, waving the letter in the air. "Yer need to find protection for yer clan, so ye tricked Kenan into handfasting with ye."

He made it sound like Kenan was a naive child who'd been led astray and made to promise allegiance for a kiss. He would rage that he wasn't so easily tricked, but apparently, he was.

Kenan's legs were braced in a battle stance, his arms crossed. "Clan MacNicol needs protection, as does our isle if Murdoc Matheson leads a campaign to take over Scorrybreac and Clan MacNicol."

Cyrus cursed under his breath. "So ye just decided, without talking to Rory or me, to make an alliance with Clan MacNicol?" Both his arms rose as if encompassing the whole Scorrybreac area. "Where is Ash? He could have sent word that he needed our support."

"Asher MacNicol has left Skye," Tierney said. "I cannot find him to ask for help. And…" She stopped before she revealed her personal stake in all this, being tied to Ranulf and possibly losing her child if he sent her away.

"And what?" Cyrus asked.

"I got him drunk," Tierney said. "And pleaded my case. I tricked him into handfasting with me."

So instead of making him look foolish enough to be poisoned and shackled, he was just a drunk fool. Kenan wanted to roar his denial, but he kept himself rooted to the floor.

Henry frowned. "Drunk?" He looked at Sara and Rory. "Ye didn't notice or question—"

"It was quick," Sara cut in, "and…Rory was drunk, too, and I didn't know about the understanding with Grace."

"There was no official understanding yet," Kenan said and looked at Cyrus. "Nothing signed, so there's no contract broken between us."

Cyrus's gaze didn't soften. "I sent word to our father that ye and Grace were betrothed when Grace and then ye seemed amendable. Father was planning an attack on Dunscaith while it lay in ruins and ye were at the wedding, and I wanted to cut him off before he proceeded."

*Well, hell.* Kenan's hand caught the back of his neck. "Ye could have mentioned that."

"I got word the night after the wedding, and I

couldn't get ye to stand still long enough to tell ye," Cyrus said and flashed angry eyes at Tierney. "Ye were determined to find out why a lass would try to steal yer glider contraption."

What would Kenan have done if he'd had the information, the threat of attack? He'd have ridden to Dunscaith before Tierney could drug him. He'd be officially betrothed to Grace. Instead of eliciting regret, the thought made his gut sour.

"I'm no longer amenable to wedding," Grace said, staring at Kenan with the full force of her condemnation. "You are a fool who gets drunk enough to handfast with a stranger in some foolish need to save her and her little, dismal clan." Grace glanced at her brother. "I'll wait outside for us to depart." She stalked through the hall, her boot heels clipping along.

Kenan walked closer to Cyrus. "Daingead, Cyrus, why did ye bring her?"

Cyrus's face was tight with fury. "She was worried about ye when we found evidence of ye being taken. When Grace makes up her mind, only a biblical flood or pestilence could sway her."

"Lord," Kenan said, rubbing a hand down over his jaw. "I'm sorry I hurt her pride."

"How about yer own pride?" Cyrus said, without softening. "Ye spoke with passion about bringing Skye together, and yet ye jeopardize everything by making an enemy of my father and sister. Ye led me to believe ye would join with Grace to create an alliance, but ye let that float away on a drunk man's lust and need to play the gallant knight."

Every muscle in Kenan contracted as shame infused him. He felt the prickle of it race over his skin, making him want to scratch it away. But he deserved this. He'd let Tierney trick him. Even if he hadn't gotten drunk, he'd still followed her out on the moor and eaten her bloody tart.

Cyrus held up his palm that showed the four scars to match the ones on Kenan, Rory, and Asher's palms. They had formed a brotherhood to escape Carlisle Dungeon built on a foundation of mutual trust and desire to bring all their clans together to strengthen Scotland.

"I still desire that," Kenan said, his voice gruff. He glanced at Rory. Did he think Kenan had dropped the cause? But Rory's watchful eyes gave nothing of his thoughts away.

Kenan looked back into Cyrus's bitter face. "First and foremost, we are still friends. I made a mistake but still strive to join the clans on Skye."

Cyrus snorted. "I disagree on both counts."

Tierney stepped up to Cyrus. Her younger brother had taken Maggie from her, and the little girl was wrestling with her twelve-year-old uncle to let her down.

"I am the trickster and used every bit of myself to coerce Kenan." She poked Cyrus's chest. "And if I hadn't, Clan Matheson would be taking over MacNicol territory on Skye. Ranulf Matheson was waiting here when we arrived, ready to use my daughter," she threw an arm out toward Maggie, "to force me to wed him so he could steal Scorrybreac. You would have another powerful clan to battle. Before you throw stones at Kenan because of your ruined plans, keep in mind I am the one who forced his hand."

Sara shook her head. "My brother doesn't agree to anything he doesn't want, even if drunk."

Tierney looked over her shoulder at Sara. "He might if he's been—"

"I decided that her need was great," Kenan said, overriding whatever embarrassing thing Tierney was going to reveal. Like that he'd allowed himself to be shackled by two lasses and a lad of twelve. "It will not do to let Ranulf Matheson invade and take over Scorrybreac."

"Ye were married to a Macqueen, weren't ye?" Rory asked her. "Will they not send warriors to help deter the Mathesons?"

"I sent word to them first," Tierney said, "asking for assistance when my parents didn't return from sea after a month of no word. They ignored my plea for help."

Sara looked horrified. "But you have a child by Wallace Macqueen, their deceased chief."

"Maggie is a lass, not a lad," Gabriel said, "and their new chief wants nothing to do with us." He held tightly to his niece's hand.

"They didn't exactly warm to me, either," Tierney said.

Kenan could imagine the condemnation she must have stirred up there, a bride shaving her head after the wedding night.

"Tierney," Henry said, his tone full of admonishment as if she were his daughter whom he held so poorly. "Yer father thought ye should wed Ranulf Matheson in an honorable alliance. And yet ye've caused all this strife." He waved his hands between Kenan and Cyrus.

Tierney stood proud, her eyes narrowing as her face flushed red. "I let my father use me once for an alliance, and apart from Maggie, nothing good came from it. I will not be traded like a broodmare again. Father wrote a clause into the Matheson betrothal contract, giving me a way out if I could find other help for our clan. So I did."

"But now ye've caused more trouble," Henry said, indicating Cyrus. "Are ye above a queen to refuse an alliance to save yer people?" Henry continued with a wave of self-righteous zest. "If ye'd thought of yer clan before yerself, yer daughter before—"

"One abusive marriage is too much for any woman to endure," Kenan said, "let alone two marriages." His voice boomed out, making Tierney's white dog bark once and move to stand before Maggie. Maggie threw her thin arms around the dog's neck.

"Tierney never consented to a Matheson betrothal, so it wasn't real." He pointed his finger at Henry. "And she courageously sought to put an end to it with me. Hold yer tongue or see it permanently held by me." His hand fisted, and he yanked his hand as if demonstrating how he'd violently remove Henry's tongue.

The man's eyes bulged, his lips closing tightly. No one in the room said anything for a moment as if waiting to see what would happen next. Kenan let his gaze move from Henry to Rory and Sara, to Cyrus. "Now, if we can rid ourselves of hurt pride and sit down, we can figure out the best course of action to keep the Matheson Clan from invading our isle through Scorrybreac and Clan Mackinnon from attacking Dunscaith."

Cyrus crossed his arms over his chest, not softened at all. "I am taking Grace home and, on the way, will try to convince her not to influence our father to take up his sword against the Macdonalds and MacLeods." He turned and strode toward the door.

Kenan took three long strides and caught up to him, his hand going to his shoulder to stop him. "Cy."

Cyrus stopped, but his face was just as hard when he turned to Kenan. "I truly didn't mean to hurt Grace or ruin yer plans," Kenan said. "A marriage alliance like the one made between Rory and Sara doesn't always work. There must be genuine regard there to bring peace, and I'm not sure Grace and I would have that."

Cyrus exhaled. "'Tis not I who will rage against ye. My father is chief, and his army has been brought up on stories of Macdonald crimes, just like I was."

"I was raised hearing Mackinnon crimes as well," Kenan said, "but we are working beyond that, strengthening our isle and country."

Cyrus stared hard into Kenan's eyes. "One of those crimes was the killing of my older brother, his heir, by a Macdonald sword."

"Patrick died of a taint and fever."

"From the sword strike," Cyrus said, shaking his head. "My father still blames Clan Macdonald. Grace is his pride and joy. I must convince her that this wasn't another crime against our clan. I'll send ye word." He turned back to the door and strode out.

"Bloody hell," Kenan murmured.

Had he truly just started a civil war on Skye?

# CHAPTER FOURTEEN

"We are each of us angels with only one wing, and we can only fly by embracing one another."

*Luciano De Crescenzo – Italian Writer, 1928–*

Tierney looked back over Fleet's rump at the trail of villagers following them, some on horseback, some in wagons, and some walking. They carried what was important to them, what they couldn't stand to let Clan Matheson burn or steal if they came while Scorrybreac was abandoned.

With a possible war with Clan Mackinnon, Kenan couldn't spare any Macdonald men to protect Scorrybreac, so the next best thing was to bring MacNicols to safer ground: Dunvegan and Dunscaith.

"You're riding so well," Tierney said to Maggie, who sat before Gabriel on his horse, her dark gray pony trotting behind.

"I think she can ride Blackberry when we stop," Gabriel said, pushing her blond hair to the side so it wouldn't keep hitting him in the face from the wind.

"We will see," Tierney said, not trusting Maggie to stay awake and not fall off her pony's back. Her eyes looked heavy from the swaying already.

Tierney's gaze slid to the line of villagers. A few had remained behind, including Jacob. He would ride as fast as he could to Dunvegan Castle if he saw the Matheson ship arrive. Some of the villagers had elected to stay with relatives living away from the village on farms, hoping the Mathesons wouldn't come out there to cause havoc. And all this upheaval was because she refused to wed Ranulf.

She felt the flush on her cheeks and turned back to face front.

*My father was wrong. I am not a sacrifice.*

Kenan's words to Henry had straightened her spine when she hadn't even realized she was bowed under the weight of shame. *She courageously sought to put an end to it with me.*

She'd been told most of her life that she was acting obstinate, not courageous. Kenan saw her differently, but she'd never have the chance to convince her father. Her heart squeezed, and she blinked away the ache of unshed tears.

Kenan rode ahead of her on his huge Percheron mare, speaking with Rory MacLeod. As soon as Cyrus Mackinnon left and Kenan threatened Henry into silence, they mobilized, and both Rory and Kenan took charge of evacuating the village.

There'd been no time to talk with Kenan about their adventures last night and the destruction of his friendship with Cyrus Mackinnon. After leaving the hall, she'd gone straight to her old bedchamber to pack Maggie's things and her own, changing quickly into a green gown with laced bodice.

In the presence of Lady Sara, Tierney couldn't bring herself to don her trousers and man's tunic. Kenan's sister was slim and could probably eat as many tarts as she wanted without worrying about stomach bulges. Tierney's body had expanded in all sorts of places when she'd carried Maggie and then nursed her, leaving marks on her skin that Kenan hadn't seen in the darkness last night.

She sniffed, raising her chin a bit. If he had a problem with how she looked naked, she'd point out his own imperfections and walk away from this farce of a handfasting.

Although the marks on his back took nothing away from the beauty of his well-muscled form. The man was like a sculpted god. Only the scars on his back, and the nicks here and there, showed him to be mortal.

"Your daughter is beautiful," Sara said, and Tierney glanced beside her where Kenan's sister rode her own horse and then followed her gaze to Maggie who'd revived at the sight of a heron spreading its wings. She was jabbering away, pointing to the bird and then wildflowers while Gabriel tried not to roll his eyes at her excitement. It was Maggie's first trip that she remembered.

"She means everything to me." Tierney felt her cheeks warm again. That damn guilt flowed through her like a fever. Did Maggie not mean enough to marry a greedy, heavy-handed man? But Ranulf would hurt her, too, either physically or by sending her away.

"I don't have a child yet," Sara continued, "but when I do, I hope I can teach her through example how to be strong and to look out for her own well-being." Sara met Tierney's gaze with strength. "I was married away for an alliance before I married

Rory. It would have seen me dead if I'd remained in it."

Tierney felt tears burn behind her eyes. She'd never been afforded kind support before. It wrapped around her heart, and she tipped her head back to look up at the trees they were passing under to keep any tears from leaking out.

"Thank you," she whispered.

"You should speak with my aunt Morag," Sara said with a knowing smile. "She supports women in a world that tries to weigh us down."

Weighed down. Yes. That was how Tierney felt. Tierney cleared her throat. "Men have the strength. Imagine what the world would be like if women were physically stronger."

"Morag would say we are stronger," Sara said. "Girl babes survive their births more than boy babes. We have parts strong enough to grow and carry and birth a babe. That's where our strength lies."

"True," Tierney said. She liked talking to Kenan's sister.

"And our intuition guides us more," Sara continued, her tone like she was discussing a recipe for bread rather than radical ideas. "We've had to learn to notice signs of strife, danger, and illness quickly to keep our children alive and to save our own lives. All that makes us strong, too."

"Does Kenan agree with your ideas?"

Sara tipped her head, thinking. "I've never asked him, but he's heard much of this from our aunt." She looked at Tierney. "And he's kind, to a fault sometimes. Our father beat him for it until Kenan was big enough to retaliate with deadly force if Father tried to lift a hand to him again. Father knew that, I think, because the beatings stopped, but not the constant criticism."

Tierney frowned, glanced at Kenan's straight back and then to Sara. "Kenan is too kind?"

Sara shrugged. "He's a rescuer and wants to save everyone, like you and your clan." She glanced at the line of villagers walking, riding horseback, or in wagons. Tierney hadn't realized how diminished her clan had become with the sweating sickness. There were so few, barely twenty.

"But Kenan can't save everyone," Sara continued. "The world is too big and full of cruel people."

A prickle rose just under Tierney's skin. Sara thought that her brother had gone with Tierney to save her, only because he was a natural rescuer, and she'd coerced him.

"I…" Tierney blinked, not sure what to say. "I'm sorry I interfered with his plans with the Mackinnon Clan."

Sara looked at her. "Oh dear," she said, noticing Tierney's flush. She reached over to pat her hand. "Don't worry about that. Grace Mackinnon is too… well, too hard to please to marry Kenan. She would require every bit of his attention when he wants to do so much for so many." She shook her head. "It would have become miserable for them both."

"You aren't trying to tell me you're unhappy we handfasted?"

Sara laughed softly. "I'm not trying to tell you anything, Lady Tierney. I but give you a little insight into my hard-to-understand brother."

Tierney stared up front at Kenan, riding easily in his great saddle. Maybe she did understand him. He would sacrifice his own happiness to save many. As a woman, to sacrifice herself meant surrendering her body, will, and soul. Something she'd sworn never to do again.

•  •  •

"I will march to Dunscaith with the few remaining MacNicol warriors," Kenan said, leaning over the table where a map was laid out in Dunvegan's Great Hall.

Afternoon sunlight filtered in through the high windows, but candles had been lit to help him and Rory study the detailed map of territories on Skye. "It takes two days to get home."

Henry paced across from Kenan. Rory's uncles, Simon and John, watched the MacNicol advisor, frowning. Rory's dog, Gus, watched Henry, too, his shaggy head going back and forth anytime someone spoke as if he were in the conversation. Tierney liked dogs. Even though Sneachda was obviously Gabriel's pet and Maggie's protector, Kenan was sure he'd lay down his life to protect Tierney, too. Perhaps he needed to adopt some dogs at Dunscaith.

"I could send a group of fifty men to Scorrybreac," Rory said. "Help keep Matheson raiders from burning everything."

"They must bring their own provisions," Henry said. "We have none at Scorrybreac."

"Yer chief's only been dead for a month," Simon called, his one good eye squinting at Henry. He'd lost the other eye in one of the battles against Kenan's father.

"Didn't he have provisions stored up?" John asked. He'd lost his left forearm in a Macdonald battle as well. The two of them had been Rory's father's advisors and had decided to stay on, much to Rory's annoyance. But they seemed to have become a fixture in Dunvegan, like the ancient tapestry of MacLeod victory and the legendary Fairy Flag.

Henry glared at the two men. "We've suffered from war and disease, losing so many people."

"Which means more food for those still alive," Simon said.

"It means there's no one to till, plant, and harvest the fields," Henry said with an air of frustration. "At the height of the sweating sickness, we had livestock roaming the fields feeding themselves because everyone was either ill, dead, or taking care of the ill and dead."

"If we decide on that course," Rory said, "they will bring their own provisions." All three elderly men continued to hold old resentments against each other's clans. 'Twas an example of how disunion weakened Skye and all of Scotland.

"Dunscaith Castle is a destroyed castle," John said, "and *ye* still have provisions." His words were low, but Henry still heard them. The old MacNicol swore under his breath and continued to pace.

Rory looked at the two advisors. "If ye two can't be civil to our guests, then ye can go back to yer cottage in the village."

Simon crossed his arms. "We can't."

"We've given our cottage to two MacNicol ladies," John said.

"Sweet ladies but with a sharp wit about them," Simon went on with a grin. "Doris and Edith."

"Edith has quite the short sword," John said and grinned, too.

"Hope she pokes ye with it," Henry murmured.

"Then keep yer comments kind or go help in the kitchens," Margaret, the housekeeper, said as she strode into the Great Hall.

"That woman can hear every inch of this place," Simon said, tapping his ear that looked like it should be sheared of hair. John nodded in agreement, but neither of them made any move to quit the room.

"Ladies Eleri and Eliza have taken the sweet child, Maggie, with them to play in the tower room that used to be Eleri's." Margaret smiled fondly. "'Twill be nice having a little one running around again. And that white bear follows Maggie everywhere."

"He's a Pyrenees dog from France, and his name is Sneachda," Henry said. "It means snow, because of his coat. He's very protective."

Kenan had heard that a Great Pyrenees could take down a wolf. "How did ye end up with a French dog here on Skye?" Kenan asked.

"Tierney's father used to travel at times to France because he had ties to the de Guise family." Henry's chin rose with pride over his chief's connections. "He brought the dog back for Tierney as a pup."

"If Chief MacNicol used to sail all the way around Scotland and down to France, he must have been an experienced sailor," Kenan said. "Seems unlikely he'd be lost at sea just sailing to the mainland."

"We thought that, too," came a lilting voice.

Kenan turned to the archway where Tierney walked out. She wore the dress that matched her green eyes, and her hair was piled in curls on top of her head, giving him a lovely view of the neck that he'd kissed through the night two days ago before the grand exodus of her clan. Cheeks rosy and golden swirls pinned up with a few tendrils down to tease her cheeks, she looked like an angel from the illuminated bible that had burned in Dunscaith's vast library.

John and Simon both stood from their seats as if Tierney was a queen.

She walked toward Kenan, her gaze, which had quickly circled the room, landing on him. Did she always enter rooms looking for danger? Like prey on constant guard?

"But they didn't return," she continued. "And none of the crew. We sent word through a bard to the mainland, asking about the *Rosemary*." She shook her head. "Nothing. After a month, we declared them lost. 'Tis been two months now."

"We are sorry for the loss of yer parents," Rory said. "'Tis a tragedy."

She bowed her head with a natural grace that he'd seen as she walked. "Thank you. We came to the realization slowly, but it was still an unkind surprise."

"She does look like an angel," Simon said, and John nodded.

"She's no angel," Henry murmured, which elicited frowns from the two men again. Those three wouldn't be playing Draughts together anytime soon. Battle histories between the clans were still raw even after decades.

Rory's gaze had risen from the map to acknowledge Tierney. His usual frown turned into a wry grin as he glanced at Kenan. "We have no use for angels here," Rory said. "Although the fallen ones," he nodded toward Tierney, "are welcome."

He referred to the glider crash, but his words could have a carnal meaning. "My sister did have quite the fall, too, after she met ye," Kenan said.

Rory chuckled. "Aye, that she did, and I'm a lucky man for it."

Tierney walked over to the table, running her fingers lightly over the map. Kenan could feel her presence, like a warmth, close to him, as if she were a flame on a cold night. They'd had no time to talk or for him to reassure her that their night together had been remarkable. She wasn't a virgin except to pleasure, and he planned to teach her every way to achieve it if she were game.

Sara came down and walked up to Rory with a knowing smile. "I am lucky you caught me."

Did everyone listen at the door before they walked in?

The obvious affection between his sister and her new husband pulsed with heat. "If ye two are going to stare at one another like that, ye should take to yer bedchamber," Kenan said.

Rory grabbed Sara's hand and began to walk away. She laughed, pulling it from him. "I'm taking

Tierney to meet Aunt Morag."

"Morag?" Simon passed the sign of the cross before his chest, and John followed the action with his one remaining hand.

"Who is that?" Henry asked, looking startled.

"A witch," Simon said.

"Aunt Morag is not a witch," Sara called out, frowning at the two men.

John's eyes were wide. "Well, I wouldn't call her that in front of her, else she turns us into newts or mushrooms or some such."

"Or she'd just plain poison us like her husband," Simon said. He turned his face to Henry and silently mouthed, *She's a witch.*

Kenan had heard the rumors of Morag killing her husband decades ago after he beat her. If the man had abused his aunt, he deserved nothing less. His own father had tortured his wife in those last years. He either pushed her off the roof of Dunscaith, or she leaped to escape him. Aye, a man like that deserved nothing less than being poisoned or, in the case of his father, decapitated. Those with power, physical or otherwise, should wield it to protect those in their care, not use it to force people into horrid situations they must endure.

"Shall we go?" Tierney asked.

Henry drew himself up as if knowing a storm surge would be forthcoming. "Lady Tierney, ye cannot visit this Morag woman."

Tierney looked at Sara as if he hadn't spoken. "Maggie is with your sisters and Cora."

Sara smiled, looped her arm through Tierney's, and they walked toward the steps that would lead them down to Dunvegan's ferry to cross over.

"I will visit Aunt Morag also," Kenan said.

Henry blustered but followed him down the steps. "Is yer aunt really a witch?"

"She has crows, and no one bothers her even though she lives alone out on the moor," Kenan answered.

"Crows?" Henry asked.

Kenan started down the steps. "Large black birds."

"I know what crows are," Henry said. "But keeping them? Like they're pets?"

"I believe my aunt sees them more as friends or her army." Kenan continued through the iron gate.

Henry sounded out of breath as he hastened to keep up with them. "How many does she have?"

"Quite a few," Sara answered.

"Has anyone asked her if she's a witch?" Henry asked.

"Not certain," Kenan said, "but there are a fair number of newts around her cottage. Food for her crows."

"Gabriel would love to meet more like Betrim," Tierney said.

"Who?" Henry asked.

"Gabriel's newt," Tierney said.

"Was Betrim his name when he was a man?" Simon called from the top of the steps.

"Betrim has always been a newt," Tierney said and met Kenan's gaze with a small smile. With her hair pinned up, she looked royal, and he couldn't wait to pluck those pins and inhale the sweet essence of her as he buried his face in her golden tresses. Maybe she would join him tonight.

"Return if ye're not a newt, Master Henry," John called, stopping at the iron gate.

On the bank, Kenan looked out toward the connecting sea while Sara explained to Tierney and Henry how the sea protected Dunvegan Castle. Dunscaith Castle, however, did not perch on a small island and relied entirely on walls to protect it. Would Mackinnon ships sail around the Sleat Peninsula to Dunscaith, attacking their port first before continuing around to the castle and village?

Kenan's gut tightened. He needed to fix the rift between Cyrus and himself, Grace Mackinnon, too. He swiped a thumb across his palm where the ridges of four scars rose, reminding him of the oath they'd taken.

And now Asher MacNicol was missing, and Cyrus Mackinnon was damning Kenan for ruining a marriage alliance with his sister. He felt stretched between Cyrus and the woman who'd crashed into his life. Was he doing the right thing by helping her?

He couldn't imagine doing anything less.

# CHAPTER FIFTEEN

"...life isn't but a feather floating in the wind. One second it's in your grasp, next second, it's floating high, wondering what is to come."

*William Shakespeare – English playwright, 1564–1616*

The cottage was made of stone and had a thatched roof in good repair. A one-story barn stood behind it, a row of crows watching. Midnight black with sunlight glinting off their wings, the large birds sat along the pointed edge and on some covered pedestals set about the yard.

There were at least twenty of them. Black eyes turned their way, judging them as they approached. Some lifted their wings, letting the breeze pick them up off their perches so they could swoop in circles over the visitors like carrion birds over a battlefield.

"A tip of their wings lifts them effortlessly," Kenan said to no one in particular.

Tierney watched Kenan as he studied the crows catching the breeze. *I will help him fix his glider.* The oath helped her inhale past the continued heaviness of guilt. It was a familiar weight after living a life of shame.

The door of the squat cottage opened, and a woman stepped outside. Her white hair looked soft, and she wore it in a long braid accented with a few wildflowers to lay over her shoulder. The touch gave her a fairy-like air. Robes of pale blue covered her, and a braided belt woven of stained leather lay on her narrow hips. Her smile was gentle and accepting as she looked from Sara to Tierney, as if she already knew her secrets and accepted her despite them. Tierney remembered that knowing smile from the day she'd been hauled out of the icy sea.

"Welcome, Sara and Kenan," the woman said, and several crows pierced the air with caws as if adding a jubilant proclamation. Henry stared up at the black birds with wide eyes. The wind blew, making Tierney's hair tug against the pinned design that Eliza had fashioned.

"And welcome, Chief MacLeod." Morag nodded to Rory and turned her gaze to Tierney, practically ignoring Henry. "You have come to introduce me to the angel who fell from the sky."

Henry gave a little snort. If Tierney had been closer, she might have kicked his shin despite wanting to appear mature and demure. Henry brought out her wicked, childish ways.

"This is Tierney MacNicol," Sara said, "and her father's advisor, Master Henry Macqueen."

"Lady Tierney and Master Henry, this is our aunt, Morag Gunn, our mother's sister," Kenan said.

Morag stared at Henry. "You came with Chief Wallace Macqueen when he wed Lady Tierney." She tipped her head, studying him. Her scrutiny made him fidget. "And you remained at Scorrybreac after Tierney was taken away."

Henry's chin raised. "Chief MacNicol asked me to stay as his advisor."

Morag looked from him to Tierney. "The trade

was unfortunate for Lady Tierney."

Henry blustered. "It was not a trade. I simply… stayed."

Tierney smiled at Morag. "Please call me Tierney."

"'Tis your title, Lady Tierney, as daughter to the chief," Henry said, his voice tired over the old argument.

"Come inside," Morag said, "before my crows think that lovely crown of shining hair is gold. They're drawn to anything that sparkles." She turned and glided effortlessly back into her cottage.

Tierney glanced at Kenan, a small smile on her lips. "I wonder what it would be like to have a crow perch upon my head."

Kenan's brows were slightly furrowed, but a grin emerged. "I imagine a great amount of tugging and pecking."

Before she could follow Sara through the low, arched doorway, one of the crows fluttered down to perch on the lintel, a glossy black feather in its beak. "Oh," Tierney said, stopping. The black eyes, which at a distance could sink into the background of its black feathers, were shining orbs that reflected the muted sun.

Morag appeared in the doorway, glancing up at the bird. "That is Madeline."

Tierney heard Rory MacLeod choke, a low curse coming from him through a coughing fit.

"Really, Aunt?" Sara's voice called from within the cottage. "You named the crow Madeline?"

Morag ignored her, keeping her smile on Tierney. "She's presenting you with a feather. They are sociable birds and like to take and give gifts."

Tierney smiled at the crow. "Many thanks, Madeline." She took the feather from the shiny black beak. It was a sleek feather that looked blue and purple when she turned it in the sunlight. Tierney quickly pulled one of the hairpins from her head and held it out to Madeline. "And this is for you."

The crow bobbed her head before leaning forward to snatch up the metal stick, flapping her wings to lift off, and several of her friends cawed, following her into the sky.

"Come in before they all want one," Morag said.

Tierney felt a heavy curl drop down from her head and pushed it behind one ear while looking at the beautiful feather. Had Madeline plucked it from herself?

Kenan bent to look at it. "None of yer crows have given one of their feathers to me."

"Me neither," Sara said.

Morag ushered Tierney into a wooden chair across the table, but she met Sara's eyes. "Even though you've also flown, you're of the flame, child." She turned her gaze to Tierney. "Crows are clever and cunning. Madeline recognized Tierney as a child of the wind and sky." She smiled, her eyes searching. "Your element is air."

"That sounds heretical," Henry said, passing the sign of the cross before himself to ward off lurking demons.

Morag's gaze rose to him where he stood near the door, an escape route. "God made the flame and the wind, as well as the water and the earth. What could possibly be heretical about that?"

When Henry didn't answer, Sara rested her hand over Morag's. "There could be unrest on the isle." Sara glanced at Tierney.

Tierney swallowed down the bitterness of guilt that slid upward from her stomach.

Kenan stood behind her. Normally she hated it when someone stood behind her. She kept her back to the wall or some large piece of furniture. But Kenan felt safe to her, despite his large form and their warlike beginning. Perhaps it was their night of passion that made her trust him. He had loved her well and hadn't hurt her at all.

"There is always unrest in our country, on our isle," Morag said.

"We may have a new enemy from the mainland," Kenan said. "Ranulf Matheson has been trying to take over the MacNicol Clan of Scorrybreac. We've chased him off, but we think he'll return with troops."

"Possibly his brother's army," Rory said.

Morag glanced at them and then at Tierney. "And he wants you, too."

Tierney nodded.

"Then he will return," Morag said.

"But they've handfasted," Henry said. "It breaks the betrothal that Tierney's father signed."

"Which I did not sign and said I refused with every inch of my being."

Morag looked up at Kenan with a wicked grin. "Handfasted. That will ruin all of Cyrus Mackinnon's plans. I saw him riding across this moor two days ago next to his haughty sister." The woman didn't look surprised. In fact, she looked pleased.

"More reasons for you to consider coming to stay with us at Dunvegan," Sara said. "Eleri and Eliza would also love to have you there."

Morag shook her head. "I'll be well enough here with my crows." She stood. "But feel free to take refuge here if *you* feel unsafe."

Henry made a snorting sound as if he was trying to hide his laughter, and Morag's green eyes narrowed like those of a stalking cat. Either the man was a fool or he didn't think their aunt could cause any harm. They may have been jesting about the newts, but Tierney could tell that Kenan's Aunt Morag would be a terrible foe to have.

Morag walked to a row of little clay jars against a wall with labels scratched into the sides. Plucking one, she walked to Rory. "For your sore tooth. Rub this in for a week, and it will help ease the swelling and pain. Then make certain to wash it well."

"My tooth?" he asked, and Tierney could see him moving his tongue behind his cheek. He looked at Sara.

"I didn't tell her," Sara said.

Morag moved past him toward the door, opening it, and her crows scattered in the yard as she walked out. It looked like more had arrived, a black cloud or a winged army. Tierney would need to start befriending crows at Scorrybreac. They were beautiful but intimidating.

"You are welcome to stay as always," Morag said, "but if your visit here was to convince me to return with you, it is over." She glanced at Kenan. "And I know you have much to do."

"Aye," he answered, looking grim.

Sara stood, and Tierney followed her out the door, the men following behind them.

"Have ye always had these black birds at your cottage?" Henry asked, waving his hands around as he followed her out. "Even when ye had a husband. I can't imagine a man putting up with this foolish rabble."

Tierney slid the gifted feather into her hair where the curved tip fluttered with the breeze. The scent of rain blew around them, making Sara's horse neigh, and she noticed a dark cloud far off over the sea. Where they stood, the sun still shone.

"My husband tried to banish my crows," Morag said, "but it didn't work."

As if being outside again had loosened Henry's tongue, he continued with his prattle. "A weak man, then." He shook his head.

Sara's face paled, and Tierney wondered if her aunt really could turn Henry into a newt. This she had to see knowing Henry was building up to his usual rant about strong women. "A man must control his wife and family," he said, "or he can't garner any respect from the men of his clan." Tierney had heard it all before. Unfortunately, her father had believed this poison from his advisor.

Morag moved swiftly across the ground. 'Twas almost as if she glided with the wind without the normal gait of a person setting feet to earth.

Pulling her hand from a pocket tied under her robes, she tossed what looked like seeds at Henry. His eyes squeezed shut, and he sputtered. The sun shone down on him, and Tierney saw that the dust had a sheen or sparkle to it. "What the bloody hell—?"

But his words cut off as twenty crows descended upon him, their black wings spread as they dove.

Henry screamed, his arms flailing as the crows pecked at the sparkling dust that had covered him.

"Aunt!" Kenan called.

Morag smiled. "They like sparkling things, like little shards of mica. Don't worry, they won't eat the mica once they realize it isn't food."

Kenan and Rory ran toward the man, waving their arms and yelling to scatter the birds. Henry's eyes were wide, and there were at least two spots of blood on his face from hard pecks. "She's a witch," Henry called. "I will see her burned!"

The crows flew back to the roofline and the stands erected about the yard.

"Aunt Morag," Sara said, "you can't send your birds to attack people."

"They weren't going to kill him," Morag said. "Just remind him to whom he's speaking his rubbish."

"I was rather hoping she'd turn him into a newt," Tierney said quietly to Sara. Sara stifled a laugh behind her hand while they all watched the stubborn advisor pat himself down and stomp, trying to rid himself of the sparkling dust. The remaining sun reflected on the tiny bits of mica, giving his skin a glittery, golden sheen.

"My husband was a weak man, Master Henry," Morag called. "He thought he could control me by beating me. But here I am, alive and well, and he is dead, rotted bones in the cold ground."

The returned threat rolled out of her like quiet thunder. Morag Gunn was definitely safe on her own with her battalion of crows ready to attack. Henry's face reddened, and he tucked his lips inward as if to stop himself from responding. He eyed the crows who watched the courtyard from all directions.

Sara gave Morag an encompassing hug, and Tierney stepped closer when they broke apart. "'Twas a pleasure to meet you, Mistress," she said.

Morag took her hand. "Come here if you need a powerful woman's protection." Her words held true invitation.

"Thank you," Tierney said, wondering if Morag would have been able to protect her and Maggie from Wallace.

Rory helped Henry rise into his saddle and handed him a rag from his belt to dab at the few blood spots.

Kenan stood looking at the road toward Dunvegan. "Someone comes."

They all turned as the hoofbeats grew louder. Two riders raced toward them.

"Jok," Rory said.

Kenan looked at Tierney. "And Jacob Tanner."

Had the Mathesons already returned to Scorrybreac? Why else would Jacob be riding as if the devil chased him?

# CHAPTER SIXTEEN

"Life is the fire that burns and the sun that
gives light. Life is the wind and the rain
and the thunder in the sky. Life is matter
and is earth, what is and what is not,
and what beyond is in Eternity."

*Lucius Annaeus Seneca – Roman Statesman,*
*5 BC–65 AD*

Jacob and another man with a red beard and hair
pulled up in the yard, making the crows fly about
before settling again. Jacob barely waited for his
horse to stop before jumping down to jog over to
Tierney.

"What is it?" Henry asked.

Jacob presented a sealed missive and a small
wooden box to Tierney. He stared right into her eyes
as if she were the only person there even though
Kenan was right beside her.

"Ranulf?" Tierney asked.

"He returned with twenty men," Jacob said.
"They ransacked the village."

Of course they did, the bastard. "Did they set
fires?" Kenan asked.

"Nay." His gaze shifted to Kenan. "He ordered
his men to do it, but one, who I think was the leader
of the warriors, said that Murdoc had ordered them
not to. If they wanted to take over a village, they

shouldn't burn it."

Tierney turned the missive over, and all thoughts stopped except one. *Father?* Pressed across the fold was a seal in wax, the profile of a hawk with tiny letters that read Scorrybreac. "'Tis my father's signet ring," she said, looking to Kenan. His face was dark with concern.

She broke the seal, unfolding the letter. Her fingers pressed against her lips as she recognized the handwriting. "'Tis from Father."

"Yer father?" Kenan asked.

"He's not lost at sea, then," Sara added from behind Tierney.

Henry stood by her other shoulder, reading over it. Kenan studied her as she bowed her head to read.

*To my daughter, Tierney MacNicol of Scorrybreac, widow of Chief Wallace Macqueen*

*We have been hostilely detained by Chief Murdoc Matheson at Eilean Donan Castle. Fannie sends her signet ring to prove this letter is from us. The crew, your mother, and I will be forfeited if you further refuse to wed Ranulf Matheson. The betrothal Chief Matheson and I negotiated overrides whatever you tried to set in place by handfasting with Chief Macdonald of Sleat. I have scratched out the clause you requested.*

*You will surrender yourself at Eilean Donan in exchange for our lives. I will then surrender leadership of Clan MacNicol of Scorrybreac*

*to Lord Ranulf to ensure your mother's safety.
Once you wed Lord Ranulf, you will continue
to be the Lady of Scorrybreac Castle at his
side while your mother, brother, and I go into
exile.*

*May God move your heart to help your
mother and the MacNicol crew.*

*Your father,*
*Chief Douglas MacNicol*

Tierney's hand clenched around her mother's
ring, and her heart spread its wings, beating rapidly
as if to rise from her chest. *May God move your
heart.* Her father had said that last part because he
hadn't seen much of Tierney's heart after he'd refused to help her escape her nightmare marriage
even after he saw the bruises. Douglas MacNicol had
turned his back on his own daughter's pleas, telling
her to endure and do her duty.

And now he wanted her to sacrifice herself again.
Douglas MacNicol knew she'd never do it for
him, but Tierney loved her mother. And the crew
was made up of MacNicol warriors, young men
alongside whom she'd grown. Jacob had been away
on another mission for her to find Asher when her
parents had sailed, answering Chief Matheson's
summons. Or else Jacob would be trapped at Eilean
Donan Castle, too. Her chest squeezing, it was hard
to draw a full breath. Her parents were alive.

Henry took the letter from her trembling fingers,
and she let him. She kept her mother's ring, sliding it
onto her smallest finger and kissing it.

"They're alive," Henry murmured, his eyes wide when he looked up from the letter. "Ye must go. Save your parents and the crew."

Tierney wobbled, and Kenan's warm hand lifted under her arm. "We will make another rescue plan that doesn't put Tierney in danger."

"Ye must marry Ranulf," Henry continued as if Kenan hadn't spoken. "Your father says the hand-fasting, or even a wedding, is null, that the clause about—"

"Aunt Morag," Sara called over Henry's noise, "do you have more of that mica dust?" She took Tierney's other arm in support.

"Plenty," Morag answered, stepping forward. "Always in my pocket for bloody jackanapes."

Henry's face reddened, his lips turning white as he pressed them together. He pointed at Tierney, his finger jabbing the air like a chicken pecking at seeds. "Ye must save them. 'Tis your duty." His gaze shifted back to Morag, and when the woman took a confident step forward, her hand already in her pocket, he ran to his horse, throwing himself up in the saddle. "Think of your mother," he added before kicking the horse to get it running along the road that led north to Dunvegan.

Tierney's heart thudded hard, an instinct to run making her feel dizzy. Whether to run toward her mother to save her or away from all of them to save herself and Maggie, she wasn't sure.

The five of them made a little circle in Morag's yard. "Ye have a ship," Rory said to Kenan.

"Two galleons and thirty smaller Birlinn ships," he answered, his voice strong.

"Birlinn ships?" Tierney asked, her voice soft.

"They are small ships with oars and a single sail," Kenan answered. "Along with the galleons, they can carry eight hundred men."

"Men who are currently rebuilding Dunscaith Castle," Sara said. "In case…" Tierney felt her glance. "In case you come under siege."

Tierney pulled her arm from Sara and rubbed her face. Kenan must surely regret rescuing her from the sea. "I would leave the Isle of Skye, take Maggie and run. Take refuge with some other clan. But those men and my mother are innocent."

Kenan remained at her side. "And Clan Matheson will still journey to Skye after they make good on their threats."

Rory nodded, looking grim. "Without a united Skye, they see their opportunity to come in and take root."

"Like a vicious weed," Sara said.

Tierney took a full breath and turned her face to Kenan. He looked so concerned for her. "I'll do anything to stop that," Tierney said, her voice stronger, "except surrender my body and soul to Ranulf."

"Of course not," Morag said. "I have some other things besides your body and soul to use against the Mathesons. I'll teach you on the journey to Eilean Donan."

And just like that, Morag Gunn, Kenan's widowed aunt with suspect ways, had decided they were going to Eilean Donan.

Everyone looked at Morag. "And yes, I am coming," she said as if reading everyone's minds. "I will have the twins watch my crows, the ones that remain

here." She walked back into her cottage as if to pack.
"I'll give them the choice to journey with me or
not."

"We must head back to Dunvegan to prepare," 
Rory said.

Kenan's fingers wove between Tierney's, linking
their hands and silently offering her support. "We
are going to war, then."

All because of her.

• • •

Morag sat at her table, the silence of the room pressing in on her. She tipped the bag of fragrant
lavender along the polished boards and smoothed
them into a circle, breathing the strong, floral scent.
It reminded her of her sister, and she wished once
again that she still lived.

Would Elspet see the spirit of air inside Tierney?
Would she wish the woman to find her way into
Kenan's bruised heart?

Blessedly, Kenan took after Elspet and not his
horrible father, Walter Macdonald. Elspet's younger
son, Gilbert, was slow witted and had been easily
influenced by his father, making the lad mean and
suspicious. That boy would end up married to a
domineering shrew, no doubt.

Kenan needed someone wise, someone who understood and supported his desire to unify the isle.
Someone who could push him out of the sacrificial
role Kenan seemed to take on too easily. First taking
his father's place in prison after the battle of Solway
Moss even though Kenan had gotten away safely.

Then he'd allowed his father and brother to ignore his guidance without rallying the Macdonald warriors against them. It would have been easy, because Kenan had won their loyalty with his fairness and honesty. Kindness was his strength even if he'd been taught that it was his weakness.

Morag chuckled to herself as she dragged her finger through the tiny lavender buds to form an *X* and four equal quadrants. The same could be said about love. It could be a person's strength, their rock in a storm, and their downfall when they sacrificed all for someone or something else. Which would Tierney be to Kenan? Because Morag had no doubt that something was growing between them. She'd seen it in the way they moved around one another, like magnets attempting not to let their sides collide but feeling the pull continuously.

"North," Morag said and set a chunk of salt crystal in the quadrant at the top of the circle. "For earth.

"West," she said, placing the small silver cup of water in the quadrant to the left. "For water."

In the bottom quadrant, she placed a small white lump of beeswax with a wick in it. She lit it with the candle sitting at one end of the table. "South, for fire." Which was her niece, Sara. She'd won Rory MacLeod, the love between the two making them strong.

In the right, or east, quadrant, she set a white feather. "And this is for air," she said and pulled the hairclip that Tierney had given her crow, Madeline. The bird had brought it to Morag, and now Morag plucked a golden hair from it that she'd seen glinting in the sun. She set Tierney's hair over the feather. Closing her eyes, she hovered her hand over it.

"Let the Celtic goddess of the sky, moon, and stars, Arianrhod, guide Tierney MacNicol." Morag closed her eyes, floating her palm over the feather and strand of Tierney's hair. She focused on the sight of Tierney soaring over the sea with the wings that Kenan had fashioned. "Earth Mother, Gaia, help me bring strength to our isle. Protect the elements and make them strong and united. Guide me as your helper in this realm."

A sudden wind gusted around the cottage.

*Crack!*

Morag's eyes snapped open as the shutters on two windows flew open, and a big wind swirled into the room, scattering the lavender and lifting the feather to the rafters. She smiled as her long white hair rose with the power of the wind. Gaia was pleased and would help Morag save the isle.

Because Morag had no doubt a war was coming.

• • •

"MacLeods will guard the coastline of Scorrybreac and Dunvegan," Kenan said, running his finger down the unrolled map in the center of the library table. His fingertip ran down to the Sleat Peninsula where Dunscaith Castle sat, and he tapped the rook drawn there. "And I will journey home and organize our warriors to sail with us over to the Matheson Clan, which is now occupying Eilean Donan Castle at the convergence of Loch Alsh and Loch Duich."

Kenan looked up at Tierney as she stared at the

map. Another golden curl slipped from her head after being loosened on their ride back to Dunvegan. Lord help him, he just wanted to inhale the fresh air that probably scented it. She hadn't said anything during the journey. A slight pinch of her brows showed turmoil, but how much was swirling around under that brilliant hair?

"My father almost conquered Eilean Donan five years ago with fifty Birlinn ships," Sara said. "About twenty of our fleet sank, and Father hadn't yet rebuilt them."

Kenan tapped the port across the peninsula where his ships harbored. "We will bring eight hundred men."

"Murdoc Matheson has more men than that," Tierney said, her fingers absently tucking her hair behind an ear.

Kenan looked at her until she raised her gaze to his. "But Ranulf does not."

"His brother does not support him?" Tierney asked.

Kenan cupped the back of his neck. "Murdoc fought at Solway Moss and told me his brother was a coward for not coming. Assuming Ranulf hasn't done anything heroic in his brother's eyes since then, my words were true."

"Murdoc Matheson must want to expand Matheson territory." Sara cast a knowing look at Kenan. "Especially if he can get rid of his tiresome brother by sending him to live on Skye." They both knew something about wanting to get rid of a troublesome brother, their younger brother, Gilbert, who'd disappeared when their father died instead of supporting Kenan's chiefdom.

"If we arrive without warning," Kenan said, "Murdoc could take it as an act of aggression."

"Send a letter to Chief Matheson that I'm coming, then," Tierney said. She swallowed. "In exchange for the crew and my parents."

*Foking nay.* Kenan's hands fisted on the table, and he shook his head.

"Don't fly Macdonald colors," Tierney continued, "and he might think the ships are my escort, although MacNicols have never had that many Birlinn ships."

"Some can hide back behind the small isle, Glas Eilean, until they hear cannon fire," Rory said.

"What do we do when we get there?" Tierney asked. Was it worry or determination in the lines of her face?

"I will escort Lady Tierney inside," Henry said.

Kenan was shaking his head, but no one was paying him much attention.

"A fool's plan," Simon said, glaring at the MacNicol advisor.

"Ye can't just hand her over," John said, waving both his good arm and his stump, his eyes wide. "That Matheson whelp will pull her before a cleric who will say the handfasting is pagan and then marry them."

Kenan's voice came out loud, a blast of sound from his roiling stomach. "Rory and I will go in first, as chiefs on the Isle of Skye, to talk with Chief Murdoc."

"They could just kill you," Tierney said while Sara shook her head.

Rory bent to kiss his wife's lips softly and pulled back. "The Lion of Skye is not so easily dispatched."

"Even a lion bleeds," Sara said.

"Especially if attacked by ten men with swords or pistols," Tierney said. "We must be clever, trick them." She released a breath, looking at Kenan, and he saw stark determination. "I could go in using some tricks Morag says she will teach me on the way over."

"That witch is not coming," Henry said, his voice rising. The man still had some mica dust glittering on his skin.

Tierney frowned. "I would rather Lady Morag walk into Eilean Donan with me than you. She won't surrender me."

"I won't surrender ye," Henry said, affronted.

"You would do so in a heartbeat."

Rapid footsteps echoed from a back hall, and Cora ran inside the Great Hall. As usual, her eyes were wide. "Tierney, 'tis Maggie."

Tierney's gaze snapped to her. "What's happened?"

"There's some sort of pit in the castle, below ground, and she's down it."

# CHAPTER SEVENTEEN

Oubliettes or Pit Prisons "were deep, narrow pits where someone could be imprisoned indefinitely. Lacking food, water, sunshine, and any means of escape, the prisoners very quickly broke—if they were allowed back out at all."

*All That's Interesting.com*

Tierney ran toward the corridor where Cora had emerged before she realized she had no idea where this pit resided. Sneachda barked, running after her, and Rory's old dog added to the barking as if not to be left out.

"That blasted dungeon pit needs to be covered," Sara said, hurrying behind her.

"You have a pit prison?" Tierney asked. What type of people were the MacLeods?

"Did she fall in?" Kenan asked, surging ahead and then spinning to look at Rory and Sara, his gaze falling on Cora. "Someone who lives here, lead the bloody way!" His voice boomed out with frustrated authority, and Rory ran ahead.

"I don't think she fell," Cora said, her breathing hard. "She's...singing down there."

"The poor lass has lost her mind," Simon said as the group hurried after Rory, the dogs' nails scratching on the floorboards as they whipped around a bend in the corridor.

Kenan and Tierney ran right on Rory's heels, following him down the dimly lit staircase into the bowels of the castle. She was halfway down, her fingers brushing the damp walls to guide her, when she realized she couldn't pull in enough breath. The mindless panic of being trapped reared up inside her. But this was nothing like being trapped in a closet.

She stumbled, her hand going out to fall on Kenan's arm. Firm and solid, her fingers curled inward as if she were once again drowning in the sea.

"Tierney?" he said.

"I...I have trouble with small places." Her breathing was too shallow, and stars began to spark around the edges of her vision.

"Mama," Maggie's sing-song voice floated up from the darkness below.

"Maggie," she whispered. "Get me down there," she said, turning to Kenan. "Go, go, go."

He continued down the steps, her hand on his arm, and she concentrated on keeping her breath even. They reached the bottom, which opened into a corridor of damp cobblestone. "I'm coming, sweet," Tierney called and hurried forward, thankful that the ceiling was higher, allowing air flow. Still, her breath was too shallow.

Sara and Rory stood looking down at a hole in the floor. "There was a rope ladder," Rory said. He tried to grab the thick rope dangling over the center of the hole, its end disappearing down into the darkness. "Where's the hook to catch it?"

"'Tis down here with me," Maggie called up. "I used it to grab the rope, and it fell down here. The ladder's down here, too."

"Does it hold weight?" Kenan asked Rory.

"Aye. 'Tis strong enough to hold a horse."

Tierney threw herself down on the stone floor, lowering a taper she'd lit from the sconce on the wall as far as she could into the hole. "How bloody far down is it?" she asked. She could just make out Maggie's lifted face and the shine of her eyes with the flamelight.

"Thirteen feet," Sara said, "and the tide comes in at the bottom. Holy Mother Mary, what is the tide right now?"

"Are yer feet wet?" Kenan asked, and Tierney realized he was right next to her on his knees.

"Yes," Maggie said. "And cold. I want to come back up. I only wanted to see how far down it went." She sounded remorseful. Her child's curiosity was more powerful than her common sense. "But I can't get back up." Tierney heard the quiver in her daughter's voice.

"We'll get you back up as fast as we can," she said. "How far up your leg is the water?"

"It wasn't deep when I got down, but now 'tis up to my ankles. Is it going to keep rising?" Her little voice squeaked with the last question.

Sara murmured a curse behind Tierney. "The tide is coming in."

Before Tierney could even stand up, Kenan rose and leaped, grabbing hold of the rope that dangled over the center of the hole. "Stand against a wall, Maggie," he called. His gaze met Tierney's. "I'll get her." With that, he lowered himself hand over hand, his legs easily wrapping around the thick rope to slow his descent.

"Stand back," Tierney called down. "Kenan is coming to save you, sweeting." When Maggie was born, Tierney's heart was no longer her own, safe in her chest behind ribs. It now resided outside of her body in the form of Maggie, vulnerable like never before.

Tierney had told herself she didn't need anyone else, that she could take care of herself and her daughter completely. But in this dank darkness surrounded by stone, when her heart wouldn't slow enough to keep her wits, Kenan was literally jumping in to save Maggie, save Tierney's heart. She blinked back tears.

"Don't fall on the girl," yelled one of the old men behind her.

"Have ye reached her yet?" the other of the odd pair asked.

"The lass shouldn't have been left alone," said Henry, and guilt sunk like needles into Tierney's middle. Everyone started talking at once.

"Will he be able to—?"

"Lady Tierney should have—"

"She can't be everywhere at once."

"I but went to the privy, and she disappeared."

"Hush," Sara called. "We can't hear."

Everyone fell silent. Only the drip of water in the corridor could be heard along with soft words below in the dark pit. Kenan's deep rumble mixed with Maggie's higher-pitched voice. The sound of water funneled up from the bottom.

"I've got ye. No more wet feet," Kenan said, and Tierney clutched her hands before her in wordless prayer.

"'Tis cold down here," Maggie said but didn't sound upset. She was merely relaying information to Kenan. "And I can smell meat cooking. 'Tis making me hungry."

"I smell it, too," Kenan said.

"I hope 'tis what we're having for dinner."

"That's to torture prisoners even more," one of the old men whispered behind Tierney. "Kitchen is on the other side of the wall so poor souls can smell food while they starve."

"We are filling this pit in with rocks immediately," Sara whispered, anger lacing her words.

"Aye, of course," Rory said.

"Like this afternoon," she continued.

"Aye, love," Rory said.

"This rope ladder doesn't help much when 'tis not attached at the top, does it?" Kenan said.

"No," Maggie said. "I should have tied a bowline knot. My simple square knot slipped by the time I got near the bottom."

Good Lord, she could have fallen, knocked her head on the stone, and drowned in the incoming tide. Tierney's lungs felt squeezed, and she struggled to take in slow, even breaths. Cold prickles spread out from the center of her body to send goose bumps over her skin.

"She knows knots?" Sara asked in a whisper.

Tierney nodded without taking her gaze from the dark hole. After another even breath, she spoke. "She will know how to survive in the forest on her own by the time she's of marriageable age."

No one asked why, although she was certain Henry knew. She'd never let her daughter get trapped in a marriage like she had.

"Can ye hold onto my shoulders while I climb up the rope?" Kenan asked.

Tierney cupped her mouth. "Wrap your legs around his waist and your arms around his neck."

"I will, Mama."

"Throw me down another rope," Kenan called. "I'm going to tie her to me."

Rory moved away while Sara whispered in Tierney's ear. "Precaution if Maggie's limbs are weak from cold."

"Coming down now," Rory called before dropping a thinner rope into the pit.

*Splash.* Tierney, Sara, and Cora leaned over the hole with Rory standing. Minutes passed as Kenan tied her to him.

"So ye sing like yer mama?"

"Yes. I love to sing. Mama only sings to me, though."

"We're going to climb now," he said. "Hold on tight."

"I will with all my strength."

The now-taut rope shook above the hole as Kenan climbed. His fists appeared first, clasping the rope, and his arms bulged as he hefted himself and Maggie hand over hand. His head appeared, and then his handsome face, Maggie's little arms around his neck. Tierney released her breath when she saw Maggie, her little face pressed into Kenan's back. The bottom of her skirts showed the water that had inched up her legs, and Tierney shivered.

Kenan held the rope with one hand while he yanked a rag from his belt. "Catch this to pull us closer to the edge." He flicked the long rag toward Rory.

Rory caught the end and swung Kenan toward the edge. "'Tis probably best to untie her first and take her from me."

"Hold me," Tierney said to Sara, who threw another rope around her middle. Rory held the dangling pair close while Tierney leaned over the wide hole to catch at Maggie. She recognized the knot and worked at it quickly.

"We've got you." The rope cut into Tierney's stomach, and she glanced over her shoulder to see the two old MacLeods, Henry, and Sara all holding the length behind her. Maggie, her little arms reaching for her, waited. Finally, the knot slipped, and Tierney pulled her off Kenan's strong back. Her little girl held onto Tierney with ferocity.

Over her blond curls, Tierney saw Kenan swing across the gap, landing on solid ground with a thump. He straightened with ease, making Tierney wish once again she'd been born with the muscles of a man. But then she wouldn't have her sweet child.

"I'm sorry, Mama," Maggie said, smashing her face against the hollow of Tierney's neck and wrapping her legs around her mother like she did with Kenan.

"Are you sorry because you climbed down there or that you didn't tie the knot that would have given you a way to climb back out?" Tierney asked, glancing down when Maggie turned her face up to her.

Maggie smiled shyly but still looked worried. "The knot."

Tierney still trembled but couldn't stop her relieved smile. She kissed her daughter's head. "We are going to have a long talk about how curious little kittens get themselves killed if they chase after everything."

"Yes, Mama."

Rory thumped Kenan's shoulder. "Valiant effort."

Kenan looked over to Tierney. "She is well?"

Tierney nodded. "Thank you." The two words didn't seem enough. She wanted to run to him, hug him, tell him how grateful she was, show him with her whole, naked body. But for now, she just stared into his eyes and simply said, "You are a hero."

"And we're filling in that pit today," Sara said. "For now, close the door over it."

Holy Joan, there was a door over the top so that a prisoner could be confined down there in total darkness. "I need to get Maggie above," she said, turning.

Two steps toward the stairs and she felt Kenan at her side, his hand gently on her arm as if he worried that she'd start to breathe unevenly again. But she held Maggie, knowing she was safe, and the world felt solid once more.

"There's a swing on a tree in the kitchen garden," Sara said from behind. "Let's take Maggie there after she's changed into dry clothes."

• • •

"She's asleep," Cora said, shooing Tierney out into the corridor and softly shutting the door behind them. "Find your own bed. I will sleep with her."

Her own bed? Where was that? She and Kenan had been given one of the rooms with one large bed, and every inch of her skin wanted to seek him out. But something had happened today when she'd watched him jump into the dark pit to save Maggie. Tierney recognized a tightening of the heart, a whispered wish to truly trust him, tie herself to him and his kind ways. A desire to break the vow she'd given herself never to allow imprisonment of any kind ever again. She'd gotten out from under her father's thumb only to be thrust under Wallace's body and wifely shackles. As a widow, she was free and would remain so.

"People will think I should be with Maggie after her ordeal," Tierney said.

Cora frowned. "Maggie is hale and hearty and can't stop talking about her grand adventure down into a water-filling pit and how Kenan rescued her like a knight of legend."

Tierney sighed. Her daughter had the same danger streak in her that Tierney now recognized in herself. "She's going to create mad plans of her own," Tierney said with a sigh.

Cora laughed softly. "We better find her a best friend who can help keep her feet on the ground."

Tierney raised an eyebrow. "If that's what you're supposed to be doing, you aren't doing a good job of it."

Cora playfully thumped her arm. "Go on now." She opened the door silently and slipped back inside. She stared at Tierney as she shut the door slowly, a teasing smile curing her lips. "I know you want to go thank him proper." *Click.*

And Tierney did, oh, how she did. Tierney felt the heat rise in her cheeks. She wanted to go to Kenan and kiss him, every inch of him. Striding down the hall, she stopped before the door of the room Margaret had given them without a backward glance about the propriety. Everyone thought they were handfasted.

Was he inside? Dunvegan Castle was silent. No voices filtered up from the Great Hall. 'Twas late, but she was restless. She rested her palm on the solid wall at the side of the door, hesitating. Should she go to him? Her body ached for his touch. But shame lay a heavy blanket over it.

*Ye're selfish*. Her father's words, repeated by Henry and then Wallace, haunted her. Her acts had possibly ruined Kenan's alliance with the Mackinnon Clan. She would never be good enough to deserve a loving relationship.

Even after Kenan had told her he was betrothed, she'd allowed him to lie to save her pride before Henry and her clan. With her swirling thoughts, shame smothered her lust. Kenan was a good man, trying to save everyone, and she had been using him. And when he'd saved Maggie without a second thought, he'd cracked into her heart. She needed to think things through before losing her mind to the thirst between them. Because she'd never be good enough to keep him for long.

Tierney turned from the door and continued down the curving staircase. The fresh air and stars called to her. Perhaps it would clear her mind. When Wallace lived, she'd spent many nights up in trees, avoiding his bed and trying to plan a way out of her marriage. She'd learned to tie herself to branches to prevent her from falling or hanging herself, something she was already teaching Maggie. Although she would never allow her sweet daughter to be traded away like she'd been.

Tierney moved like a shadow through the sparsely lit corridors of Dunvegan Castle, through the kitchen with the snoring cook, Fiona, and out into the open air of the garden where Sara had pushed Maggie on the swing earlier. The ten-foot-tall wall around it prevented people from trying to climb out and into the sea, but the tree holding the swing had grown above it. The sturdy boards held aloft by chains would never get her as high as she wished, so she stood upon it in her slippers, head tipped back to search for a branch.

Grabbing a thick limb with the crook of her arm, she swung a leg up to it, her petticoat fanning out. She hoisted herself and got her feet under her to stand, reaching for another branch. She didn't look down, only up to where she longed to be. Where the breeze could cool her shameful flush, and she could think.

The summer leaves rustled, and the sound of gentle waves below in the darkness soothed. The unblocked wind off the sea moved the branches and rushed by her ears.

"Are ye planning to sleep there?"

Tierney's heart galloped at the sound of Kenan's deep voice below her. With the wind in her ears, she hadn't heard his approach. Had he followed her?

"Perhaps."

"With all the fine beds at Dunvegan? My sister will be embarrassed that her guest couldn't find comfort within her home." His words were teasing, but there was an underlying hardness. Not anger but…hurt, perhaps.

"I came out here to think, and I do that best up in the air."

The limbs quivered as Kenan grabbed onto the same branch she'd used, making it dip with his weight. He hoisted his large form up, climbing another level so that his face was even with hers. The darkness shrouded them as much as the fluttering leaves. "And what are ye thinking about?"

She looked away from him. It was easier that way. "I think…you should do what is good for your clan. Dragging you into the mess of my life was dishonorable. I didn't mean to cause strife between you and your friend and certainly not war. If you want to say we never handfasted, I will admit it as true." It would mar her reputation, but she didn't have one of modesty anyways. She was also a widow, which gave her some social freedom to act loose without condemnation.

The wind had increased, making their perch sway and creak. Tierney could feel rather than hear Kenan drawing closer to her, his boots balanced two limbs below. It was as if he gave off heat or some energy that made her skin come alive and her breath halt, waiting for his touch. She tried to keep her attention on the quickly moving clouds outlined in the sporadic moonlight, but her body tingled. Lord help her, she couldn't control her reaction to him.

"And that's why ye're sleeping in a tree?"

The hint of laughter in his voice made her face snap to his, her frown in place. "Do I look like I'm sleeping?" Mo chreach. She wasn't angry at him. She smoothed her voice. "I'm just thinking and regretting some of my choices."

"Like drugging and shackling a man ye don't know?" He leaned in closer to her face, and she held her breath. "Instead of jumping right to plan number three?"

His lips were mere inches away. Kind eyes met hers despite her waspish tongue. His cheekbones were defined and his jawline firm. Only the bump of a poorly set broken nose could be considered a flaw, although she didn't. That and the scars on his back meant he was human, fallible, and experienced with pain like her.

"I don't think plan number three would have worked," she said. "Not with Grace Mackinnon waiting for you at the wedding celebration."

His hand rose, and she felt his callused thumb stroke her cheek. An urge to press her face into his palm nearly overwhelmed her, but she kept her seat on the limb, her fingers curling into the bark of the trunk to steady herself. "Grace Mackinnon was only ever an alliance," he said.

"A duty," she said, remembering her own sacrifice for an alliance with Clan Macqueen. Although at first, she'd been naively hopeful, infatuated with Wallace's dashing good looks. Things with Kenan had been reversed. They had lain together before any legal entrapment had been sprung. And it had been…wonderful, a memory she would cherish.

His thumb brushed her lower lip, and she felt herself leaning toward him. The wind seemed to blow against her back in a push, and she didn't fight it.

"A duty that ye saved me from." Kenan's arm went behind her, helping with the wind to pull her off the limb to balance in his arms. Her legs slid down his, her slippers resting on his boots. "I know now that wedding Grace would have been a mistake."

Her heart danced at his words. "Truly?"

"It would have ended in war." His hand cupped her face. "Ye saved that from happening."

Her face lifted and their lips met. Her eyes shut to the feel of being surrounded by this man and his kind strength. She slanted easily against his now-familiar mouth, and the fingers of her free hand curled into his tunic, holding herself to him where they balanced. Heat flared instantly, burning past guilt, shame, and any regret. Tierney knew where she wanted to be, within Kenan Macdonald's arms.

Kenan shifted, pulling her completely off her branch to balance with him on his limb. The wind shook the tree, rushing around them, mimicking the wild dance of blood and aching Tierney felt thrumming through her. This did not feel selfish, not when Kenan pulled her to him, and she gave in to the need.

*Creakkkk... Crack!*

Tierney's breath caught, and her instinct was to clutch onto Kenan. But he was no match against nature, and they dropped, the limb falling down from under them.

# CHAPTER EIGHTEEN

"When the oak is felled the whole forest echoes
with its fall, but a hundred acorns are sown in
silence by an unnoticed breeze."

*Thomas Carlyle – Scottish Philosopher, 1795–1881*

There was no time to react to the cracking, not while
holding onto Tierney. Kenan pulled her into him, his
hands spreading around her head as they dropped
through the tree to the ground. He bent his knees on
impact like he did when practicing falling off his
huge horse, taking the jolt hopefully without breaking bones.

The heavy limb hit the ground, and his feet flew
out from under him. He hardened all his muscles to
protect him and Tierney. The impact jarred through
his body, a grunt coming out of him, and Tierney
gasped. His training made him curve just so, but the
log under them made it impossible to roll with the
force of the fall.

Breath knocked from his chest, he made himself
relax all his tightened muscles. His lungs opened,
and he drew in the wind whipping the leaves over
and around them. Thunder cracked at the same time
lightning severed the clouds above. As if ripping the
bottom off of a full rain bucket, the cloud dropped a
deluge of water.

"Saint Margaret's foking tears," Tierney said

against his chest, her warm body stretching within his arms.

Relief that Tierney was well enough to curse helped Kenan breathe. "Are ye allowed to use fok when talking of a pious saint?"

She was silent for a moment, the rain slamming down through the leaves. "She birthed King David, so she must fok."

Laughter poured out of him. Tierney pulled herself up his chest, lying over him. Rain saturated her hair so that it hung down in a wet curtain. From the light of another lightning flash, he saw that she was laughing, too.

"What the bloody hell is going on?"

Kenan tipped his head way back to see an upside-down Rory running out toward them, Sara standing in the doorway to the kitchen, a robe wrapped around her. Rory stopped to stare down over them, worry on his face. "Are ye well? What happened?"

"Yer tree is not strong enough," Kenan said.

Rory looked up and then back down at them. "To hold the two of ye up there, tupping like squirrels? Nay, 'tis not."

"We weren't—" Kenan began.

"Like the bed at Scorrybreac," Rory said over the wind. "The two of ye are destructive like rampaging whirlwinds."

Tierney pushed up off Kenan. "Can you move?" she asked, grabbing one of Kenan's hands.

Kenan took a few seconds to wiggle toes, fingers, and his limbs. "Aye."

Rory grabbed the other hand, and the two of

them leaned back to help Kenan rise from the leafy branches spread across the yard. The limb that had cracked had been long, the end lying across the herb garden.

"Fiona's going to have words with ye," Rory yelled over the thunderous rain. "Now get inside." He pivoted and jogged back to the doorway where Sara backed up to let him in.

Already soaked through, neither Kenan nor Tierney moved toward the shelter. When he turned to her, she was staring at him, still holding onto his hand. He pulled her back into his arms, the warmth of her body instantly welcoming with the chilled wind and rain whipping around them. "We should get ye dry and warm," he said near her ear.

She nodded but made no move to pull away, so Kenan continued to hold her for a long moment. "Are ye afraid of the cook waiting for us in the kitchen?"

Tierney laughed against him, and he felt her take a full inhale. He let her pull back to look up in his eyes. She blinked as rainwater ran down her forehead, past her brows. "I don't know where to sleep." The smile that had been on her lips washed away.

Where to sleep? They'd been given a bedchamber together. He studied her, trying to see past the portrait of drowned beauty. There was so much more to her words. He felt the weight of them. 'Tis why she'd come outside to a tree in the first place.

But her kiss had been full of desire, and he was too wet to untangle all her worries right then. So he pulled her back into his arms and kissed her long and without hurry, his hands cupping her face. When they stopped to breathe, he looked down into her face, its paleness a stark relief against the dreary night around them.

"Ye will sleep with me, Tierney, until ye only feel cold when ye think of me."

"What if I never feel cold when I think of you?"

He leaned in and kissed her chilled forehead. "Then ye will always know where to sleep."

His words were a poetic ending. He wanted only to lead her inside up to their assigned room, stripping the wet clothes from her. Would she turn away from the passion he felt in her kiss? Would he be able to let her go?

Before he could try and probably fail to give more arguments for her coming to bed with him, Tierney slid her hand down his chest, his tunic sticking to the wet skin underneath, to grab his hand. "Then I think 'tis time for us to get out of these wet clothes," she said. She tugged Kenan, striding toward the frowning woman in the doorway. "I will help right the herbs in the morn, Mistress Fiona."

"See that ye do," Fiona said, and on closer inspection, the woman had a twinkle of mischief in her narrowed eyes. "And the swing will need to be tied to another branch," she called after them as they wound through the labyrinth of kitchen tables. "And the other branch thrown over the wall."

"I will be down in the morn to do just that," Kenan said, his long strides nearly making Tierney run to stay ahead of him.

Long snores came from the two sleeping advisors who sat in chairs near the dying fire in the keep. The wolfhound's head rose and lowered back once he saw that they weren't enemies. The squish of Tierney's slippers on the steps was accented by the clip of his boots.

They made it to the door of their room, and she pushed inside without hesitation. Did lust pulse through her like it did he? As she entered, she stopped abruptly as she spotted his surprise by the fire. He'd forgotten as their passion nearly killed the tree.

She turned slowly toward him. "You ordered a bath?"

A smile slid across his mouth. "I ordered us a bath in the largest tub Rory had made."

"For us? What if I hadn't come?" She walked toward it. He knew it was filled with barely warm water, but there was a cauldron of hot water over the coals in the hearth.

"Then I would have enjoyed a bath in a tub big enough to accommodate me." Lifting the cauldron by two wooden handles on the sides, he strode to the large wooden structure lined with linen and dumped in the steaming water.

Tierney looked from the surface of the bath to Kenan. "It has been a long time since I've indulged. I usually bathe in the creek behind Scorrybreac."

He set the cauldron down and grabbed several drying sheets. "I would like to stay, but not if ye'd like to be left to enjoy it alone." He wasn't going to act as if he didn't care. He wanted Tierney, and with her past he'd never want her to think herself undesirable.

The lass had been abused inside and out by people who should have protected her. She deserved more than pity, more than a bath on her own. She deserved respect and the ability to decide for herself how much she was willing to give. And he would give her both tonight.

Tierney stood in silence, her wet hair brushing against her shoulders. The tie at the top of her smock had come undone, allowing the skin sweeping across her collarbones to glow with creamy paleness. They were alone behind thick stone walls, sur-rounded by sea, at night in a storm. There were only the two of them, and his blood thrummed quickly. His hands clenched, impatient to touch her, but it was her turn to cross the line to him. He had set up the room and bath. If she decided that being with him threatened her freedom too much, he would find a pallet in the Great Hall on which to sleep. Anything else might send her into another tree.

Her fingers rose to the ties of her bodice, and she began to unlace them. "There is no one else I would rather share my bath with." She shrugged out of her bodice and reached behind herself to untie the pet-ticoats weighted down with rain over her hips.

Kenan's body tensed with reined in hope. "Ye can use it all alone. 'Tis a gift with no presumptions."

Her brow rose, and she grinned with a sly tilt to her lips. "You said it was a bath for *us*." Her wet pet-ticoats dropped with a thump around her ankles, and she stepped out.

He shook his head, and she held up one finger. "Only if I want to share."

With a sweep of his arm, he peeled the wet linen tunic off over his head, letting it thump to the rug. He'd have to change no matter her decision.

Her gaze slaked down his bare chest, his own nipples peaked from the chill that came with the dampness. Her look was voracious as if she were planning to devour him. Heat rushed under his skin.

Tierney stepped out of her petticoats and untied her stays. Only then did he bend to untie his boots, shucking them off one at a time without looking down. "So the us," she continued, "makes the bath not just a gift for me."

She was baiting him. He could tell by her tone and the fact she continued to undress. He couldn't speak when her stays slid off, revealing her damp smock. The white undergown, edged with lace, was nearly transparent, and Tierney's peaked nipples stood out under the gentle cinching around her breasts.

"'Twas a mistaken word," he said. "A hope, a wish, but 'tis yer choice. The gift is yers." Kenan waited, his hand on his belt. Once he freed it, his heavy pleated wrap would drop, and he'd be naked, his cock thrusting high. If he were a betting man, he would guess he was staying, but Tierney had a dark history and an unpredictable streak.

Tierney stepped over to the tub and ran her fingers through the warm water. Her eyes brightened. "'Tis so warm." With wet fingers she caught the hem of her smock and pulled it off over her head. He watched as her arms came down to her sides.

She was exquisite. He shook his head. "Someone should sculpt ye, Tierney. A lush angel fallen from the divine."

Her lips slowly rose at the corners. "You are a poet, Kenan Macdonald." Before he could answer, she stepped one long leg into the tub. "Holy Joan," she whispered, stepping in with her other leg. Her hair, which was starting to curl as it dried, fell around her shoulders as she stooped, lowering into the hot water. A sigh came from her as she leaned back against the one curved end. "'Tis heavenly." She looked at him, smiling. "One could say 'tis divine."

She sunk down, and Kenan watched her entire head slip under the water. When she emerged, her hair slicked back, the heat from the water had rouged her cheeks. She blinked water-spiked lashes as she cleared her eyes.

He brought over a cake of soap that Sara had given him when he'd ordered the bath. It had a definite flowery scent, as if she knew the bath was for Tierney. Holding it out, her wet hand wrapped around his, sliding the soap off. *Plop*. It dropped into the deep, warm water. She kept his hand and looked into his eyes. "Perhaps you could get that for me."

*Clunk*. His heavy, woolen wrap hit the side of the tub on its way to the floor.

He leaned down, meeting her lips, and Tierney's arms went around his neck, pulling him. Kenan's hand went down into the water, his palm lowering onto the edge of the slippery soap. It slid out from under the heel of his hand when she pulled, and he fell forward, his face going past her shoulder to hit the water.

He lifted his face out of the water, his hair covering his eyes. Tierney's laughter shot through him, filling him like wind filling the sails of a ship.

Pinching the water from his nose, he pushed forward. She shrieked when he slid over her into the bathing tub, his bulk sending the water to the rim. He slipped to the side of her, pulling her naked body before him, her back against his chest as he held her on his lap. "That's better," he said, his arms wrapping around her middle. "I have caught a mermaiden."

She turned in his arms so she could peer up into his face, her smile seductive. "I am no maiden."

His body was on fire. There should be a cloud of steam rising up from the water with the heat he felt, the lustful ache. Her hands found his shoulders, and she turned in the water to slide along his taut body, rising up to kiss him. He lost himself to the feel of her against him. The bathing tub was long enough that he could straighten his legs if he was sitting, but he sunk down, his knees bending so he could cradle her as she straddled him. His cock sat up hard against his belly, pressed between him and the soft curve of her stomach. She rubbed her mound against the base, and a small moan passed her lips as she lowered her mouth to his.

Their kiss turned wild, her arms clasping him as the water helped her rise and fall, rubbing more. He stroked down her back, tracing the outline of her spine until he reached her lovely, rounded arse. His fingers sought her, and she arched, her knees splayed open across his lap.

"Yes," she purred against his lips as his fingers slid into her from behind. She was just as hot and wet inside as out.

Kenan sucked in breath when her hand wrapped

around him, moving briskly. Her tongue slid along his as she pulled her body forward, positioning his cock against her opening, the buoyancy of the water holding them. Kenan grabbed her hips without releasing her mouth and slowly pushed her down onto his straining cock. The pleasure was maddening, and he grabbed her body to him, completely impaling her.

"Oh God, yes," she breathed as he began to slide her up and down his length. She rose up so that she sat upon him, her wet, gleaming breasts moving, peaked and tantalizing, above the waterline with each thrust. She bent forward so he could suck a nipple into his mouth, her fingernails scratching through his hair to his scalp. His hands were free to explore every bit of her skin, every nook and cranny, even the taboo.

With a breathy moan, she climaxed on top of him, her body squeezing every inch of his length. Grabbing her hips, he took over the rhythm, pushing her up and down his cock. Water sloshed over the side with the rising tempo, and the explosion rocked through him. "Mo Dhia," he growled as he released deep inside her, and her body continued to milk every last bit of him.

He pulled her to him, and she rested her cheek against his rapidly rising chest. They sat entwined in the warm water, bathed in languid satisfaction. He felt her hand move around along his leg, and it broke the surface.

She smiled triumphantly, holding up the rough cake of soap. "I found it."

He met her smile with his own, wrapping his

arms around her to hug her to his wet chest. He breathed in, and the words tumbled through his mind.

*Marry me, Tierney.*

But he didn't say them. If he did, this night of pleasure would probably end, and Kenan wished to wring more moans from her lips.

# CHAPTER NINETEEN

"It is not light that we need, but fire; it is not the gentle shower, but thunder. We need the storm, the whirlwind, and the earthquake."

*Frederick Douglass – American Social Reformer, 1818–1895*

Tierney rode toward battle. She shouldn't be smiling, but it was difficult to keep the memories of her nighttime adventures with Kenan from spilling across her lips. *I am not cold, not an ice queen.* At least not with Kenan Macdonald.

He'd called her beautiful more than once, his words full of authentic admiration. She marveled at the lightness filling her, as if happiness was possible in this life.

She peered ahead where Kenan rode next to Rory MacLeod. Henry and Jacob rode behind them, followed by John and Simon Sutherland. Once the two elderly advisors found out that Doris and Edith were accompanying Kenan's twin sisters to Morag's to help guard them and Morag's crows, they'd ordered their own mounts saddled. They would protect the ladies.

Tierney rode several rows back with Sara, Eliza, and Eleri, letting their chatter wash over her like the rustle of leaves, soothing and musical. Sara had insisted on accompanying them so she could see how

her childhood home, Dunsciath Castle, was progress-
ing as it was rebuilt. She also wore one of the lighter
swords that Gerard had built for the women and
older children.

The smell of mud and fresh grass tangled with
the breeze after the rain the night before. Tierney
preferred the slight sprinkle of mud on her skirts to
the clouds of dust a traveling army could scatter. She
could have worn her trousers, but she'd felt prettier
in the simple blue gown. It was something she hadn't
cared about for a long time.

As Henry approached the cottage where Morag
stood, swathed in flowing green robes, patterned
with stitched rose-hued flowers, she raised her hand
as if pretending to throw a handful of mica dust.
Henry squeaked, maneuvering to the other side of
the path. He made the sign of the cross before his
chest. Morag laughed, pushing her long, gray braid
off her shoulder to settle down her straight back.
She turned to Tierney, beckoning her to break from
the line. She followed Sara and the twins and Doris
and Edith toward Morag. The two elderly ladies
stared curiously at the crows along the rooftops.

"The devil's birds?" Edith asked.

John stopped, dismounting awkwardly with one
hand. "She's always had them."

"Killed her first husband for striking her," Simon
added, dismounting.

Morag wore a tolerant smile. "They are my army
who protects innocents, especially when I am absent."

"They will pluck eyes right out," Simon said. "But
not this one." He pointed to the patch he wore over

his missing eye. "This one was a battle wound."

"Damn Macdonald sliced down it," John said. "Blood pouring down his face, soft eye matter—"

"The details are best kept being regaled around the fire at Samhain," Sara said with a sharp look.

Doris and Edith stared at the men as if envisioning the slaughter, their eyes wider and almost respectful.

Simon patted his chest. "Well, 'twas gruesome, but I survived."

"Eleri and I will take good care of your crows, Aunt Morag," Eliza said, cutting the man off. She gave the regal woman a hug. Morag's strong features softened into a kind grin as she hugged back.

"A number may follow me," Morag said, "and the rest can take care of themselves."

"I will use your stretching contraption while you're away," Eleri said, dismounting. Eleri's spine had been curved at birth, and Morag had shown her exercises to strengthen the muscles to stabilize it and reduce pain. "It helps me with my poses."

"Excellent, my dears," Morag said. She glanced at Kenan and pointed to two large satchels. "These must accompany me."

Kenan shook his head. "We don't pack but one set of clothing when we travel on campaign."

His aunt flapped her hand at the leather bags. "They are my weapons and poisons, things we can use. They will all accompany us, every single one of them." She didn't wait for agreement but turned, the twins following her into the cottage. Doris and Edith glanced at each other and proceeded after them. Simon and John followed.

Would the four elderly people protect Eleri and Eliza, or would the twins end up taking care of the elderly?

"We should have one of your warriors remain with them," Sara said, speaking Tierney's concern aloud. "Rory?"

"I've already asked two remaining MacLeod warriors to arrive here within the hour after we move through," Rory said. "They will send John and Simon back to Dunvegan and camp out here to guard the ladies."

Sara smiled, her eyes full of respect for her husband. Could Tierney ever feel content tied to another man? Not just any man. Could she be content with Kenan? Marry him?

Not that he'd asked her. But if he did, would she?

The idea tightened her chest, and she rubbed her wrist that had been bruised so many times by Wallace's grip.

"Have the men continue," Kenan said. He had taken charge of the moving armies even though most of them were MacLeods and they were rescuing MacNicols. But Rory's respect for him had transferred to his armies. Gabriel had remained behind with Cora to guard Maggie inside Dunvegan with its inaccessible sea moat.

"Lady Tierney," Morag called from the cottage door. "I would see you here for a moment."

Tierney swung her leg over Fleet's backside and dismounted as if she wore trousers, her petticoats catching air. They belled out around her, and she smoothed them. Kenan's gaze followed her, and she passed a grin to him while keeping her face forward.

Morag clasped her hand, pulling her to the side of the cottage. There was such a cacophony of voices inside as the elderly ladies decided where they would all sleep and what to do with their horses if there were only two stalls, that Morag rolled her eyes. "Let them figure all that out," she said. "We have more important matters to discuss." She pulled something out of one of her satchels. "This is for you to wear when we enter Eilean Donan Castle."

Tierney's brows rose, and she glanced around to see if anyone had heard. "We are entering the castle?"

Morag stared hard into her eyes. "They won't expect you and a little old woman sneaking in, will they?"

"Kenan wants me to stay on the ship."

Morag squinted at her. "And what do you want?"

Tierney glanced at the armies walking by, some pulling supplies of food and cannonballs. "I think a lot of blood could be shed if we attack outright."

Morag nodded. "Men like to go in blasting because they have strength. They are raised to respect muscle and power and use the agility they've practiced if things go awry. Women use their cleverness from the start. Men are ready for men to attack but not for women to use their innate power."

Tierney looked down at the oddly shaped lump under the wrapped linen. "This will help me use my power?"

Morag smiled and patted the item that felt soft and heavy like something made of leather. "This will be your armor."

• • •

Kenan inhaled as they broke through the forest line, his gaze riding ahead down the green slope to the village before Dunscaith Castle, or what used to be Dunscaith Castle. Right now, it was only a shell of what it once was.

"Your home?" Tierney asked. Since that morning when they left the overnight camp, she'd ridden up-front with him, leaving Rory to ride next to Sara behind them.

"Aye." He cleared his throat, trying to rid his voice of any trace of anguish. "'Tis not currently at its proudest." Dunscaith was the most vulnerable it had ever been. Burned from within, all four stories rendered to ash. Cyrus's father, Chief Hamish Mackinnon, could swarm in, attacking his people and taking everything.

"Show me," she said and pressed her horse forward.

For a heartbeat, Kenan watched her fly away from him, her blond hair slipping from the leather thong with which she held it back. The wind lifted the silky mass like a flag, pointing back at him, drawing his loyalty.

"Siuthad!" Kenan called and leaned forward. Freya shot off after Tierney.

They slowed as they reached the path that wound through the thatched-roofed cottages making up the broad village. Flowers accented stoops and window-sills, and the thatching was clean and full. Whatever Dunscaith Castle had suffered, his village was sturdy and whole. Right now, anyway. If the Mackinnons rode through with torches, those roofs would burn.

People came out of their homes, the women waving, and the children running alongside. A few picked flowers before their scolding mothers shooed them away. They ran forward to hand them to Kenan. He leaned down to take them.

"Chief Macdonald has returned!"

"Hail Kenan Macdonald!"

"Our chief is here!"

"All is well!"

Various proclamations rose from both sides as they walked their horses through the streets leading toward the open gates of the hulking castle. Kenan sat straight and proud, the bunch of flowers before him, even though guilt and concern made his shoulders want to round forward. If he hadn't met Tierney, saved her, been tricked by her, and then loved her body so well it felt imprinted on his own...

If he hadn't done all that, he'd be betrothed to Grace Mackinnon with the force of the Mackinnon Clan ready to help rebuild Dunscaith and protect his people until Kenan had his defenses back in place.

Did his people think Tierney was Grace? Word would soon reach them that she was no savior, bringing over a thousand warriors to protect them. Instead, she represented their vulnerability, the very symbol that heralded an attack by those thousand Mackinnon warriors.

Kenan continued forward, his face turned to the blackened stone walls of Dunscaith Castle. He glanced back at Tierney, who also held picked flowers before her. Her face was stoney, as if she'd realized what her plan to save Clan MacNicol meant to these people.

Their horses clip-clopped into the bailey. The tang of damp ash carried on the breeze, but there was also the smell of freshly hewed planks. The pounding of a mallet against nails came from somewhere deep inside. Kenan knew he must focus on the revival and not the death of the castle, but 'twas difficult not to remember the flames and destruction.

He dismounted and walked around to Tierney who still sat upon Fleet. "Wish to see the rebirth of a castle?" he asked.

She looked down at him, and he saw a glimmer in her eyes as if tears sat there. "Your people need you," she said. They were words he had spoken to her, but it had taken the sight and smell of the devastation for her to truly understand.

Kenan reached for her waist, his hands wrapping around where they had last night, and lifted her down. "There is need across the whole isle, Tierney, but if we come together to unify, our isle will be strong against any outside foes."

Her gaze remained on the charred walls. "Like the Matheson Clan?"

"Like England."

She looked at him. "How can we stand against England when we stand against other clans in our own country?"

"Exactly." This was the terrible problem Kenan had discussed with Rory, Cyrus, and Asher while they survived in Carlisle Dungeon all those months. The clans of Scotland were often separated by the mountainous terrain and sea, making it difficult for the country to unify. With the young Queen Mary Stewart being raised in France, and James Hamilton holding tooth and nail onto the regency with Mary's mother, Marie de Guise, attempting to take over, there was little effort in trying to unite the Scottish people. A fractured country would always crumble under the solidified heel of its enemy.

Kenan took her hand. "We make alliances and support each other."

"Against other Scottish clans."

"Until they agree to unite."

She scoffed, rubbing her nose as if it itched from a forbidden tear. "It seems impossible."

"I take one step at a time, one clan at a time."

"Like marrying Grace Mackinnon." Tierney's words came as a statement, not a question. He heard an underlying of hurt there.

Kenan stepped before her, catching her face with one palm so that she met his eyes. "I am not marrying Grace."

"The Mackinnons would support Clan Macdonald then," she said, "instead of warring against you."

"I doubt she'd consider me now."

"She would unless she's a fool."

"I will not marry someone I do not wish to share a bed with."

Tierney closed her eyes for a moment and then looked pointedly at him. "Women have been made to share beds with unwanted partners for thousands of years."

He leaned closer to her. "Which has been wrong for thousands of years. It hasn't ended war. It hasn't even united countries when the husband and wife are not suited. Grace and I are not suited."

"How do you know that?"

Frustration squeezed him, and he dropped his hand but didn't move back. "My cock doesn't even twitch when I think of her."

Tierney narrowed her eyes. "Haven't you been told not to listen to your cock when making important decisions?"

Of course, he'd been told that, and he never had before. "How about my heart, then?" he asked, realizing how foolish he sounded but going with the truth anyway. "Or my head. I can't get ye from my mind, Tierney. And my head and heart, and possibly my cock, too, are all in agreement that I will only bring war on my people if I wed Grace and we end up despising each other."

"You may grow to love her."

"Impossible."

Her voice rose, filling the bailey. "Very possible with her glossy brown curls and curvy body and one thousand warriors."

She also brought thirty thousand crowns and twenty head of Highland cattle. But that didn't matter. "For some reason, I prefer a blond-haired fallen angel and her twenty warriors, including two old women with short swords." His words met her own in volume.

Her face tensed with pained anger, and she blinked as if tears threatened. "Then you are a fool, Kenan Macdonald."

Someone behind him cleared his throat, and Kenan turned to see Tomas, his second in command, standing just inside the castle. "The men would like to show ye the progress on the Great Hall. After ye're...uh...done." He scratched his head.

"We are done," Kenan said and traipsed forward. The weight of anger and obligation lay heavily on Kenan's shoulders. Tierney, willing and eager to follow all his suggestions in bed, wouldn't even consider his plans involving her when they were fully dressed—at least not plans involving her being tied to him legally.

When he reached the archway, he looked back to beckon her to follow for the tour, but she'd turned away. She jammed her foot in Fleet's stirrup and rose into her saddle with graceful ease and guided her horse out of the bailey.

He wanted to call after her, but he'd already been called a fool loud enough for everyone to hear. He didn't need to prove the label true.

# CHAPTER TWENTY

"Look for me in the whirlwind or the storm."

*Marcus Garvey – Jamaican publisher, 1887–1940*

*We are done.*

Kenan's words repeated in Tierney's mind, making her chest clench.

*We are done.*

She walked amongst the small fires that her men and the MacLeod warriors had set out on the moor above Dunscaith Village. Darkness had fallen, and she had no idea where she should lay her head to rest that night. With her men on the hill? With Sara and Rory who had been given a cottage with Morag in the village?

She continued to walk aimlessly. "We are done," she whispered. He'd been talking about their discussion in the bailey, but the words had felt like the final note in a tragic ballad.

She spotted Jacob with some of the MacLeod warriors. Lord help her, she couldn't go over there. Jacob would jump on the opportunity to find her a place to sleep near him. Perhaps she should go to Morag and Sara.

A rider breached the hill and slowed. Foolish anticipation caught Tierney's breath, but then she saw it was a Macdonald warrior, the one she'd seen in the bailey right before she left. The one who'd heard their exchange. *We are done.*

The rider stopped before Jacob and the men with him.

"Tier is out here?" she heard Jacob say, his voice loud enough to carry on the breeze.

"Daingead," she whispered and traipsed away from the fires, hoping the shadows would hide her from him.

"Lady Tierney," the man from earlier called, and she stopped, unwilling to look like she hid, even if that was what she'd been trying to do.

The man was Tomas, Kenan's second in command. He had a kind smile set in a hard face. He dismounted when he saw her and guided his horse toward her. He bowed. "Lady Tierney."

"Yes?"

"Chief Macdonald wants to know," he lowered his voice so it wouldn't carry, "do ye feel cold when I say his name?"

"Pardon?"

Tomas straightened. He didn't seem to know what to do with his hands. They moved against his legs until he finally crossed his arms. "Kenan. Kenan Macdonald."

She stared at him. "Yes?"

"When I say his name and it makes ye think of him…does it make ye feel cold inside? That's what he said to ask."

*Ye will sleep with me, Tierney, until ye only feel cold when ye think of me.* Kenan's words from Dunvegan's garden teased her. Would she ever feel cold when she thought of the broad, courageous Highland chief? She hadn't felt cold or indifferent, even when she was furious or frustrated, and never afraid. Even with his final words today, her face had felt hot.

And now the man was willing to make himself look like a fool to his friend, to his second in command. If she lied and said she felt like she was turning to ice just talking about him, Tomas could mock him and his prowess for years.

"Is he so lazy that he does not come to ask himself?"

Tomas's mouth quirked. "I told him I should come so it would be easier for ye to choose honestly."

Her mouth relaxed. "And what are the choices?"

"If ye are not cold to him, he bids me fetch ye. And if ye are cold to him, he still bids me to fetch ye so ye can sleep comfortably and warm this eve."

She couldn't help the small chuckle that she masked as a sniff. "There is little choice but to ride away with you. Will you take me to the same bed either way?"

"Aye, but I will drag Kenan out of the room if you wish it. His orders."

He'd ordered his friend to remove him from her as if Kenan wouldn't have the strength to do it on his own. *Holy Joan.* The man could be a chivalric poet.

"Since I have not been given a pallet yet," she said, indicating the men beginning to sprawl out under the stars, "I will come with you, Master Tomas."

"And yer decision on whether I must draw my chief from yer side?"

"I will decide when I see him."

He mounted and offered her a hand up. She

climbed on behind him in the long saddle.

"Well, I hope ye choose not to make me carry him away, because I'd probably need six more warriors with me to do so."

"Six?" She laughed. Kenan's friend was loyal and trying to make him seem like a giant of iron and brawn.

"Give or take," Tomas said, and they broke into a canter back down the sloping meadow to the village of Dunscaith.

The houses glowed with hearth light while the formidable shape of the castle remained dark. Tomas slowed but didn't stop along the paths lit by light spilling from glass windows not yet shuttered. Tierney held loosely to him but used her strong thighs to keep her from having to hug him. Tomas rode directly for the dark castle, slowing to clop into the bailey where she'd left Kenan earlier.

She spotted him by the doorway, a torch in his hand. He didn't advance.

"Yer decision, fair lady?" Tomas asked as he brought his leg over the horse's head so he could jump down and offer her his hand.

"Is there a comfortable and warm bed somewhere in that rubble?"

"Aye," Kenan called but didn't come any closer.

Without a word, she walked away from Tomas toward Kenan. She was curious, and her heart seemed to flutter around in her like a lass being asked to dance at her first after-dark festival.

"The lady has not yet made a choice," Tomas called from his mount.

"I will once inside," Tierney said without turning

back. She kept her gaze on Kenan and his flame. "Don't worry, Tomas, you can go. I can make Kenan leave if that is my choice. I don't need six more warriors to see it done."

Kenan's brow rose. "Six?" He glanced out at Tomas over her head.

A moment later, the *clip-clop* of the horse departing floated to Tierney. She stopped close enough to feel the warmth coming off the torch. "Has enough work been done on the castle for people to sleep within it?" she asked.

"Aye." Kenan offered her his arm, and she slid her hand along the muscles there before resting it on his forearm. Heat bloomed through her, but she kept her formal distance. They clipped along a newly laid floor toward an arched alcove that was blackened by soot.

"Is this what I will be cleaning?" she asked. "As part of my promise to make amends?"

"Aye," he said. "'Tis dirty work. Ye might need a bath afterward."

His words sizzled through her with the memories of the other night at Dunvegan. They had dripped from the bathing tub to the bed, wrapping first in drying sheets and then throwing off all the bedding with their love play. Luckily, the bed hadn't collapsed.

"Do you have one of those large bathing tubs here at Dunscaith?" she asked as they climbed the turning steps. Most of these stones had been cleaned and awaited fresh plaster.

"I've commissioned the building of one," he said with the same serious tone one would use to talk about commissioning a new war ship.

A lightness filled her at this quiet banter. Even in the early days of courting, she'd never had that with Wallace. Nothing about Kenan reminded her of her monstrous husband.

They reached the first floor, and Kenan brandished the torch before them as they walked down to an open doorway. "It will be a new library, eventually. For now, 'tis the chief's room, which I give over to ye, Tierney."

There was a large bed made up with pillows and quilts pushed up against a wall. A chest sat at the end of it, and a writing desk was placed diagonal to the hearth where a small fire crackled. Opposite was a privacy screen. But what caught Tierney's attention were the bookshelves built into the walls on three sides, broken only by a pair of large windows. All of the shelves were empty. She looked at him, his gaze on her. "All your books burned in the fire?"

"Aye." His voice held a note of sorrow. "A cauldron of burning pitch was poured out in the keep, and the fire spread both upward and downward through the entire structure. It spared nothing." His smile was sad. "But Dunscaith will rise from the ashes."

*Unless it is attacked again.*

His smile faded as if he read her mind. "Tierney, ye can sleep here, with or without me."

"I...I wasn't certain," she said. "Today, in the bailey...when you said we were done."

He stepped closer, his brows pinched over searching eyes. "That was to say we were done arguing, but Tierney..." He let out a breath. "We will never be done."

"Even if you marry someone else." Her words were soft.

He slid the torch into a sconce and walked over to her. "If ye feel heat or warmth or kindness toward me, we will never be done."

This man, full of power and muscle, was leaving this up to her. 'Twas a gift more impressive than the bath or saving her people. He was offering her freedom to decide. At least how she slept.

Without a word, she stepped into his arms and reached up to pull his face to hers. The kiss was slow, and tingles spread throughout her body. He was giving her the gift of freedom if even just for the night. In return, she would give him the gift of pure pleasure.

. . .

Kenan watched from the porch of the customs house as men boarded his galleons, the *Sweet Elspet* and the *Tempest*, in an orderly fashion. His gaze scanned down the extensive docks that had been built on the opposite side of Sleat Peninsula during his grandfather's time. Thirty smaller Birlinn ships were tied along the extensive jetty, men being assigned to each.

The ships would be overcrowded with Macdonald, MacNicol, and MacLeod warriors, but men would be needed if they were forced to raid Clan Matheson at Eilean Donan Castle. A contingent remained behind at Dunscaith in case the Mackinnon chief coordinated an attack before their return. Kenan didn't even want to consider that disaster.

A group of villagers had already evacuated toward Dunvegan, although they'd have to skirt Mackinnon territory to get there. Both war and peace were complicated. Was the first worth the second? Both required risk and courage.

"Risk and courage," Kenan murmured.

"Risk and courage?" Rory asked, coming up to stand next to him. "Tierney has plenty of both already. Courage or madness to have locked ye up."

Kenan snapped his gaze to Rory. "Pardon?" Rory knew about the abduction?

Rory grinned back. "Gabriel is sweet on Eliza and told her how Tierney tricked ye, drugged ye, and forced ye into coming to Scorrybreac. Eliza then told Sara." Rory's smile flattened some. "So...she chained ye. That must have brought out yer not-so-kind side."

"'Tis a testament to her courage."

Rory nodded, growing more serious. "Or her desperation."

The sound of several galloping horses pulled Kenan's attention to the wide path that they had traversed from Dunscaith early that morning. "Daingead," he said, inhaling briskly. "'Tis Cyrus and his men."

Both Rory and Kenan looked toward the forest line. "No troops," Rory said.

"Not here, but they could be at Dunscaith," Kenan said. He was already descending the wooden steps and jogged to meet Cyrus.

"Ye're sailing to the Mathesons at Eilean

Donan?" Cyrus asked from his horse, his voice raised and tinged with the same anger he'd displayed since finding Kenan in bed with Tierney. He must have journeyed first to Dunscaith before being directed across land to the docks on the peninsula's eastern side.

"Are yer father's troops at Dunscaith?" Kenan asked.

"Nay," Cyrus said, and relief funneled through Kenan's body. "'Tis just me and my men." He indicated the six other men who remained mounted behind Cyrus. "Attacking the Matheson Clan? I thought we were all about uniting the clans of Scotland." He held up his hand to show the scars.

Kenan ignored the tone that called him a hypocrite. "Chief MacNicol, his wife, and twenty MacNicol warriors are being held captive, along with their carrack ship," Kenan said. "Chief Murdoc Matheson is threatening to kill them unless Tierney marries his brother, Ranulf, and the clan gives up Scorrybreac to them."

Rory stood next to Kenan. "Ranulf is determined to get a foothold on Skye."

"Why are ye here," Kenan asked, "and not yer father?"

"Father fell from his horse," Cyrus said. "Broke his leg and bruised his organs. The physician won't let him up from his bed, not that he's in any condition."

"And ye've come to tell us?" Rory asked. He kept the same irritated tone that Cyrus had, showing without words that he was supporting Kenan in this madness.

Cyrus looped his horse's reins over the saddle and dismounted, walking over to stand with the two chiefs. "Father asked me to swear to wage war against Clan Macdonald of Sleat if he cannot."

"For the sake of all that's holy!" The three men turned to see Sara, Tierney, and Morag striding toward them. Sara had spoken, her face red. She stopped before Cyrus, her hands on her hips. "Cyrus Mackinnon, we have more important issues than your sister being unhappy because my brother chose not to wed her. There are people's lives at stake."

"And my father," Cyrus said without missing a beat, "is obsessed with ending Macdonald lives."

"You can tell him no, you won't war against Kenan," Tierney said, meeting Cyrus's gaze.

Cyrus wouldn't look at either woman. "My father has always wanted to wage war against Dunscaith, and he's using Grace as an excuse."

Morag pushed her way through Rory and Kenan to stand right before Cyrus, forcing him to look at her. "Your father was a good friend of my husband's. In fact, Hamish Mackinnon came to see me right after Bruce died. He met my friends." She pointed upward where a circle of her black crows swooped and squawked, making Cyrus's men look nervous. They ducked when one flew low toward them. One Mackinnon passed the sign of the cross before himself.

Morag's layered robes fluttered around her with the wind, her white hair tied in her usual long braid. "Remind Hamish Mackinnon that Morag Gunn is a Macdonald of Sleat even if I live closer to Dunvegan. That there are more powerful weapons than men with swords. There are weapons that can damn the soul."

Kenan's aunt had always reveled in scaring people with her witch-like ways. One day her actions and threats would get her into trouble. But right now, they were making Cyrus's large men grow pale.

"I will remind my father," Cyrus said with a bow of his head. Whether he believed Morag or not, he knew how to show respect to an elderly woman.

"Good," Morag said and pivoted around. "Let us board."

Tierney met Kenan's gaze for a moment. Her lips looked so soft, and the afternoon sun shone in her hair. They hadn't talked last night, but they had come together with slow, languid strokes, stretching the pleasure out. He'd held her the rest of the night, and she'd let him.

"I will sail with those planning the excursion," she said.

"The *Sweet Elspet*," Kenan said, pointing to the ship with black sails. The *Tempest* had white sails.

Morag looped her arm through hers, and the three women strode down the slope toward the docks. Kenan tried not to watch the sway of Tierney's hips. She wore trousers that cupped her sweet, rounded arse that had cushioned him as he thrust into her from behind last night.

Rory's elbow poked into him, and Kenan turned away only to catch the Mackinnon warriors staring after her.

"Trousers are easier to ride and sail in," Kenan said, his voice gruff enough to make the men look back to him.

"I need to get Sara a pair," Rory murmured.

Kenan turned back to Cyrus. "Again, I am sorry I offended ye and yer sister, Cy, but I broke no oath. The only oath weighing upon me is to our brotherhood and our quest to unite Skye. Help us defend our isle."

Rory raised his palm to show his set of four scars. "Ye've made the same oath, Cy."

"Bloody hell, I know," Cyrus said and ran his scarred hand through his hair to cup the back of his head. His lips were pinched as he studied the sky as if looking for answers. Finally, he turned to his men. "William, ride to Dun Haakon to tell my father that Clan Matheson is an enemy of Skye and that I am sailing to prevent them from invading our isle. And send Morag Gunn's greetings."

"Aye," William said, his stoic face revealing nothing. He turned his horse and rode away.

"The rest of ye can come along to defend our isle," Cyrus said. He looked back at Kenan. "Hopefully, my father will be too ill to act while I'm gone."

• • •

Tierney stood next to Morag in the cramped captain's cabin on the *Sweet Elspet* while it maneuvered up Kyle Rhea waterway. They were nearing Loch Alsh, and the sun was dropping. Her heart thumped too high in her chest, feeling close to her throat. Partly because she hated being confined in a small room with only one exit, but mostly guilt overrode her familiar fear of being trapped.

All these men were going to war, because she wouldn't marry Ranulf.

*They don't want Clan Matheson on Skye, either. They're going to war for Skye.*

The timing was terrible with Dunscaith being left burned and without its full army. And she'd brought war to Kenan's doorstep by taking him away from Grace Mackinnon.

*I saved him from Grace Mackinnon. I'm not selfish, and I haven't lied. He knows I won't marry again.* The mental tirade back and forth within her head drowned out the sounds around her.

"And ye will stay on the ship so there's no chance they'll capture ye," Kenan's voice cut into Tierney's thoughts.

Morag stepped up next to Tierney. "After the woman has provided you with a map of the castle and grounds?" She pointed to the drawing that Tierney had unrolled after they'd gathered, one that she'd made months ago after her father demanded she wed Ranulf Matheson.

At the time, she was afraid she'd be carried off to live at Eilean Donan with the Mathesons. So when the bard, Reid Lewis, had come to visit Scorrybreac after leaving Eilean Donan, Tierney had questioned him tirelessly on the land there. If she were forced to go there, she'd know as much as she could in order to create an escape plan.

Tierney's chin rose as she felt a battle brewing. "I know the layout of the castle and the grounds, and those imprisoned are my people."

Kenan's sharp gaze rested on Tierney. "Ye will stay on the ship. 'Tis too dangerous for ye—"

"You plan to march in and spill blood," she interrupted him. "No diplomacy?"

Henry stood beside Kenan over the map that showed the position of Eilean Donan Castle on the bank where Loch Alsh and Loc Duich met. "We could use Lady Tierney to enter the castle without beginning the night with bloodshed." For once, Tierney agreed with her father's old advisor.

"Nay," Kenan said, keeping her gaze. "Tierney will remain on the *Sweet Elspet*, and nay, we will not start with bloodshed. We will walk in to speak with Chief Murdoc and request the prisoners be released. We must try diplomacy first. Otherwise, we go against our goal of uniting Scotland." He glanced at Cyrus Mackinnon and Rory MacLeod. "The presence of three chiefs from three clans on Skye will give power to our request."

"I'm not a chief," Cyrus said.

"Ye will be," Rory said. "And Murdoc doesn't know how yer da fairs."

"That's right," Tierney said, her words succinct. "Murdoc will see chiefs from three powerful clans on Skye walk into Eilean Donan. How much easier it will be for him to take over our isle after he seizes and kills you three."

"I have no intention of being killed nor seized," Rory said.

Tierney opened her mouth to retort, but Sara spoke first. "And you can fend off a hall full of Matheson warriors all on your own?"

"Kenan and Cy will be with me and our most able warriors."

Sara huffed. "Lovely. That would be about six of

you against…fifty of them." She looked at Tierney. "Fifty men could probably fit in the Great Hall at Eilean Donan, don't you think?"

"'Tis rather large," Tierney said. "Perhaps more, but I would think twenty against six would be sufficient enough to kill them and hand three quarters of Skye over to Clan Matheson."

Both Tierney and Sara crossed arms over their chests and turned to Kenan and Rory, waiting for their response to the obvious. Silence sat in the packed cabin. Outside, the taut lines creaked with the snapping sails as the ship cut through water and wind.

Tierney narrowed her eyes to meet Kenan's hard gaze. Her words came out slow, calm, and hard. "Murdoc and Ranulf will not negotiate. Someone must sneak in and release my parents."

Kenan didn't back down. "If Murdoc agrees that the betrothal is null and releases yer parents, the Mathesons will not retaliate by coming to our isle to burn Scorrybreac."

"The Mathesons will not agree—"

"Ye've only met Ranulf," Kenan interrupted Tierney. "Murdoc has seemed more level-headed in the past."

Henry cleared his throat. "So…perhaps sending Lady Tierney in first would—"

"Lady Tierney is not going within a hundred feet of Ranulf Matheson," Kenan said without breaking their stare. "We will ferry more men to the shore. And Murdoc's lookouts will report that they see dozens of ships in the loch."

Kenan finally looked down to move little carved

Birlinn ships up to the harbor on one of the maps. "They will all light beacons to announce their presence when our large bell on the stern is rung." He raised his gaze back to Tierney. "Ye can be responsible for ringing the bell."

*Bloody hell.* He was treating her like a wee lass being given an easy job to feel included. Anger infused her cheeks with prickly heat. "I do not plan to remain on board the ship." Tierney met his gaze without blinking.

"Ye will."

"I will not," she answered. She wouldn't let their total agreement in the pleasure arena soften her resolve to save as many people as she could.

Kenan rested his hands on the edge of the table. "I will lock ye in a cabin."

"I have loyal friends who will liberate me."

Kenan's nostrils flared like when she'd kept him chained in the cottage. "I will shackle ye to the deck of the ship," he said, leaning forward.

She learned forward, too. "I will burn this ship down around me."

Faces of those in the room volleyed between them with each verbal strike. Each one was fantastical, but the emotions behind the threats were very real.

"I will tie ye in a Birlinn and sail ye back to Dunscaith."

"I will jump overboard and swim back to Eilean Donan."

Morag's laugh sounded like a cackle. "The lass won't be contained, nephew. Leave her with me. My crows and I will keep her safe."

"Ye would both be safer staying on the ship," Rory added to the press. "Ringing the bell to signal the other ships is important."

Kenan might be her nephew, but Rory was only her niece's husband. Morag narrowed her eyes at him. "Tierney isn't a crow, enthralled by the shine of a polished bell. She's a goddess of the sky, Aranrhod, or an angel, neither of which will sit on a ship to ring a bell."

Sara, who had been standing to the side behind Tierney, leaned to whisper in her ear. "I'm a phoenix, so sky goddess seems appropriate."

Sara straightened and raised her hand high in the air. "I will take the important bell ringer position." She sounded completely serious, making Tierney want to laugh. "I'm quite qualified to yank on rope."

Cyrus made a popping sound with his lips, and Tierney saw him hide a smile behind a pitying look toward Rory and Kenan. "When they support one another, ladies are unstoppable," Cyrus said.

Kenan crossed his arms over his chest and looked at Tierney. "What would ye do on shore?"

"I can go inside with—"

"Nay, not inside Eilean Donan," Kenan said.

*Stubborn boar!*

Morag wrapped her arm through Tierney's. "Eilean Donan doesn't have a large enough dungeon for the crew. They must be kept somewhere in the village. Tierney and I can find them, release them."

No one said anything, and Morag continued. "Truly, if you want to keep Tierney safe, don't leave her on a ship that will probably receive pistol fire."

Kenan ran a hand over his head as if it pained him and released an exhale.

"Lady Sara can remain in this cabin," Rory said. "Someone else can ring the damn bell."

"Holy Saint Margaret," Sara said, her eyes rolling heavenward. "I've already been demoted."

Rory pulled Sara into his arms. "I don't want to lose my wife of a fortnight. Give me a few more decades to tire of ye, lass."

Her brow rose. "Only a few?"

"Ten decades or so," Rory said and kissed her forehead.

"A century, then?"

"At least," Rory answered Sara with a serious tone. Their loving banter just made Tierney's chest tighten with envy over the couple's obvious love and respect for one another.

Tomas entered the cabin, adding to the cramped feel of the small room. "Master Sawyer says we've reached the mouth of Loch Duich."

"Order all sails dropped," Kenan said, confidence in his tone. "Send out two dressed as fishermen in a dinghy to find where the prisoners are being held. Meanwhile, have a meal served on all ships. Full bellies win conflicts."

"I'll go myself," Tomas said and pivoted, leaving the room.

*God speed, Tomas.* Tierney prayed the man who'd been so kind in bringing Kenan's message last night would remain whole and well. *If I went in his place, they could all go home to defend Dunscaith.*

Morag took Tierney's arm, tearing her from her remorseful thoughts. "We will rest and eat and prepare as well." Before Kenan could ask again what they were preparing for, Morag hurried her out of the room.

Tierney took a full inhale of the briny air, thankful for the breeze that refreshed her. Sara followed, and the three women made their way to the stern of the ship, avoiding seamen who coiled ropes as they collapsed the sails. Tierney leaned against the rail, her gaze on the sun setting off to the west. A distant castle was seen jutting out from Skye at the western end of Loch Alsh as the ship floated east.

"That's Dun Haakon Castle," Sara said, "the seat of the Mackinnon Clan on Skye. Let us pray that Chief Mackinnon doesn't mobilize his forces before we return or at all."

With her fear of small spaces receded, Tierney felt the guilt once again flood through her body. She turned to Sara and Morag. "By my soul, I beg your pardons for pulling your clans into fighting." She dropped her gaze to the rail under her curled fingers. "I do feel that the Matheson Clan would come and war on Skye if they take Scorrybreac, but my actions from the start have been selfish."

Morag sniffed. "Selfish? A woman protecting herself and her child, protecting her young brother, going to great lengths to obtain an army when hers was defeated by disease and war. I see nothing selfish in that."

"But in my heart…" Tierney shook her head as she gazed out at the flaming red ball of sun sliding below the horizon. "I won't have a man rule me again, not to save my people, not to save my parents."

"You're protecting Maggie," Sara said. Her hand rested on Tierney's on the rail, squeezing it.

Tierney met Sara's eyes. "Even if I didn't have Maggie."

Morag's weathered hand came down on Tierney's other one. It was cool but strong. "A woman should never have to choose to give up her body, mind, and soul to be tortured in a union of abuse. And a union with Ranulf Matheson would be just that." Tierney met Morag's stare. "That is not selfish," the wise woman said. "That is fierce and brave and strong."

"But if I walk into Eilean Donan and agree to wed, my parents and men will be released, and all these good warriors can sail home unbloodied."

Morag's serene face tightened with a sharp, stubborn look. "If you think that Ranulf and his brother will lead a peaceful life after taking you and Scorrybreac, you're as naive as England's King Henry thinking Scotsmen will honor their promises to support him taking over their country. You will sacrifice yourself for nothing."

Tierney nodded, and Morag's hand relaxed on top of hers. She inhaled fully, bringing the misty air deep inside herself. "Then what's our plan?"

# CHAPTER TWENTY-ONE

"When you see something that is not right, not fair,
not just…do something about it. Say something.
Have the courage. Have the backbone. Get in the
way. Walk with the wind."

*John Lewis – American Politician, 1940–2020*

"He will not negotiate."

Tierney repeated her view from her spot on the bottom of the Birlinn ship as the men rowed alongside the dock at the shore of Loch Duich. "He will willingly release my parents if I surrender."

Kenan glanced down where she and Morag lay flat, staring up at the naked mast, its sail lowered as they rowed. "We will try diplomacy first while ye release the crew. I don't want ye anywhere near Ranulf."

"Maybe we should surrender Henry Macqueen in exchange," Rory said, making the man glare at him.

"I have no value to the Mathesons," Henry said.

"And yet ye demanded to come with us," Cyrus said, his tone low.

Henry drew himself up. "I can hold a sword, and I represent the current chief Gabriel as his regent."

"Bloody hell, Henry, if anyone is Gabriel's regent, 'tis I," Tierney said and nearly sat up, but Morag stilled her with a hand on her arm. They were arriving covertly so Murdoc's warriors at the dock couldn't report that two women were part of Kenan's party.

"Diplomacy first," Kenan said and crouched down next to Tierney as if being closer to her would make her understand. "We will explain how they will enrage three powerful clans making up most of Skye."

"Say four," Cyrus said with a gusty exhale. "I'll convince Father somehow to support ye."

Rory clamped his hand down on Cyrus's shoulder in a silent show of gratitude.

"And what if they don't let you leave Eilean Donan?" Tierney asked from her hidden position.

"Diplomacy and then battle," Kenan said, straightening as they neared shore. If they went in with swords drawn, there was no hope of change to the hostility between the clans of Scotland.

The Birlinn ship bumped along the dock, and Kenan stepped out. Rory, Cyrus, Henry, and three other warriors followed him: Tomas, Jok, and one of Cyrus's men, Bartholomew. The deep-water dock was long with room for several galleons.

"That's the *Rosemary*," Henry said, shaking his head. "Chief Douglas's ship. And here we mourned as if the sea had taken it and all aboard."

Kenan looked at the top of the Birlinn's mast where four crows blended into the shadows, catching a ride instead of flying. No one else seemed to notice them. He looked down at his aunt, and she smiled softly but didn't say a word. They were going to release the men from the cave that Tomas had discovered. The task had to be big enough to keep

Tierney occupied but far away from Ranulf's grasp.

"If they have the ship, they have the people," Rory said.

"And the desire to take Scorrybreac and move onto Skye," Cyrus said. The proof of the jeopardy seemed to help Cyrus see the truth in Tierney's concern.

"State yer business," a man with a sword strapped to his hip said, striding toward them. Three burly Highlanders followed him.

"I am Chief Kenan Macdonald of Sleat."

"I am Chief Rory MacLeod, the Lion of Skye."

"I am Cyrus Mackinnon...Chief Cyrus Mackinnon of Dun Haakon."

"And I am Henry Macqueen, regent for the MacNicol chief."

Kenan stepped forward. "And we are here to discuss Scorrybreac and the threats made by Chief Murdoc of Clan Matheson."

A moment sat before them, and Kenan kept the man's stare. Finally, the guard nodded and turned. "Follow me. Geoff, run ahead and inform the chief that he has visitors."

Kenan kept his gaze from moving back to the Birlinn ship two Macdonalds guarded. After they boarded the ferries to enter the seawater-surrounded castle, Morag and Tierney would float out of it like wraiths in the night. His aunt swore she would keep Tierney safe as they worked their way to the men housed in a garrison cell apart from the castle. Tomas had brought information back about the guarded cave. Jacob, the second scout, remained in the village, prepared to jump in to fight if Kenan and his men weren't allowed to disembark at the dock.

They strode briskly through the dark street leading to the ferries that took people over to the isle where Eilean Donan Castle sat. From the shadows between two cottages, Jacob Tanner nodded to him before he turned and ran off into the darkness to meet up with Tierney and Morag.

*Keep her safe.* Kenan had made the man swear this. The infatuated youth would keep Tierney safer than he would keep himself.

Kenan turned to focus on the hulking shadow of Eilean Donan Castle. Just like Dunvegan, the castle sat on a little island off the coast, so a natural seawater mote surrounded it. The only way in or out was over water. Unlike Dunvegan, though, the island was large, allowing for a kitchen garden, an orchard, and a treeless meadow before the bailey where invaders could be shot. The keep was three stories tall, its walls fourteen feet thick in some places. A poorly kept curtain wall surrounded part of it but had turned to rubble in other places.

'Twas a MacKenzie holding, but the old Matheson chief had sworn to protect it. His son, Murdoc, had apparently taken up the post while enjoying living in the fortress as if he were the rightful owner.

As they walked through the quiet village, several men came out from cottages to follow behind Kenan's group. Their party of seven was now outnumbered. Would Murdoc Matheson attempt to take all three chiefs and a regent hostage because of his arrogant belief that their clans would not act without their leaders?

Kenan's hand curled around the hilt of his sheathed sword. So far, they hadn't been made to surrender them. They stopped at the set of three ferries, each with a Matheson poleman tasked to take visitors across.

"The ferry only fits the three chiefs and MacNicol regent," the leader of the guards said, "along with us."

"Then ye will take the next ferry," Cyrus said. As if his word was final, the warriors from the Isle of Skye surged onto the ferry.

The poleman stepped off, letting two Matheson guards onto the ferry in his place. "If I wasn't under orders…" one of the guards said, narrowing his eyes at Cyrus. He left his threat hanging.

Cyrus shrugged, tilting his head in question. "Ye'd…introduce me to yer sister?"

Kenan stepped in front of Cyrus before the guard could shove him into the sea. "He's a bit peevish over having to leave our bonny isle," Kenan said. "Last time he was off it, King Henry threw him in a hole for eighteen months."

The guard snorted. "One of those willing to sign the English king's agreement to turn yer back on yer own country."

Cyrus looked around Kenan's shoulder, and Kenan could hear the sneer in his voice. "Nay, I slit a guard's throat with a sharp rock and left a pile of shite for King Henry after wiping my arse with his agreement."

Kenan resisted rolling his eyes, which would take all the venom out of Cyrus's words, and he wouldn't do that to his friend even if he was lying. There had been killing, but none of them had enough food in them after eighteen months in Carlisle Dungeon to leave a decent shite for King Henry.

The other Matheson guard stifled a chuckle. Then only the lapping of the water made noise as they were poled across the watery gap by one of the guards. Torches flickered at the landing, and they disembarked. Kenan, and the others, strode across trampled grasses toward the bailey before the keep.

Three men walked out from the bailey with guards flanking them with lit torches. As the torchlight shone across them, Kenan inhaled, pushing past the boulder now in his chest. He paused, letting them finish walking toward him across the small island. He knew Ranulf and assumed the balding man next to him was Murdoc, but it was the third man that made Kenan release his breath in a huff.

"A declaration of war *and* a family reunion." Gilbert Macdonald grinned at Kenan. "Welcome to Eilean Donan, Brother."

• • •

Tierney kept the hood of her cloak pulled low over her forehead as she walked along the shoreline south of the castle. Two guards stood watch at a darkened set of bars across the mouth of a cave. Tomas had discovered from one drunken villager that it was the dungeon for the MacNicol crew.

Tierney's boots crunched on the broken shells and gravel as she walked up the path by herself. "Pardon me," she said and lowered her hood, exposing her blond hair. "I am looking for Ranulf

Matheson. He sent for me."

The two guards, burly men, glanced at each other and then back to her.

"Well, now, little lass, we can take ye up to the castle," one said. He raked his stout fingers through his unkempt beard, making it stick out unevenly.

"But ye have to give us each a kiss," the second guard said, rubbing his lips that seemed to have bits of food still attached.

She smiled sweetly. "I would rather be strapped naked to an ant mound."

They frowned almost in unison. "I can help with the stripping ye naked part," the bearded guard said.

"A little lass like ye wandering all alone in the night," the second man said. His hand slid down the front of his wrap as if checking that he still had a jack.

Had she hooked them enough? She took a step back, but they didn't follow. The first guard glanced at the bars where she saw several faces peering out. They must be MacNicols, but they didn't say anything to give her away. "I suppose I'll have to find Ranulf by myself," she said.

The second guard looked at the bearded man. "Ranulf owes me a favor, and he doesn't mind sharing." He leered back at her, lifting his wrap to show his erect jack. "I'll take ye to him after we have a little fun first, lassie."

Holy Joan! At least one of them was a predictable savage. The other one remained near the barred entrance and could light the warning fire at his shoulder, sounding the alarm that something was amiss. She needed to get them both away from it.

"I am Lady Tierney MacNicol," she said and dropped her cloak. She wore her trousers and tunic over the thick leather armor Morag had given her. It fit like a second skin under her clothes, like stays except that it swooped under and between her legs, protecting her from lusty bastards like these guards.

The man kept walking toward her, and the second one came, too. "Lady Tierney? Cane, ye best leave her be. She's to be his wife."

*That's it, follow me.* Tierney turned and ran farther up the dark path that curved around the rock. When she looked over her shoulder, the one named Cane still had his hand on his jack like it was a sword to slay her.

As he ran after her, Jacob stepped out of the shadows and hit the bearded guard by the cave's entrance with a rock to the head. He dropped without a word, so Cane kept running after her.

Tierney reached Morag, who strode past her wearing a set of white gloves. Her hood dropped back, revealing her wild, loose hair and bared teeth. Cane stopped short in surprise, and Morag reached forward, grabbing hold of his jack in a solid grip.

Cane yelled as the burning ointment Morag had applied to her glove soaked into the tender skin of his jack. But Jacob threw a gag over his head, catching it in his mouth and tying it tight before throwing a sack over his head. Within minutes, Cane was tied to a chair with his jack out and burning next to the iron gate over the cave entrance, his fellow guard tied and unconscious in a more dignified position next to him.

Jacob found the key, handing it to Tierney. "For

ye. Let yer men free." For all his annoying ways, Jacob understood her. Did Kenan? If he thought she'd sit on the ship waiting to ring the bloody bell, he did not.

"Lady Tierney," a man called, his dirt-covered face between the bars.

"Mathew," she said, keeping her voice strong even as she blinked against the tears swelling in her eyes. "I'd thought you and the others were lost to the sea."

"Nay," another voice said, and a face appeared a couple bars over. "Damn Mathesons tricked yer father, milady."

"Darby," she said, reaching through to squeeze his hand.

"Aye, milady. Ranulf said that since ye weren't on the ship, we were all forfeit."

Guilt itched up inside her chest. "Well, I'm here now to get you out."

"Ye've always been the clever lady," Mathew said. Her heart swelled at the compliment.

She shoved the iron key into the heavy lock and used both hands to turn it. "Is everyone from the *Rosemary* in here?"

"All 'cept yer parents," Mathew said.

She swung the iron gate wide, and Jacob leaned in with a torch to light the cave. Twenty sets of eyes blinked back. They'd been living in filth and cold for nearly two months.

"Everyone alive?" Jacob asked.

"Aye," Darby said, "although some are poorly."

A young warrior named Wendall bobbed his head to her. "Good to see ye."

"I sent word to your mum," Tierney said, "as soon as we heard the crew was alive."

Wendell had just started working on the ship and was barely old enough to grow a scraggly beard. He smiled. "Thank ye, milady. I worried about her with Da gone."

"Jacob," Tierney said, "see that these men get onto the *Tempest*." She placed her hand on Wendell's narrow shoulder. "With food and blankets."

"Blankets without rats chewing on us," Wendell said, his toothy grin almost skeletal in the dark.

"Without rats," Tierney said and ignored the shiver that ran through her.

Jacob leaned toward her ear. "Ye're coming, too, aren't ye?"

Tierney bobbed her head in greeting to the men emerging silently from the cave, their clothes and faces filthy but their smiles wide with relief. "Mistress Morag and I need to ensure the three chiefs of Skye aren't murdered." Saying the words, her heart felt too low in her stomach. Kenan and Rory might die because of her.

"Ye and the crone?" Jacob asked, his eyes wide. "How will that help?"

Tierney tipped her head to the hooded and gagged guard sitting against the outer cave wall with his deflated jack out. "The crone knows how to handle scoundrels."

He leaned closer to her, his words nearly spitting out his whisper. "What? She'll just go into Eilean Donan grabbing cocks with a poisoned glove?"

"You say that like 'tis a bad idea when it

obviously worked." She flapped a hand at Cane, who grunted as men kicked him as they passed by.

"I would spit on ye, ye bastard," an older shipman said, "but I won't waste what little water we've been able to lick off the bars on ye."

She leaned closer to the assaulting guard. "Perhaps you should think better about tormenting those you guard and attacking women with that sorry jack of yours." She stood back, and Mathew, being the last to leave the cave, stomped down hard on the man's exposed groin. Cane doubled over, rolling to the side in anguish.

Jacob lifted the unconscious man, setting him in the cave. Then he and Mathew picked up Cane, putting him inside, too. Tierney relocked the cell and threw the key into the dense bushes growing farther out from the rockface.

Morag stood along the path, handing out bladders of drink to the hostages. The men guzzled, passing them around to each other. Two held a third man between them, another helping him drink.

"Where did you get those?" Tierney asked her.

"I carried them under my cloak." She pulled it aside to show a hanging basket attached to a thick strap around her neck.

"I could have helped," Tierney said.

She waved a hand. "It helped me walk like an old woman." She stretched her back, the poisoned glove off and tossed aside.

"Lead them back to the Birlinn ship to go to the *Tempest*," Tierney said to Jacob.

He grabbed her arm. "I can't leave ye here. Kenan thinks I'm staying to help, and ye're going back to the ship."

Kenan wanted her to stay protected while he jeopardized himself and his two friends, along with three clansmen from Skye. But this was her tangle, and she must help where she could.

"The bard told me about a way in through the orchard on the north side. I won't just sit on the ship waiting for them to return."

Jacob rubbed his hair hard as if his brain itched. "I will stay here with ye. Keep ye safe."

She squeezed his arm. "You always have, Jacob, as much as you could. You were the only one who helped me…with Wallace." His eyes widened, and she nodded. "I know. Thank you." She continued before he could respond. "But I need you now to get these men back to the ship. Their lives depend on you, Jacob."

"Kenan will rage when he realizes ye didn't go with them."

"Kenan controls his rage, and…I left him a note," she said.

Jacob exhaled. "Bloody hell, Tier."

"'Tis in a poem in case someone intercepts it."

# CHAPTER TWENTY-TWO

"The pessimist complains about the wind;
the optimist expects it to change;
the realist adjusts the sails."

*William Arthur Ward – American Writer, 1921–1994*

The night wind blew across the treeless spit of land, making the flames flaring up from the torches dance and dim before straightening again. "How *kind* of ye to come visit," his younger brother, Gilbert, said, knowing how their father had punished Kenan anytime he deemed his son kind.

Kenan breathed through his rising anger and studied Gilbert. He hadn't seen him since the day their father had been killed and Dunscaith burned. He was the same stout, heavily browed brother he remembered, although his hair was shorter, and he was keeping his beard in better shape. Gilbert had disappeared with Winnie Mar after their father had been killed.

The woman was wily, fanatical, and probably aspired to be queen of the entire world if she could just poison enough people. She'd yanked Gilbert along with promises of passion and devotion, things Kenan's stocky, dark-hearted brother lacked.

"Is Winnie here with ye?" Kenan asked over the hard thumping of his blood, his body ready for battle. "And her brother, Reid?" Reid had helped Sara survive her ordeal with the MacLeods and their own father, but Kenan still didn't trust him.

"My wife," Gilbert said, stressing the title, "has journeyed to our Macdonald kin here on the mainland to acquire help in resurrecting Dunscaith for us."

"Us?" Rory asked. "As in ye and that conniving traitor taking over Dunscaith?"

Gilbert didn't acknowledge him. "Winnie and I will move in once 'tis completely restored."

"Are ye challenging me for the chiefdom, then, Little Brother?"

"If there's a need."

His brother, who knew very well Kenan had the loyalty of their army and superior skill with the blade, must have another plan in mind that turned his tone arrogant. Perhaps it involved Murdoc and Ranulf Matheson.

Kenan looked at Murdoc, ignoring his brother's boast. "Chief Murdoc Matheson, steward of Eilean Donan Castle, I am Chief Kenan Macdonald of Sleat on the Isle of Skye. Chief Rory MacLeod, Chief Cyrus Mackinnon, Henry Macqueen, and I have come with our warriors to retrieve what was unlawfully taken: Chief Douglas MacNicol, Fannie MacNicol from the Clan Lindsay, the crew of the *Rosemary*, and the ship. To garner a strong Scotland, we are willing to retrieve the MacNicols without bloodshed."

"And that's yer problem, Brother," Gilbert said. "Everyone but ye wants bloodshed."

Without warning, Kenan drew his sword and leveled the point at Gilbert's thick throat. "If ye so desire." Behind them, more men poured out of the bailey.

"I had heard ye were the reasonable chief," Murdoc said, his tone calm as his warriors filed along the path to Eilean Donan, "with a desire for peace."

Kenan leaned forward, the tip breaking the skin of Gilbert's neck. Just a bit more, and he could sever an artery.

Gilbert jumped back. "Foking Christ, Kenan." He grabbed his neck where blood squeezed out of his blotchy white skin.

"Lower ye sword and come inside," Murdoc said.

"Did ye bring my bride?" Ranulf asked.

"Who?" Rory asked.

Ranulf's lips twitched, and he looked at Henry, who'd remained silent. "Lady Tierney MacNicol, did ye bring her as requested? Is she on yer ship?"

"She's handfasted to me," Kenan said, "so she cannot be yer bride."

"Is she here?" Ranulf raised his voice, staring into Henry's eyes.

"Lady Tierney is near, but as Chief Kenan Macdonald says, he's hand—"

"Which is not supported by the church or the government," Murdoc cut in.

"'Tis been a tradition since the beginning of time," Rory said.

"I have a contract," Ranulf said, stepping forward, which was foolish since Kenan still held his sword level, tip outward. Murdoc's arm went across his brother's chest as if holding him back or trying to save his irritating life.

"A contract never agreed to nor signed by the lady," Kenan said. "A contract that has a clause saying it is null if she marries a clan chief."

"Douglas MacNicol reconsidered that clause and crossed it out. Ye were requested to bring Lady Tierney here," Murdoc said. "To buy back her family and clan. Ye'll bring her from yer ship."

Kenan gave Henry a dark look and spoke before the arse gave more information away. "Master Henry does not know where she is."

Ranulf sucked on his teeth, making a wet suction sound. "She likes to hide, like a timid mouse, but I thought the life of her parents and clan might make her brave enough to come."

"If ye think Tierney is like a timid mouse, ye know nothing about her," Kenan said.

Kenan lowered his sword so he wouldn't be tempted. If he attacked first, the Mathesons around them, ten now behind with more on the steps above, would kill him and then Rory and Cyrus. His friends knew the risk going into this, which was why diplomacy must be suffered.

"Let us discuss this inside like civilized men," Murdoc said and turned, yanking Ranulf's arm to follow. Gilbert glared at Kenan but turned, striding across the grassy stretch of land before the gate leading into the bailey. Kenan kept his sword out and ready, but Rory gripped his arm.

"Tempting, I know," Rory said, "but we're committed to trying diplomacy first because they are Scots. If they were English, we'd slice them through."

"Bloody diplomacy," Cyrus muttered.

Rory looked at Cyrus. "When it involved Matilda,

our jailor's daughter at Carlisle, ye were all about diplomacy."

"Her name was Mirella, and she couldn't help she was born English. And I, too, want to discourage Scots fighting Scots," Cyrus said and exhaled. "Which is why I must convince my father not to war."

Kenan looked across at him, but the shadows hid his face. "I am indebted."

"No matter what," Cyrus said, "don't drink anything my sister hands ye. She's less forgiving than our father."

"Warning taken," Kenan murmured.

The three strode across the bailey, ignoring the dozens of Matheson warriors holding torches inside the bailey, watching in silence. Henry trudged behind them, keeping up with much grumbling while Tomas, Jok, and Bartholomew followed. They were outnumbered seven to fifty.

Rory slid a small parchment from his sash and whispered, "I forgot. Tierney gave me this for ye."

Kenan's brows furrowed as he took it. "When?"

"Right as we parted at the dock, and then we got busy," Rory answered.

Kenan tried to read it, but the scrawl was light, and shadows covered almost everything. "Did ye read it?"

"Of course not," Rory said.

As they walked beside the torches set in iron sconces flanking the gate, Kenan stopped. "Give me a chance to read this," he whispered, and Rory strode faster ahead.

"Pardon, but I need to take a piss before going in," Rory called to the guard. "Maybe we all should."

Kenan stared at the looping scrawl.

*Plan Number Four – Ignored but not forgotten.*

*An angel,*

*her wings clipped by a lover's fear, falls toward the briny sea.*

*A crow,*

*her wings black as moonless night, answers her warrior's plea.*

*Angel and crow fly together*

*under the vacant moon.*

*Clothed in cleverness, armor, and magic,*

*They will land on the mountain soon.*

*When the crow comes calling, I beg you to take heed.*

*Fly home upon its wings, with your power three.*

"Daingead," Kenan said. "She's got another plan."

• • •

With the MacNicol crew headed back to the Birlinn ship and freedom, Tierney and Morag walked arm in arm with their hoods up over their heads. Anyone glancing out in the night would see an old woman being helped by a younger one.

"Your armor in place?" Morag asked, her voice so soft it could have been the breeze.

Tierney patted her stomach. The leather casing

made only a gentle thud under her palm. "Yes, although 'tis not comfortable." The thick girdle wrapped between Tierney's legs, across her backside, and ran all the way up her torso to cover her breasts with thick straps that lay over her shoulders. It was a full covering of protection, the likes of which she'd never seen before. It hugged her body and curves and had two locks, one at the top sitting between her breasts and one low at the top of her pelvic mound.

"Are you certain it would work against any man?" Tierney asked, sliding her hand over her trousers where the worked leather rubbed the skin at her hips.

Morag pulled her into a dark space between cottages, her hands rising to Tierney's shoulders to tug on the straps. She yanked around her breasts and then fingered the edges under Tierney's trousers, checking that nothing slid.

"I had this made by Gerard at Dunvegan when Bruce threatened to punish me in bed," Morag said.

"You wore this to bed?" Tierney wiggled her body, but the leather held her firmly in place.

"Aye, after hiding the keys. No one can get inside unless you unlock the contraption. I think every woman should have one. Protection against cock-wielding madmen."

"What did Bruce do when he discovered you wearing it?"

Morag didn't say anything for a moment, and the silence felt heavy there in the shadows between the low buildings. "He reacted poorly, but he didn't get what he wanted." Morag patted her arm in the dark. "And now I pass it to you to use when going into the proverbial lion's den of vile devils. Even if Ranulf finds you, he can't threaten you with what that guard had in his wicked mind."

Tierney smiled in the darkness, thinking of how furious Ranulf would be if he got her in that position and discovered the barrier.

"And if he tries to stick anything in your mouth," Morag continued, "bite down hard."

Tierney heard the woman's teeth clack together. Holy Joan, Morag Gunn was fierce.

"Sound advice," Tierney said, wondering how her marriage to Wallace would have ended if she'd had Morag's courage. Although she'd also been protecting Maggie. Every woman's circumstances were her own.

Above them, wings fluttered, and Tierney looked up to see several black crows sitting on the thatched roof. Morag laughed softly. "My army."

Morag looped her arm again through Tierney's, and they crept to the corner of the sleeping cottage before venturing into the street. Everything was quiet as if the townspeople locked themselves away at night.

A shiver ran through Tierney as she remembered her father's bedtime stories about dragons roaming the countryside on the mainland of Scotland. The beasts would pick up stragglers at night with their talons, carrying them back to their young to eat. That was long ago when Douglas MacNicol still cared to spend time with her.

Tierney and Morag walked silently, their boots coming down with gentle steps so as not to crunch the gravel along the road. They neared the ferry station where a Matheson poleman stood, his gaze on the torches burning on the opposite side.

"We need passage across," Tierney said, keeping her hood up. Next to her, Morag let out a piercing whistle.

The man jumped at the sudden noise. Tierney kept her hood raised while Morag lowered hers. "I am a soothsayer sent for by Chief Murdoc Matheson." Her arm swept upward. "He wishes me to read his fate in the stars this eve since 'tis clear."

The man was young, tall, and thin. "Chief Murdoc has guests this eve. Come back on the morrow."

Morag *tsk*ed, her arm still raised. With a great flapping, one of her crows landed on her sleeve, black wings outstretched. Four more landed on the ground around them, and Tierney could hear the birds circling above.

"Holy Mother Mary," the guard swore, crossing himself. "Demons."

"They are birds, not demons," Morag said as if the man was an imbecile. "And we were called to come this eve so we cannot wait. Perhaps we were called because of these guests."

The guard continued to stare at the large crow, which hopped to the ground with the others, all of them walking with stick-like legs, stretching their wings before Morag, sentries guarding their queen.

"If the guests are potential enemies, the chief would like us to reveal them," Tierney said, using a wispy voice that she hoped sounded mysterious or witch-like. Her heart thumped, making her want to twitch or run, but she forced herself to remain still.

The guard bent to try to see past the shadows

into Tierney's hood, but Morag swooped her arms, making the crows expand their wings, lifting themselves into the air before the man. He gave a little squeak and jumped onto the ferry.

"Call yer demon birds off me, and I'll take ye across," he said.

Morag settled her hood back on her head and preceded Tierney onto the flat ferry, one of the crows stepping sedately along the planks to follow her.

"They're coming, too?" the ferryman asked, glancing between the one on the ferry and the others flying around, their black wings blending in with the inky night.

"Madeline goes where I go," Morag said, and the man made another sign of the cross.

The poleman threw his weight into moving the ferry quickly. On the other side, Morag and Tierney disembarked, but the crow remained on the flat boat, flapping her wings as if part of the plan.

"Take yer bloody birds with ye," the man called, but the two women strode down the wooden dock, climbing the rocks that led toward the castle. 'Twas mid tide, so the ferry had taken them close to the broken outer walls. While Madeline flapped and lifted off when the man tried to jab her with his pole, Tierney and Morag climbed the uneven rocks where the torchlight didn't reach. They squatted behind a low wall that was no longer fortified, waiting until the ferryman poled his way back over to get away from the crow.

They did not speak as they moved from rock to rock, climbing the incline, avoiding tufts of washed-up seaweed with bulbous, wet leaves. In the silence, Tierney could hear the slight squeak of the leather armor hugging her body under her trousers and tunic. She hoped she wouldn't have to use the privy before getting the contraption off. Even with the chilled night breeze coming off the sea, she wasn't cold, not with thick leather encasing her like a sausage.

Ahead, torches outlined the broken wall that used to surround the fortress. It hadn't been kept up in recent centuries and provided cover as they neared the orchard along the north side of the keep. Reid Lewis hadn't lied.

They reached the rustling leaves of the apple trees growing in rows. A small wall enclosed the bailey, leaving the keep only protected by the sea on the western side.

Tierney walked briskly amongst the trees. She inhaled the smell of apple mixed with the brine off the water. If at least one tree was close enough to the keep that she could use it to climb inside a second-level window, she could enter without anyone knowing. Reid had said he'd been able to reach out to pluck an apple from one when he'd visited.

Morag met Tierney at the last row of trees. Tierney exhaled, her rapidly beating heart sinking inside her. The trees were too far from the windows of the keep. Perhaps the tips of the limbs could reach, but not limbs strong enough to hold a person.

"On to our second plan," Morag said.

"The next plan is actually number five," Tierney said.

"Whatever the number," Morag said, "we need to

get you inside. If not through a window, then a door."

Tierney thought of the diagram she'd drawn of the keep. "My parents will be held probably on the third floor in one of the sleeping chambers or in the small dungeon below. My guess is the bedchamber, or the letter would have mentioned their poor accommodations."

"You will need a distraction to enter through the kitchen garden on the seaside," Morag said, pointing past the end of the orchard to the right. "I will walk in the front bailey and say I am a soothsayer come to read the stars. I can get inside and chant so loudly that everyone in the keep will come to see my predictions."

Tierney stared at her. "You can make that big a distraction?"

"I have been walking the edge of acceptable behavior my whole life." Morag's voice held a wicked smile. "Distraction is second nature to me."

Tierney looked to the right. There were no guards walking the perimeter on that side. Murdoc and Ranulf must feel secure with the sea around them. Kenan had ordered several dinghies to be silently rowed to that shore if an escape was needed.

Tierney turned back to Morag. Even though the moon was merely a sliver, the older woman's eyes seemed to glint. "I'll wait in the back gardens until I hear your distraction."

Morag slid her black cloak from her shoulders and motioned for Tierney's crimson-colored cloak. "Wear my black one," Morag said. "There are helpful things in the pockets tied underneath."

Tierney exchanged the cloaks, putting the black one over her tunic and trousers. Her hand slipped into the cinched pocket. "A key?" She pulled it out.

"It fits most door locks but not the locks on your armor."

A small velvety bag was heavy. "Coins?"

"Always good for bribes," Morag said.

Tierney jerked her finger out of the pocket. "Something sharp." She couldn't see the bead of blood that must sit upon her poked finger.

"A long, sharp pin. 'Tis one of the best weapons, along with an awl." Morag made a jabbing motion. "'Tis good for poking into eyes."

Tierney nodded slowly. "With you by my side, Mistress Morag, we could take over Scotland."

"I am merely interested in protecting my isle." Morag patted her arm and turned, disappearing into the orchard toward the entrance to the bailey.

Tierney kept to the trees, moving in the opposite direction around the north side of the keep where a kitchen garden was planted. There didn't seem to be any animals on the small isle, so all she had to watch for were raised tree roots. A low wall surrounded the garden, dividing it from the orchard. Morag's black cloak transformed Tierney into a shadow. She blended in with the thick, twisting apple trees, moving with the night breeze.

Tierney swung her legs over the wall, pulling her cloak around herself, and slid to the ground in a crouch. No one was about, so she moved along the wall until she reached the door cut into the stonework of the castle. If Reid had been correct, this led to the household kitchen, which had a back staircase for servants. The door didn't fit well, leaving a crack under it and at the top. Leaning close, she could hear muted conversation, splashing water, and a rhythmic thudding on wood.

What was going on in the Great Hall at the front of the keep? Had Morag entered yet? Had Kenan read her note? He'd either think her quite talented or completely mad.

If Ranulf found the poem, she doubted he was clever enough to understand it. But Kenan would know she was the angel and Morag the crow, and he'd know they were coming to Eilean Donan. He'd know that he and the other chiefs should leave after Morag shows up, because Tierney knew Ranulf wouldn't just release her parents through negotiation, not without her surrender.

And Tierney wouldn't surrender. Nor would she let Kenan pay the price for her decision. "Just stay alive," she whispered so softly the rustling leaves hid any trace of her.

# CHAPTER TWENTY-THREE

"It is not in the stars to hold our destiny
but in ourselves."

*William Shakespeare – English playwright, 1564–1616*

"The crone says she's a soothsayer, and the stars tonight give warning, milord."

Kenan glanced toward the archway where a
cloaked figure stood. Tierney or Morag? *Be neither.*
But Tierney's poetic note left no doubt that she had
another plan in mind. *Daingead.*

If the soothsayer was Morag, her identity
wouldn't remain hidden with Gilbert there.

"Let her enter," Murdoc said. "I would hear this
warning."

"Gilbert Macdonald," Kenan called with a voice
that would reach her, "I did not know ye searched
the stars for predictions." The soothsayer continued
to step slowly over the rug-strewn floor toward
them, nearly gliding, silent even, when she traversed
the floorboards. She showed no hesitation walking
between two guards.

Gilbert frowned at him over the gold-rimmed
goblet in his thick hand. They sat at a long table better suited for a thirty-person banquet rather than
the four chiefs, Henry, and the troublesome brothers.
Murdoc sat at the head, Ranulf to his right and
Gilbert to his left like a kingly trio.

"I do not," Gilbert said. "I make my own fortune." But he eyed the woman gliding across the hall as if he were just as frightened of witches as in his youth.

The cloaked figure walked right up to the end of the table. The guards had stopped near the entrance where Jok, Tomas, and Bartholomew stood watching the stiff exchanges. The soothsayer wore a crimson cloak with the hood covering her head, hiding her face. *Daingead!* Tierney had been wearing a crimson cloak when they came over on the Brinell.

The woman stepped onto the chair and then onto the top of the table as if she were climbing the steps to her throne, as if standing on tables was a natural occurrence for queens of darkness.

Murdoc stood so abruptly that his chair tumbled backward, clunking on the floor. "What is this?" His voice carried throughout the hall, and his men ran closer to the table. The maids carrying pitchers of ale and bottles of wine stopped to witness the show.

The crone raised her arm, her cloak tightly fastened with silken loops and knots down the front. A wafting of wings breezed into the hall, making maids scream and swords slide free. The currents of an unnatural wind blew through the hall, flickering the torches. By then, everyone at the table was standing as the giant crow flew across the room under the rafters to land on the table before the crone. On stick legs, it turned to stare out at everyone.

The figure raised her hands. One was covered with a glove and the other bare. The bare one was knobby with age. *Morag.*

"Beware, Murdoc of Eilean Donan," she said, her

voice ringing out with proclamation. "I have seen your end."

"Who are ye?" Murdoc yelled.

"Do not be fooled by those closest to you."

Murdoc instantly looked at Ranulf and then Gilbert.

"Why?" Murdoc yelled.

"Traitors seek to take your seat." The crone walked along the table with small, gliding steps, the crow hopping out of her way.

Gilbert's eyes were wide, and he half bent when the crow flew overhead.

"Remove yer hood," Ranulf said. "I would see the face of a lying witch."

The woman lowered her hood. Morag stared out with stony eyes.

"Aunt Morag?" Gilbert said and looked at Kenan. Kenan just shrugged his shoulders.

People had gathered to see the spectacle at the entrances to the hall. Was Morag a distraction for Tierney?

"She is yer kin?" Murdoc asked, anger tightening his face. "She warns me of yer betrayal."

"She is Kenan's kin, too," Gilbert said, flapping his hand at Kenan.

"I'm no hidden traitor, though," Kenan said. "I openly dislike ye."

"Enough of this," Murdoc said. "Woman, be gone."

Morag didn't look like she planned to step down anytime soon. Her crow grabbed a bun from the platter at the center of the table, flapping its wings to gain altitude. Morag ignored the bird and walked toward Murdoc. The only noise she made was when her cloak hit the goblets, knocking them over and sending the wine and ale running in rivulets over the table.

"Bloody hell, ye old witch!" Ranulf yelled.

Morag turned her gaze on him. "Help me down." She extended her gloved hand.

"If it will get ye the fok out of here." Ranulf grabbed her hand.

"Nay," Gilbert said, but it was too late.

Ranulf yanked his hand back where a white substance covered his palm. "It burns!"

"Grab her," Murdoc ordered, and his men ran forward.

Morag spun around and unclasped the top of her cloak, letting it fall.

White hair in a braid down her back, she held onto the cloak with her bare hand as she walked back down the table. The other hand was still gloved and coated in poison. The rest of her was completely naked.

• • •

As soon as Tierney heard a commotion inside, followed by the patter of slippers and then silence, she worked the latch on the door, the key in her other hand. Unlocked. *Thank you, Saint Joan.*

She slipped inside, her gaze sweeping the warm kitchen. A cauldron steamed over a fire in the hearth, sending the aroma of thyme and garlic into the air. Lumps of bread dough lay abandoned, deflated on floured tables. But unless Morag was burning down the Great Hall, stabbing Ranulf's eyes, or creating some other catastrophic havoc, the cook and maids would return quickly.

"Stairs? Where are you?" she whispered, stepping between tables toward the back corner that sat in shadows. Reid said he'd been taken to the kitchen for broth and saw a door that opened when a maid was bringing down a tray, steps behind her.

"She's what?" a voice came from the hallway beyond. "Is she mad? Poisoned glove and a crow." Morag was certainly causing a stir in the great hall. Was Kenan heeding the warning and making his reasons to leave?

Tierney spotted the door toward the back corner and hurried to it, pulling the latch and sliding inside. She stood for a moment at the bottom of the narrow stone staircase, the stones rough without plaster since it was for the servants to use. They were also steep. Tierney stepped up them on the balls of her booted feet, quickly but without a sound. One complete turn brought her to another door, which would be the second floor. She continued around another turn and a half before reaching a door that must lead to the third-floor corridor.

Tierney listened, her ear against the wooden planks, her hand on the latch. Heavy footfalls came her way. *Holy Joan!* She looked around wildly. Even if she tumbled down the stairs, she wouldn't make it in time before—

The door swung toward her, missing her by inches as she leaped down two steps. The middle-aged woman at the top, wearing an apron, gasped.

Tierney held a finger to her lips, but the woman

opened her mouth to scream. Tierney waved her hands before the woman's face. "I am Chief Murdoc's...paramour, concubine." What other words were there for a hired woman of ill repute?

"What?" The maid looked confused.

"His whore."

"He already has two lasses in his bedchamber." The woman's lips pinched in a scolding, judgmental twist.

"I...suppose I'm number three."

The woman looked down Tierney's front where her cloak had opened. "Ye don't look like a lady the master would want. Ye're wearing a tunic and trousers."

"Chief Murdoc requested it," Tierney said. "A special...type...of...performance. I'm to kiss one of the other lasses, only to reveal I'm a woman."

The elderly maid stared at her, blinking rapidly.

Tierney nodded. "I'll tie my hair up to help my disguise. 'Tis why I keep it shorter than most."

"I had no idea his lordship was so...imaginative," the woman said.

"Oh, yes. Sometimes, we dress as wild animals and chase him around."

"Oh my." The woman flattened a hand over her chest.

"I best get there before he comes above."

The woman flattened herself against the wall so Tierney could move past. Tierney looked back at her. "Which is his room?"

"Last one on the right...uh...miss."

Tierney nodded, striding down the corridor. The woman kept watching her, so she went to Murdoc's room and pushed inside. Two ladies sat at a small table playing cards, wineglasses in hand. Tierney leaned back against the door, breathing hard.

"Who are you?" a blonde with pouty lips asked. Her large breasts teetered on the edge of her bodice.

The other one had loose brown hair that was seemingly given to curl. She stared at Tierney with wide eyes.

Tierney dug around in Morag's pocket and pulled out some coins. They plinked on the table when she dropped them. "Someone who hopes you're able to leave Eilean Donan if you wish. Find Morag Gunn on the Isle of Skye if you need refuge."

She turned away, hoping they wouldn't sound an alarm and hoping the coins would give them freedom. Tierney cracked the door and looked over her shoulder. "Do you know which room is occupied, maybe locked, maybe with prisoners in it?"

The blonde was dividing up the coins with the brunette, using her finger to separate the coins evenly. "Near the servants' stairs down on the left."

"Thank you." Tierney slipped out the door and hurried back the way she'd come. Reaching the last door before the stairway, she pressed the door handle. Of course it was locked. Would there be a guard inside?

*Rap. Rap.* "I have your evening meal," she called through the door.

Movement inside, and then someone spoke with terse, measured words. "Well, use yer bloody key. We don't have one."

Tierney's heart clenched, and it took her a moment to draw in a breath. 'Twas her father's voice.

She yanked the key from the tied pocket in Morag's black cloak and shoved it into the lock under the door lever. A sprinkling of something shiny came out with it, falling on the floor. Mica dust.

She jiggled the key in the lock. "Please, please, please," she whispered. The sound of the scraping tumbler sent relief pulsing through her. She turned it completely and pushed into the room, being careful to tuck the key away.

"Bloody hell," her father said, grabbing a pillow from the bed to hold before his genitals. He was completely naked.

"Da?" she asked, not sure of what to ask, the shock of catching a glimpse of her father without a shred of clothing too disturbing for words. Her eyes glanced around the spartan room. "Where's Mother?"

"I'm here," she called, coming out from behind the privacy screen in the corner. She had a blanket draped around her. Fannie MacNicol's hair was down in loose curls that hung to the backs of her knees, and the skin exposed in the *V* made by the clasped quilt showed she was naked, too. Even her toes were bare.

She ran awkwardly over to Tierney to hug her while holding the blanket, her hand squashed between them.

"What are ye doing here?" her father asked, his voice quieter as he hurried to shut the door. "Did ye give in to Ranulf and Murdoc's demands?" From his tone, she couldn't tell his preferred answer, so she didn't give one.

Tierney looked between them, one holding a

pillow before his jack, his gray hair curling over his chest. The other wrapped like a woman caught naked with a lover. "Why are you naked?" Tierney asked. "Both of you? Completely...naked."

# CHAPTER TWENTY-FOUR

"Be a mirror, absorb everything around you and still remain the same."

*Leonardo da Vinci – Italian artist and scientist, 1452–1519*

Tierney had never seen her parents naked. They were not the naked, frolicking in the summer flowers and swimming in the loch type of people. She had even heard the maids talk about how her mother took baths while wearing her smock, sliding the soap underneath. The only evidence that her parents had ever taken off their clothes with another person was that they'd created Gabriel and herself.

But here they were, in their enemy's lair. Her father all pale and hairy with a bulging stomach and knobby knees and her mother flushing red and trying to pull the blanket up to her chin. "What happened to your clothing? Your shoes?" Tierney asked, fury beginning to burn away her surprise. She looked at her mother. "Did someone…attack you?"

She shook her head and looked at Tierney's father, Douglas. "We were…locked in here." She turned back to Tierney when her father didn't jump in with explanations. "To get food, they made us remove all our clothing. They said it was so we wouldn't dare try to escape."

"It was to humiliate us," Douglas said, his tone hard. "But it also has the added security of us not trying to break out of our room."

Tierney untied the cloak at her throat and pulled it off. "Put this on." She handed it to her mother. "Wait." Tierney untied the bulging pocket hooked underneath. "Now go put it on."

"They will take it away," Fannie said.

Tierney blinked at her parents, her mouth slack with surprise. "I thought it was clear I'm rescuing you," Tierney said. Both her parents stared at her. "Is that so surprising? I have already released the crew from the cave."

Fannie's hand went to her mouth. "They're still alive. Thank God."

"How are ye here? Rescuing us?" her father asked, still holding the pillow before his groin. "Dressed like…" He didn't finish. Perhaps because Tierney was yanking her tunic over her head.

"Put this on," she said, tossing the tunic to him and pulled the knot on her trousers. "And these. I have no desire for nightmares that involve seeing my father's…" She flapped a hand at the pillow before him.

"What in heaven is that you're wearing?" Fannie asked, fastening the cape down her front.

Tierney glanced down, her thighs feeling the chill. She wore stockings gartered just below her knees with low-cut boots on her feet. Her skin was bare up to the joint between her legs and hips where Morag's armor hugged her hips, torso, and chest, keeping her breasts covered. The armor was snug, hugging her and leaving no hill or valley hidden.

"'Tis armor made from leather."

"'Tis scandalous," her father said.

"Says the naked man." Tierney tapped the lock at her pelvis. "I'm locked up tight." She fingered the one snug between her breasts. "No man can get it off without the key, and the key is not here. Therefore, I am safe from any scandalous attack."

Her parents stared at her, and she looked down to make sure the snug suit still covered all her bits. Yes, everything was covered. "I think all women should have one."

With the tunic down to his knees, Douglas dropped the pillow and shoved his spindly legs into the trousers. They wouldn't close over his gut, and he had to tie them, leaving the flesh of his lower abdomen exposed, which he covered with the long tunic.

Tierney slipped off her boots, handing them to her mother. "Take these. I will just wear stockings. You'll need them to climb over the rocks outside to make it to the dinghies waiting along the water on the far side of the castle."

"But you—" Fannie started.

"I will climb without." Tierney nodded to her father. "Same with you."

"What ship did ye bring?" Douglas asked to Tierney's back as she helped her mother fasten every available loop on the cloak.

"The Macdonalds of Sleat have two galleons and thirty Brinell ships waiting off the coast in Loch Duich."

Fannie's fingers slid along the line of leather that disappeared between her legs. "Doesn't this chafe?"

she whispered.

"Macdonalds?" her father said, his voice louder. He glanced at the door as if realizing the need to stay quiet.

"No, Mother." At least not yet, but this was no time to worry over chafing.

"And yes, Father." She looked at him. "There are warriors from the MacLeods, Macdonalds, and Mackinnons who've accompanied the twenty remaining MacNicol warriors."

"Our enemies," her father said, his voice stern.

"Who are risking their lives to free you."

"I don't want their help," he said, his face turning red. "Gilbert Macdonald is one of Murdoc's supporters. The Mathesons plan to help him establish another group of Macdonalds near Scorrybreac if he can't immediately oust the Macdonalds on Sleat."

Kenan's brother was at Eilean Donan? "Gilbert Macdonald?" She pressed her fist against her chest where a pain suddenly beat. "How do you know this?" she asked, her gaze going back and forth between her father and the door as if she could see down below in the Great Hall.

"Before we were locked in this blasted room, Murdoc tried to force me to give up Scorrybreac. To save yer mother, I had to cross out the clause about the contract being void if you married another."

"The contract tying me legally to Ranulf without my consent," she added.

Her father's lips pinched, ignoring her comment. "Gilbert was there, discussing plans with Ranulf."

Tierney controlled the rage welling up inside her.

They were running out of time, especially now that Gilbert could expose Morag as his aunt. Murdoc would think Kenan was playing a game. *Holy Joan! Bloody hell!*

Heart thumping hard, she turned back to the door, needing to go, needing to do something, and needing to do it now. "I came for the crew and Mother. You can choose to stay." She threw her arm through Fannie's and tugged her to follow her to the door. Morag was probably already discovered.

Her father blustered behind her, but she heard his footfalls following her out of the room. She opened the door to the narrow staircase. "These are for the servants. You're on the third floor. Go to the first. It opens in the kitchen. Run through to the outside door before anyone can stop or question you. You will have to run through the kitchen garden, orchard, and over rocks to the western side of this small island. Go through the tumbled-down gate facing the sea. Find the dinghies there to pick you up."

"What if someone tries to stop us?" Fannie asked.

"Use this pin to stab them, most preferably in the eye." She handed her the pin that kept poking her leg through the pocket she'd tied to her waist.

"Good Lord," Fannie murmured and stuck it through the fabric of the cape.

"And where will ye be?" Douglas asked.

Tierney couldn't leave Kenan to deal with her plan blowing up. "I need to get the chiefs out."

Her father grabbed her arm. "I'll help. Ye take yer mother to the ship."

She stared into her father's hard eyes. She didn't trust him to aid three clans he'd been raised to hate even if they'd come to Eilean Donan to rescue him. "No. This is my plan to get you out of here. And damn it, this plan is going to work." She ended the word with a harsh *K*. "So get Mother to the ship."

"Listen to her," Fannie said. "She has gotten this far."

"Nearly naked," Douglas said.

Tierney gave him an incredulous look while she flipped her hand to indicate his own lack of clothing. "Once again…" She left the words unsaid.

He frowned but took her mother's arm. "Daughter," Douglas said, and she met his gaze. "Be safe." The softening in his voice caught her off guard. "Ye…ye've…done well to rescue yer mother."

*And you and the crew.* But she merely shooed them down the steps. Her mother in the full-length cloak and her father in the ill-fitting trousers and bare feet hurried down. For a moment Tierney watched them go and then looked back along the corridor.

Plan number five had been for her to go with her parents once they were free, but she hadn't counted on Gilbert Macdonald being friendly with Ranulf and Murdoc. She'd literally dragged Kenan into this, drugging and shackling him, too, and now she and Morag had worked behind his back. She wouldn't leave him behind when plan five had to be falling apart.

She turned to look back down the corridor, trying to decide which way to go.

• • •

Kenan jumped up from his chair like the rest of them, mouth agape. Morag's long, white-and-silver hair swung in a braid against the lower edge of her arse. Her legs were pale with a few blue veins visible through the translucent skin. Slim and regal, she walked with determined grace toward the door. The only sign of weakness about her was a scar on her back. He recognized a flogging scar since he had his own.

"Good God," Henry said, watching his aunt, his eyes wide as moons.

Those before her must see her heavy bosom and the crux of her legs, but no one turned away. The gloved hand, slathered in some type of poison, remained apart, and her boots rose to her mid-calf. Otherwise, his aunt was naked.

She stepped down the same seat she'd used to mount the table and walked with clipping dignity. Her crow glided back and forth over her head, closer than when it had come inside. It appeared like a sentry or guard, ready to defend its vulnerable mistress if any approached her.

"Ye brought Aunt Morag," Gilbert yelled at Kenan. "The witch of Skye." He ran toward her as if he couldn't believe it was her. Morag kept her face straight ahead. "Aunt Morag? Why are ye here?"

*Daingead*. Tierney hadn't known Gilbert would be there when she put her newest plan in motion. Kenan glanced up at the steps leading above. Was

Tierney up there trying to release her parents?

Murdoc's face hardened. "She's a distraction."

"Fok!" Ranulf yelled, holding his red hand with a handkerchief as if it still burned. "Stop her!"

"Time to go," Kenan said to Cyrus and Rory. Cyrus and Rory moved with him after Morag, Henry following in a blustery trot.

"Stop them!" Murdoc yelled, and the guards within the hall filled the space before the archway to the steps leading out of the keep. They were outnumbered, even with the three warriors who'd come with them. Only Henry drew his sword, both hands wrapped around it like a shield.

Morag pushed open the doors beyond, and a flurry of wings and screeches from out in the bailey kept anyone from running after her. She disappeared into the blackness.

Kenan turned back to Murdoc. "We came to negotiate, and ye hold us hostage? Ye better check yer harbor before deciding to detain the chiefs of three powerful clans."

Murdoc kept his severe frown. "Ranulf, check on our prisoners above. John, go look at our harbor and light the signal fire to gather our warriors." Ranulf ran toward the steps leading above while one of the guards turned, jogging through the entryway—the angry sound of cawing crows filtered in as he opened the doors.

Hopefully, Douglas and Fannie MacNicol and Tierney were already outside and headed to the dinghy along the shadowed shoreline.

Hopefully, another would be waiting there for them, one that she arranged. That woman was going to be the death of him and possibly two of the brotherhood working to strengthen Skye.

*Bloody foking hell.*

"While we wait, why don't ye take yer seats?"

They did not move, but Kenan heard Rory whisper to Henry. "Put yer damn sword away."

"I thought… Oh," Henry whispered and returned his sword to its sheath.

Kenan's mind ran through their assets: six trained warriors and one old man with a sword, two galleons, thirty Brinell ships moving along the seaside of Eilean Donan, and Morag's questionable powers if she hadn't fled the isle.

Had Tierney finished her plan and left with her parents? Even if they did make it back to the ship, the MacNicols needed the other clans on Skye to keep the Mathesons from coming to overtake Scorrybreac. If she was the reason the three chiefs did not return to the ships, she'd have an impossible time convincing them to aid her.

She should have told him her plan. *Daingead. Would I have listened?* The answer was no. Now this tangle might leave the Isle of Skye more vulnerable than it had ever been, and all because he couldn't stop wanting to protect Tierney, so much so that he wouldn't listen to her. He was a fool like Cyrus had said.

Despite the thoughts churning in Kenan's head, he needed to show a calm, level-headed countenance. "I don't know why Morag Gunn arrived here or left like she did except to bring ye a warning, Murdoc." He opened his hands wide. "That was completely on her own. I would never ask my aunt to bare her body to anyone, let alone a room of men."

"She's mad," Gilbert said. "She and her bloody birds."

Kenan walked slowly back to the table. He sat and grabbed a roll, taking the eating knife out to slather soft butter onto it. Cyrus and Rory followed, and finally Henry. Kenan took a bite and pointed the roll at Murdoc, who still stood as if ready to jump into action. "But ye must have guessed we would bring our troops to retrieve Chief and Lady MacNicol, which includes ships with cannons and men." He swallowed and motioned with the roll toward the back wall. "Which are just about now sailing up Loch Duich, positioning themselves to fire."

"Eilean Donan won't fall," Murdoc said, leaning forward on his palms placed on the table before him.

"Perhaps not," Cyrus said, taking a roll himself. "But yer docks will be obliterated and then men will storm the shoreline."

"We don't take the invasion of the Isle of Skye quietly," Rory said, his amber eyes staring at Murdoc.

"The clans of Skye do not defend one another," Gilbert said. "They war with one another."

Rory looked at him. "An outdated strategy that left yer father without his head."

"Ye foking bastard," Gilbert yelled, rushing toward Rory, who stood in defense.

But before Gilbert could reach him, Kenan stepped before him, his fist pulled back. *Crack!*

Kenan's fist connected with Gilbert's face. With the additional momentum, the impact shook through Kenan, but he remained standing while Gilbert dropped like a basket of bricks.

Kenan turned toward Murdoc, continuing as if his brother's unconscious body weren't lying at his feet and his knuckles weren't bleeding. "My brother loses his temper, which makes for a bad leader. We should discuss and strategize like disciplined men if we are to guard Scotland against its true enemy, England." Kenan stepped over Gilbert's extended hand and took his seat.

Murdoc, brows furrowed, moved back to his own chair at the top of the table. "Ye want to take on England?" One of Murdoc's men dragged Gilbert away from the table, leaving him lying on the floor.

"Nay," Kenan said, reaching down the table to grab his half-eaten roll while Cyrus and Rory retook their seats. "I want Scotland to be strong and united so the English bastards don't come up here and do what ye're trying to do on Skye, infiltrate it so ye can control it." Kenan glanced at Gilbert. "With men like my brother, Scotland will always be weak against foreign foes."

Murdoc tilted his head, his tongue sliding up behind his lips across his teeth. "Ye have a brother like I do, one ye would rather have somewhere else."

Kenan had guessed this. "So ye sent him to Scorrybreac."

"It seemed like a reasonable plan." Murdoc studied the three of them.

"Not when the three most powerful clans on

Skye are ready to go to war against ye for doing it," Rory said.

"Now it seems rather *un*reasonable," Cyrus said.

"And what if the chiefs and their second in commands," Murdoc indicated Jok, Tomas, and Bartholomew who now also sat at the table, "were to…disappear?"

# CHAPTER TWENTY-FIVE

"The higher the hill, the stronger the wind: so the
loftier the life, the stronger the enemy's
temptations."

*John Wycliffe – English Theologian, 1320–1384*

Tierney stood at the back staircase, listening to her
parents descend. *I should follow them.* Kenan and
the others could already be out of Eilean Donan.
Ranulf could be downstairs, and no amount of armor would stop her nightmares that combined
Wallace with Ranulf. The idea of seeing him again
made her skin itch.

As if conjured by the thought, Ranulf appeared
at the top of the main staircase at the end of the corridor. Tierney's heart lurched, and she felt suspended
in time as she took in the surprise on his face. Every
muscle in her body contracted, and her fingers dug
into the side of the door.

His surprise turned to predatory rage and promises of some type of deviant torture. "Tierney
MacNicol." He lunged forward, charging toward her
down the corridor.

Her body, mostly bare, twisted to throw herself
down the servants' steps. There was no lock on the
door, so she abandoned the thought of trying to hold
the door closed. *Run!* She shot down the steps, her
stockinged feet slapping the stones as she rounded

the curve in the narrow spiral staircase.

With any luck, her parents had already run through the kitchen. That's what Tierney planned to do. Was that plan number five still or had she moved onto plan number six? "Run, run, run!"

She was fast, but she'd given her mother her boots, so the uneven steps bruised her feet. And Ranulf was fast, too. By the time she'd reached the second-floor doorway, he was at the top of the stairs. There was no handrail to hold, and throwing herself down the stone steps that curved would only see her dead. So she continued as fast as she could while hitting each step evenly. Above her, it sounded like Ranulf was taking at least two at a time, his grunts and thuds echoing in the contained space.

*Holy Joan, help me!*

The door to the kitchen was ahead, but Ranulf's huffs and curses were so close now that he was nearly upon her. If she could just make it to the kitchen, there would be witnesses to his crimes against her, because Tierney knew there would be crimes even if he was unaware that she'd already freed his prisoners.

The wooden door was before her, her fingers reaching for the handle, when she felt his hand graze her braided hair. Her hand pushed the handle down as her shoulder hit the door, and she flew through the space with Ranulf following her. The two of them tumbled over the brick floor, a jumble of scrabbling and cursing.

Gasps and brief screams overrode the hissing of the steam pots and sizzling meat on the hearth. The thumping of the bread halted, and at least one crockery bowl hit the floor, shattering.

"Ye foking bitch!" Ranulf yelled, yanking Tierney up, his hand grabbing her braid, coiling it around his fist. If she didn't rise, he'd pull it right out of her scalp, so she got her feet under her. He pushed her against the plastered wall. "What are ye doing sneaking around Eilean Donan?"

"Trying to find my parents and the crew you detained," she said. No reason to let him know she'd succeeded.

"Master Ranulf, what are ye doing with that lass?" It was the older servant that Tierney had met on her way up the steps when she'd been fully dressed.

"This is my betrothed," he said, "so I can do whatever I wish with her."

"I am not your betrothed, Ranulf. Get that through your numb head."

He shoved her hard against the wall, and she was thankful for the leather corset that padded her, although her head would have a bump.

"Ye can't treat yer…mistress, betrothed, or any woman like that," the maid said.

"Hold yer tongue, woman, or I'll see it removed." Ranulf kept his focus on Tierney, his hand sliding down the leather armor. "And ye're nearly naked." His mouth curved into a leer. "Time to wash away any touch from that damn Macdonald ye've been foking." Like she was a territory to be claimed by pissing or spreading his seed all over it.

Heart thumping wildly, she forced a grin. "You'll find I'm locked up tight."

Ranulf pushed his hand between her legs. The

pressure nearly made her panic, but she breathed through it, knowing he couldn't get through. He yanked on the leather at her pelvis. "What is this contraption?"

"Armor against your lust."

He tried to pull the bodice down, but the thick straps over her shoulders kept it in place. If he yanked enough, he would be able to get that down, but there was no way he could access her pelvic region.

He leaned into her face. "Then I'll cut it off ye."

From what Tierney could see past his shoulders, the kitchen had emptied of witnesses. So much for getting help from the maids and cooks. She was on her own once again. Instead of accepting that fact as part of her life, sadness and then anger mixed with the fear within her.

*I don't want to be alone.*

She screamed, a ferocious yell, and Ranulf yanked her from the wall to push her over the edge of a table where the cooks had been working. Bending her backward, he shoved the heel of his hand against her mouth. Unfortunately, he'd caught her lips partway closed so she couldn't bite him. She sucked large pulls of air through her nose and winced at the cut of Ranulf's fingernails as he tried to move the leather armor from her crotch. Tierney moved her head left and right, trying to dislodge his hand.

If she could reach her dagger, she'd plunge it into him. It was tied into her garter just below her knee. Her fingers slid down the outside of her thigh as she tried to reach the blade.

*Clink.* Shite! The blade was now on the floor, far from her reach.

*I need a weapon! Something. Anything.*

Her wild eyes slid to the lumps on either side of her head. Bread dough. The cook's assistants had been kneading dough for the daily bread. Without debating the effectiveness of bread dough against a violent foe, she grabbed one and used all her force to shove it into Ranulf's face.

When he lessened his hold, cursing, she grabbed the one on the other side to join the first. Both hands full of floury dough, she shoved with all her might.

• • •

Murdoc's voice was more curious than threatening, so Kenan kept his voice the same as he, Rory, and Cyrus slowly stood from their chairs. The three guards followed their example, as well as Henry.

"If the six of us fail to return from Eilean Donan—"

"Seven of us," Henry put in rapidly, pointing at the three other warriors and himself.

"Then there will be war against Clan Matheson," Kenan said. "And if ye think that we could not breach Eilean Donan, remember that my aged aunt did with no trouble at all."

Murdoc let his gaze trail over them, weighing them, not just as warriors but as leaders.

Kenan continued. "We have a chain of commanders behind us, Murdoc. We have thousands of troops who will be fighting to keep ye off our isle, and quite a few who wouldn't mind taking over Eilean Donan after ye're routed, even if 'tis yer brother leading his attack. They all know the chief who sent him."

Murdoc rubbed his short beard. "This all started with the request for a marriage alliance from Chief Douglas MacNicol. He did not wish to be aligned with the clans of Skye."

"Now that ye locked him, his wife, and his crew up and stole his ship, I think he won't hesitate to align with the clans of Skye out there in the harbor," Kenan said, his gaze direct.

*Please let Tierney be out there, too.*

Even though he was furious with her acting on her own, the thought of her being harmed made his blood rush. He wanted to run through the castle searching to make certain she wasn't there. *I won't leave Eilean Donan without her.*

"Maybe we should involve Chief MacNicol in these discussions," Murdoc said.

On the floor, Gilbert groaned. Murdoc looked to one of his men. "See if Wilcox is at home in the village." Murdoc looked to Kenan as the man ran off. "He's a surgeon for yer brother. Meanwhile, let's find Chief MacNicol above." He stood. "I wonder why Ranulf hasn't returned." He looked sideways at Kenan. "What were ye attempting to do with sending yer aunt in here?"

"Again, I don't know what was going through her mind," Kenan said, standing up to walk with Murdoc. Cyrus and Rory followed, along with Henry and the three guards. "She insisted on coming on the ships. Perhaps she truly had a premonition concerning ye."

"'Twas a bloody bad warning," Murdoc said as they walked, and he scratched his head. "I would like to hear more about uniting Scotland, how ye imagine that happening." Murdoc stopped at the archway leading to the stairs and glanced at Kenan. "My cousin died at Solway Moss. 'Twas a ridiculous loss. Fifteen thousand Scots to three thousand English and yet we lost." He rubbed his bearded chin. "Ye're right that we need to align."

"And yet ye are starting war with the MacNicols?" Kenan asked.

Murdoc's lips pinched tight. "'Twas Ranulf's plan to detain them when they sailed here. He was irate to find his betrothed handfasted to ye."

"Tierney never agreed to the betrothal."

Murdoc frowned. "Her father said she had."

"Her father lied." Outrage seethed inside Kenan. Did a father like that deserve to be rescued?

Murdoc's face darkened. "I do not like liars."

Before Kenan could agree, a woman ran around a bend in the corridor, her eyes wide and frantic. "Oh, Chief Murdoc, please come quickly." She waved her hand, barely noticing all the men with her employer.

"What is it, Hazel?" Murdoc asked, starting to follow her. She must be someone of rank in the castle for him to immediately change course.

"Master Ranulf is attacking…one of yer…ladies."

"One of my ladies?" Murdoc asked. "Where?"

"In the kitchens."

He began to stride down the tight corridor, and they all followed. "Which lady?" Murdoc asked.

"The one dressed like a lad in trousers and tunic," Hazel said. "Well, she was dressed that way." She waved her hands about in the air. "Now she's wearing…I don't know what it be."

"Ye have a mistress who dresses like a lad?" one of the Matheson guards asked.

Murdoc looked confused. "I don't believe so."

"She said ye like her to…interact with the other ladies in traditional dress."

*Tierney*. Kenan's chest clenched. Who else would be dressed like a lad and give such an explanation? Kenan charged off into a full run toward the end of the corridor where several younger maids peered into the kitchen.

They squeaked and flattened themselves against opposite walls as he ran past into the room. He slipped on spilled flour and caught himself on a workbench, pulling his sword free. "Tierney?" he yelled.

Tierney didn't look up as she pressed Ranulf backward over a low table, using her body weight to hold him down. She wore some sort of leather corset that came down over her back and arse, curving between her long, bare legs to continue up her front. But what was even more surprising was what she was doing. She held bread dough, shoving it into Ranulf's face. The dough covered his mouth and nostrils as if she tried to push it inside him. Unless he could breathe through his wide eyes, the man was being suffocated.

Kenan saw one of his hands was stabbed to the worktable with a dagger so that only one hand tried to fend Tierney off, and her knee was planted between his legs. As she continued to shove the dough into his face, her knee also continued to push forcefully into his cock and ballocks.

"Well, shite," Cyrus said, stopping next to Kenan.

Rory stood behind them at the doorway. "Doesn't look like she needs much help."

"Lady Tierney!" Henry admonished as he burst into the room, but she didn't turn his way.

"Should we let her finish?" Cyrus asked.

But Kenan rushed past them, grabbing Tierney's shoulders to pull her backward. She struck out at him with her fists, but Kenan caught her to him.

"Tierney. Ye won, lass." He felt the frantic in and out of her breaths. As if finally registering that it was Kenan, she went limp, scarcely standing. Kenan held her to him, his fury at Ranulf barely controlled.

"I'm going to gut ye, Ranulf," Kenan said, his voice low, menacing. "From yer ragged beard to yer cock. Ye foking evil bastard." Rage burned all Kenan's negotiating skills to ashes.

Kenan used one hand to yank his tunic over his head and pulled it down over Tierney's head. It was long enough to cover her to her knees. Even her bloody boots were missing. Where were her clothes? Had Ranulf ripped them away? He wouldn't have bothered with her boots.

Murdoc held his hands out as if trying to part the sea. "No one's gutting anyone right now."

Ranulf's face was white with flour and pieces of dough. He gulped raspy breaths and sneezed, a chunk of dough flying out one nostril. "She's mine! We are betrothed!" His words were breathless croaks.

"If ye wed her, ye'd be dead within a week," Rory said.

"Och, Roar, less time than that," Cyrus said. "Two days at most. One if Kenan's aunt visits."

"Marry me and give me Scorrybreac, or ye will never see yer parents again," Ranulf said, spittle leaving specks on his floury chin.

Tierney straightened, turning in Kenan's arms to cast a sneer at Ranulf. "I'm not marrying anyone, especially not you, you barbaric whoremonger who treats women like herd cows to be used and sacrificed."

"Your parents will die by my blade tonight!" Ranulf yelled back.

"Bloody hell, hold yer tongue!" Murdoc yelled. "I'm the chief and won't allow it."

Tierney pulled away a bit, and Kenan dropped his arms. She leaned slightly forward toward Ranulf. "Keep them. My father abandoned me twice before and was trying to do it again. Keep them." She turned, grabbing Kenan's arm. "We are leaving." She glanced back at him and then to the other non-Matheson men. "All of us."

"Lady Tierney! Yer parents," Henry said.

"Stay if you'd like to wed Ranulf, Henry, otherwise move your arse out of here," she said.

As much as Kenan wanted to bloody Ranulf, Tierney was already rushing through the kitchen to the door in the outer wall. Something had happened. Tierney had surrendered her clothing and had completely changed her plan to save her mother.

Kenan caught Tierney's hand at the door. "Were

yer parents in need of clothes?" he said close to her ear.

She met his gaze. "They were stark naked."

"Rachamaid dhachaidh," Kenan said, and his men followed. Even spluttering Henry walked briskly after them, unwilling to be left behind.

Out in the dark, without light from the new moon, the orchard trees almost blended in with the shadows. The slight glow of torches from the small wall around the bailey cast the only light.

"The sea gate is through the orchard to the west," Tierney said.

"I know." His voice was terse, still full of anger against Ranulf, against Tierney for acting on her own, and against himself for ignoring her own plans.

Tierney was moving slow, picking her way around the roots of the trees, and he remembered her lack of boots. Without a warning, Kenan picked her up and began to run toward the sea wall. "I hope there is a dinghy waiting or 'twill be a cold swim."

"There should be," she said, her arms holding around his neck. "I can—" she started, but he cut in.

"Not without boots."

"I'll keep up."

"For all the gold in Christendom, just hold yer tongue and let me help." He headed toward the darkness along the barely lit white stone of the crumbled wall, which must be the old sea gate.

"So you happen to have all the gold in Christendom?"

"Nay, but I knew ye couldn't hold yer tongue." They climbed over the fallen rocks at the sea gate.

"My hands are full. Make a bird call."

"A bird call?"

"Any bird."

Tierney held her hands to her mouth. "Hoot, hoot."

He would have laughed at the odd sound, but he was concentrating on keeping his footing on the boulders while carrying her.

"Cora makes much better bird calls," she said.

Lanterns flickered from three dinghies sitting just off the shore.

"I will teach ye," he murmured. The woman was clever, courageous, and able to escape deadly predicaments. Maybe she would need him for making proper bird calls.

He set her on the shore and helped Jok, Tomas, Bartholemew, Cyrus, and Rory pull the thick ropes that the men in the dinghies threw to shore. One of them was Jacob Tanner, his gaze scanning the shadows until they fell on Tierney.

"But yer mother," Henry said. "At least ye would negotiate to save her."

"She's already on the *Tempest*," Jacob said, "along with Chief MacNicol."

Tierney climbed into Jacob's boat without a word for her father's old advisor.

Kenan followed her. "Take us to the *Tempest*," Kenan said.

"No," Tierney answered. "I prefer to have a few hours before confronting my father. To the *Sweet Elspet*, Jacob."

Jacob and the other rower pulled hard on the oars.

"Bloody foking hell, Tierney," Kenan said, his words a lowered yell. "Diplomacy was never yer plan." Kenan stared out at the ships lit on the surface of the dark loch. Relief to have her safely heading to his ships warred with his anger at her for putting herself in such danger.

"If you'd listened to my plan, you would have realized that."

"The goal was not bloodshed, only diplomacy."

Tierney snorted. "Ranulf doesn't respond to diplomacy."

Anger shot around inside Kenan, poking holes in his relief. "Murdoc Matheson wants peace for Scotland," he said through stacked teeth.

She turned her face to him. "By invading Skye to take over Scorrybreac? By abducting the chief and lady and crew? By stealing our galleon?"

"'Twas Ranulf who convinced Murdoc to detain the crew and yer parents. Murdoc felt that a true betrothal had been broken. Yer parents would have been released by the end of the evening. My plan was working. Negotiating was working."

She narrowed her eyes. "You have no way of knowing that. He could have been lying, waiting to kill you all."

"A chance I was willing to take. Rory, Cyrus, and I knew that before we walked inside Eilean Donan. But without taking a chance on peace, it will never happen." He shook his head as she stared at him, her face belligerent in the light of the torch. "Tierney, ye are all about being independent, taking risks great enough to see ye dead." He leaned in to her face. She didn't back up. "But ye don't work with anyone, don't trust anyone, and that's dangerous. Not only for ye but for everyone in yer path."

Tierney turned her face away to stare out over the sea. For once, she didn't have a reply.

# CHAPTER TWENTY-SIX

"True love is like ghosts, which everyone talks about and few have seen."

*Francois de La Rochefoucauld – French Writer, 1613–1680*

Tierney pissed with great relief behind the privacy screen in the small room she was sharing with Morag and Sara. Rory, Cyrus, and Kenan shared his captain's cabin. Prying off the armor over the scratches from Ranulf hadn't been pleasant, and she was now dressed in a smock and petticoat again.

"And you stuffed bread dough up his mouth and nose?" Sara said, her voice full of humor, unlike her brother. Kenan had been furious. Even in his whispers to her on the dinghy, he'd thrown daggers at her. She still felt sick from the blood loss.

She swallowed past the familiar guilt. "'Twas the only weapon I could reach, and you can't breathe through it, and bastards can't assault when they can't breathe."

"Clever and quick thinking," Morag said. The kind words didn't lift Tierney up like they should. She wished she could be alone to think and to do something with the blasted press of tears behind her eyes.

Sara shook her head. "I cannot imagine your poor mother being naked for a month."

"They should both be examined for cuts and bruises and taint along with the ship's crew," Morag said.

"We didn't retrieve the ship, did we?" Tierney asked, letting her shoulders slump forward as she sat on the edge of a hammock.

"No," Sara said. "Kenan felt we should depart with the rescued people and negotiate for the ship's return."

There was that word again. Negotiate. Would Murdoc Matheson act with honor when Ranulf surely wouldn't?

*Rap. Rap.*

All three looked at the cabin door, but Morag went to it, pulling it open.

Kenan stood there looking damp, and Tierney noticed the sound of rain above. "Lady Tierney," he said. "A word."

"I highly doubt it will be *one* word," Tierney said as she rose from her seat. Her voice sounded firm, irreverent, but inside she felt the hollowness of regret.

Sara lowered her heavy cloak over her shoulders, and Tierney followed Kenan up the narrow ladder to the deck where a gentle rain pattered down. They stopped at the aft gunwale that was partially covered by raised sails. The water whooshed and gurgled behind the ship as they sailed through the cold, dark waters of the loch.

They stood in silence for so long that Tierney jumped when Kenan spoke. "We weren't able to speak freely in the dinghy."

"You seemed to speak fine," she said,

remembering his biting words. She looked at him. "Or are you going to yell at me now that you aren't worried about your men hearing?"

"Damn it, Tierney, ye could have been killed." He wasn't yelling, but his words were full of force. "Ye were assaulted." He looked out at the darkness. "I will kill that bastard."

"You could have been killed, too," she said, her heart thumping.

"I am a warrior."

"So am I, but your death is acceptable? You can risk your life, but I can't? You wouldn't even consider my plans. Ignored them. Wanted me to ring a damn bell."

He ran his hands through his hair that was getting wetter with the rain blowing down around the sail. He huffed. "When I saw ye…fighting for yer life, saving yer own life…my gut all but dropped out of me. I would have given up everything…" He rubbed a hand down his face. "Would have turned my back on uniting the clans to save ye, to take revenge upon Ranulf."

She looked up at him. "But you didn't. You didn't retaliate."

He shook his head. "I was so close." He held his thumb and forefinger an inch apart. "I could have easily killed Ranulf before his brother and jeopardized our chance of peace."

"Because of me."

"Ye were only to release the crew and get to safety. It was a good plan."

"But you weren't safe."

"But ye would be."

"I've never been safe!" she yelled. "My whole life is dangerous. I've learned to fight for my freedom despite being told no. I've learned to do it alone."

"Ye do not have to fight alone. I am here to protect ye."

"I don't want you protecting me!"

"Why not?"

"Because one day you will stop, and I'll be alone again." Her voice had risen over the sound of the increasing rain. "On my own, trying to protect Maggie and me and Gabriel." She thumped her fist into the middle of his chest with each name as words tumbled out of her. "You will treat me like…like I'm everything to you until I'm not, and then I'll need to survive without your help. So I never stop fighting. I never let my guard down. I won't fall for that again. I just won't!" She felt the words tear out of her like a sob, and she stepped to the rail, her face turned up to the rain to wash away the unbidden tears.

Her breath came in shallow inhales as she stared blindly out into the stormy night. Kenan came up beside her. His face bent near hers, his lips at her ear. "I'm not yer father, Tierney. I don't love ye until someone better shows up."

Love? Did he say love? Her heart clenched hard, making her want to throw up. How dare he lie to her?

She turned to him, blinking, her face fierce. "I know you are not my father. It isn't that." The denial came out even though her tears came with it. Tears that showed he'd pressed the festering open wound.

He wouldn't look away, tethering her with his gaze. "Aye, I think it is. He left ye once he had a son.

Stopped taking ye hunting, to that cottage in the woods, teaching ye things when Gabriel came around. Cora told me he stopped doing everything with ye, turned his back on ye. And then he married ye off to a monster. Someone ye might have thought would be good to ye, protect ye, but then ye ended up having to protect yerself and Maggie from him."

Tierney felt a cracking inside as if the pitcher holding her tears of frustration and hurt were being broken, smashed with the hammer of his words, and the deluge of emotion was beyond her control. She stood stiff there in the tempest growing around them, the sky mimicking the monster of sorrow, hate, and distrust that lived within her.

*No, no, no! I can't… I'm fine. I'm better alone.* She concentrated on pulling air through her lips and releasing it as hard sobs came unbeckoned and unwanted. 'Twas like a purging.

Kenan pulled her against him, his arms wrapping around her. Even though she wanted to be strong enough to yank back, his warmth and strength drew her, allowing her to be weak for a moment. Just a moment. She would regain control soon.

*Right now. I will turn away.*

Control and strength and independence would fill her again. She waited, letting the sobs subside, but the tears continued, adding salt to his already drenched tunic.

Tierney curled in on herself, her arms tucked as he held her against him. He didn't ask her to stop, didn't try to usher her somewhere else. He just held her, a rock in the storm. Slowly her arms opened, and she slid them around his waist, her fingers curling into the back of his wet tunic.

"Chief Kenan," someone called. "The storm's a right banshee. We will have to put in near Dun Haakon for the night."

She tried to release him, but he didn't drop his arms. "Tell Cyrus Mackinnon," Kenan said over her head.

"Aye," the man said, and Tierney could hear him striding off, the thumps of his boots disappearing quickly under the sound of the ship cutting through growing waves and wind.

With a full breath, Tierney released his tunic and lifted her head. She stared up into Kenan's face. It was hard to see him in the deep shadows, but he was looking at her. His hand came up to brush a strand of wet hair from her cheek, taking the time to slide it behind her equally wet ear. The gentle touch made her heartbeat tremble. He leaned in but didn't kiss her, his mouth moving to her ear. His breath was warm. "When ye're ready to believe I am who I say I am, that I'm speaking truth to ye…marry me, Tierney."

He didn't wait for an answer but turned, his hand finding hers. He slid his fingers through hers, weaving them intimately as he led her back to the room where he'd found her.

*Rap. Rap.*

Sara answered the door, her eyes growing wide. "And we just got her warm and dressed." She gave her brother a scolding look. "I don't even know if we have more dry gowns."

Sara took her from Kenan's arm, looking back and forth between them before giving her brother a withering look. "What did you say to her?"

"I must see to the storm," he said and turned away.

Sara closed the door and hurried over to Tierney with a towel. "What did my awful brother do to you?"

Morag came to stand before her while Sara mopped Tierney's face. Tierney looked down at her folded hands. "He asked me to marry him."

• • •

"So ye truly want to wed the woman who drugged and shackled ye?" Cyrus asked as he climbed over the side to descend into the dinghy tied to the *Sweet Elspet*.

Kenan's eyes narrowed as he looked at Rory, standing beside him at the gunwale.

Rory shrugged. "I thought it best to let Cy know ye hadn't just run off from my wedding with her in an effort to avoid Grace."

Kenan looked back at Cyrus. "She had honorable reasons."

"Good thing she didn't have any bread dough to suffocate ye with," Cyrus said as he climbed down the rope ladder.

"I wouldn't have done her much good dead."

"Ye still might want to lock her out of the kitchen when ye marry," Rory said.

When? It was definitely more of an *if* they marry.

Cyrus grinned and gave a small shake to his head. "I'll tell Grace that ye aren't the man for her." His smile flattened as he sat in the small boat where

Bartholomew had already taken up the oars. "And I will stop Father from sending troops to burn Dunscaith. Somehow."

"Thank ye," Kenan said, and Cyrus nodded.

Cyrus and Bartholomew would walk the rest of the way back to Dun Haakon along the shoreline. The rest of the Mackinnons who'd accompanied Cyrus would journey back to Dunscaith's port to ride their horses home. Cyrus was anxious to see how his father fared and if he'd made plans to attack during the few days he'd been gone.

"Sails to be raised," Tomas called out, taking his cue from Kenan's nod. Voices repeated the order down the *Sweet Elspet*. *The Tempest* and half the Birlinn ships had already moved down the strait of Kyle Rhea toward the Sleat Peninsula.

A rotation on both ships had kept watch through the storm and into the morning to see if the Mathesons would launch a naval attack after them, but the seas had remained vacant. Kenan had no idea how Murdoc would react after finding Tierney's parents and the MacNicol crew liberated. Prior to that, he'd sounded reasonable and as annoyed with Ranulf as Kenan was about Gilbert. The two second sons should be stranded on an isle to rule it together, away from the rest of Scotland.

The sails snapped, raining water upon them on deck, as they caught the wind. Rory stood beside Kenan at the rail, letting the sailors move around the coils of ropes and supply crates. With the addition of the *Rosemary's* crew split between both ships, there were more than enough hands on deck.

Kenan watched, but his mind played out the

conversation from last night. He'd pushed her to tears, but after what she'd endured, Tierney needed to bleed out some of that pain. He knew one conversation wouldn't be enough to lighten her past, but hopefully it was a start. The fact that she hadn't pushed him away, had finally clung to him, added to the hopeful flame in his chest.

"Has she given ye an answer yet?" Rory asked.

"I didn't ask her to marry me."

"Sara said ye did."

Kenan steepled his fingers on his forehead, leaving his thumb free to push into his temple that had begun to ache. "I told her that if she decided she could marry someone again, she should marry me. That's not asking her."

Rory shrugged. "Tierney told Sara and Morag ye asked her to marry her."

*Daingead.* What an awful proposal if that had been one. "If I was really asking, I wouldn't have done so in a downpour on the deck of a tossing ship."

"I'm just saying, Tierney, Sara, and yer aunt think ye've asked for Tierney's hand."

"Did Tierney tell Sara if she'd answer aye or nay?"

"So ye did ask?"

"Bloody hell, Rory, I don't know. Maybe I did. I don't really care about the asking, only the answer."

Rory's brows rose. "Ladies care about the asking."

Kenan made a sound like a growl, causing several men nearby to glance his way. "Have ye seen Tierney this morn?" He had gone to her cabin at first light but didn't hear any movement inside and didn't want to disturb the ladies if they were sleeping.

"I saw Sara," Rory said, "down in the hull behind some crates." He gave a wicked grin. "'Twas quite a nice way to wake up."

Kenan stared at him without blinking until Rory continued. "Sara says Tierney was still asleep. She has bruised feet from running on rocks, scratches from Ranulf that they've treated with an herbal paste, and bruises the shape of fingers around her upper arms and shoulders. Otherwise, she is well."

"I should have run that bastard through," Kenan said.

"It would have felt good." Rory nodded. "But we decided to try for peace instead of conquest. Leaving him alive was the best, even though I get the idea that Murdoc wouldn't mind his brother being gone."

"Like me with Gilbert, a thorn stuck in my foot. Annoying as hell with the possibility of tainting my blood and killing me."

"I wonder where Winnie Mar is and her brother, Reid," Rory said.

"One thorn at a time," Kenan said. Right now, he was completely focused on another problem, a fallen angel with a brilliant mind, the courage of a goddess, and a stubborn streak as long as Hadrian's wall.

A fallen angel he was beginning to think he couldn't live without.

# CHAPTER TWENTY-SEVEN

"Human misery must somewhere have a stop; there
is no wind that always blows a storm."

*Euripides – Greek Poet, 480 BC–406 BC*

The next three days consisted of treating the crew of
the *Rosemary*, writing letters to gain support for
peace on the Isle of Skye to thwart a possible attack
by Clan Matheson, and avoiding Kenan. *He wants to
marry me, even after I foiled his plan. 'Tis a trick, a
cruel trick that will tear me apart when he walks
away.*

Tierney had longed to go to Kenan, find him
among his men, pull him aside and… What? Entice
him to bed? Say again that she will never marry
anyone, tying herself to a man? Or would she play
the fool and say she'd marry him? How could she be
so foolish as to even consider that? Every man she'd
known had hurt her. *Except the man you drugged,
chained, and coerced.*

After all that, she didn't deserve him. "So foolish," she whispered.

"Not foolish," Henry said. "Just hopeful." Henry,
who'd been silent for so long that Tierney had felt
alone in the cottage, held out one of the missives
she'd written to the new chief of Clan Macqueen on
the northern end of Skye. "Ye think a tribunal of
chiefs will work?" Henry asked. "And that Kenan

Macdonald would be the first leader." He shook the brittle paper toward her. "And ye want to resurrect the title Lord of the Isles."

She looked down at the letter she was penning to Cyrus's father, who was currently still alive. "I know what's in it, Henry. I wrote it."

"Ye can't send this without yer father looking at it. And Kenan Macdonald and Rory MacLeod, too, probably Cyrus Mackinnon."

"I have no intention of bribing a rider to carry these letters out in secret." She'd had enough of executing rash plans in secret. "But someone needs to start this process."

And she was bored. Bored of waiting for herself to decide what to say to Kenan. She'd gone over and over their discussion on the deck of the *Sweet Elspet*, yelling and then whispering over the actual tempest swirling around them and pelting them with rain. Every time she heard him in her head say that he wasn't her father, she felt her chest tighten and the ache of tears form in her eyes. That had to mean he was somewhere close to the truth.

"What does yer father say about this?" Henry asked, nodding toward the field beyond the window where Douglas MacNicol trained with the other warriors. Tierney sat in a cottage where she was staying with her mother, Fannie, and Morag. Kenan had given the bedchamber in Dunscaith to Rory and Sara and was sleeping with the warriors, as was her father.

"I haven't spoken with him about this since he doesn't listen to anything I say anyway." She dabbed her pen in the inkwell. "I assume he'll support peace with Clan MacLeod and Clan Macdonald as allies."

Henry's face reddened. "Lady Tierney, ye need to speak with him about…what occurred."

Tierney swung her face up to him. "Which part? The part where he ignored me as soon as he had a son? Or when he married me off to someone who assaulted me nightly and threatened his grand-daughter? Or the part where he refused to help me and Maggie escape from Wallace even when I came to him with a swollen lip and blackened eyes? Or when he tried to give me away a second time to Ranulf Matheson?

"Or maybe I should ask him all about how he survived being naked for a month at Eilean Donan. Did he enjoy it as much as when Wallace did the same to me, locking me naked in a closet?"

Henry's face went from red to white, his lips pinching tight. "I am sure he did not—"

"Know? He knew about Wallace's abuse. Jacob told him."

"I was going to say he did not intend for ye to be harmed."

"He did not lock me and my daughter in a room to die, but he might as well have since he was told about it."

"Only after the fact." Her father's voice made her quill freeze, hovering over the paper.

Tierney's face snapped up to the open window. Morag stood next to Douglas MacNicol. Morag's long finger extended to Henry. "You come out here so these two can discuss through the window in pri-vate."

"Through the window?" Douglas asked, glancing

at her.

"I can't guarantee she's unarmed," Morag said. "You better stay out of reach."

Henry left, shutting the door behind him, and Tierney turned her face back to the letters flattened on the table before her. Her gaze danced across the scrawl where she'd been copying the initial plan for the chiefs of Skye to meet at an assembly to discuss creating a strong isle.

After she picked back up where she was writing, her father's words stalled her scratching. "I heard all ye said to Henry just now."

"If you don't want to hear the truth, don't listen at open windows."

"Kenan's witch of an aunt didn't give me much choice."

Tierney responded without looking up. "That witch helped get you out of Eilean Donan."

"As did ye."

She glanced at him. "I was being a naughty lass, Father, something you won't stand for."

His face was red, and his nostrils flared as he inhaled. "I was trying to help ye be a respectable lass. Ye were too wild as a child, and I was teaching ye to be even more wild when I took ye hunting and shooting."

"I will always be too wild for you, Father." She looked back down at the paper but didn't really see it. "And I don't think I will be able to change at this point in my life."

"That's...all well, then." Douglas began to pace outside the window. "When we go back to Scorrybreac..." He cleared his throat. "I would like to include ye in strategy discussions. Ye've been very clever in how—"

"I am not returning to Scorrybreac," she said, raising her eyes to him. "Maggie and I will remain living with the MacLeods of Dunvegan. I've already asked Lady Sara. Then ye can have Gabriel all to yourself to mold into a chief."

He curled his fingers over the edge of the window. "Tier," he said, using her shortened name like he had when she was a child. It caused her face to bloom with heat. "I've...I've been...wrong in a number of ways, especially when it came to raising a daughter."

She stared at him. "That's part of it. You needed to raise a person, not a daughter. I will never be the daughter you want me to be, someone who flounces about in ribbons and does what she's told to do."

"My mistakes have been explained to me quite clearly by that wit— Mistress Morag." He exhaled through his nose. "And Wallace was a mistake. Ye seemed agreeable at the beginning. Perhaps I wanted to convince myself you'd eventually be happy."

Tierney's chest felt tight, and her skin prickled. She blinked. *I will not cry.* "Wallace was a mistake, and so was using me to align with Clan Matheson by trying to give me to Ranulf."

He nodded, his face drawn. "I see that." He looked over his shoulder toward the fields where Kenan and Rory worked with the warriors. "And I see the need for working peacefully with the clans on Skye to make our isle strong. Kenan Macdonald makes some very good points, and he has a way about him that makes people agree with him." He scratched his thinning hair. "He is a good man."

Tierney stared at him. His endorsement meant nothing. Except that pride swelled in her. Kenan Macdonald was a good man. *And he wants to marry me.* Even though he'd seen firsthand that she wasn't one to behave and follow orders without question. "He's a natural leader," she said. "People listen to him, and he's wise and kind and brave."

"Sounds like a perfect candidate for Lord of the Isles," Douglas said.

He had heard about her suggestions, about bringing the position back to keep the Isle of Skye strong and eventually including the rest of the islands.

"Not sure if he believes that."

Her father shrugged. "He needs a good advisor to make it work, someone clever and daring, someone who does things that people don't expect with such commitment that they realize it was the only thing to do." He nodded to her. "Like ye." He smiled at her, and Tierney's chest felt hot as he nodded. "I see the value in that now."

She didn't say anything. She couldn't without tears breaching her eyes and embarrassing her. Her father thought she was clever, someone who could help in an important way. She squeezed her eyes shut.

"I will go back to helping organize the lads now," Douglas said at the window. "Whatever ye may think, Tier, know that…I do love ye." He turned then and marched back out toward the field.

Tierney wiped a quick finger under her eye, her hardened heart feeling cracked in a thousand pieces.

• • •

Kenan stood in the growing darkness on the newly slated roof of Dunscaith where his glider had been hauled. The wings were actually in good shape. Only a few leather straps had broken with the force of the impact into the sea. He laced a new one in place to tie tightly.

*Tierney promised she'd help me with this.* Should he go find her?

It had been four days since he'd held her on the deck of his ship in the rain, four days since he told her she should consider marrying him.

Four days since he sent Cyrus back to Dun Haakon with a letter for Grace explaining he could only ever marry one woman while kindly saying that it wasn't her. Four days of preparing for war with Clan Mackinnon and awaiting retaliation from Clan Matheson. Four days of waiting because Sara said he should give Tierney space to sort her feelings.

"Mo chreach," he murmured and ran a hand through his hair to cup the back of his head and stretch his shoulders. If he gave Tierney more time and space, she'd leave, take Maggie, and disappear into the mist. She could do it. Hunting for food. Sleeping in trees. Beating off wolves with her bare hands.

To hell with waiting for her to sort her feelings. He dropped the ties and turned to the stone steps that led down into the slowly resurrecting castle and froze.

"Tierney," he said, and for a moment he

wondered if he'd conjured her only in his mind. She stood in the glow of the torch set into the wall that he'd lit. Her hair was down around her shoulders, and the flamelight shined against the golden streaks in the waves. She wore a simple gown that laced in the front and slid against the hills and valleys of her body, skimming her where he wished to touch her.

He watched her chest rise and fall with her breath as if she'd charged up the three stories of steps. "You are up here," she said.

He motioned behind him. "Working on my gli... der," the word stretching out as she walked toward him. The breeze picked up the edges of her hair so that she looked like an angel lowering from the sky.

She didn't say anything but walked right up to him until he could feel the softness of her form against him. She rested her forehead against his chest, her arms by her sides, and he breathed in the fresh scent of her hair.

*I need her.* The realization yelled through him.

Kenan's arms came around her gently as if worried the pressure would make her disappear into mist. But she remained solid.

She tilted her face up, and his hand cupped the side of her face.

*Don't disappear. Don't be a dream.*

He'd had dreams about Tierney, dreams that had left him panting and depleted when he woke.

Tingles raised the small hairs along his arms as she lifted her hands to rest on his chest, sliding over to his shoulders.

"I will never be a meek lass," she said, "a woman who will follow what she's told to do, having bairns and keeping her opinions to herself. I cannot be that woman, that wife."

"I don't wa—"

She pressed a fingertip to his lips, stopping him.

"I need to tell you all this." She waited until he nodded and lowered her finger. He wanted to hear her thoughts, too, and this was the first time she seemed to be opening up.

"My father wanted me to be…different than who I am. I was always told I was behaving too brash or I was talking too much or I had too many opinions. For a while I tried to stop being too much of…everything. I even thought I could be a proper wife to Wallace. That's what I was focused on instead of seeing him for who he was before I trapped myself into marriage with him."

She looked down at his throat. "I thought I could try to be…proper, but I can't. Eilean Donan proved that." She snorted softly. "I can be a partner, but I won't be silent nor yielding when I don't agree. I'm working on compromise." She tilted her head side to side and then lifted her eyes to his. "But I will likely always be somewhat bad."

"Bad?" he asked, his brows rising.

She moved her hand. "Fallen, naughty, probably even broken."

Kenan watched the firelight flicker across her face, and his chest squeezed at the worry he saw dragging down her smile. He slid his thumb over those lips. "I don't see bad, Tierney. I see clever, strong, brave, and someone who won't sit by and let the wrong thing befall the people ye love."

"You're wrong," she said. "I am—"

He put a finger over her lips to stop her. "My turn."

He waited until she nodded to drop his finger, although he had a feeling he'd have to stop her again. She looked like she was waiting to refute anything he said.

"And I like naughty," he said, giving her a wicked grin. Her lips twitched like she fought a smile of her own.

"I think we make a good team. I've been called," here he hesitated around the word he'd hated, "kind. And I've been told that being considerate of others makes me a brilliant negotiator." He tapped his own chest. "And ye, Tierney MacNicol, are clever, stubborn, and someone who takes risks, which makes ye a brilliant warrior and protector." He slid his hands up and down her arms. "We can work together on yer idea of bringing back Lord of the Isles. It could unite the clans, at least on Skye and the isles."

She drew closer to him. "So you don't mind that I'm not a proper woman?"

"First, I'd like to say I love that ye're not whatever ye think is a proper woman." The teasing leer was evident in his voice. Then his smile softened. "But I believe that most people aren't good or bad. They are just who they are."

She released a full breath and pressed against him. "So 'tis not improper if I…" She slid her hand lower between them, stroking down over his cock beneath his plaid.

He groaned, his hands climbing up to comb through her heavy locks of golden hair. "Mo Dhia, if that's improper, I love improper." He lowered his mouth to hers. She kissed him back with open passion as if she'd been hiding her wild nature before.

He lifted her against him, fitting the crux of her legs around his throbbing cock. He turned and walked them back toward the middle of the newly finished roof. He'd brought up a pile of blankets with which to cover his glider to protect it from rain. Setting Tierney down, he broke the kiss. "Don't disappear." He waited for her nod and then sprang to the folded pile of blankets and returned, snapping them open across the roof.

She pulled him down to the middle of them, her mouth finding his again. Lord, she was warm and soft and smelled of flowers and spice. He tried to roll over her, but she planted an open hand on his shoulder. "You watch the stars," she said and pressed him back.

He shoved another blanket under his head and watched her lean over to blow through his lantern, extinguishing the light. "To better see the stars."

The rooftop was swollen with darkness. Only a scant curve of moon had returned. Tierney leaned down over him, her hair tickling the sides of his face, shrouding them. Her lips pressed against his, and the coolness of her skin warmed. The kiss slid immediately into wild, hold-nothing-back merging of lips and tongues and tastes.

"God, lass, ye taste like heat and need and everything wanton," he said against her.

"Not good or proper," she whispered.

"Absolutely perfect."

She sniffed a little laugh, and he heard joy and lightness in it, as if a burden had been lifted. But then he was awash in sensation as she straddled him, rucking up her skirts, and he couldn't think anymore. Only the wool of his plaid separated his cock from the heat between her legs.

His eyes had adjusted enough to see her fingers pull the ties of her bodice, loosening them. There were no stays underneath, only a lace-edged smock. With a gentle back and forth of her shoulders, both fell down enough that the perfect moons of her breasts came out.

Kenan pulled her back to his mouth, his hand palming one warm orb while he tugged his belt open with the other. The belt loosened, the buckle thudding softly on the blanket next to his hip, and he pushed his plaid open.

A rustle of petticoat was the only sound above their lips moving against one another. He raised his knees and felt the fabric of her skirt go over them and her hot slit flatten against his cock, pressing it to his abdomen. He groaned, and his fingers dug their way past all the layers of dress until he reached her inner thigh.

Tierney slid up his bare body until his lips captured her nipple. She moaned as he sucked, and gasped softly as his fingers found her heat. Holy Lord, she was ready, slick and open, her body already moving in a rhythm that would milk him dry. He held his cock so that the tip touched her.

"Yesssss…"

Kenan rubbed himself along her and up to her sensitive nub. "Holy Joan," she whispered. Her breathing was heavy, and he broke the seal over her nipple.

He looked up and saw her poised above him, her breasts out, nipples hard, and a petticoat billowed out around them. He pulled her forward again, kissing her as he held his cock, aiming true. He thrust upward as he pushed her hips down.

Her breath caught, the gasp turning into a long moan, and she sat up, completely impaling herself on him as she sought to catch her breath. His need for her surged up inside him, his need to slam into her over and over, his need to touch her very soul.

Reaching up to squeeze her breasts, Kenan's thumb and forefinger pinched her nipples as she began to move up and down his length. She leaned forward, her hair again cascading around them, to hold onto his shoulders. With each rise and fall, her wet channel gripped him, and her sweet breasts bounced. He reached forward under the petticoats and rubbed his thumb briskly over her sensitive clitoris.

"Oh God, yes," she crooned, her breaths shallow and fast. As she sat on top of him, she held her breasts, cupping and palming them herself as he worked her flesh below. Hair dancing in the night breeze, the sliver of moon highlighting her pale skin, unembarrassed to show him her passion, her want of him. She was the most beautiful creature he'd ever seen.

She tried to find him through the layers of skirts. "Too many clothes."

Kenan reached behind her and tugged open the strings of her petticoat. She slowly rose off him, breaking contact to yank the layers of fabric off her body. And then he watched as her naked form straddled him again.

Poising at the top of his cock, her body totally open and dripping with want, she looked down at him. "Catch me," she said and dropped down over his shaft.

Kenan couldn't breathe for a moment with the lust that rolled through him. She leaned forward across his chest, and he caught her hip bones in his hands. She was on top, but he was moving her back and forth over his body. She panted and moaned, propping herself again on his shoulders, her pale breasts moving before his face. Her clitoris was pressed against his pelvic bone as he met each thrust, rubbing her there until he felt her channel contract around him.

"Yessss," she moaned, and he felt her climax from the tip of his cock to the root. And he exploded inside her.

He held her over him as their rhythm slowed, loving the feel of her against his skin, the feel of him still inside her.

Tierney shivered and rolled to her side, taking Kenan with her, their legs entwined. Her head nestled against his other shoulder as their bodies cooled in the chilled air, and he pulled another blanket over them.

He looked up at the stars, knowing all the constellations could have watched them writhing together, climaxing together. Would Orion be jealous or achy from watching?

"That wasn't too improper," she said, her breath against his chest.

"If ye plan to take the holy vows as a nun, then perhaps."

She slapped his arm playfully and pushed up onto her elbow to look at him. "I am a wanton creature, Kenan Macdonald," she said. "With you, anyway."

He cradled her head as he rolled them over and looked down into her beautiful face. "I want ye exactly how ye are, Tierney MacNicol."

She studied him, and her hand rose to his cheek. He leaned in and kissed her before falling back to lie beside her. He heard her sigh in what sounded like contentment. Perhaps they would stay up there together all night since Rory and Sara had his bed below.

"Look," Tierney said, her fingertip rising to point. "A lucky star."

Kenan caught the long tail that streaked across the night sky. "Morag says to make a wish when ye see one," he said, his voice deep but quiet.

"Did you wish?"

"Aye."

"What for?"

"One's wish is one's own."

Tierney released her breath, and they lay together in silence, looking up at the millions of sparkling lights in the heavens.

"Kenan?" she said.

"Aye?"

"The answer is…yes."

The finger that he'd been absently stroking her arm with stilled. "Yes?"

"Yes," she repeated. "If your star wish was to marry me."

Kenan's head turned to hers on the makeshift

pillow, and for a long moment he couldn't seem to move. Then a smile slowly curved his lips. "Come here, ye perfectly imperfect woman, soon to be my wife."

She laughed as he pulled her back across to drape over him. Hope burst inside Kenan. If she married him, she would eventually love him. And that was imperative because he realized he was completely in love with Tierney MacNicol.

# CHAPTER TWENTY-EIGHT

"Love shows itself more in adversity than in
prosperity; as light does, which shines most where
the place is darkest."

*Leonardo da Vinci – Italian artist and scientist,
1452–1519*

A week had passed since that clear night when the
stars witnessed Tierney's proposal, or answer, or
whatever the amazing interlude had been. Even in
the light of the next morning, she hadn't retracted
the idea of marriage, informing her parents that she
wished to make the handfasting something more
official.

Kenan stood on the hill above Dunscaith, waiting
with the rest of the wedding party and spectators.
He saw Jacob Tanner amongst the MacNicol warriors. "I'll be right back," he said to Cyrus and Rory
and walked over. Kenan hadn't spoken to Jacob except for a few words since their fight. He'd been
waiting for an opportunity to catch the young man
alone since he'd picked more details out of Tierney
about her life with Wallace.

"Jacob," he said. "A word." The man didn't move.
"It will be quick."

"Go on," said one of the warriors. "'Tis his wedding day."

Jacob kept his frown but walked over to him

away from the crowd. Kenan held out his hand, but Jacob just stared at it, so Kenan dropped it. "I just want to thank ye, Jacob, for being a good friend to Tierney." He met Jacob's permanently narrowed eyes. "Especially…what I'm thinking ye did to help her out of her marriage to that bastard, Wallace."

Jacob's eyes opened wider for a moment. "Don't know what ye mean."

"I'm grateful," Kenan said. He rested his hand on Jacob's shoulder as if he were passing him to walk away, but he stopped. "That Wallace Macqueen happened to lose his footing on those cliffs, and that ye happened to go directly to find Tierney and Maggie locked without food or water in that foking closet."

His hand squeezed Jacob's shoulder as Kenan tamped down the fury that rose up whenever he thought about it. "I…am truly grateful." Without glancing at him, Kenan walked away, back to where the priest, Father Bright, stood with Cyrus and Rory. They were all staring down at Dunscaith Castle.

"Ye think she will emerge?" Cyrus asked as Kenan walked up. "She'd sworn never to marry anyone ever again."

Rory playfully punched Cyrus's arm. "Stop worrying him."

"I'm just saying," Cyrus continued, "she has a history of surprising us, changing plans, climbing trees—"

"Hold yer tongue," Rory said again, the humor out of his voice. "Can't ye see he's growing pale?"

Kenan watched the gate of Dunscaith for a sign of Tierney. She'd asked Sara if she could get ready in the bedchamber, and his sister had made Rory move out immediately. So they'd had the bed together for the week.

Sara had just arrived out of the castle, holding Maggie's wee hand. She waved at Kenan as if to tell him he had nothing to worry about.

Tierney had sent for Cora, Gabriel, and Maggie, along with the twins, Eliza and Eleri, to watch the ceremony. Even Rory's two old advisors, John and Simon, had come, escorting Doris and Edith, who still had their swords strapped to their sides like elderly warrior maidens. And Father Bright had been recalled from the mainland to perform the ceremony.

Henry stood as far away as he could from Morag, where several village children held bits of Bannocks out for her crows to nip from their little hands. Tierney's father waited for her at the gates with her horse, Fleet, who'd been groomed and beribboned for the occasion.

Sara trudged up the hill and came to stand next to Kenan. "Brides always take some time to prepare their hair and costume. I left her mother with her just now." She patted his arm. "Perhaps Fannie is giving her the talk about what to expect on her wedding night."

Kenan's face turned to her, and he saw the humor in her gaze. "She still wants to marry me."

"She seems to," Sara said, nodding, but the humor left her face. Lowering her voice, she said, "But Tierney's been through a lot, trauma that she's still working through."

He stared at her. "Did she say something just now? Hinted that she doesn't want to go through with the ceremony?" A coldness tinged his words, but his sister knew him well.

She shook her head. "Of course not. I'm simply saying she's been through a lot, especially when she was married to a sadistic, diseased wolf of a man, and she might be a bit nervous and take her time coming out."

Kenan inhaled, releasing the breath. "I would kill him if given the chance, slicing off piece after piece until he stopped twitching."

She patted his chest. "Somehow such sentiments don't seem appropriate for a wedding."

They both looked out toward the gates where Douglas MacNicol and Fleet waited.

• • •

Tierney stared at herself in the polished glass and barely recognized the beauty staring back. Sara, Cora, and her mother had helped Tierney alter the magnificent wedding costume Sara's mother, Elspet, had worn to fit Tierney's slender frame better. The flowing petticoat had bluebells and birds stitched into the overskirt that parted in the front to reveal a panel of blue satin, studded with pearls. Old lace had been replaced with satin ribbon around the edging, giving a crisp, new look. A panel of sheer fabric was removed from the wide neckline, leaving Tierney's collarbone exposed from shoulder to shoulder. And they'd added a train of ivory satin edged with blue to match the gown. A crown of bluebells and perfect daisies sat in Tierney's hair. Half her golden curls were lifted and woven to sit inside the crown while the rest of the curls cascaded down to the middle of her back. Even her slippers had been decorated with matching ribbon roses in ivory and blue.

"You are exquisite," Fannie said, smiling brightly.

Tierney's heart flipped at the memory of her mother saying the same sentiment when she'd wed Wallace. That day, she'd just wanted to make her father proud.

*That's not why I'm marrying Kenan.*

"I am so glad I talked you out of wearing that leather contraption underneath," Fannie said.

Tierney had considered putting on Morag's armor to surprise Kenan, giving him the key as a symbolic gesture. But the neckline was low enough that the edge of the armor might show. She'd save it for another night when she wanted to tease him a bit.

"'Tis…beautiful," Tierney said, holding out the full petticoats.

Fannie walked closer, her slim hand touching her cheek. Her fingers were cool on Tierney's warm skin. "*You* are beautiful." Tears sat in her mother's eyes. "And you've always deserved love. Kenan loves you. 'Tis obvious to everyone who witnesses him looking at you."

"I…I love him, too," she whispered, and her mother's tears swelled out. Tierney had to blink to keep her own back. She smiled. "I do. I love him. I will tell him in a few minutes."

Fannie nodded, dabbing under her eyes with a handkerchief. "Then let's get you out there." Her mother walked to the door. "I'll let your father know you're coming. I fear we've taken longer than we thought to get ready. Poor Kenan will wonder." She hurried out of the room as Tierney looked at herself in the mirror.

*I love him.*

The words blew through her chest like the inhalation of a fresh breeze. "I want to marry him," she whispered to the woman in the mirror.

In the reflection, Tierney caught a movement near the door. Perhaps her father had grown weary of waiting and had come to fetch her. Things had been better since he'd stood at the window of the cottage. Just releasing the betrayal she'd felt and seeing him sad about his poor judgment had made it so she didn't roil with fury every time she saw him.

She turned, enjoying the feel of the full skirts billowing out around her. And then her heart thumped like someone had kicked it.

"Aren't ye a bonny lass?" Ranulf Matheson stood in the doorway. He took two steps inside the room and shut the door behind him. "'Twas almost like ye knew I was coming."

• • •

"Perhaps she will steal yer wings again," Cyrus said. "Watch the roofline."

Rory picked up a pebble and threw it at Cyrus. "I don't remember ye being such a foking pest when we were in Carlisle."

"Starvation and smelling like a neglected animal took away my humor," Cyrus said.

"Her mother just came out," Kenan said, relief relaxing his fists. He'd been holding them so tightly they tingled now. "She's taking Chief Douglas's arm." He exhaled. Nothing was wrong. Tierney was just taking her time getting ready.

He had half expected her to call things off this past week. Every time he woke to see her staring down at him, her features wary, he wanted to ask her if she truly wanted to wed. But it would make him sound doubtful, and he was definitely not doubtful. Kenan wanted nothing else but to wake up next to Tierney every morning for the rest of his life and see what unexpected thing would pop from her rose-hued lips. He loved to watch her talking with Maggie, her little self. She treated her daughter with such respect, as if everything she said was important. Tierney would never disregard the thoughts and feelings of her children.

And in bed, Tierney was adventurous. Even though she wasn't a virgin, she'd known little of pleasure, and Kenan was determined for her to feel every ounce of sweet torture and release he could wring from her. Och, but life with her would never be boring again. He smiled just thinking about it and quickly adjusted his cock through his plaid.

A man trotted up the hill, and Tomas intercepted him, taking a folded paper.

"A note from yer father, Cy?" Kenan asked. "Wishing me wedded bliss?"

Rory snorted.

"If my father sends a message," Cyrus said, "'twill be some poorly written threat of war." Hamish Mackinnon was still feeling poorly, but a letter from Grace the day before said he was improving. Kenan would not wish ill on his friend's father, but Hamish's old vengeance made peace difficult. And he controlled a large section of territory on the Isle of Skye.

"Maybe 'tis a response to Tierney's letter about the Lord of the Isles Council," Kenan said.

Tomas ran over but stopped before Kenan instead of Cyrus. "Message from Eilean Donan."

All eyes turned first to Tomas and then to Kenan. He looked at the seal, the fist holding a tri-cross identical to the one he wore on his own finger, the Macdonald family crest. "Gilbert."

Kenan broke it and unfolded the crisp sheet.

*First Day of September in the year of our Lord 1544*

*Kenan Macdonald of Sleat*

*This is notice that I, Gilbert Macdonald, have started a new sect of Macdonalds on the Isle of Skye. The land along Trotternish is now part of my territory, which will encompass Scorrybreac. I have the full backing of Clan Matheson as well as the Macdonalds from Islay Isle. Any resistance you devise will be met with force, and it will be civil war. Keep to the Sleat Peninsula, Brother, and your brazen angel will continue to breathe.*

*Chief Gilbert Macdonald*

A prickle slid along Kenan's spine as his blood shot through him, readying his body for war. "Tierney," he said, the letter dropping from his hand as he ran down the hill toward the castle. There was cursing and loud questions behind him, but all he could focus on was getting to Tierney. His legs churned through the tall grasses and bobbing daisies, his arms pumping at his sides.

*Your brazen angel will continue to breathe.*
Gilbert wrote it as if he held her captive.

Were Mathesons in Dunscaith Castle or sneaking
through the streets of the village? Had Ranulf and
Gilbert already taken her? But her mother had just
emerged moments ago. The questions bombarded
him, and he breathed deeply, pushing them away. He
could only focus on getting to her, holding her, seeing her safe.

Kenan ran, his well-conditioned heart giving him
all the blood and energy he needed to get there as
fast as humanly possible. He barely felt the ground
beneath his feet.

"What's going on?" Douglas MacNicol asked as
Kenan skidded into the bailey.

"Good Lord," Fannie said, clinging to her husband's arm.

But Kenan didn't stop, didn't even slow. *Tierney!*
He flew through the open doors and across the
Great Hall. Up the stairs he thumped toward the
bedchamber. "Tierney!" he yelled.

He caught the frame of the door, swinging inside
the room. It was as if a cannonball had shattered
through the dressing table. The water pitcher and
chairs were upended on the floor. Flowers and pins
lay scattered across the rugs. Two of the thin drapes
on the bed had been ripped down, the bed trampled
as if someone ran across the smoothed quilts, one
forgotten slipper in the tangle.

But Tierney wasn't there.

A crown of flowers lay on the rug before the mirror.

*I'll be the one in a crown of bluebells tomorrow*, she'd told him this last night when they parted, him celebrating and sleeping with his friends while she slept alone the night before the wedding.

"Daingead!" He spun around and ran out of the room, his gaze flying both ways along the corridor. Where would Gilbert take her first? Because it hadn't been long.

Rory and Cyrus met him on the stairs. "She's not in the bedchamber," Kenan said. "Have the ship who brought the message stopped."

"Already ordered," Cyrus said. "I'll check these rooms." He ran down the corridor.

"Ye go to the roof," Kenan ordered Rory and leaped down the stairs he'd just climbed.

*They would drag her down.*

There was no escape going up. Kenan's feet barely touched the steps. He used his hands braced on the walls to keep him from tumbling.

*Focus, daingead!* He needed to control the rising panic within him. In battle, he achieved total concentration by taking emotion out of it. There were only those who must be stopped and those who were trying to kill him. Ranulf was both of those, because losing Tierney would kill him.

His churning legs brought him to the bottom where a single table had been erected for the workers who were still scrubbing the walls of the Great Hall. The grayness from light filtering through empty windows and the tang of burned furniture and tapestries added to the grisly, hollow feeling of the room. And it was empty. If Tierney were there, she'd be fighting and screaming.

Kenan ran through the archway toward the still-intact kitchen. Its reinforced wall had kept the fires from the Great Hall. He ran toward the open door.

"'Tis a trap!" Tierney's yell ended in the sound of a small yelp.

Rage, hot and all-consuming rose up in Kenan, but he made himself slow and think. He wouldn't let her warning be given in vain. His sword was already drawn, but he re-sheathed it. He picked up speed again and then fell back onto his hip, letting the momentum slide him through the kitchen doorway.

Ranulf's blade whizzed over Kenan's head as he brought it around with enough force to decapitate him if he'd been standing. Ignoring the bruising on his hip from the stone step he'd slid down, Kenan leaped up, unleashing his sword.

Ranulf spun toward him, delivering another blow, but Kenan deflected it. He wanted to look for Tierney, see if she was hurt, but he couldn't look with Ranulf baring down on him with slash after frenzied slash. The man's face was bright red, spittle on his snarling mouth. He was out of control.

"Sneaking into Dunscaith to steal Tierney away." Kenan ducked and kicked Ranulf backward with his boot to his gut. "Ye'll lose yer foking head today."

"Ye were meant to die that night at Eilean Donan!" Ranulf yelled as he straightened, holding his sword out as he sucked in large amounts of air.

"Murdoc wants Dunscaith, too?" Kenan asked. Daingead! He couldn't see Tierney.

Ranulf snorted and wiped his upper arm across his sweaty brow. "Not my weak brother. He wants peace like ye. Gilbert and I were going to kill ye at the ferry. We had men waiting there for when ye left."

If Tierney hadn't interfered, and they'd have left out the front of Eilean Donan, they'd have been attacked in the dark, probably by twice the number of men or more.

"Tierney?" Kenan called without looking.

"I am well," she said from somewhere behind him. The slight slur in her speech didn't sound well, but she was there, and she was conscious.

Bursting fury at whatever was causing the swollen sound in her voice made Kenan lunge toward Ranulf. The man got his sword up in time, and both swords struck so they were face to face between crossed blades of steel. "Where's Gilbert?" Kenan demanded, yelling in Ranulf's contorted face.

But Ranulf didn't answer. He didn't have to, because Tierney screamed.

# CHAPTER TWENTY-NINE

"He who would learn to fly one day must first learn
to stand and walk and run and climb and dance;
one cannot fly into flying."

*Friedrich Nietzsche – German Philosopher, 1844–1900*

The scream came from Tierney's open mouth before
she could stop it. The last thing she wanted was to
distract Kenan as he deflected Ranulf's sword. But
the arm that snaked around her middle wasn't gentle
as it yanked her up against another man.

"That's it," the man said in her ear. "Get my
brother to turn around so Ranulf can finish him."

Gilbert Macdonald hauled her backward. His
fingers curled into her side, bruising her. She tried to
keep her feet under her as he dragged her toward
the door of the kitchen that led to the neglected
gardens.

Tierney wasn't going without a fight. She'd fought
when she'd been matrimonially chained to Wallace.
She'd fought to keep her daughter safe when
Wallace only wanted a son. She'd fought her father
with threats and readiness to take Maggie and flee
when he'd signed the betrothal contract without her
consent. And she'd fought Ranulf and his clan when
they'd come for Scorrybreac, devising a plan to abduct the chief of a powerful clan who was known to
be kind.

*I am a warrior.*

Her arms flailed out, reaching for anything. Unfortunately, there was no baking going on in the empty castle, and much of the kitchen had been removed for cleaning. Tierney sunk her nails into Gilbert's forearm. He grunted but didn't lessen his hold.

He got her to the door, and she reached to the sides to capture the doorframe, stopping their exit.

"Foking bitch, let go!"

Before her, Kenan parried Ranulf's thrusts expertly, never turning his head toward her. She didn't want him to break his concentration. He'd be killed, and she'd never forgive herself. No, she needed to take care of Gilbert on her own, a man twice her weight and five times her strength.

A breeze whooshed from the interior doorway through the kitchen to the open back door, pushing against her as if Morag's mother goddess wished to help Gilbert take her.

*A child of the wind and sky. Your element is air.* Morag's words had seemed poetic and fantastical. But if there was truth in it…

Tierney pulled against Gilbert's backward thrust, her hands holding tight to the doorframe, as the wind blew in her face. Having lost her slippers, she braced her bare feet on the sides of the doorway. Using all her might, she suddenly reversed direction, rearing backward.

*Crack!* The back of her head slammed into Gilbert's face, and her momentum, added to his tenacious pull to get her outside, made him fall backward. They crashed together onto his back.

Tierney wasted no time in rolling off him when his arm loosened, even though her head ached from the impact.

Gilbert groaned. "Bloody foking hell."

She didn't wait to see how badly he was hurt, and she wouldn't run. Barefoot through untended briars and weeds wouldn't help her outrun a trained warrior. This was likely her only chance to stop him.

Scrambling in the dirt, her fingers locked on the edge of a rock. It was good enough for David against Goliath and heavier than bread dough. Gilbert's hand grabbed her ankle.

"Ooof!" She fell over his chest. Without anything but instinct to survive, she lifted the rock with both hands before he could catch her arms, and swung down with all her might, gravity her fellow warrior.

*Crack!* The rock slammed into the front of Gilbert's head. He grunted, and his arms dropped to the side.

Blood poured from Gilbert's nose and a cut on his forehead where the rock had hit. His skull seemed whole, but he wasn't moving.

Tierney scrambled back from him, her dress dragging in the dirt. She ripped off the back ivory train that was speckled with blood from Gilbert's nose and ran back into the kitchen.

"Keep fighting!" she yelled. "I'm well." She ran to the hearth, grabbing a poker that remained there, and stood with her back against the wall.

Kenan kept his gaze on Ranulf, and Ranulf used his force and skill against him. They were both excellent swordsmen, but Ranulf didn't have her in his corner.

Without making a sound to distract Kenan, she leaned down to pick up a piece of something charred, perhaps a nut. Moving to the side, she hurled it at Ranulf's forehead.

*Plunk!* It hit him right between the eyes. He blinked, his snarl pinching into a grimace, and he slowed his attack in confusion. It was the opening that Kenan needed. With a two-handed grip, he ducked slightly and sliced his sword, his well-muscled body turning with a powerful follow-through. The blade slid right across Ranulf's middle.

Ranulf doubled over, dropping to his knees, his sword clattering to the stone floor. Kenan didn't even wait for him to topple before spinning around. "Tierney." He dropped his own sword, rushing through the kitchen to her.

She dropped the iron poker, and he was on her, pulling her into his arms. "I thought...I thought they'd taken ye."

All the muscles in her body gave way with relief. "There was a moment I thought they would."

He pulled away, his hands reaching to brush the tumbled curls back from her face. His gaze slid over her. "Where are ye injured?"

"Bruises only."

"She's here!" someone yelled from the kitchen entrance.

Cyrus and Rory, swords drawn, rushed inside.

"Gilbert's unconscious just outside the door," Tierney said as Kenan continued to hold her, scanning her for injuries of which she might not be aware.

"Ye have blood on ye," he said.

"'Tis Gilbert's."

"Tapadh le Dia." He exhaled with relief, his forehead leaning into hers.

"Ranulf's dead," Rory said.

"Gilbert's not looking too good, but he's breathing," Cyrus said, leaning over him.

"I broke his nose with my head and then hit him with a rock," Tierney said.

Kenan stroked her cheek. "He didn't stand a chance, him trying to take ye." He wrapped her in his arms, and she pulled in his strength as he held her.

"I'm sorry," she said against his chest. "He's your brother."

"He's an enemy first if he was trying to hurt ye," Kenan said.

"They're in here!" Tierney recognized her father's voice and then her mother's gasp as they entered the kitchen battlefield.

Cyrus's face appeared over Kenan's shoulder. "Ye all right, lass?"

"I believe so."

Rory appeared over the other shoulder. "Thank God. Kenan's a sensible man, but if ye'd come to harm, peace in Scotland would have been a fading possibility."

"She's well?" Douglas asked, coming up beside her with her mother. "Tier, are ye well?"

"Yes, Father."

"Are ye still getting married?"

• • •

"I need some air," Tierney said as she and Kenan exited the door onto the roof of Dunscaith Castle. The clouds raced across a blue sky that peeked out as they passed. She inhaled the breeze, ridding her nose of the smell of blood and dirt.

Kenan walked beside her, letting her lead them to the wall. She could see the crowd up on the meadow, their wedding guests. Rory and Cyrus were jogging up the hill to alert everyone about the delay.

Delay? No, 'twas an attack, one that could have seen them both dead.

She trembled slightly. "Ye'er cold," Kenan said and yanked one of the blankets off his glider. He shook it and draped it over her shoulders.

She watched as two groups of men jogged away from the wedding spectators, half running to the dock where a rowboat must sit that led to a ship sitting somewhere off the coast. The other group ran for the castle.

"They probably didn't come alone," she said.

"My men are doing a search of the village. We will ferret out the bastards."

"How did they know we were marrying today?"

Kenan huffed. "Perhaps from our request for Father Bright. He was near Eilean Donan when I sent a rider in search of him. I paid to have the banns waived, but word still travels."

Ranulf was dead, Gilbert in custody. She should relax, but her shoulders were still stiff and high. Tierney concentrated on breathing in and out, letting the cool air calm her as she hugged her own arms.

Kenan pulled her gently against his side. "Today

is not the day."

She studied the rugged outline of his profile as he watched the warriors disperse to search for Mathesons below.

He turned his face to her, his eyes searching. "Blood shouldn't be spilled on a wedding day."

"No," she answered, remembering the tale of Sara's first wedding to Rory's brother. "And my gown is stained and torn, my hair a vermin nest, and I've lost my flower crown and slippers."

He shook his head, never leaving her gaze. "I don't care about any of that. I'd marry ye covered in dung."

A small smile tugged on her lips. "I wouldn't marry *you* covered in dung."

He grinned. "I'm less choosey."

She sniffed a little laugh and looked back out at the field where clusters of people waited to see if the wedding would take place. "They will be disappointed."

"They will understand," he said. "We can marry on the morrow."

The familiar tightening pulsed through her middle, the one that made her breath come faster, her lips parting to suck in air. She thought she'd banished her worry about binding herself to another man. She trusted Kenan. He'd never hurt her and accepted her for who she was.

But her heart still raced at the idea. Sara had called it trauma. Morag said it would fade in time. Right now, Tierney just wanted to run away, but she didn't want to leave Kenan, couldn't imagine leaving him.

"What if this is an omen, Kenan?" She looked at him with a gentle shake of her head. "What if we shouldn't marry?" She splayed her hands out to her blood-speckled gown. "I vowed never to wed again, and look what's happened right before I was about to replace that vow with a new one."

She felt tears in her eyes and wondered if they would have come as she stood on that hill with Father Bright asking for her pledge, asking her to break her vow. "I...can't marry you."

They stood in silence, the wind the only sound reaching up four stories from the ground.

She waited for Kenan's reaction. Anger would be appropriate, but she didn't fear him.

Disappointment, sadness, betrayal. They might all be displayed on his face. She inhaled and turned to him.

He'd been staring out at the village and mass of people beyond, but he turned to face her. The curve of a smile still lingered on his lips, and he took her fisted hand. He slowly opened each of her fingers so they could weave together with his own.

"Then we won't marry."

Her breath stalled, and panic made her eyes open wider. "You will send me away." The thought tore through her. "I didn't mean..." Her mouth opened, and tears swelled out of her eyes. "I don't want to lose you, Kenan."

Kenan captured both her cheeks in his hands, cradling her face as he bent in. His thumbs brushed away the tears, but more fell. Was she emotional because of the attacks below? She'd never given in to tears so unstoppable.

"I will never send ye away, Tierney. Ye are part of me, and I am part of ye. We will live together and love each other, but we do not need a priest to bless us before family and friends."

Her heart clenched on the word "love." Did he love her? "But we won't be truly united. The clans will think badly of us, that we are sinful and the alliance between Macdonalds and MacNicols is weak."

"I don't care what others think." He shook his head without breaking eye contact. "After what ye've lived through, ye need freedom in order to trust me enough to give me yer heart, so I will never take yer freedom away."

She stared up into his stormy blue eyes and saw the truth in his words. "You want my heart?"

The corner of his mouth hitched up. "Ye already have mine. I love ye, Tierney. Marrying me or not marrying me won't change that. And if ye feel free and happy not being married, then that is what I want."

*He loves me.* She inhaled, the ache in her middle lessening. "I love you, too."

His grin spread into a large smile, and she saw his shoulders relax. "And ye'll stay with me even if we don't get married?"

Her smile grew to match his. "I promise."

"Even if times get tough or we fight?" he asked, looking serious again. "Ye will stay and talk things out with me?"

She nodded. "I won't leave. I start fights all the time, and only half by accident."

He chuckled. "I will stay, too, even if I'm angry or we disagree. To work it out."

She leaned into him, lifting her lips to his, and he kissed her. There on the roof, before only the sky and God, they pledged to stay together. Had he just tricked her into marrying him? She didn't care, because he understood her need to be free, and he loved her as much as she loved him.

The wind swirled around them, gentle but insistent, and she felt the hair lift and tug around her face. They broke the kiss, and she tucked a strand behind her ear. "Your aunt said I am a child of the sky and air."

"Does that mean ye'd like to fly?"

She glanced behind them at the glider. "One day, with you."

Kenan looked between her and the wings and then went to them, dragging the blankets off. "Life is too short not to fly when given the chance." He smiled at her. "Help me drag this over."

Tierney's eyes opened wide. "You're going to fly? Now?"

"Nay." He smiled broadly. "We are."

"I'm not dressed to fly."

"Take off as much as ye can and still be decent." He grinned. "Ye don't want to make Doris and Edith swoon."

Tierney began untying the heavy outer petticoat. "They'd be more likely to slice you, thinking you were trying to kill me." The petticoat dropped to the slated roof. Reaching under the inner petticoat, she yanked down the extra layers that added bulk to keep the heavy skirts out from her legs. She was left in a simple petticoat and her bodice over her smock and stays. She shook out her hair, releasing the rest of the updo, pins falling around her.

"The best I can do."

Kenan stood, staring at her, and she blinked as a clear patch in the sky released a ray of sun upon her.

He walked back to her. "Ye look like an angel, Tierney."

"You know I'm no angel."

"A gloriously wicked, fallen angel, then."

She tipped her head to the side, her lips curved. "Better."

He took her hand, and they hurried to the glider. "I worked with the builders to create this launch space," he said, unlatching a wide, wrought-iron fence. He walked it inward and hooked it open through a ring built into the stone wall, leaving a flat stone surface of about ten feet in length with two steps leading up to it.

Kenan lifted the glider, sliding it into place on the edge of the castle. Tierney lifted her skirt and ran up to it, looking over the side. Her heart sped but not from fear. She remembered the feel of the wind under the wings when she'd tried to steal the glider before. How freeing and incredible it felt to be lifted. And the knowledge that this handsome, kind warrior loved her enough to not marry her filled her with brilliant light.

"I'll strap in first, and then ye can climb in," Kenan said.

"There's room for us both?"

He grinned. "I made it adjustable. Ye'll be strapped to my back."

She laughed, her heart so light she might float up without Kenan's glider. He loved her. He understood her need for freedom, and he accepted it.

He put out his hand, and she placed hers in it. The warmth filtered down through her. She was loved. She was free, and she was ready for adventure next to this amazing man.

. . .

Wind whipped through Kenan's hair, and he couldn't stop smiling. Below them, the houses and people looked smaller. Pressed against his back with leather straps binding them together, Tierney laughed, the sweet notes being carried in the rush of wind around them as they soared, the great wings catching the invisible currents.

"I'm turning us. Don't worry about us tipping," he said. He turned the horizontal control stick he held between his hands, and the wings tipped. He felt her arms squeeze tighter around him, but falling off him was impossible with the three straps secure.

The breeze off the sea caught easily under the wide, light wings, and they turned.

"Hooo raaaa!" Tierney yelled, the joy obvious in her tone.

Below, people pointed and ran under them. Children cheered, leaping in excitement at the spectacle as he and Tierney swooped in a gentle arch over the tree line to head back over the moor. Kenan had studied enough of da Vinci's notes to make the wind currents work to lift them back up anytime they began to descend.

They circled the moor above Dunscaith Castle. From up there, he could even see the ship anchored off the coast, waiting for Ranulf and Gilbert. How long would they wait before finally leaving? Because neither would be returning.

Ranulf was dead and Gilbert injured and arrested.

But those were thoughts for another time. Right now, he was light as a leaf caught in the early fall breeze.

"I love you!" Tierney yelled out.

"I love ye, too!" he called back.

• • •

Eight Months Later – 9 May 1545
The Moor Above Dunscaith Castle

"What?" Kenan yelled the word as he dropped his training sword. "We still have three weeks. Aunt Morag said three weeks."

Cora threw her hands in the air, dashing after him. "The bairn's coming early. Only God knows the exact timing."

Kenan didn't wait for the woman, his breath coming in gusts as he charged toward the castle. Tierney was as ripe as an overrisen yeast bun, and he'd left her sleeping this morn in their large bed. She'd tossed through the night, trying to find a comfortable position, so he'd left her undisturbed when he rose to go to the training field with his warriors.

Had she actually been laboring through the night?

"All is well!" Cora yelled out to concerned villagers as they ran through the streets. "Lady Tierney is having her bairn."

Was it Kenan's imagination that people sighed in relief over the end of Tierney's prickly mood? Just the other day, she'd yelled at her horse for being too tall for her to mount in her condition. Fleet didn't look hurt by her comments, but Tierney burst into tears, hugging the horse's neck. 'Twas the constant discomfort of her size, curtailing her ability to fly with Kenan, that brought out her irritation at mundane things. Besides himself, only Morag, Cora, and Maggie stayed by her side, immune to her outbursts.

Kenan ran through the open gates. With Murdoc Matheson's letter of alliance arriving, Gilbert's exile, and the continued convalescence of Cyrus's father, the gates remained open more than closed these days. The burned shell of Dunscaith was almost scrubbed free and rebuilt. But Kenan's focus was not on the colorful tapestries hanging on the walls of the Great Hall when he ran inside, nearly tripping on a thick rug when he halted. His focus was on a dourlooking Father Bright, standing before the burning hearth where he held his hands out to capture the warmth.

"Father Bright?" Kenan's heart dropped in his tightening chest. "Ye were called?" Was Tierney in peril? The bairn? Did one of them need last rites because things were taking a dangerous turn?

The priest shook his head slowly. "I was called to come. No explanation."

Cora ran into the Great Hall, huffing, her cheeks red from the early spring cold and exertion. Both men turned to her.

"Ye called the priest?" Kenan asked.

"Yes, Tierney requested Father Bright. The two of you are to come up to the bedchamber together."

Father Bright passed the sign of the cross before him, concern tightening his face. His lips moved in a little prayer that Kenan wouldn't accept.

"Nay," Kenan said, shaking his head. "Tierney was fine last eve. She was eating sweetened scones and jam."

But Cora was already hurrying to the steps. Father Bright was suddenly next to him, his hand on his shoulder. "Be strong, son."

Kenan felt weak and ready to explode with violent power at the same time. *I can't lose her. I can't. I'll die with—*

"Come along." Father Bright tugged on his arm. "Lady Tierney needs ye by her side."

"Aye." Kenan surged ahead of the priest, running up the steps two at a time to reach the door that he'd softly closed that morn, leaving his love sleeping after a night of discomfort. Pausing, he prayed. "Please God, keep us together. Keep me strong for her." With a full inhale, he opened the door. "Tierney, love."

The room was full of smells: burning peat in the hearth, lavender, some tangy herbal concoction, and the scent of blood and fluids that he'd smelled before on the battlefield. This was Tierney's battlefield masked to look like an ordinary bedchamber. A mother's battlefield to bring forth life and fight to keep her own.

A ribbon of crisp spring freshness wafted in from the two windows that had been opened a crack, allowing the air to move. He strode over to her in the bed where she was propped by a multitude of pillows.

Tierney's hair was pulled back into a haphazard bun on top of her head. Her face was flushed and damp with sweat, and her chest rose and fell under the smock she was wearing. A thin sheet covered her bent knees.

"Kenan," she said, her face pinching again as she started to huff.

He sank to his knees next to her, taking her small hand in his two large ones. "Tierney, I'm here."

"And Father Bright?" she asked, her voice pinched as pain made her whole body tighten.

"I'm here, my child."

Morag's head suddenly appeared from under the sheet, causing the priest to gasp softly. "The bairn is almost breaching."

Tierney grabbed Kenan's hand. "There's no time. Father?"

"Aye?" he answered with a tremor in his voice.

Tierney's eyes were bright with determination, not weakness. Her skin glowed with perspiration and health, not the paleness of one losing too much blood. She spoke to the priest but held Kenan's gaze. "Marry us. I will not have my bairn born a bastard, not when I love his father with all my heart."

"Marry?" Kenan said.

A weak smile played over her lips. "Marry me, Kenan Macdonald. Right now."

In Kenan's mind, they had married back on the roof before they flew together the first time, but it wasn't official in society's eyes. He was pretty sure

God considered them pledged to each other.

"Are ye well, then?" he asked. "No last rites for ye or the bairn?"

"Last rites?" Tierney looked at Father Bright. "No. Wedding vows before the church and witnesses." Her hand floated up to point to Cora and Morag and little Maggie, who seemed suddenly older as she carried clean linens to Morag.

Kenan doubled over, his forehead touching the edge of the bed as relief exploded within him. "Wedding vows. Not last rites."

Tierney began to blow large exhales, and he lifted his head. Her narrowed eyes stared at him. "Well, what's your answer, Chief Macdonald? You better decide quickly before your son is born."

Kenan took her hand, and she squeezed it with so much strength that he felt a bit of the pain wracking her body. "Lass, in my mind, and I'm sure in God's, we are already married, but absolutely, if that's what ye want, not for the bairn but for ye."

She sucked in through her nose, a smile lighting her eyes if not her lips. "Yes. I want to marry you officially, Kenan. I am certain."

"Then you better do it now," Morag said. "Before your own bairn is a witness."

Father Bright began talking behind them as Kenan knelt at the altar of Tierney. She was sweaty, straining, and the most beautiful a woman could look.

"Do ye, Tierney MacNicol, take this man, Kenan Macdonald, chief of the Macdonalds of Sleat, as yer husband? To love, obey, and cherish for as long as ye both shall live?"

"I'll obey when I agree, but I will love and cherish and always stay truuuuuuue." She dragged out the last word on her groan.

"I see the head," Morag called.

Kenan didn't wait for Father Bright to catch up. "And I, Kenan Macdonald, take ye, Tierney MacNicol, as my lawful wife to love, protect, and cherish for as long as we both live on this earth."

"I protect him, too," Tierney yelled through a wave of pain that broke more sweat over her face. Och, but if he could take her pain, he would. She clutched his hand with crippling strength.

"The bairn is on its way out," Morag said.

"Father Bright?" Tierney yelled so loud that the priest jumped.

"I pronounce ye husband and wife, and all yer children are legitimate."

"Push, Tierney," Morag said.

Tierney grabbed the front of Kenan's tunic, yanking him down to her face for a hard kiss on the lips. As he pulled away, she groaned. The sound changed into a roar when her body contracted, and then her guttural gasp and the sound of fluid announced the release of the bairn.

The breathy cries of their bairn grew louder under the sheet draping her legs. Kenan's heart swelled with gratitude and pride as he looked at the woman before him, his wife, his angel, his true love. Kenan leaned over Tierney, wiping the damp hair from her face. Her hazel eyes looked brilliant green and damp. "Wife, my beautiful angel."

She breathed as if finishing a long-distance race. "You lie, husband. There's nothing beautiful about me right now. And whatever you do, don't look under that sheet."

He leaned in and kissed her lips, tasting the salt. "My wife, the warrior, and aye, 'tis beauty and strength and bravery I see before me."

"'Tis a girl," Cora yelled, her hands clapping together into a look of thankful prayer. She rose onto her toes.

Kenan's smile expanded. "A wee lass as strong and passionate as her mama."

Tierney kept his gaze. "I will raise her to be a chief one day." There was no question in her voice, but he saw it in her eyes.

He kept his place by her side, holding her hand. "As will I. A Boudica, warrior queen, to guide her clan, if that is her wish."

The wee Boudica cried with acceptance or just annoyance at being pulled into the cold, bright world. Morag wiped the bairn briskly and cut the cord tying her to Tierney.

"Here now," Morag said, setting the crying bairn on Tierney's chest.

Tierney looked down at their daughter with such love that Kenan felt his own swell within him, releasing in one tear that he would probably never acknowledge. "She's a beautiful warrior, too," he said.

*Thump!*

Kenan looked over his shoulder to see Father Bright slump onto his arse on the rug by the bed. The hand clutching his crucifix slid away as he limply fell to his side. Maggie ran over to him while Cora helped wipe the feisty bairn's mouth with a cloth.

Maggie looked up from her crouched position by the priest. "He's well but might have a bump." Rising, she ran back to look at her sister with Kenan and Tierney.

Kenan took in the small circle of his family and beamed, his entire body filling with the lightness of joy. 'Twas a lot like flying.

He kissed the bairn's head, then the top of Maggie's head. He lowered gently over Tierney and kissed her. She stared into his eyes, tears swelling out of them, making them look even greener. "I love ye, my fallen angel," he whispered.

"I love you, too," she answered, her smile growing, "husband."

Their kiss blocked out the bustle around them as the bairn was taken to be washed, overseen by Maggie. Nothing else in the world could make him feel more joy than at that moment.

He and Tierney, together in every possible way, forever.

Thank you for coming on this journey of building trust between Kenan and Tierney. Without trust and respect, love is hollow and fragile. But to trust, especially after trauma, requires a huge leap of faith.

Make sure to continue the adventure through the Brotherhood of Solway Moss series and the quest to unite the Isle of Skye with Cyrus Mackinnon's story. Laria is a child of the water and Lady of the Loch.

• • •

To stay up to date on Heather's writing projects, sales, conference schedule and more, please subscribe to her once-a-month newsletter at:

https://www.heathermccollum.com/about/newsletter

# ACKNOWLEDGMENTS

Thank you, readers, for continuing to follow the adventures and love in my new series! By reading, you bring my characters to life, and I will forever be grateful for you.

Thank you to my beautifully supportive writing pals who understand when my word well goes dry and who push me to keep going. Thank you to my own Highland hero, Braden, who reminds me that when I say, "This book is crap," my dismay is part of my process, and it will all work out wonderfully in the end. You've always been right. And thank you to my always-looking-out-for-me agent, Kevan Lyon, my supportive and understanding editor, Alethea Spiridon, and my team at Entangled Publishing who puts my words out there in the world.

Also…

At the end of each of my books, I ask that you, my awesome readers, please remind yourselves of the whispered symptoms of ovarian cancer. I am now a thirteen-year survivor, one of the lucky ones. Please don't rely on luck. If you experience any of these symptoms consistently for three weeks or more, go see your GYN.

· Bloating
· Eating less and feeling full faster
· Abdominal pain
· Trouble with your bladder

Other symptoms may include indigestion, back pain, pain with intercourse, constipation, fatigue, and menstrual irregularities.

*Don't miss the exciting new books
Entangled has to offer.*

*Follow us!*

**f** @EntangledPublishing

**◎** @Entangled_Publishing

**♪** @EntangledPub